TYPHOON

Version 2.0 — November 2010
ISBN 978-1-926959-00-9
© 2010 1889 Labs Ltd.

Earth photo on cover courtesy of the Image Science & Analysis Laboratory,
NASA Johnson Space Center (ID #STS059-218-44)
http://eol.jsc.nasa.gov

Ship design by Andrew King; 3D model by Cyril Meusy.
Cover composition and design by MCM.

Published by 1889 Labs Ltd.
Visit our website for free books and other fun stuff:
http://books.1889.ca

For Eli, Jan and Anna

Table of Contents

TYPHOON

BY MCM

1889
LABS

November 3, 2042

Terror Plot

No one noticed the blood stains on his jumpsuit. All eyes were on the sky above, on the clearing in the middle of the buzzing crowd, sleek and shabby cars pushed out to the edges of Times Square as organizers struggled to make room. Ayoub pushed through the packs of onlookers, racing towards the distant podium where a dozen Secret Service agents kept watch with professional unease.

He fell into a pair of revellers who smelled strongly of beer at noon, wearing t-shirts and shorts in the crisp autumn air, cheeks rosy for one reason or another. He tried to find his footing again, but nerves got the better of him, and he fumbled forward into a woman wearing a what looked like a rocket ship — foil messily wrapped around chicken wire mesh on her body.

"It's here, dahling," she said with empty eyes. "Ain't it grand?"

He shoved her aside, trying to ride atop the wave of the crowd, rather than in it. Oblivious strangers jabbed into his ribs from all sides, but he was moving faster, and for a moment, he almost smiled at the prospect of reaching the podium in time.

From the left, he heard static: the NYPD had noticed him, and they were radioing it in. He saw his window closing; suddenly his goal got much further away. He ducked down and ran, clipped by elbows and purses, moving unseen for a few steps, until he bumped headlong into the chest of a very broad police officer.

"Where you goin', sir?"

Ayoub turned, saw another three coming towards him. They were calm, casual, but he knew the glint in their eyes. The look of a brawl waiting to happen. "I need—" he began, but then stun sticks were drawn, and he started to back away. The closest one grabbed him by the arm, fingers cutting into his frozen skin.

"What happened to your shirt?" asked the officer.

"It's not what you—"

"Base, we've got a situation here," said the officer, talking into his radio and waving a hand in the air so he'd be visible to the command centre, somewhere in the surrounding buildings. "Can you see me out here?"

Ayoub couldn't hear the answer. He tried to look, but his head was shoved down roughly by another cop. His teeth were chattering from the cold, so loud he could barely hear anything else. Someone somewhere shouted "There it is!" but there was no sound, no roar, no boom. He struggled against the captors.

"…Arab male, late thirties, five-nine. Checking fingerprints now—"

Fingerprints. No.

Ayoub swung his head back, hit the man behind him in the teeth. Something cracked, and his arm was let go. The one with the fingerprint scanner had no time to react before Ayoub's foot caught him in the chest, sent him flying into the others, and their prisoner leapt into the crowd again, pushing revellers back to block the pursuit.

"No time left… no time…"

The Secret Service saw him coming from their perches on the gleaming metal stands around the podium, towering over the crowd like an archaic oil rig, decked out to look majestic for the Big Apple. The steps to the upper level were blocked by the most ominous of agents, watching, begging him to try. They wouldn't touch their guns until they'd had a chance with their fists. He knew he'd lose that battle, too.

He scrambled onto the roof of a car, foot slipping, then cracking the windshield before leaping onto a TV van. The cameraman almost fell off the edge in shock. "Be safe," Ayoub said, patting him on the back, only to hear a quiet *twip!* and the feeling of something spraying his hand. The cameraman slumped forward, a small wound in his jacket leaking blood. The gunshot had made no noise. Ayoub didn't pause to check the skyline. He had to move.

His ankle seared from the rough jump from the windshield, and his footing was bad, but he managed to throw himself at the scaffolding at the side of the podium, pulling himself up halfway until he saw a pair of polished shoes only an arm's length away.

"Secretary Weiss!" he yelled, trying to see the man's face.

A stun stick hit his leg, his hands convulsed, and he dropped onto the pavement below, surrounded by agents in dark suits, assessing him gravely. Gravel dug into the back of his skull, his too-long hair doing nothing to stop the pain. He bit down on his lip and tasted blood.

"Threat contained," said a voice from a direction he couldn't place, the world swimming around him. He was dragged, limp, to his knees.

"Wait…" he slurred, tongue not ready to move yet, "I'm… I have to—"

A fist put him back into silence, and he sucked down the blood, avoided looking them in the eye. His beard, wild and itchy, burned like mad all of a sudden, but he couldn't scratch it. He stomped his foot on the ground like a petulant child. "There's a bomb in the—"

Then the sound. A roar, sudden and shocking. Windows in all the skyscrapers shook, and though he couldn't see it, he knew what was coming. The crowd was in awe, stunned by the sight, and he fought to get loose, to get to the podium.

"Run him," said a voice from behind, and a scanner hit his finger, though he tried to make a fist to stop it.

"You said a bomb?" asked another agent, grabbing his chin and looking him in the eye. "You speak English, right? You said something about a bomb. A bomb where? Here?"

"Y-yes," said Ayoub, shivering. "It's here."

The agent looked over his shoulder, nodded. "Check the back door to the Hilton again," he said, earpiece buzzing audibly over the hum of the crowd. "I want that area locked down."

"Sir," said another, "We checked it twice. Nobody got in there before the—"

"It's not in the Hilton!" Ayoub screamed. "The bomb is right here! In the crowd! You're all going to d—" Another blow to the face, and his eyes had trouble focussing afterward.

"You shut the hell up," said the close agent. "Just shut up. Somebody cuff him so I can get back to work!"

There was a cheer from the crowd, and he tried to see over his shoulder, see what was going on, but a rough hand turned his head around.

"There's no time…" he cursed. He kicked out at the agent in front, hitting him in the groin, and yanked an arm free. He clipped another agent in the face with his elbow, grabbed a gun from the closest holster he could find, and pistol-whipped his last opponent to the ground before taking off.

"Suspect is armed!" shouted voices from behind. "Shoot to kill!"

Ayoub grabbed hold of the railings and pulled himself up onto a gangplank that led to the main podium. Nobody but the agents saw him do it. The crowd was starstruck by the sight in their midst, on the giant reproductions on the screens around the Square. He'd have looked too, but he had no time.

"Secretary Weiss!" he shouted, gun tight in his hand. "Secretary Weiss!"

The second gunshot made a noise.

THREE YEARS EARLIER

Have to Run

Kani was not awake. The faintest trace of light came through her shuttered windows, drawing long blue rectangles on the floor, up her bed, and onto her face as she tried to ignore the morning. The clock above her bed showed a soft "5:10AM", but the terrible, grating, screeching noise that passed as an alarm came from her computer across the room.

"Snooze," she muttered, and it began to fade. Briefly.

"Snooze disabled," it said calmly.

She sighed. "Cancel disabling."

"Command not found."

"Undo snooze lock."

"Command not found. Say 'help' for help."

She sat up, eyes narrow and puffy, teeth locked in fury. She kicked her covers onto the floor and stormed into the bathroom, slamming the door. The computer went on with its day, playing an assortment of soft music like there was someone there to hear it.

The lights in the bathroom started dim, but as the lightbulbs got their mojo back, Kani's eyes were forced to squint more and more until she was nearly blinded by reality. She washed her face in the sink, hair pushed away from her face so half-heartedly it couldn't mask the look of sheer exhaustion about her. She dried her light brown skin, caught a last drop of water before it fell off the tip of her nose, and sighed.

"Good morning," she said, trying to convince herself. "Good morning."

By the time she was done with her early-morning routine, her computer was fully on, showing a list of messages she'd missed overnight. She swished through them as she brushed her teeth, finding nothing worth reading, and closing the mail window. She tapped the news icon, started putting on her track suit.

The computer began displaying articles, scrolling lazily, hard to read against the burgundy Trudeau High background. She took the toothbrush out of her mouth. "Shpook noo," she said, trying not to spray.

"Command not found."

"Shpeee noo," she repeated, then stormed into the bathroom, spat and rinsed, and leaned back out. "Speak news!" The computer started speaking the articles, but in a quiet voice that wasn't audible against he running water. "Louder!" she called. The voice got a fraction of a decibel louder. "Forget it! Play news video!"

"Please specify playlist," it said.

She put her head around the corner. "Default," she glowered, then cursed as it put a question mark onscreen. "Of course. Preference file corruption. As always."

"Please specify playlist," repeated the computer.

"Just pick some random stuff. Random. World news."

"Random world news," it said, and then the familiar tune to the IPN World News played softly, and a robotic voice introduced Kana Choi.

"This is a IPN News Refresh for 1100 SST," she said in a voice that almost put Kani back to sleep. "Top stories at this hour: Gossamer trial to proceed against threat of violence; Typhoon Koshi gains strength off Korea; UN pledges to revisit issue of—"

Kani put in an earbud and tapped the mute button on her computer. The earbud picked up the broadcast from there, lagging a bit as she crept through the darkened hall, down the stairs and into the kitchen. The lights gradually came up, to soften the blow of the early hour. She wished her bathroom did the same.

Kana Choi was still talking: "... Constitutional scholars remain divided on the issue of jurisdiction, despite assurances by Attorney General Deborah Warner that Gossamer is not being tried as an enemy combatant..."

The fridge was mostly empty, and the cupboard too. Kani pulled a bundle of bagels from a drawer and searched for a clean knife to cut them with. The kitchen was in disarray, and it got worse as the lights came up.

"I'll make it," came a voice from behind. "Don't worry about it." She didn't turn to look, because she knew what she'd see. Her father was forty-three but looked much older, after years of working late nights at a pre-fab facility that never caught up with its deadlines. The yard to their house would have been an overgrown jungle if the company didn't send gardeners to maintain it — an unspoken admission they realized they were working him to death. She hated seeing him like this, especially early in the morning, after getting home only one or two hours before. "If you can, you should," was his motto, but coming from the mouth of a veritable zombie, it seemed more like a curse.

"I don't have time for that, dad," Kani said, checking the dishwasher and pulling out a crusty knife, still trying to avoid looking at him. "Gotta go."

"I'll drive you," he said. "You'll be fine."

She gave him a deadened look, trying not to wince at dark the circles under his eyes. She wanted to call in sick for him, force him to sleep, but it never worked. "You in a car right now is a public safety issue," she said. "Besides, I'm meeting Stacey at the train station. It's way out of your way."

"How is Stacey?"

"I won't know until I see her," Kani said with a faint smile.

"Is she still... I mean, did she ever..."

"The police talked with her step dad last week, but she won't talk about it yet. She's still at home, though, I think."

"You haven't talked to her?"

"She hasn't been at school. Had a cold or something. But she wrote to me yesterday and said she was fine, and I believe her. She's fine."

Her father nodded, rubbed his eye. "Well, the offer stands. We've got an extra room."

"She knows."

"All right," he said, stumbling onto a stool at the counter. "Let's get this show on the road. I just need some coffee and I'll be ready to roll. What time is it anyway?"

"A little past 5:30," she said, scrubbing the crust off the knife. The sponge smelled awful. She wondered if the company would spring for a maid, too. She got home too late from school to do much cleaning these days. Like father like daughter, apparently.

"Mr Longbottom is an evil, evil man," said her father, rubbing his face with his shaking hands. "I think we need to... to do something nasty to him."

"You sound like the rest of the team," Kani sighed.

"Who starts practice at six in the morning?"

"Someone who lives across the street from the school. I hear half the girls sneak in and sleep in the locker rooms overnight so they don't have to get up so early."

"That's just *wrong*."

"Yeah, well…" Kani said, giving up on the knife and ripping the bagel in half by hand. Her father watched her for a second, then shook his head, started for the fridge.

"You can't get by on just that," he said. "Sports take energy. How about this: you make me some coffee, I'll make you a proper breakfast, and we'll get in the car, pick up Stacey, and get to school on time."

"Doubtful," she said wearily.

"What do you want? Country ham? Biscuits, sausage gravy? I don't know what we have."

Kani grabbed her bag off the counter, waved to her father. "We don't have any of that, dad. And what's more, I don't think you know how to cook any of that. So let's skip it. I hereby relieve you of your fatherly duties for the day."

He sighed, rested his head on the counter and started to snore. Kani grabbed her gym bag from the hook by the door, dimmed the lights and went outside. She had made it to the driveway when the front door opened, and her father stumbled into the brisk morning air.

"Don't forget about tonight!" he called, and she stopped short, wincing.

"What's tonight?" she asked, though her voice said she knew the answer.

"The Prabhakaran memorial," he said. "Your grandfather asked if you were coming."

"I'm…" she said, taking a shaky breath. "I'm busy tonight, dad. I'm gonna have to skip it this year."

"Kani," he said, coming further outside, waking up too damned fast, "You know it's important to him."

"Yeah, well, I'm busy. Sometimes these things happen. What can I do?"

He was close now, spoke quietly, determined. The opposite of the faltering father from inside. "Kani, it's important."

"What's important?" she snapped. "Worshipping a war criminal? Or better yet, getting on the news while worshipping a war criminal?"

"It's not worshipping—"

"It looks that way!" she said, dialling her voice down in the quiet of the morning, trying not to wake the nosy neighbours who would stand by the edge of their windows, hoping not to be seen. "It looks that way to anyone watching. 'Hey look! There are those crazy Tamils, praising a mass murderer...' It does wonders for my social circle at school, let me tell you."

"Your friends will understand," he said.

"Will they? *I* don't even understand!"

He exhaled slowly, took a step away, rubbed his hands across his face. Kani crossed her arms, not ready to give in. They stood in silence for a moment. "Your grandfather wants you there," he said. "We're family, Kani. We take care of each other. Every other day of the year, you can be whatever you like. Today... no, *tonight*, we take a few hours to remember our history."

"You never even *lived* in—"

"That's what history *is*. You don't need to agree with it, but you need to respect it. It defines who you are."

She waved him off, turned and walked to the street.

"You're coming, right?" he called.

"I don't know yet!" she called back, and then started jogging away.

Kana Choi kept her company on the way to the train station, talking about the latest songs by pop stars she couldn't identify without video, and movies she didn't have time to see. The streets in the overgrown suburbs were slowly starting to wake up: cars backing out of driveways, lights turning on in bedrooms and kitchens here and there, a handful of stubbornly nostalgic homeowners, wrapped tight in housecoats, ducking outside to snatch the morning newspaper. No one looked up to say hello this early in the morning; it was an unspoken rule that the way you looked and behaved before seven in the morning was strictly your own business. Kani checked her watch, saw she had fifteen minutes to go 'til the 5:45 train, and doubled-timed her pace as she got to the highway, leaving the sleepiness behind.

Cars zipped past her, switching lanes back and forth before rush hour set in and all movement ground to a halt. Some made a high-pitched whining noise as they approached, others a soft purr. Some had broken speaker systems, so they made no sound at all but the soft shifting of their wheels on the concrete. One vintage car with Michigan plates — a quarter-century old and looking every year — tore through a red light, engine revving fiercely and a faint trail of exhaust from its tail pipe. At any other intersection, it'd have been a ticket for sure, but this one's camera had been broken for months, and everybody knew it.

The trees were turning colour already, in the subtlest of ways, so the green you saw last week was just a little yellower than it was today. If you really thought about it, you'd see it happening, but nobody took the time to see those things anymore. Except Kani. She had a good long walk to the train station every day. Even in the summer, trucking down to the CRA office in the north end of Toronto proper, she watched the world change around her. Tall grass to short, short grass to pavement, smooth streets to potholes, and cleanliness to anarchy. The sights you saw were the only things that kept you company.

That, and Kana Choi. Her voice was smooth and precise, a kind of British-American mix no one could quite place, but it made Kani feel like the world was under control. After a further update on the Gossamer trial and a brief piece by a reporter named Peter Lacroix — embedded with the SEF for the fifth time — the news turned back to the latest UN summits, which sounded very much like the old summits, and soon Kani lost interest. She turned off her earbuds as she rounded the corner to the train station, cutting through the half-empty parking lot as she fished for her train pass.

Half the stalls in the station were broken at one time or another, but today's surprise was a spray of vomit right at the base of the only working entry point to the platform. A woman in high heels was trying to find a way to navigate the mess, but every time she swiped her pass, she took too long to get through, and the tall glass doors closed on her again. Kani checked her watch quickly, then tapped the woman on the shoulder.

"Give me your shoes," she said, swiping her own card. The woman looked her up and down, then smiled with relief, slipped her heels off, and handed them over. Kani cleared the vomit easily, then held the glass doors open with an elbow, nodding back. "Ready!"

The woman backed up, holding her expensive alligator-skin handbag close to her chest, and ran. She landed safely next to Kani, getting a bracing hand under her arm. "Thank you," she said, receiving her shoes. "You're a darling."

"You're welcome," Kani smiled. "I think."

She and the woman parted ways on the way down the long tunnel to the east-bound platforms, where a collection of vending machines offered to sell the unwise traveller a collection of snacks, power juices and condoms for exorbitant prices. Kani was contemplating an orange drink to get her energy up when she caught sight of the flashing clock on the wall, and it made her flinch: 5:45.

"What the hell..." she muttered, and checked her watch, only to find it had stopped at 5:30. Her eyes shocked to life, and she ran up the stairs, stumbling on the last step as the train's doors closed, giving her a clear reflection of the state of her face, mouth hanging open. "Wait..." she squeaked, but the train lurched forward, picking up speed, and shooting down the tracks without her.

She leaned her head against the concrete wall, sighed deeply, and pushed the earbud back in her ear. She tapped through to Stacey's name on her phone, slid it back in her pocket, and waited while it rang. "Hey Stace," she said unhappily. "It's Kani. Just missed the train. Hope you're on it. Tell Mr Longbottom I'll be—"

A hand grabbed her shoulder, and she nearly fell down the stairs. She turned and gasped at the sight of Stacey, bruised face and tears in her eyes, gasping for breath.

"Stacey..." Kani said, holding her friend's arm. "What's going—"

"Run," Stacey said, hands shaking. "We've got to *run!*"

Execution

Kani's bag dropped from her shoulder as she raced down the steps, stumbling and falling into a stranger, nearly toppling into a free-fall as Stacey pulled her forward. They dashed through the hallway, straight past the stalls, and out into the parking lot. Sweat was pouring down Stacey's face, skin so pale it only served to make her injuries look worse. Kani was about to ask her about them when she was pulled off again, trying to hold on to a little bit of control in her suddenly-crazed life.

"What's going on?" she gasped, but Stacey wasn't answering. She smashed into the gate by the station, pushed and rattled it until the latch gave way, and they tumbled into the tall grass in the field by the tracks. The morning sun was burning off the moisture on the stalks, but the pinpricks of water were enough to give Kani a chill, making her fear feel even worse.

They ran faster than they could see ahead, skipping over rocky patches and quick dips in the terrain, finally coming to a stop in a small indent in the ground near a dead tree. Stacey pushed Kani close to the ground, peered over the grass nervously.

"What's going on?" Kani asked, and Stacey hushed her quiet.

"I'm in trouble, Kani," Stacey whispered with a trembling voice. "So much trouble. I don't know what else to do. I've got to run."

"Where have you been the last few days? Everyone's asking, but I—"

"I told my mom I was staying with you."

"Oh," frowned Kani. "Well that's—"

"I didn't know what else to do," Stacey said, tears in her eyes. "I really don't know what to do anymore…"

"What's wrong? Is it your step dad? I swear to god, if he hit you again, I'm going to—"

"No! No, it's not him. It's not him. It's... god, I don't know how to say this."

Kani grabbed Stacey's hand and squeezed, brushed blond locks from her friend's swelling face. For a moment, Stacey seemed to flinch at the contact, ready to fight, but she calmed, her breath slowed, and she nodded, bit her lip. She wasn't wearing her sweats or her uniform; she had on party clothes that looked two days old, crinkled and dirty, blue material accented with drops of blood. She had no shoes on, and the soles of her feet looked ragged. Wherever she'd been, it had been some time she'd been home. She looked at Kani with deep, pleading eyes, and spoke in a whisper that was all that was left of her voice: "I owe money."

Kani nodded. "Okay. Money. How much money?"

"Twelve thousand dollars."

Kani nearly choked. "Excuse me? What?"

"Twelve thousand. I know. I know, but—"

"Stace, seriously... how is that even *possible*?"

"It's not what you think."

"Oh sure," Kani said, almost laughing at the thought. She didn't want to do this, but it was just too absurd. The frustration boiled over and she let loose: "I'll bet it's *perfectly* reasonable. Sometimes you just can't resist those new shoes, and—"

"I'm being serious, Kani!"

"Really? Because seriously, I don't know how you can possibly owe *anyone* that much money. You're eighteen! That's insane!"

"It's... complicated," Stacey offered, and started to cry.

Kani took a sharp breath in, shook her head. She had to get a hold of herself, because like it or not, her friend needed help. She softened her tone, tried to be as constructive as she could. "Okay," she said, taking Stacey's hands in hers. "Can't you tell whoever it is you'll pay them back as soon as you—"

"It's the mob," Stacey said, quieter now. "The Italians. I owe *them* the money."

Kani nodded, peered over the grass. No one at the gate, in the parking lot, even at the platform. Another train raced out of the station, rattling the air. If the mob was involved, they had to get to a downtown police station, and soon. Nostalgia for the "good old days" meant the Italian mob was increasingly volatile and dangerous as they struggled to overtake their Russian counterparts. But the Russians owned the city, so if they had to hide, that was where they had to go. She took her phone out of her pocket without letting Stacey see. She needed to call her dad, get him to drive them. Anything else was taking a risk.

"They did this to you?" she asked, motioning towards the bruises. "That's what this is about? We should get you to a hospital—"

"When I told them," Stacey stammered between sobs, "... when I told them I couldn't do it anymore. I couldn't—"

"Couldn't what?" Kani asked, looking again at the party clothes, the heavy make-up, the ripped stockings. She held her breath.

"It's so hard, Kani," Stacey whimpered. "I don't know what to do..." She put her face in her hands, and Kani rubbed her back softly, face not nearly as sympathetic as her touch. She squeezed her phone in her hand. "I was trying to get away," Stacey said, so quiet she was barely audible. "I needed to get away from him, but I needed money."

"You don't need to do... *things,* you know. You can stay with us and—"

"No! No, I can't do that to you guys. I can't do it, and he wouldn't let me. He'd make your life a living hell, Kani. You have no idea."

"Stacey. Come on. You've got a family. You've got friends. Whatever's gone wrong, we can help you fix it. Nobody's going to judge you if you felt you needed to—"

Stacey looked at her friend, tears in her eyes. "You don't understand," she said "This is too big. I screwed up too bad."

"So you borrowed twelve thousand... that's not too—"

"I borrowed half a million."

Kani's breath left her. She grabbed Stacey's chin, turned her face up so they were making eye contact. "You *what?*"

"It's... complicated. I pay it off as I work. But when I'm done, Kani... when I'm done, I'll have millions of my own! I can get away..."

"You can get away *anyway,* Stacey," Kani said, shoving her phone back in her pocket. She quietly cursed herself for not seeing it sooner. There *was* no mob, no twelve thousand dollars, none of it. When she was ten, Stacey had come to school and said her parents had died in a car crash, and she was staying with her alcoholic aunt. Friends took turns sheltering her for weeks before someone saw her mom at the store, alive and well. Since then, Kani was the only one who really listened to her anymore, got to hear her new fantasies come to life. Sometimes she believed them, sometimes it was too easy not to. The only constant was her step-father and his drunken rages, and that was the thing that kept Kani was abandoning her, too. Reality was hell for Stacey, so it was easy to sympathize with the imaginary world she made for herself. The mob, half a million dollars, all this… it was the same old routine, amped up to an absurd degree.

Kani squeezed her hands, spoke softly. "Stacey, you need to call your mom and tell her what happened. And if she won't listen, you really need to go to the police. Your mom will understand."

"He's *not hitting me!*" Stacey yelled, then covered her mouth as if she could pull the sound back in.

"This is all just a fantasy," Kani said solidly. "A fantasy to avoid—"

"It's not a fantasy," Stacey cried. She pulled a small bank book out of her pocket, flipped it open to the first page. The top entry, handwritten in blood-red ink, was "LOAN: $512,000", followed by dozens of lines slowly chipping away at the total until she was left with just under twelve thousand dollars in her balance. Kani took the book, skimming through the rest of the pages, seeing odd scratches and notes, then looked her friend dead in the eye. She had no idea what Stacey was doing to earn that much, but it was a lot less imaginary than it had seemed a minute ago.

"Okay," she said, voice distant. "Okay, so you owe twelve thousand out of half a million. That's not great, but it's pretty good. You must be raking it in. I… I don't want to know how you're doing it. You don't need to tell me. But you're doing okay for yourself, and everyone has a bad day once in a while. Your… boss must know that. Everyone has a bad day. Why not ask for an extension or something?"

Stacey started crying harder. "It's not the way it works," she sobbed.

"Listen," Kani said, pulling her phone out again and taking Stacey by the arm. "We need to go to the police. This is too serious to handle on our own."

"No!" Stacey yelled, then cursed to herself. She grabbed Kani's arms, squeezed tight. "We can't see the police. Please, Kani, you need to help me. We can't go to the police."

Kani watched her warily. Stacey's phone started chiming, and she shuddered when she saw the address. She turned it off, put it away. "Who was that?" Kani asked. "Was it them?"

"No," Stacey said, wiping the tears from her eyes. She suddenly looked confident, in control… or at least scared of something else. The name on the phone almost flipped a switch in her, and Kani wanted to know *why*. Stacey blinked as if waking up. "Listen," she said. "It's not safe here. Can we go somewhere safe? Someplace we can hide? Just until things calm down?"

Before Kani could answer, a loud voice boomed out from the distance, and though she couldn't understand the words, by Stacey's reaction, it was clear they'd been found.

They scrambled to their feet and ran through the field as the shouts got louder, more persistent. There were two voices Kani could pick out, and a third coming from ahead, to their right.

Stacey stopped suddenly, and Kani did too, grass brushing against her knees as they swept their gazes across the horizon, looking for options. The panic was back in Stacey's eyes, and Kani squeezed her hand tight, trying to infuse some bravery she didn't feel herself. She pointed at the river in the distance. "There," she said. "Let's go!"

They raced across the field, Stacey checking over her shoulder every few seconds, nearly falling because she couldn't make herself look where she was going. "Stacey," Kani gasped between strides. "Police. Please..." Stacey just kept running.

They arrived at the edge of an embankment, a long, gnarled concrete slope going down to the river's edge, drains built into the upper levels as a failsafe in case the thing ever flooded. The river was too dark to have colour, and was moving fast, dragging trash and foam along as it rushed to the city reservoir. It was probably two metres across at the edges, but each side of the embankment added another three. Kani checked behind them and finally saw their pursuers: dark figures in the distance, closing in fast.

"There's no time!" Kani said. "We've got to jump. Can you make it?"

"I... I think so..." Stacey breathed.

"Jump as far as you can," Kani said, zipping her sweater all the way up. "Try to hit the water. It looks deep enough. I can't see the bottom."

"Okay," nodded Stacey.

Kani backed up, tightened her fists, and filtered out the shouts from behind, the panic in Stacey's voice, the sound of her own mind racing. She slowed her breathing, listened her heartbeat, made it calm... calm...

She took off, foot touching the edge of the concrete, and threw herself into the air, legs still pumping as she flew. For a moment she thought she might even clear the river, land on the other side, and she inhaled a hopeful breath, a smile on her face. But then she hit the water, choking as it filled her lungs, and struggled to bring herself back to the surface.

"Hurry!" she shouted up at Stacey, spitting out a mouthful of putrid liquid.

Stacey nodded, took two steps back, and then started to jump without even close to enough momentum. "Wait!" Kani yelled, but it was too late. Stacey barely cleared the ledge, foot catching in one of the drains, and sending her slamming into the concrete with gut-wrenching force. She cartwheeled down, losing her bag along the way, cracking her shoulder hard and skidding into the water.

"Stacey!" Kani shouted, splashing forward as her friend went under. She dove down, saw Stacey floating, face twisted in pain, not trying to get back to the surface, like drowning was a viable solution to her problems. Kani screamed at her, furious. She grabbed her by the arm and started to pull, but Stacey shook her head, eyes wide with fear. She tried to wrestle free, but Kani was stronger, held on to her grip, and pushed her to the surface ahead of her.

Just as Stacey's head made it up, she was suddenly yanked clear of the river, out from Kani's hands. Kani yelped, swam up herself, and sucked in as much air as he lungs could manage while trying to see what was going on. A hand grabbed her hair, wrapping tight, and pulled up until her shoulders were out of the water.

"What's this?" asked a man she couldn't see, his voice thick and saucy, an Italian cadence in every word. "One of your girlfriends?" The only thing she could make out was a tattooed arm close to her face, and the barrel of a gun touching her forehead. Nothing else would focus.

"Don't need *you*," continued the man. "Good thing you're already in the river. Saves me some work."

Kani closed her eyes as the safety clicked off.

Waiting for Death

"Wait!" barked another voice: a man with a higher, nasally voice, with grit around the edges like he'd smoked every day since birth. Kani blinked back beads of water, tried to see him, see what was going on. As her vision cleared, she saw a small man in a scratched and dusted black jacket kneeling over Stacey, jaw set tightly.

"Leave her alone!" Kani yelled, and was dunked under water again. She struggled to get free, but couldn't escape the tattooed man's grip. She choked as she screamed, only to be pulled out, gagging and wheezing.

"You shut your trap," said the tattoo.

"Bring her out of there," said the small one. "This is not good. Look at this." He held up Stacey's arm, and Kani gasped at the sight of blood.

"What did you d—" A slap to her face ended the protest.

"This is not good," repeated the small man.

"Who are you people?" Kani asked, watching the big man with the tattoos carefully. He had on small round sunglasses that made his head that much more bulbous. The words across his arms weren't English, but they looked angry. He dropped her on the concrete, nudging her away from the water with his foot. He was easily twice Kani's size, looked like he was made of brick wrapped in pale skin, and he smelled like old, used mint gum. "What do you want?" Kani said, looking over at the big man's boss.

"I'm Augusto Fantoni," said the littler one, puffing his chest to make himself look tough, and failing. He was the kind of person who was scary because of the quiet rage you could see just beneath the surface; the kind that would explode out of nowhere and hurt anyone in sight. He just didn't seem to recognize it himself, so he played at being a tough guy. He threw Stacey's arm to the side and stood up to full height — a few centimetres shorter than Kani. "I'm the one in charge of your little friend here. She tell you about me?"

Kani shook her head.

"It don't matter now. I'm your new best friend."

"I've called the cops," she said, voice wavering below the defiance. "Let us go and I'll forget this happened."

"You're tough for such a little girl," Fantoni grinned. "I like that. I can make good use of you."

"Not interested," Kani said, scowling.

"Oh, but you do not know the family yet! We are good people, and we'll treat you very good!"

"Yeah, I can see," Kani said, looking at Stacey on the ground, face battered and arm mangled. Fantoni looked over, too, and shrugged.

"We treat you good if you treat us back," he said, as if it was a viable excuse. "Like I said, we are like family, yes? I'm the pappy, the one who knows best. This paisan who helped you out of the water, he is like your big brother. We call him Erlenmeyer."

"*Erlenmeyer*?"

"He spend time in Germany—"

"Austria," said Erlenmeyer.

"Whatever. It make no difference. He is a good guy. Strong guy. Always does what he's told. Does good work. Unlike *you*!" Fantoni kicked Stacey in the stomach. She yelped, but kept quiet. A bone was sticking out of the back of her hand, and blood was seeping towards the river. She was pale, shivering.

"She needs a doctor," Kani said.

Fantoni and Erlenmeyer laughed. "Doctor! That's funny! You a funny kid! I like you. You an' me, we gonna get along very well, I know. You can call me Pappy if you like. I can see you and me, we are going to be very close."

"You can go to hell," Kani spat, and Erlenmeyer slapped her again. She fell to the ground, dazed at the impact, cheek burning fiercely. Fantoni crouched down next to her, held her chin, spoke to her like she was a child. "Stacey's hand is busted. Even with a doctor, she's no working any time soon. Can't hold things, can't work, no? You know what that means?"

"You're a bastard?"

"It means she can't do what I pay her to do. She's no good to me no more."

Stacey bent her head up, reached towards Fantoni with her trembling, mangled hand. "They know about me…" she said. "Please, we need to stop. They know…"

Fantoni sighed, scratched his chin, then nodded to Erlenmeyer, who slammed a foot down onto Stacey's hand. She cried out in agony, curled into a ball and whimpered to herself. Kani wanted to go to her, but when she looked back, she saw Fantoni with a knife in his hand, digging dirt out of the cracks in the concrete between them. He was much scarier when he forgot to be tough.

"Since Stacey is no longer useful," he said, almost absentmindedly, "with the broken hand, I have a problem. She isn't free and clear until her debt is paid, and like this, I don't think she's going to be paying much. But you see, that money, it *needs* to come in. Broken or not, it needs to come in. So what I'm thinking is… *you* can take her place."

Kani's face flushed red and it took all her willpower to keep from lunging at him. "Screw you," she said. "I'm not going to be your whore."

Fantoni's face twisted into a smile, and he looked over his shoulder at Erlenmeyer, who was already laughing. Kani reached for the knife while he was distracted, hoping she could slip it out of his hand, somehow use it to fend them off … but they had guns, and she had nowhere to run, and if she left, Stacey would—

"You a pretty girl," Fantoni said, flipping the knife away as he turned back. "But that kind of work won't pay what I need. That ain't it." Kani looked at Stacey, but he snapped his fingers and drew her attention back. "It's touching you think so much of your friend, that she would do that. But no. What I need is someone to fly in her place."

Kani jerked to attention. "Fly?"

"Do not worry so much, it's very easy. If Stacey can do it, you can do it no problem. You already look much smarter than she was, digging this hole for herself." He snapped his fingers, motioned to a third man who was just stumbling down the embankment, gun in hand. "Find the bottle."

Stacey groaned as she was rolled over, her bag taken from under her. Books and papers fell across the ground, along with a large bottle of painkillers with the label ripped off. Fantoni scooped it up, shook it. "This is for you," he said, opening it up and handing it to Kani. She looked inside the bottle, saw a collection of huge pills, all different shapes and colours, rolling around the bottom. Any one of them could be poison, or something else to make her more complacent. Regardless of what Fantoni said, she wasn't going to trust this wasn't some elaborate scheme to get her into a party dress of her own, stuck in some club somewhere until she'd paid off Stacey's debts. She rattled the pills around in the bottle, looked at Fantoni.

"Take 'em," he said.

She dumped the pills into the river.

Fantoni looked back at her, eyes narrow. "You have fire in you."

Kani said nothing back. She was shivering all over, both from the cold of the water, and the intense adrenaline rush she got, facing off against a monster like this. She felt like she was sprinting along the edge of a cliff, ready to fall at any time, but not really believing it could happen.

"It will be your funeral," Fantoni shrugged. "I can appreciate fire, but not with such a short deadline as this. You can be fiery when it's done, but for now, you do what I say, you fly this one time, and you get to go home."

"And Stacey?"

"Yes, yes. Stacey too. She gets to go home."

"And if I say no?"

Erlenmeyer aimed his gun at Stacey's head. There was so much blood, she was barely awake at all to notice her life being threatened, but Kani yelped. "Wait!" she pleaded. "I don't know anything about flying! I don't even know what you're talking about! I'm just a teenager, I don't—"

"It's not hard," said Fantoni. "They make it easy these days. Here…" He fished Stacey's phone off the ground, turned it on, held it forward, but paused. "If you drop *this* in the water, you both die. No joking. Do not cross me."

Kani paused, nodded reluctantly.

"You take this phone, you ride the westbound train to the Guelph express stop. Get out there, and there's a big field behind you. Look west, walk about three kilometres through that field…"

"Wait, what am I doing there? What am I looking for?"

"You keep your mouth shut, and I tell you."

"Fine," Kani grumbled.

"Three kilometres in, you will find a shack. Wooden thing. Looks like it was built by Erlenmeyer's mamma, yes? You find the ship, plug the phone into the dashboard and—"

"Hold on," Kani said. "What ship? What's this about?"

"You plug it in, it takes care of the rest. You just punch in the code when it says to. Right? Right, Stacey, girl?" He prodded Stacey with his toe. She barely reacted. Kani's breathing got more urgent, furious. "Any funny business, and we kill your friend. And maybe your family, too. I can't decide. I will let Erlenmeyer decide."

Erlenmeyer chuckled to himself.

"I don't know what you're talking about," Kani said, taking the phone and pocketing it. "How am I supposed to do what you want if I don't *understand* what you're after?"

Fantoni laughed, and his men joined in. He started up the embankment, glancing into the sky with a wide grin on his face. "You don't listen well, do you?" he said. "You're flying for me. Up there. Bringing home... how does it... yes, bringing home the bacon."

"What bacon?" Kani called as he reached the top.

"Minerals, I think. I don't know, I don't do that part."

"Wait, *asteroid* minerals?" she gasped, taking a step back. Erlenmeyer caught her before she fell into the river again.

"That's the one," he grinned. "For today, you get to play a pirate. It'll be fun, right? I think it'll be *loads* of fun."

On the Last Line

A pool of water was forming under Kani's seat as the train pulled out of the station, heading west. She pressed her head against the glass, catching a glimpse of Fantoni shoving Stacey into a black truck in the parking lot below. Seconds later, the parking lot was gone, the station too, and all she saw were lazy fields stretching off into the distance. She stared at the horizon as if it could comfort her, instead of looming ominously.

She rested her forehead on the seat in front of her and pulled her arms in close, trying to warm up. The train's air conditioning blew from all sides, making the chill worse. The last great heat wave of the season had rushed through the area, prompting cheers after such a frigid summer of cold rains and even a freak snowstorm; but sitting in an ice box of a train, Kani couldn't help but wish this September were more like the rest. Colder outside meant warmer in. She wasn't sure she'd make it to Guelph like this.

She couldn't decide if she wanted to take off her sweater or keep it on. It felt cold on her skin, but the jersey she wore underneath wasn't going to help much either. She started to unzip the sweater, then caught sight of a businessman out of the corner of her eye. He sat across the way, newspad in hand, watching her more than the words on the screen. She shrugged at him, and he jerked to attention, went back to reading. Uneasily. She knew he wanted to know what happened to her, but he didn't know how to ask, or to even bring it up. She wouldn't know how to answer, either. She laughed at the conversation unfolding in her mind, awkward and halting, and then found herself crying, silently she hoped, at the answers she would have to give.

She caught her breath, held it, and all in a rush, the weight of the past hour came pounding into her. She covered her mouth just in time to stop a loud sob, lowered her head down towards her knees, wrapped her arms around her head, and cried. She kept having flashes of the gun at her head, Stacey's hand, the blood… just when she thought it had passed, that gun came back into view like lightning… a flash of terror, and then gone. It was more real than real for the second it happened, and it made her shudder every time.

She calmed herself, stowed the panic away, and wiped the tears from her eyes with her soaked jacket sleeves. The businessman was watching her again, finger hovering over the newspad like he was trying to decide between helping her and continuing with his day. She looked out the window, huddling close and hoping she could vanish from people's minds, like she had every other day on the train.

She fumbled in her pocket, pulled out her phone, checking the waterproof case had kept it safe from the river. Its sleep button pulsed softly, and she slid her finger along the edge to wake it up. It listed her "favourite" contacts in a neat list, the top being home, and the word drew her in. In the cold reprocessed air of the train this early in the morning, help seemed so far away, but all she needed was to push that button…

She looked up. Various eyes glanced away, pretending to mind their own business. Kani wiped more tears from her eyes, leaned back in her seat like she belonged there, and sniffled. Let them think she had a broken heart, or she failed a test, or she couldn't get the car for Friday night. Problems not worth a second glance. Please let them think that. Anything but the truth, because the truth was so awful and unexpected, she still couldn't wrap her mind around it.

No, she said to herself, shaking her head. No, she could wrap her mind around it. It was a problem that could be beaten. She could beat it. She was fine. She was going to be fine. She gripped the phone in her hand and tried to be fine.

The train rocked side to side as it straightened from a turn, lights flickering off as the pre-set schedule figured dawn was over and daylight would be bright enough. Above the nearest doors, a thin strip of fluorescent paneling illuminated a poster, scratched on with black marker: How to pick out a pirate. Asteroid pirates. Worst of the worst. Terrorists, murderers, more hated than the most notorious criminals of the last two centuries combined. Ruining lives, pushing up unemployment to extreme levels, costing the world economy its foundation, and threatening the future. Asteroid pirates were the kind of myth everyone knew, but nobody knew personally. And here, two feet away, Kani looked at a poster of a pirate, and felt her stomach tighten. The photo was nothing like her: a gravely-looking man with a scar on his face, cigarette hanging from his lips. Somehow, she and this man were the same.

She read the address on the poster, an easy-to-remember link meant to stick in the mind long after you'd first seen it. She keyed it into her phone with shaking hands, thought for a moment, and then hit "go." The site came up: slick and friendly and designed to comfort instead of intimidate, but failing on all counts with her. She tapped through to a page called "See the signs," wondering how much of herself would come through. A video began to play, and she popped in an earbud to hear.

"... can be anyone, anywhere. Always be on the lookout for these telltale signs... Excessive vitamin use. Because of their unsafe vehicles, pirates are exposed to high doses of solar radiation, which can cause serious health defects if not treated. To counter this, many criminals consume large quantities of specially-fortified vitamins to help them survive their time in space..."

Kani clasped her hands together, shaking. The pills in the water. She looked at the sun, and it felt cold. She wondered how important those pills really were.

"... An abnormal work schedule is often a warning sign. Because of the unpredictable nature of unlicensed mining, pirates will often need to leave work at strange hours, and stay out for extended periods of time. Sometimes you—"

A hand landed on Kani's shoulder, and she flinched back into the wall, dropping her phone. An old man stood there, patchy stubble framing a rotting mouth. He put his hand out to her, brown with caked dirt and sunburnt cracks, and breathed putrid air at her. He was speaking, but she couldn't hear. She took the earbud out, grabbed her phone from the floor.

"Can'ya spare some, dear?" he asked.

She glanced around. "I don't... I don't have any money," she said.

"Not money, dear. Tea. Can'ya spare some tea?"

Kani smiled nervously. She shook her head. "Sorry," she said. "I don't have any tea, either."

The old man sighed and sat next to her. She pushed herself as far against the wall as she could manage, trying not to touch any part of the filth settling in next to her. He began massaging his thighs, humming softly to himself, like he'd forgotten she was there.

"Mood swings?" he said suddenly.

"Excuse me?"

"Mood swings? You have them?"

She looked around. A few other people on the train were watching them, cautious or amused, she couldn't tell. She leaned as close to the old man as she dared and whispered: "Sorry, what?"

"Your phone. It said 'mood swings'. You have them?"

She looked down, stopped the video from playing, put away the phone. "No," she said. "No mood swings."

"I like swings."

"Sure," she nodded.

"When I was a boy, I jumped off the swing, did you know? I jumped off the swing, and I landed on my face. Right here… can you see the scar?" He pointed to just under his nose. Kani smiled at him, nodded. He tapped two teeth around an empty space on his gum line. "Lost my first grown-up tooth that way. M'mother was livid. Absolutely livid."

"Yeah," Kani agreed, looking out the window again.

"Do you have a mother?"

She closed her eyes, turned her head halfway to see him, pushed some wet hair from her face. "No," she said. "No I don't."

"She was lovely," he said. "My mother was lovely. She bought me things at my birthday."

"I think that's normal," Kani said, the edge in her voice piercing through. "Listen, I think that guy up there has some tea."

The old man's eyes shot forward. He got to his feet. "Tea? Really?"

"Yeah."

"I don't see him! Where is he?"

Kani pointed forward, squinting. "He went into the other car. He's up there. He had a cup of tea. A kettle, too. He looked happy."

The old man waved to her and rushed out of the car, laughing the whole way. Kani looked at the other passengers and shrugged. They smiled back, went back to their reading. For a minute, she felt like a normal teenager again, just one of the crowd, totally undeserving of any attention.

"Guelph express station," said the train gently. "Please prepare to exit."

Kani got up, checked her seat in case she'd left anything behind, and slipped off the train onto an abandoned platform. The air was thick with the smell of trash, wet and rotting in the overstuffed cans at either side of the exit. The train shifted off, kicking dust up into swirls as it went, and she watched it until it was just an impossibly-thin line in the distance, and then nothing at all.

She looked west, through a farmer's field, one of the greenbelt farms they'd built to help the local economy in the last recession. Some of the bigger trees were still there, perched in the middle of the plantings, the odd-looking concession to environmentalists who'd fought so hard to save the forests. All the way beyond her view, there was nothing but corn. No shack, no ship, no danger.

She looked around herself until she was certain she was alone, then walked down the stairs, out to a parking lot that was completely empty, and had been for some time. Grass grew out of cracks in the pavement, and the parking meter signs were all bent over or missing, long forgotten since Guelph got a proper station closer to downtown. She watched the cars swish past on the highway, the big box stores lighting up for the morning rush, and it was like it was any other day, just in a different part of town.

She stood at the wooden fence blocking her way into the field and thought for a minute, running her hand along the edge. This was the moment, she knew. The moment she could turn around and try something else. Anything else.

She put a foot onto the bottom rung of the fence, and lifted herself over into the field. The ground was wet and muddy, recently-watered, she guessed, and it sucked on her sneakers like it wanted her to stay put. She started walking, slowly at first, but then faster and more urgently, leaving the safety of the paved world behind. Leaves hit her face, and she pushed them aside, hopping every so often to see over the stalks, trying to see what was coming.

Ten minutes later, just as she was beginning to wonder if she was lost, she shoved through the thicket and nearly collided with a beaten old tractor, rusted and broken, looming over her like a scarecrow for humans. The thing looked strangely out of place, just sitting amid the corn, one of its massive wheels bent around a rock. She carefully moved around it until she was standing at the edge of a clearing. It was barely bigger than her back yard at home, shorter grass drawn loosely in the countryside like it had been half-planned and forgotten decades before. In the centre was a sizeable wooden shack, like a barn, boards coming off the sides, painted blue and yellow, but so faded it was almost impossible to tell there'd been colour at all. Out from the front of the shack, heading straight for her, was a long stretch of crumbling asphalt, giving way to nature at the edges, ending at the tractor on the rock. Kani walked around the shack slowly, trying to guess if this was it. She stopped when she saw the name painted on the left side: "Eli's Air Patch." She nodded to herself. This was it.

The side door was open, swinging in the wind, back and forth, squeaking at the tail end of every move. As she approached, something inside the shack rattled. She paused, held the door still and leaned in. "Hello?" she called. "Is anyone in there?"

Silence. She leaned in further, tried to see through the darkness. Bright shafts of light from the ill-fitting boards made it impossible. They pushed the contrast no matter where she looked. "I'm Stacey's friend. Is anyone there?"

Another shuffle.

She looked over her shoulder, back at the field, and for a brief moment, thought about running. But where would she go? Home? What could her dad do? What could the police do? If she ran, Stacey would die, and even if she told herself otherwise, she'd know it was her fault. She couldn't run. She had to do this. It didn't matter who was in there, she had to face them.

She stepped in, letting the door sway again, and listened. The wind made a faint whistling as it passed through the roof, and she thought she heard a dripping sound, but there was nothing else. No breathing but her own, and even that was stalled to help her hear better.

She took another step, and tripped over something, fell to her knees. She turned around and saw a dusty bin of chocolates, left right by the entrance. Department store chocolates, the tape still around the seal. She'd bought Stacey one just like it for Christmas last year, and wondered if this is where they'd gone to. Tossed on the floor of her secret life. Kani was about to push them out of the way, but paused and looked at the door, realizing this was an impromptu early-warning system. She slid them back where they were. Back on her feet, she brushed the dirt off her knees, and looked around.

A huge tarp, stitched together from different materials and textures, was draped over an oddly-shaped vehicle at the centre of the room. Only the giant wheels peeked out the bottom, hinting at what it might be. She pulled at the tarp, and it came off easily, revealing a dull, patchy metal underneath. She pushed the tarp to the side and stood back, taking it in.

It was a jet fighter, wings folded up in a triangle above it, cockpit speckled with dust and dirt. It looked like the old fighter planes from World War II, re-done by lunatics fifteen years ago, and left to rot. Nostalgia had been big with the designers of the space tourist boom, Simon had told her. To her, it looked unsafe. The metal seemed rusted, pitted even, decorated one way and then reworked by so many others that it was impossible to tell what colour it was trying to be. Along the side, the letters "F-422" were half-removed, painted over by playing cards and fiery patterns. Running below the edge of the cockpit, it said: "Incessna," and below that, "Tundra."

She ran her hand along the edge of the glass and found a latch. She pushed it in, and the cockpit hissed, opening gently and easing to a stop with just a palm's-width space from the ceiling.

She glanced around herself, listening for a rattle again, but heard nothing.

She climbed the side of the ship, kneeling over the opening like she was trying to decide whether to jump into the water or dip a toe. The cockpit was a mess of buttons and screens, and she felt a panic at the thought of climbing in there, having to make sense of it all. A flight suit and helmet were folded on the seat, waiting to be used, and since it was the least-imposing part of the view, Kani snatched them up and dropped back to the ground. Anything to escape those buttons.

She looked around one more time and then eagerly stripped off her clothes in favour of the flight suit. They'd gone from wet to damp to clammy, but the smell of the river wouldn't give up, and there was something about them she just couldn't stand. Painful memories. She moved her wallet and keys from her slim pockets to the big, baggy zippered beasts on the flight suit, and fastened it up everywhere she found a latch. The suit was too big for her, but she rolled up the sleeves and legs until they fit, and strapped the gloves on as best she could.

The front doors to the shack rolled open easily, as if they'd just been greased, coming to a rest and locking into a slight groove in the ground. As soon as the first door was open, a small creature — almost like a cross between a hedgehog and a monkey — scurried out and into the field. It looked back at Kani, turned its head to the side, and made a little noise that felt so alien, it was like she was in another world altogether. She blinked at it, and it disappeared into the corn stalks. There was no reason left to delay: she turned back towards the fighter.

It looked worse in full daylight. Vintage cars had a look about them that said they were built to last, and would hold themselves together out of principle... but this thing, it looked like it felt every minute of every day of its incredibly-stressful life. If it could make it off the ground, it would be a miracle. If it could survive in space...

She put on the helmet and sat herself in the cockpit, closing the lid. She fumbled the phone into a cradle in the console, and the dashboard lit up. The phone said: "Please dial."

"Dial?" she said to herself. "Dial what?"

She looked around for something that looked like an address to dial, but found nothing but a small scrap of paper with a drawing of a pickle wearing a dress. She smiled at the oddness of it, turned it over, and saw the hand-written note: "M-27."

"M-27," she said. "Memory 27. Okay, I get it. That makes sense."

She went into the phone's memory banks, tapped through until she found entry 27. Unnamed. She took a deep breath, and hit "dial." The glass in front of her flashed to life, showing a text overlay with quick words scrolling by faster than she could read. Like a really old computer booting up overtop reality. A peaceful logo faded onscreen, proclaiming: "Centrix Interface System 4.2 — Better Than Old School™."

Without warning, the jet powered up, making Kani jerk back in her seat, heart racing. She gripped the sides of the cockpit, suddenly realizing she had no idea how to get out if she wanted to. The jet started rolling out of the shack, making her panic all the more severe. She checked behind herself, saw the wings unfolding as the ship cleared the shack, rotating around and locking into place with a jerk. The left wing had to try the locking process twice before it got it right, which was not calming at all. A second later, the engine roared loudly, and she felt herself pushed back into her seat.

"Please fasten safety harness," said a pleasant voice, not unlike her computer at home. "Please fasten safety harness."

She pulled the belts over her shoulders, fumbling with the latches as the engine got louder, and clicked them into place. She had only had a second to spare before the jet picked up speed and tore down the runway, straight at the rusted old tractor!

Recalibrate

Kani braced for impact as the tractor raced closer, putting her feet on the console and covering her head with her hands. At the last second, with a whir, the ship jerked into the air, knocking her feet loose, and pressing her down into her seat like nothing she'd ever felt. Her bones almost creaked from the pressure. She let out a rattled breath, turned her head until her helmet knocked against the canopy glass, and watched the corn field shoot past in a blur.

"Coordinates locked," said the computer. "Requesting satellite coverage. Confirmed. Changing course. Please be patient." The ship banked to the left, and Kani's head knocked sideways, on the other side. Faster than she would have imagined, she saw the field give way to dark green forest, sporadic lakes and rolling hills, and then slowly, frost, snow and giant oceans of ice.

"Where are we?" she asked herself, then spoke louder. "Computer, where are we?"

"Command not found," said the console.

"Figures," she muttered.

"Updating satellite information," said the console. "Confirmed. Changing course." The ship banked left again, and again she swayed to the side.

"Hey! Warn me next time," she said.

"Command not found."

"Shut up. Yeah, yeah. Command not found."

All the snow outside began to look the same, so she started looking around the cockpit for things to do. The screens were all working away, showing data she couldn't understand, and the buttons were content to exist without her interaction, so she let them all be. The paneling seemed to be made from a kind of rubberized metal, soft when she pushed it, but not so soft it would bend very far. It was far newer than the rest of the ship, and in thin strips around the edge of the canopy, she could see where the old cockpit fittings had been replaced, swapped out for this newer, friendlier design. Small pockets and compartments littered the cockpit, as if you'd bring knick knacks and a picnic with you into space, but after an exhaustive search, Kani found most were empty. She discovered a tube wedged into a small slot on the left side, and inside was a rectal thermometer. She blinked at it through her helmet. "Oh Stacey," she said. "This is so not how I want to remember you."

She looked out the window again and noticed they were much higher now. The finer details of terrain were missing, and off in the distance, she could see the faint edge of the continent, though she couldn't tell what part. It was beautiful, whatever it was. Rich, dark blue and a kind of green noise she couldn't put a word to. The sun reflected brilliantly off the Pacific ocean.

"Course correction," said the console, and they banked right. She knocked her head on the edge of the cockpit.

"Stupid goddamn…"

"Please avoid pressing buttons during autopilot stage," said the console.

"Stop knocking me around, then," she snapped.

"Command not found."

She began to get impatient at her situation, strapped into such a cramped space with nowhere to go. She thought back to her last trip in an airplane, and what she'd done to amuse herself. That'd been a three-hour flight to Calgary, which had been just enough time to watch a movie. Inspired, she tapped the phone, and it came to life exactly the same way it would had it not been plugged into a massive wedge of pressured metal. She searched through the media folders and found a copy of Stacey's favourite movie, *Fragment Man*, but when she played it, she found the sun was causing such a glare on the screen, she couldn't see anything. She turned off the movie in disgust, then flicked through to music, and hit the shuffle option.

She jerked to attention at the first song. A mopey, traditional country tune. She tapped the screen and read the title, squinting in disbelief. "*All My Exes Lives in Texas*?" she said. "I don't know which is worse, Stace, the thermometer or this. Holy crap."

She let it play, glancing out the window again, and in the distance, saw a mass of swirling white in the middle of the ocean, moving yet totally still. "The typhoon…" she said to herself. "That must be Korea. Where the hell are we going?"

She began to realize her arms were floating, not resting at her sides anymore. The helmet was putting faint pressure on her chin rather than the top of her head, and she suddenly felt ill. Horribly, painfully ill. Airsickness, but worse, like there was no up and down, and no limit to nausea.

She closed her eyes and took deep breaths, blowing out slowly, trying to work past the feeling. "It's all in your head," she said. "It's all in your head. There's no reason to be sick. No reason to be sick—"

"Microgravity alert," said the console.

"Shut *up*! Shut up! Just stop talking!"

"Enter mute mode?"

"Yes! Mute mode! Do it!"

The console didn't reply. It flashed an "OK" on the glass above her, and went back to its business. She looked up for the first time and saw... black. Pure, deafening black. The cockpit lights dimmed until she could barely see her own reflection anymore, only the enormity of nothingness. In its presence, her sickness evaporated, replaced by an overpowering fear she couldn't bear to acknowledge.

Off to her right, a small pinprick of light twinkled, shining more as her ship moved into space. The pinprick was moving, too, moving over the curved horizon, too big to be a satellite, but too regular to be anything but man-made. "The space station," she said, smiling to herself. "Got it."

She looked over her shoulder towards the sun, and everything went black very suddenly. Red letters flashed over her vision: "Warning: Avoid direct exposure to sunlight." She turned away. Her body felt... toasty.

"Good to know," she said.

A sudden noise shook her awake. It was digital, like a glass breaking over a long period of time, coming from behind and arcing over her, off into the distance. She looked around, couldn't see anything, but then a second noise pierced the silence, moving the same direction. She wondered how she could hear this, given the helmet, the cockpit, and the vastness of space. Whatever it was, it was unnerving, and she wanted it to stop. She reached to the console, searching for something to mute all audio at once. Instead, four buttons with pictograms on them caught her eye, and she pushed the first one that looked like a grid. Suddenly, the darkness of space filled with a set of digital wireframe axis planes showing three-dimensional space.

"Wow," she said. "That's pretty cool."

She tapped the second button in the sequence, and a long rectangular trough appeared before her, running off into the distance. She was moving along it, she could see, at a rate that seemed impossibly fast. Beside the green trough were two others, both yellow.

"What are those things?" she asked, but the console only wrote "Command not found" on her visor.

The last button clicked down and Kani nearly fell back from the shock of what she saw. Dozens — if not hundreds — of tiny markings, all over her vision, showing every bit of *everything* space had to offer. Another sound shot by, and she watched a small red square arc into the distance, labelled "debris." She was surrounded by debris. It was stunning. Junk, satellites, unknown objects of various shapes and sizes. She saw one item called "STS-142 Screwdriver", and wished she could get closer to see if it was true. The ship was swivelling left and right to avoid things, and she only barely registered the motion. It wasn't banking like in the atmosphere, it was actually *shifting* itself in clean motions, effortlessly. Her airsickness started to return as her eyes started to recognize what was happening, but her body didn't feel it.

The visor read "Autopilot ending" and suddenly a long pole with a sphere on the end extracted from the side of the cockpit, and a second stick, like a gear shift, appeared at her left hand. She had no idea what to do with them, but it seemed like she was being told she had to try. She reached out and held the gear shift, and wrapped her fingers around the handle at the side of the sphere to her right.

"All right," she said. This makes sense. I think."

She turned the sphere clockwise, and the ship mimicked the motion perfectly. She wasn't swooping like an airplane, she was simply rotating in space while moving forward. When she stopped, the movement stopped. She turned back, just to be safe, until the digital corridor outside stayed beneath her, rather than at her side. She turned the sphere again until her hand was on top, and the ship flipped downwards. She could still see the green corridor directly in front of her, the nose of the ship cutting through it. She was moving the same speed, same direction, just not with the same orientation. It was extremely unnerving. Unnatural. She almost threw up.

"If this were a game, I'd return it," she muttered. "The UI sucks."

She pushed the stick to the side, but the computer put up a warning saying, "Fuel loss expected. Please correct course." She put herself back on track.

"Crybaby."

Ahead, a series of green triangles appeared, but without identification. She motioned to them. "Can we magnify that?"

"Command not found. Please reduce speed."

"I'm saying, can we magnify that before I get there?"

"Please reduce speed."

"Seriously? Just—" But then she noticed it: they were approaching much faster than she expected. In a moment of panic, she realized she was going to collide with them in a matter of seconds. She pulled back on the throttle, and jerked forward as the ship slowed down. It finally eased into a reasonable velocity, and ahead of her she saw what appeared to be other fighter ships, floating in loose arrangement, the green triangles positioned over their cockpits by the console. Finally, something useful.

A ping echoed in her ear, and she heard a voice that was not the console for a change. It sounded African-American. Rough, curt, and not amused.

"Who are you?" said the voice.

"Um… I'm here because—"

"Answer the question," repeated the voice, and she could finally see who was talking: every time the voice spoke, the green triangle over top a ship in front of her changed hue slightly.

"I'm… um… Tundra?"

"You don't sound sure, *Tundra*."

"Feeling a bit sick," she said, noticing the other ships around her, all facing her. She felt late to a party.

"Sick?" said the voice. "How long have you been doing this?"

Kani glanced at the phone, as if it might tell her, but she had no time for that. She began to speak, but then her console flashed red. Weapons lock, it said. Evasive manoeuvres recommended, but she had no idea *how*.

"Too slow," said the voice. "Now we've got to blast you out of the sky."

Stranglehold

"Wait!" shouted Kani, feedback loud in her ears. "Hold on, I *am* Tundra!"

"Where have you been, then? It's almost twenty minutes past."

"I was… held up," Kani said.

Silence. The fans on the console began whirring to life, strained from rendering the busy slice of space ahead of her. Kani checked the other ships nearby, trying to see what her chances of escape were. One was a twin-bodied vessel with long wings spread between the two nacelles, painted blue and marked with kangaroos and Australian flags. Another was long, gleaming and metallic, like a mirror in space, almost invisible but for the blue of the Earth and the white of the sun. The last ship was very much like her own, but nowhere near as wretched-looking. The major problem was that all these pilots were likely much better at flying than she was, and given they were pirates, they'd have no issues with killing her.

"Does anyone know her?" asked the angry man again. A chorus of "no"s came across at once. One woman, two men. "No one to vouch for you," said the man. "You're out of luck."

"Now hold on there, Rook," said a man with a higher-pitched voice. Australian accent. The kangaroo man. "I don't *know* her, but I have some mates who do. Let's give 'er a test, see if she fits."

Kani glanced between the two ships, waiting for the reply. The weapons were still locked on her, and she had no idea how to fight back. If she even *could* fight back.

"Fine," said the angry man — Rook — unhappily.

"'ello, darling. I'm Spastik. How's it going today?"

"Skip the pleasantries, Spastik," said Rook.

"They're the best part!"

"Shipments in three," warned the third man.

"Fine, right, okay," said Spastik. "Tundra? Can you tell me who was the last player the NHL let go without a helmet?"

"What kind of question is that?" snapped Rook.

"Shush, you," said Spastik. "It's a test."

Kani considered checking the phone for the answer, but knew the signal wouldn't work in space. She tried thinking back to all the NHL information she'd ever been exposed to in life, but all she remembered was that the Maple Leafs never won the Stanley Cup.

"I… I don't know," she said, watching the guns mounted on Rook's wings with dismay.

"She passed!" laughed Spastik.

"She *what*?" said Rook.

"Oh, definitely a pass. I heard from Ricochet that Tundra was a hockey newbie. Couldn't tell a puck from a football if you drew'er a picture."

"I don't see," growled Rook, "how the two issues are connected at all."

"Logic, mate. Logic."

"Let's put this off," said the third man. "Tundra, welcome. I'm Elvis, and Chenne is in the Tigris over there."

"H-hello," Kani said nervously. The weapons lock was still on her, Rook's ship looking straight into her, daring her to make a mistake. Slowly, the other ships started to part, moving off the green corridor, to either side and out of view. Kani didn't follow them, just kept staring at her opponent, terrified.

Finally, Rook slid his ship to the side, too.

"You might want to move, Tundra," said Elvis. She was about to ask why when her screen flashed red, and she instinctively jerked her controls to the side, sliding off the corridor as four green triangles appeared in the distance, moving fast towards her.

"Let's get up to speed, people," said Rook. "You *do* know how, right, Tundra?"

"Yes, sir," muttered Kani.

"Wahoo!" yelled Spastik, taking off, back towards Earth. Chenne and Elvis followed, but Rook stayed close by Tundra, watching her, she could tell. She glanced out her window at him, trying to see who he was, but his cockpit was dark. She might have expected it, but it made her even more nervous. She pushed the throttle and took off, trying to escape him for a while. Out of the corner of her eye, she caught sight of something big, and before she could think of what it was, a giant ship raced past her, following by two more. They were massive boxes, at least six storeys tall and more gnarled and pitted than her own ship; their sides were made up of large octagonal plates that seemed burned and warped, like they'd been to hell and back. The fronts of the ships were like ramps moving up into a point at the top, and down at the base were enormous hinges that looked at least as big as a bus. There were no windows, no cockpits, no signs of life. These were the freight containers of space.

"Decell in ten," said Elvis. "You're in the turn zone, Tundra."

Kani looked around, couldn't see anything, no markings, no corridors... she checked above herself, but...

"Move on up, kid," said Spastik cheerfully. "And quick-like." She lifted the sphere, and her ship floated upwards, until the massive ships were clearly below her, flying in a staggered row, the edge of the Earth silhouetting them brilliantly.

They all blew powerful streams of mist out of bell-shaped jets on their sides, and in perfect synchronization, they spun themselves around, facing backwards, their gigantic matte-black thrusters bearing down on the planet. It was all so graceful, like a bulky mechanical ballet... and just like watching ballet, Kani felt like she was missing half the story without a programme.

"Freighter decell stage one complete," said Elvis. "Get ready for burn."

Kani was just about to ask what that meant when the rear thrusters on all three freighters lit up... giant, bright bursts of flame burning so bright her helmet tinted to protect her eyes. And then, in an instant, they were gone. So far behind her she couldn't even see their triangles anymore.

"Good evening, friends," came a new voice. Deep, Russian, jovial, even. "Nice to see you all again."

"Hello Redux," said Rook. "How are the freighters?"

"No problems," said Redux. "Minor deviation at halfway mark, but I fix, so we are good now."

"Excellent. Thank you for your work."

"No," said Redux, "thank *you* for taking care of them from here. I will sit back and relax, if okay."

"Tundra, your speed is high," said Rook. "Slow it down." Kani pulled back on the throttle, but her speed stayed up. She pulled back on the sphere too, and that did it.

"So what's this I hear about you retiring, Redux?" asked Elvis. "Too good for us now? Is that it?"

"Yes, is always," laughed Redux. "But no, my time up here is over. Is now day to pass mantle to young pilots, yes?"

There was a long silence, and Kani knew everyone was staring at her.

"So if you go," said Spastik sharply, "who's gonna be the slowpoke in our group? Not me, I can tell you that. Rook? You feel like bein' slow?"

"Ignore Spastik," Rook said.

"Always do," said Redux.

"I hate to break up the party," said Elvis. "But I need to remind you all we're coming in on the dark side of the planet today, so you need to be extra careful in the Earth's shadow."

Kani looked at the Earth, looming large in her viewport. She could see a sliver of light along the edge, but the rest was like a pit of darkness. "Careful how...?" she whispered to herself.

"Four minutes to splashdown," said Elvis, and then static filled Kani's ears, loud and piercing. The sound resolved itself somewhat, but she heard Rook say through the mess: "Channel nine, switch now."

She searched the console for a place to switch channels, but couldn't find anything. The other ships were starting to break off and fly in strange patterns, but she didn't know *why*. She smacked her head against the headrest, and noticed on the ceiling, a little display for comm channels. "Oh," she said, and switched to channel nine to urgent noises and Rook booming his voice over the cacophony.

"... Elvis on backfire and Spastik—"

"Yeehaw!"

"— do whatever you want," Rook sighed. "Good." Kani pulled away from the freighters, trying to follow the others. "Tundra!" he snapped. "Stay with the freighters! You're the spotter, remember!"

"Oh, yeah. Sorry."

"Is your voice changer on?"

"My what?"

"Voice changer. Dammit. Double-check before we—" The radio filled with static again, but this time resolved itself very quickly to a voice speaking in a clear American accent, calmly and dispassionately.

"...2028. Section 4.3 dictates a maximum travel speed of 62,920 kilometres per hour; further, section 6 requires proper certification for extra-terrestrial activities." Up ahead, five yellow squares began their approach. They were in tight formation, and closing fast. Next to each was an identifier: UN-SEF-01, UN-SEF-02... "In accordance with section 4.2, the Space Enforcement Fleet is hereby making the following requirements of you..."

"Tundra," said Rook. "Stay on the freighters. Copy?"

"Copy," Kani said, and went back to listening to the enemy — the good guys — speak: "First: surrender your freighters to our control by transmitting the corridor codes. Second: eject any and all weaponry on your vessels in a way obvious to SEF forces. Third..."

Kani watched the battle start: Chenne charged at the SEF ships, blasting them with something that sent giant plumes of smoke into the air around them. Smoke? The mist cleared quickly, and the ships were all still intact, just positioned strangely on approach. Drifting towards each other...

"Stay in formation," said the SEF leader carefully. "Repeat, stay in—"

The leftmost SEF fighter broke off and started charging after Chenne. A second later, two more followed Spastik. They wove around the darkness with unreal movements... nothing like this would have been possible in the atmosphere. Kani was mesmerized by the sight of it, as terrifying as it was. It was a kind of beautiful, imprecise dance on a black backdrop. Stunning.

By the time she realized she'd been drifting, it was too late: the fourth SEF ship charged at her, and her ship shuddered loudly, from dozens of impacts. "I'm hit!" she shouted. "What do I do, I'm hit!"

"Relax," said Elvis calmly. "It's just ice. Turn yourself so you get the sun, and you'll be fine."

Kani looked at her windshield and realized it *was* ice. Thick, awful-looking ice, but just ice. She turned the sphere to angle herself, but the ship didn't move the way she expected. She dropped down, close to the freighters.

"Whoa there," said Elvis. "Watch it until your RCSes are unblocked. Baby steps."

"Sorry," said Tundra.

"Don't be," said Elvis kindly. "Just take it slow. We don't need the political fallout from you dying up here." By his tone, it was a joke. But it wasn't really.

In the full light of the sun, the ice melted off her ship almost instantly. When she nudged the sphere, her ship moved as expected. It was strange, thinking the spaceship's controls could be "expected", and she almost laughed at how easy it really was. Maybe this is what Stacey had liked about it. It was deadly, but *easy*. She turned herself around and saw the green and yellow markings of a dogfight in action.

"Thank god I'm not out there..." she said to herself, and moved further back, behind the last freighter, trying to keep an eye on everything. Spastik was spiralling in and around the enemy, firing ice almost at random, sending ships scattering for cover. Chenne stayed at the periphery, making quick jabs into the fray, coating an SEF fighter heavily, and then winding back out of danger. Kani had lost sight of Elvis, but she saw Rook now, making a long arc around the convoy on his way back to the dogfight. Kani gasped when she realized an SEF fighter was coming at him from below.

She didn't know what to do... he was technically her teammate, but he was about to get attacked by one of the good guys, so should she really get involved? She bit her lip, playing through the options... if Rook was somehow captured, would the mission still be a success? Would Stacey's debt be paid off? She wasn't sure, but she also wasn't ready to take the chance. She started to call out to Rook to warn him when the SEF fighter blasted him with ice, knocking his ship sideways. He tried to adjust his course, but he was heading straight for a freighter, glass canopy first!

"Rook!" she yelled.

Time to Go

Kani turned the sphere and shoved the throttle as hard as she could, and was pushed back into her seat as she rocketed towards the freighters. Rook's ship was sputtering, trying to turn, but with all the ice, it wasn't going to make it in time.

Kani felt a small button on the back side of the throttle, and hoped it controlled the weapons like she thought it did. She pushed it down and her ship made a horrible grinding noise like it was eating itself whole, and a moment later, a long burst of bright white ice pellets shot out of the nose of her ship, bounding into the freighter.

She glanced up and noticed a small cross where she'd been shooting. Targeting. She adjusted so it was pointing at Rook. She fired again, straight into the nose of his ship. The force of the blast spun him down, and pushed him clear of the freighters.

"Tundra!" he shouted. "Are you on the freighters?"

She looked back, saw how far she was off-target, and smiled weakly. "Um, no, sir?"

"Jesus, newbie! We're two minutes out here! We don't have time for this!"

"But you were—"

"If your brains were made of dynamite you wouldn't have enough to blow your cap off! Get back there! You don't get points for saving me! Move it!"

"Yes sir," she said, and took off again, back into position where she could see the whole field. The dogfight had been left behind, so the only thing between the freighters and Earth was a lone SEF ship, floating in the void. The commander kept announcing orders, but none of his fighters seemed to care.

"Return to formation!" he shouted. "That's a direct order, and I—"

Chenne careened past him, blasting him with ice, before taking off back towards the convoy again. Another SEF ship chased after her, missing with every blast. She ducked in and out of the massive frames of the freighters easily, like inertia meant nothing to her... but the SEF pilot was no so lucky.

On a quick turn, he missed his mark and cracked his right wing against the edge of a massive bell rocket. The impact spun him around and he bounced forward, skidding off the side of the freighter.

"All stop!" Rook shouted. "Everyone stop!" All the pirate ships paused in mid-motion, even as the SEF ships continued.

"This is Ares!" yelled the SEF captain "All stop! All SEF fighters, stop right now!" Slowly, the field became still. The broken fighter kept twirling away, small bits of debris leaving a red trail behind him in Kani's visor.

"Fireball! Report!" said Ares.

Static.

Kani held her breath. Space looked so much bigger suddenly.

"Lost a wing," said Fireball, finally. "Dent on the nose, but pressure intact. Going to try and stabilize."

"Pressure is definitely safe?" said Ares.

"Definitely, sir. I'm good."

Kani exhaled with the rest of them. It seemed strange, going back to fighting, after that. She stayed still, waiting for instruction.

"Can I just say," said Spastik through the silence. "That Fireball... is a damn stupid name for a pilot."

"Here we go again," sighed Elvis.

"I mean holy tempting fate, right?" laughed Spastik, taking off and chasing another SEF ship with expert cruelty. "Who wants to play trivia time?"

"Spastik..." Rook warned.

"Trivia time! Chenne? Chenne, darling? I'll take your silence as a yes. Love ya. Good, then. Trivia time!"

Kani kept close to the freighters, watching the end of the corridor hit the edge of the planet beyond. Suddenly, a little light flashed on her console: "Enter splashdown code."

"What code?" she asked, looking around the cockpit for some kind of note, scrap of paper, or something. She remembered the phone, turned it on, and started paging through screens as fast as she could, desperate for answers.

"Trivia numero uno," said Spastik. "Ferrets: are they rodents?"

"Shut up," said one of the SEF pilots.

"Sorry, incorrect!" laughed Spastik. "Anyone else?"

Kani found a number in the notes app that had no explanation to it. She tried typing that into the console keypad, hit "enter". Red light. Incorrect. "Dammit," she cursed.

"Ferrets," declared Spastik, "are actually mustelids. Not rodents. You're welcome."

"Spastik," said Rook, "leave the channels clear except for—"

"What is the significance of the following numbers? 0, 1, 1, 2, 3, 5, 8?"

"Your IQ test scores," laughed another SEF pilot.

Kani found a second number, punched it in, and this time the light went green! "Yes!" she laughed, and then rocked sideways as her ship was blasted by heavy ice cover. She blew past the freighters, far off to the left, and the green light turned red again. The SEF had overridden her code. "Dammit," she cursed, and tried to turn herself to melt the ice.

"Fibonacci sequence!" said Spastik. "Come *on*, people! Make an effort!"

Kani entered the numbers again, got control of the ship back, turned the sphere, and punched the throttle. The SEF ship that blasted her was in sight, racing away at top speed. She kept at him, nudging the controls just enough to keep her crosshairs in place, a grin growing on her face. He'd caught her off-guard, but she was going to teach him a lesson he'd never forget. All she knew how to do was aim and shoot, but that's all she needed. She waited until it was carefully aligned, and then —

The SEF ship spun completely around and, not losing speed, blasted her instead! She screamed off target, vision blocked by ice, and tried her best to fall into the sunlight. "Gotta remember they can do that..." she muttered, waited for the ice to burn off.

Once her controls were responding well, she punched the throttle and took off after the ship again, learning the subtle difference between accelerating and accelerating too much: in a frictionless environment, you could easily overtake your prey, but if they switched directions suddenly, it was incredibly time-consuming to follow. Flying in space was so simple to do, but so hard to do *right*.

She fired broadly over the enemy's right side, then the left, pinning it into a straight trajectory, right to into the shadow of the Earth. The SEF pilot spun again, but she rotated her ship out of the way in time, laughing at how seamless it was, and returned fire.

The first ice pellets hit, and the plume they gave off shocked her so much she jerked back, slowed herself. For a second, she felt incredible guilt at what she was doing: she was attacking the good guys! The police! What kind of person was she becoming? But then, through the fast-dissipating mist, he returned fire, grazing her wing.

"Dammit," she said, losing any sympathy for her target. "Learn to stay down." She held down the trigger as she approached, layering him with so much ice it was hard to tell the features of his fuselage anymore. She shot past him into the darkness, his ship barely visible but for the yellow square on her visor.

She stuck her tongue out at him. "See ya later!" she laughed, and pulled up the code from the phone again. She entered it confidently, hit "enter", and gasped in shock when the light turned red. The code wasn't accepted. She tried again, carefully this time, but got the same response.

"What the hell?" she gasped, and looked to see how far she was from the freighters. Maybe she had to be closer for the code to work, or…

They weren't there.

The freighters *weren't there*!

Pathetic

"See ya later, guys! Nice chattin' with ya!" laughed Spastik, twirling in circles as the SEF disappeared into the distance. "Next time you bring the trivia!"

Kani flew herself back to the group, but not too close. Rook was arriving from further afield, and she wanted to be as far away from him as she could manage.

"I missed re-entry. Was it all clean?" he asked. There was a long pause as Kani tried to think of how to explain, but before she could speak, Elvis cut in.

"We didn't make re-entry," he said. "I don't know how, but we lost the freighters."

Someone groaned, and Rook roared so loudly, Kani wanted to take off her helmet to escape it. "What happened?" he boomed. "We were at the finish line!"

"The SEF hijacked the freighters somehow," said Elvis, trying to infuse calm into a situation quickly getting out of control. "They overrode the splashdown codes. I've never seen it before but—"

"Tundra!" snapped Rook. "You entered the code. Tell me you entered the damn code."

"I…" said Kani quietly. "I… they chased me, and when I came back, the freighters were—"

"Dammit!" shouted Rook. "I *knew* we couldn't trust her! Dammit!"

"Everyone calm down," said Elvis. "We can't just blame Tundra for this. She really *was* being chased, so—"

"Yeah," said Spastik. "Let's blame *you* instead!"

"Me?" said Elvis.

"You're supposed to be her guard, aren't ya? Where were *you* when all this was goin' down?"

"There were… it was crazy out there, and you—"

"That's enough!" shouted Rook. "That's it. That's enough. There's nothing to be done about it. It's a damn mess, but there's nothing to be done. I'm sorry, Redux. I know this must hurt you most of all."

There was a long pause, and Kani held her breath waiting for Redux's reply.

"As you say," he said. "Nothing to be done." He took off towards the planet, leaving the rest of them in silence. Kani rested her head against the side of the cockpit, trying not to cry.

"Everyone go home," said Rook. "I'll… I'll work out the details, see what can be done for everyone. And don't worry, I know who pulled their weight today. Nobody's reputation will suffer because of—" Chenne's ship dipped into the atmosphere, lighting a re-entry flame as it disappeared. It felt like a slap in the face, and Rook's voice reflected that. "We'll figure it out," he said, then left, too.

Elvis said nothing for a minute, then turned his ship towards the dark side of the planet. "One job at a time, kid," he said.

"I'm so sorry," Kani cried.

"Yeah, well…" he sighed. "One job at a time."

He disappeared as well. Kani sat there in the darkness, hearing the faint noises of debris around her, the fan on the console shutting off in the relative calm. She exhaled and fogged her visor, closed her eyes and breathed as slowly as she could.

"Computer," she said. "Take me home."

Nothing happened. She opened her eyes, saw the words "Command not found" on her visor. She sniffled, adjusted the helmet.

"Mute off. Computer, autopilot on."

"Command not found."

She slammed her fist down onto her knee — afraid to hit anything else — and swore under her breath. "Dammit, just get me the hell out of here!"

"Coordinates set. Autopilot engaged. Please be patient."

The ship started moving back towards Earth, down through the atmosphere, down through the clouds and into the hangar she'd entered all those many hours ago.

She didn't notice any of it until the canopy opened.

She sat there in the late afternoon light, helmet in her lap, hearing the crickets chirping outside the hangar. The sunset was red, and the clouds above were lined with a brilliant pink, blurred at the edges by the air over the city.

Somewhere out there, somebody hated her. She'd never had that feeling before, and it was awful. She closed her eyes and sunk deep into the sound of the crickets.

The corn field was hard to navigate on the way home. She stayed off the worn path she'd taken in, and stumbled through the thick vegetation. Maybe to get lost, maybe just to punish herself. The soil wasn't muddy anymore, but it was uneven, and halfway to the station, she tripped, landed on her knees and curled into a ball for so long her legs went numb. Her dried clothes were stiff and awkward, feeling wretched against her skin as she stretched back out and carried on her way.

The world kept spinning beneath her, at first she thought it was panic or guilt or something in between, but after the third time, she realized it was physical, like vertigo, and she started kneeling in the dirt until the feeling passed. She felt like throwing up, but wouldn't let it happen. Suffering seemed like the least she could do.

Her phone rang as she approached the train station, and she nearly dropped it trying to see who was calling. It was her father. She gripped it in her hand, finger over the "answer" button, but couldn't make the last move. She waited until it stopped ringing, then put it back in her pocket.

She climbed the steps to the platform, one heavy step at a time, as the two cars in the parking lot started up and drove away, turning it back into a ghost of its former self. Three steps from the top, she heard the sound of a familiar phone, but it wasn't hers. She checked her pocket and pulled out Stacey's handset, turned it over to see it ring again, and put it to her ear.

"Hello?" she said, tentative.

"Hey," said Fantoni. "You're back."

"I'm back," she said quietly.

"How'd it go?"

"Is Stacey safe?" she asked. "I want to talk to her."

"She's sleepin'. Had a nice meal of Greek yogurt with honey and cranberries. Can't stand Greeks, but their food is delicioso. How was the flight? I need to know."

"It was okay," she said.

"Okay-okay, or just decent?"

She stopped walking, pressed her back to the wall to stop the spinning. "It was fine," she said. "Everything's great. Let Stacey go. I did what you wanted."

Fantoni laughed so loudly she took the phone from her ear. "Not a chance, girly," he said. "I'll wait for the money to appear, and *then* we'll talk about the rest. Understood?"

Kani continued up the steps. "Yeah," she said.

"Don't go and do something stupid now, okay?"

She arrived at the platform, lit by flickering lights and the setting sun. No one was there. "Yeah," she said, and hung up, put the phone away. The next train was due in five minutes. Next to the time was an ad for Chromoco Mining Corporation, the leaders in asteroid mining. The ones you saw when you wanted to go *out there* the legal way. "Forging a Brighter Future," it said.

"Don't I wish," she sighed.

The train pulled in, and Kani set herself at a window, looking out at the darkening fields, the city in the distance, the lights fighting off night. She felt cold, exposed, alone. She took out her phone, stared at the keypad, the nine, one, one. She could call for help, she could let the authorities sort this out, and she could go back to being herself. Hell, she'd go to the damn memorial if it made this disappear. She hovered a finger over the nine.

Her stop was called before she found the courage.

The sun was low on the horizon and the evening chill was setting in as she walked back home. She shivered, picked up her pace and came around the corner to her street, glad to finally be home, to have a chance for some rest.

There were five police cars parked outside her house.

All You Can Do

PARIS, FRANCE

He left the ship locked in the hangar outside town, and with it, the name Redux. In his suit and tie, he walked less comfortably, spoke more cautiously, felt less secure. By the time he got home, he was sweating.

The streets were quiet, light rain giving people an excuse to stay inside, the streetlights glowing a pale orange and giving the place a warm aura the city didn't deserve anymore. Shops all along the route home were closed, windows papered over, boarded, posters advertising cheap tickets out of town, or bargain-basement prices on luxurious condos, abandoned and impossible to heat through the winter with electricity as expensive as it was. A drunk pissed on the front doors of a bank, singing *Frère Jacques* at the top of his lungs, but all the words were in Bulgarian. He went to sleep in the same spot, cradling an empty bottle of wine in his arms.

The steps up to the apartment were old and creaky, some bone-dry and worn, some drenched in water that leaked from the roof except in the direst of droughts. Up he went, heavy frame bending the boards until he reached his floor, never a beautiful place to live, but never as bad as this. The door to the apartment was unlocked, and he opened it slowly, ducking through to the frigid air inside. Down at the kitchen table, Sabina was shoving a sweater into a packed suitcase, eyes red and hair a mess. She turned when he came in, shook herself out of a daze.

"Yuri," she said. "You're home."

He put his keys on the table by the door, loosened his tie. "You are off to hospital?" he asked, voice coarse and dry.

"Yes," she said, and zipped up the bag. "You didn't answer your phone again."

He patted his pockets, sighed. "I am sorry. It was long week. I thought it was on."

"It's never on, Yuri. Never with you."

"It was simple mistake," he said, trying to take her small hands in his. "Please, Sabina, you know me."

"I know you," she said, and pushed past, getting her coat from the hanger beside the door. "I know you too well. I can't take it anymore, Yuri. It's too much. Anya's been in intensive care for a week, and where were you? Where were *you* while I was keeping everything together?"

"I... I was working," he sighed.

"Fine!" she snapped. "Fine. Working. Your contribution. Always the same. Always the same. But tell me, Yuri... how is it work just doesn't cover what it used to, eh? Why don't I feel like you're making a difference any more?"

"Is... is complica—"

"Where else is your money going?" she asked, accusation flaring in her eyes. He had nothing to say. He slumped his shoulders, shook his head lightly, and she cursed under her breath. "I knew it." She tried to go, but he caught her arm, kept her in.

"Sabina," he said. "Don't. Is not your fault." She squeezed his hand, and moved it off.

"Anya needs her gene therapy soon," she said. "This week. We cannot wait longer. The doctors are worried."

"And coverage?" he asked.

She shook her head. "Denied."

"No!" he cursed, pounded the door with his fist. "Why this time?"

"It's because neither of us are *from* here. Why *would* they give us expensive treatments for free?"

"I pay taxes, that's why!"

"You're naïve, Yuri. So naïve." She opened the door partway, then closed it again. "Will we have the money soon? Will they pay you soon?" He said nothing, put his hand to his forehead and stepped away from her. The kitchen faucet was dripping a methodical *pat pat pat*, it was infuriating. "Yuri," she said. "What about the money?"

"Business had setback," he said. "We lost... client. My manager cut pay for month."

"No!" Sabina cried, covering her mouth. "No! Not now!"

"I'm sorry," he said. "I will—"

"No!" she yelled. "No, you just… you don't…" She slumped into the door, and started to cry. The suitcase dropped beside her. "I should have listened to my mother," she whispered. "I knew it. I knew she was right."

Yuri sighed. "What," he said. "What did she say?"

"She said I should divorce you and move back to Germany. That Anya would be covered if you were gone."

"If I were gone," he repeated.

"It's true, isn't it? You're the thing keeping her in that bed! It's you!"

"I did not give her leukaemia," he said quietly.

"You didn't cure her, either!" she shouted, and opened the door again. "Be her father, Yuri. Be her father or get the hell away from us! Before *she* hates you too."

She didn't close the door behind her. Yuri stood there in the dim light, listening to the faucet, staring at the photo on the wall of the three of them on vacation in Cannes. Sabina in her red dress, Anya in the little tank top and skirt, white with black spots like a cow. She was wearing his sunglasses, beaming proudly as they dwarfed her face, but she kept them up with her tough little fingers. You couldn't even see the world behind them, it was so bright. So unlike Paris. He barely breathed.

By the time he let go of the tension, he was at the bar around the corner, a beer cold in his hands, just enough money in his pocket to pay for it. He stared into the mirror across from him, saw himself there, greying beard and hollowed eyes, and lowered his head against the glass. The oxygen in the ship was flaky, giving him less than he needed, but just enough to survive. He knew this beer would flood his system, hit him harder than it should, and wipe away the past few hours in a swirling mass of confusion. He knew what he was doing, but he still didn't like it. It felt like cheating. But he didn't know any other way.

Beside him, loud men with English accents were chanting a chorus, some football song with a poor excuse for a tune, and swaying themselves around like fools. Paris was unaffordable for its residents, but for tourists, it was the cheapest place in western Europe. Ten euros could get you anything you wanted, and if you found the right part of town, quite a lot more. It was a city of transients, the homeless, and the nearly-homeless. The best thing to do was to keep your head down, and not make a sound.

Yuri slid over into a seat away from Englishmen and started drinking. He finished the first pint without pausing, the cold freezing his throat and filling him with a chill that felt like heaven. He slid the glass back, nodded until he knew the booze was working, and asked for more. He couldn't afford it, but he no longer cared.

The English fools were crowding him again, sloshing around their drinks and stumbling over each other. The closest one, wearing a red and white jersey and a military cut, held his glass high and shouted "To the menthol monk!" The rest of them cheered loudly, began to sing again. The close one stumbled, and fell sideways, spilling his drink over Yuri's lap.

The Englishman quickly recovered, standing back and taking in what happened. He wavered slightly, frowning as the images churned in his brain, then stood a bit straighter as he realized he'd dumped his drink all over a stranger.

"Is nothing," Yuri said without looking or reacting. "Don't worry about."

The red-shirted man took another step back, then slammed his glass into the bar. "It *is* a problem!" he yelled drunkenly. "That's a damn expensive drink, you moron!"

Yuri took his second beer from the bar tender, sipped it carefully. He made no move to react to the provocation.

"Hey!" said the red-shirt. "I'm talkin' to you! You hear me?"

Yuri turned his head, face blank. "I hear you," he said. "What do you want me to do? I cannot make you un-spill."

"Buy me a new one," he said, and his friends cheered him on. "And buy some for me mates, too, while you're at it!"

Yuri looked at his mates, looked at him. "No thank you," he said.

"Excuse me?" slurred the red-shirt. "What did you say?"

"I say no thank you. You can buy own drinks."

"Piss on *that*," said the man, and punched Yuri across the face.

Yuri didn't move. He stared straight ahead, eyes not looking at anything but the fierce determination he had to stay in control.

"I will not fight you," he said calmly.

He was punched again, and this time, he turned his head slowly, eyes narrow, and stared directly into the red-shirt's face. "I am not here to fight—"

Another punch, straight to the forehead.

Yuri straightened his jacket, and stood up. At his full height, he was almost half a metre taller than the red-shirt. And twice as wide. He looked down on his opponent and sighed.

"All right," he said, and punched the Englishman straight into his friends. They all backed up, shocked at the rush of reality in their drunken revelry. Locals never crossed vacationers. That was the cardinal rule of Paris. They never crossed them, and they certainly never punched them. The surprise of it took a moment to wear off, but when it did, their faces twisted with fury. They roared as a group, threw furniture out of the way, and charged at him, fists ready.

He took down four with a pair of blows meant for two, caught one of them by the shirt and threw him clear across the room. A fifth stopped, face white, and then ran for the door, bouncing into the glass before stumbling through, into the night. The others were crawling away, too, moaning and dazed and uncertain what had happened. Yuri fixed his collar and reached back for his beer when the red-shirt pulled himself off the ground and produced a switchblade from his pocket. He flicked it open and smiled, inching forward.

"You bit off more than you can chew, old man…"

Riot

"Stay out of it, old man!"

Yuri took a step back, back towards the crowds. The chanting was louder, the voices angrier, and the signs being used as weapons now. Chants of "No! No! WTO!" became less concrete, more violent. The thugs crowding the old woman were wild with energy, ready to pounce.

Yuri watched them as they pushed her into the wall, circling like jackals, and shook his head. "No," he said, grabbing the back of the closest one's jacket and pulling him away. The punk lashed out at him, spat in his face.

"Beat it, gramps!" the punk snarled.

A massive fist broke his nose. He crumpled to the ground while his friends broke away from the old lady, ready to defend their comrade. The streets were filled with protestors, shops afire, car alarms blaring, so there was no one who'd hear what they were going to do. This was righteous justice, and no one would care.

"I only ask," Yuri said, struggling with the words. "Leave lady alone."

They moved in on him, manic eyes shining in the light of burning effigies, and charged. He caught the first one in the face, but two others leapt on him from behind. They pounded on him, trying to make him break, so he threw himself onto his back, using them as cushions. They screamed, frantically trying to get free, to no avail.

The riot police arrived as he was finishing off the last, throwing him into a wall and turning, furious, into a shield and baton to the head. They cuffed him and dragged the whole lot of them off to detention vans along the

Champs-Élysées. His vision swirled for hours, but no medics came to check on him, and he took to counting back from one hundred, just to be sure he could. When police came, they came to drop off more rioters, until the van was too packed to breathe, and they were trucked off out of the city.

By midnight, he found himself in an open-air jail cell somewhere in the suburbs, a quiet park ruined for the sole purpose of housing the riffraff from kilometres away. Bright spotlights shone down from above, keeping everyone awake, washing away any secrets or privacy, except those done in the dark shadows on the grass. Yuri's block was mostly empty, only a young woman in the cell next to him. He glanced at her once or twice, taking in her spiked pinkish-red hair and torn black clothes, marked with white paint that equated the G20 with swastikas. He laughed to himself, rested his head on his knees and tried to sleep.

"What's so funny?" asked the woman, her French impossibly fast. No matter how much he studied, he'd never get to be that fluent. He looked her up and down, and shrugged. "Are you laughing at me?" she asked.

His gaze fixed on the large ring through her bottom lip. Then, her unhappy eyes. He shook his head.

"You are," she snapped. "I can tell. You think we're wrong. You think they're right? The capitalists? You're one of them, right?" Yuri shrugged, went back to resting. "How do you feel about the rape of the developing world?" she said, her voice rising. "Do you like seeing children starve? Do you get off on it? Is that what you like?"

He sighed, didn't move.

"The Big Five have a stranglehold on the natural resources of the world, and who's going to do anything about it? Not you. You like your comfy life, with eco-friendly cars and your spotless home. But you're *killing* people with your car. *Killing*."

Yuri looked to her, rubbed his eyes and sighed.

"You should talk less," he said.

"You're Russian, aren't you?"

"You are quick," he said.

"What are you, then, part of the G20?"

He laughed, turned away from her.

"Scared to fight fair?" she called. "What's wrong? Harder to rape me to my face, isn't it?"

"Rape *you*?" he said, turning around suddenly. "I… you are not—"

"I work in solidarity with those who—"

"You know nothing about it," he snapped. "Keep mouth shut, please. And thank you." He turned back again.

They sat in silence for a while. He could hear her plotting, whispering arguments to herself to try them out. He leaned against the fence, considered sleeping. The ground was ruined, grass interspersed with mud and worse, so there was no place to lie down. Maybe by accident, probably by design.

"Do you know the Bonn Convention?" she asked, just as he was dozing off.

"You still speak," he said.

"It's a treaty, signed by most of the world, and it criminalizes *true* free enterprise. It makes it virtually impossible for smaller players to bring back ore from the asteroid b—"

"If safety issues, maybe for best," said Yuri.

"You're a fool. Do you even know what you're talking about?"

He looked over to her. "Do *you*? Have you been in space?"

She looked down, seemed hurt by the question. She regained her bravado, sneered. "I have a job down here," she said. "I have to fight for the people without a voice. Against people *like you*."

"Who am I?" he sighed.

"You're one of the fascist pigs behind it all."

He shrugged. "Believe what you like."

They sat in silence for another few minutes. A guard came by, checked on them, leaned down to walk to the woman. "Having a good night, Rache?" he asked. She spat in his direction, and he laughed. He walked to Yuri's cell, motioned back to Rache. "A regular," he said, and left.

"Fascist pigs," Rache muttered.

Yuri turned towards her, began to speak, but stopped himself, turned away. Rache sneered at him. "What?" she said.

"Is nothing."

"What? You have something to say, so say it."

He shook his head, then shrugged. "Is illegal to fly in space, yes?"

"Yeah," she said.

"No, is not illegal. Is *hard*. Must meet safety needs. Like to fly in airplane, is not illegal. Only hard. Yes?"

"It's an order of magnitude harder," she said.

"Order of magnitude more danger," he said. "Lose cabin pressure in propeller plane, is big deal. Lose cabin pressure in spaceship, and you die."

"Splitting hairs," she muttered.

"No, is not splitting hairs. Regulations in place for reason. Protect people from danger. You want to mine asteroid for poor people, you go ahead, have your fun. But to bring home, you need to be safe, yes?" She said nothing. For a change. "Is like for everything. Supply, demand. First movers, they have advantage of setting rules. Chromoco set up shop, make rules, protect investment. You want to play game, you have meet ante, yes?"

"It's *wrong*," she said.

"Right, wrong, no matter. Is capitalism."

She spat at him.

"You have gland issue," he said.

"You don't know what you're talking about," she snapped. "You're making excuses for the rape of—"

"You keep using word, but you do not understand meaning. Maybe too young."

"To you, anyone's young."

He laughed, leaned back to stretch his legs. "I am not so different than you. I think rules are unfair, and I protest too. Just without… you know… putting holes in face." He tapped his lip, and she put a hand to hers, fingering the ring. She sneered and turned away, pouting probably.

"They can keep us here forever, you know," she said. "They can lock us up without cause and just forget we ever existed. Just because we were protesting."

"I was not protesting," he said. "I save old lady from protesters."

She looked over at him. "You what?"

"Punching them in the face, yes?"

"Oh Jesus," she sighed, and turned away again. "You're worse than I thought."

"Is not my fault. They pick on old lady. You talk about injustice, this is injustice. Old lady, she do nothing wrong. Bunch of fascists."

Rache laughed, but stopped herself. "You're an idiot, old man."

"You are not so dumb yourself, Rache."

The guard came back, knocked on the edge of Yuri's cell, unlocked it and opened the door. "You're free. An 86-year-old woman came in and ID'd you. Said you saved her life."

Yuri looked over at Rache.

"This is what I tell you," he said.

She grumbled in her solitude.

"Good luck out there, old man."

"And good luck to you, Rache. I hope you will find better life to live."

Trapped

Kani was walking briskly. A careful kind of fast, not likely to attract attention, but not so slow as to be seen. She worked her way down to Bolton Village, stayed out of the streetlights, close to the buildings.

The Village was a kind of carefully-crafted mini-town, with monolithic buildings carved up to look like homey shops, little patches of lawn and benches set here and there to give the illusion of unexpected growth, as opposed to an architect's careful scrutiny. The place was busy during the day, and only a little less so at night, though it was never on any teenager's list of hangouts, due to the prevalence of freewheeling security guards with stun sticks and very few rules. Normally, that wouldn't be appealing, but if things went wrong, Kani had a feeling they might come in handy.

She looked at Stacey's phone in her hand, trying to decide what to do. She'd been taking even, calm breaths since she left her street, trying to keep from having a meltdown, and hoping she at least looked the part. The phone, so central to her experience in space, felt dangerous, somehow tainted, and she desperately wanted to throw it in the nearest trash bin and run away. She closed her eyes, trying to think of a way to get out of the mess she'd gotten herself into. When she opened them again, she still had no answer.

A woman across the way was closing up her shop, turning out the lights, but staring at Kani fiercely. Kani kept still, just outside of a streetlamp's glow, trying to disappear. The woman flipped her "open" signed to "closed", glaring through the glass, one hand floating near the phone at her belt. Kani smiled at her, moved on, turning a corner and climbing some stairs to the second level of the place.

She slid her finger along the edge of the phone and searched through the memory banks, through all the names of people she didn't know, back to the start again. Some of the names were vaguely familiar, but no one she could trust to call. Some were just pure gibberish, but she was afraid to dial something so unknown. Especially on this phone. Especially today. She paused at number twenty-seven, the entry that had started the fighter, and bit her lip. There was no reason to do it, and so many not to. She pushed the call button anyway, and put the handset to her ear. It rang twice before picking up with a noisy background.

"Hallo!" came a heavily-accented voice. "Wong Mushu Chicken Factory! Home of Magnificent Cheesecake! Can I take your order?"

She pulled the phone back, frowned at it. "I…" she began.

"No, just kidding," laughed the voice, accent gone. "I love that one. Every time I do the Italian accent I sound like a Nintendo game. Still funny, just not the same."

Kani blinked. "Who is this?" she asked.

"Who is *this*? Who are *you*?" he asked.

"It's T—"

"Rhetorical question, sorry. Never… you know what? Hold on."

The phone went dead. She took it away from her ear, checked it, then slid it into her pocket. It was probably best this way. Talking to strangers was not going to get her out of this mess. She had to find a way to talk to her father, to explain what had happened, and maybe he could find a lawyer — no! the company had great lawyers! They'd help him for sure! Then she could explain the situation, the police could save Stacey, and she might even be able to provide some kind of help identifying the pirates. There were rewards for stuff like that. Not that she wanted the reward, but it was nice to know this whole ordeal might yet pay off…

She reached for her phone, but Stacey's rang instead. She took it out, checked the number, and saw it was from "Wong Mushu Chicken Factory." She answered.

"Hallo!" said the voice. "Wong Mushu Ch… yeah, it doesn't work the other way around."

Kani stopped walking looked around. "I think I have the wrong number," she said.

"Wong number! You made a funny!"

"It's not funny," she said.

The voice grunted. "You're no fun. Why am I helping you again?"

"*Are* you helping me?"

There was a long pause.

"I think I'm helping you. Tundra, right?"

Kani took a step into the shadows. A couple across the street watched her, frowning. She smiled at them, but they wouldn't stop frowning. She didn't know why, and it was making her shiver.

"How do you know who I am?" she asked.

"*You* called *me*, didn't you?"

"I… Where *are* you?" she asked, looking around, into the sky. The stars were out, bathed in a dark blue that felt so comforting, Kani couldn't describe it. Not like the pitch black of space. The absence of blue would be a big part of her nightmares from now on, she could tell.

"You ever heard of Monitor City?" he asked.

"No," she said.

"No one has," he sighed. "But that's where I am."

"Is that a made-up place?"

He cleared his throat. "Listen," he said. "I don't go making fun of you because you called yourself Tundra. I mean honestly, between the two of us, I'm the more grounded, I'd say."

"So what's *your* name?"

"Kaso."

Kani said nothing.

"Okay fine, I have a strange name too," he said. "You're getting me off track here. I'm supposed to remind you about security. Do you remember security?"

Kani winced. She smiled into the air. "Which part?" she asked.

"The part about not calling this number?"

"Ah. Right."

The phone went dead again.

She held it back, and it rang. She answered, put it to her ear carefully. "Hello?"

"Sorry, wrong key."

"Listen," she said. "I don't mean to be rude, but I have a crisis here and I need some help. Can you help me, or is there someone else I can call?"

"You're talking about Espey, aren't you?"

"Who?"

"Espey. You're dissing me to my face. Well, not my actual face, but virtually *and anyway* no. I'm what you've got. Now let's go over the security protocols. What's your emergency?"

Kani ducked into the doorway of a closed shop, peered around for security cameras. When it seemed safe, she whispered: "There were police at my house."

"Do you live at a donut shop?"

"No."

"Just checking. Okay. What's your Plan B?"

Kani leaned against the door and closed her eyes. The wind was picking up, and she was hungry and had never felt so tired in her life. "I don't have a Plan B," she said, voice wavering.

"Nobody ever has a Plan B," Kaso muttered. "It doesn't matter how many times you tell them, nobody ever thinks they need one. And then here we are, sitting around in the night, wishing we had one. *I* have one, and I live in a bloody autonomous city state. I don't *need* one."

"Are you going to help me?"

"Hold on. I need you to do something first. There's an Off License shop across the street, right?"

Kani looked over, saw the sign, nodded blankly. "How did you—"

"Go in there, walk to the back of the store, and pick up two bottles of Screech."

"I'm not old enough to—"

"I didn't say *drink them*, I said pick them up."

Kani sighed, but didn't have much choice. She ran across the street and ducked into the store, the harsh lights making her squint after so much time in the dark. The clerk watched her with narrow eyes, chewing a long pepperoni stick that made the whole place reek of processed plastic meat. There were rounded mirrors placed here and there, giving him a clear view of every corner of every aisle, which he watched with quick, darting eyes. Kani felt him watching her, waiting for her to make a mistake so he could push a button, call the cops, and make his evening a little more exciting.

The TV was on in the corner, the evening news refresh playing on demand, queued up heavily with sports and entertainment, but a breaking news bulletin had cut into the program, and it made Kani pause.

"... defence lawyers insist the medical emergency is genuine, and are asking permission to transport Gossamer to a facility outside Detroit for further testing. There is no word from the White House whether the request will be granted, though many senators have already gone on record opposed to the deal, saying it risks national security and…"

Kani slipped into the back, found the whisky aisle, searched up and down for Screech. There was nothing. Nothing that said Screech. "I can't find it," she said into the phone.

"It's with the rum," Kaso said, sighing loudly. She ducked around the back to the rum section, scoured to the bottom until she found the Screech: big, heavy bottles of something that looked almost black. Horribly unpleasant. She picked up two bottles.

"Now what?" she asked.

"Turn a bit to your left."

She turned, paused. "Why am I—"

"Ooo," said Kaso appreciatively. "You're quite the looker, aren't ya?"

She saw the security camera ahead of her, and her face went dead. She put down the bottles, gave the camera the finger, and left the store, smiling to the clerk in as calm a way as she could. She snorted at her, went back to his magazine until the sports came back on.

"So here's my plan," said Kaso, once she was outside and moving again. "Since you're good looking — ooh la la—"

"Shut up."

"— but with a poor, poor excuse for a personality, I'm going to suggest the following: you need to find yourself some cheap booze, get brain-smashingly drunk, and pass out in a public washroom somewhere."

Kani stopped, looked at the phone, and then put it back to her ear. "That's not a plan."

"It's a great plan. Listen: nobody would know when you started drinking, so it's as good as an alibi. Honestly, the cops won't be looking at any teenager for you-know-what if they can help it. Give them a reason to go elsewhere, and they will."

Kani sighed. "It's not just that, though. There's something else…"

"What?" asked Kaso. "What else?"

Kani knew telling him about Stacey was a bad idea, but she also knew she was running out of options. Now that he'd seen her, the pirates would be able to find her, so going to the police might be even more dangerous than before. She honestly had no idea what to do, but given the circumstances, it the truth might be the best way to go.

She took a deep breath and turned around, but didn't get to say another word, because she found herself staring straight into the face of a very angry Erlenmeyer. He plucked the phone out of her hand and turned it off as Fantoni came up behind him.

"The money didn't come through," said Fantoni. "Time you saw what we do to failures in this biz…"

Only Ashes

The truck jumped the curb and nearly shredded the lawn, jerking to a halt right in front of the driveway. The door flew open and a man threw himself out, adjusting his tie and running across the small field to the gates to the cemetery.

"Wait!" he called to the old man closing the doors. "Wait! Just a second!"

The groundskeeper turned stiffly, scratched his neck, back curled forward after years of the same routine, fingers locked from arthritis. His face was lined heavily, like he'd spent his life laughing. This was not one of those times. "Place is closed," he said. "We open at ten."

"Please," said the man in the suit, catching his breath, "please, I just need a few minutes. It has to be today. Please."

The groundskeeper checked his watch, shook his head. "Last time I let someone in past hours, the tombstones got spray painted. Tagged, as they say. Got me in a big heap of trouble, you can imagine."

"That won't happen," said the other man. "I promise. I'm not like that. I'm not here for that."

"That's what they'd all say, Mr…"

"Major. Major Freeman."

The groundskeeper nodded. "Where to?" he asked.

"Mexico. Afghanistan before that."

"Tough spots. I was in the Marines myself. Back in '05."

"Iraq?"

"Yes sir," nodded the old man.

"Tough times," said Freeman.

"They're all tough times. Listen. I've got to take a leak. Takes me a good ten minutes to do that. You think you can wrap it up in that window?"

"Yes sir. Thank you, sir."

The old man patted his shoulder. "No problem, Major. You did good."

Freeman slid through the gate and turned on a pen light, cutting a thin line through the darkness. Just enough to navigate by. The rows were neat and orderly, small patches marked with headstones of varying shapes and sizes, but none straying from the perfect rectangle everyone was afforded. He passed names he knew without reading: Dana Turner, killed in a biking accident ten years ago this March. Her father never said much until you asked about his little girl. Then he couldn't stop. There was Miguel Esposito, years spent as a POW in Mexico, back in the States ten days before a heart attack finally bowed him. His wife spoke no English anymore, like an entire language had been carved out of her mind by the grief. That's what this place was: the fresh grief, the raw grief, the kind that all the visitors shared. It wasn't a place to visit and fondly remember, it was a place to come when you wanted to feel pain again.

He made his way along, head lowered in respect, until he stopped at the edge of a rectangle he knew too well. A tall white tombstone stood almost as high as he was, flowers growing in the plot at its base. He stood there, staring at them in the dark, wondering if they were getting enough water, what their colour was like in the daylight, if they were as alive as he wanted them to be.

He stepped onto the stone in the middle of the patch, leaned close to the tombstone, dusting off the screen embedded in the marble. It flickered to life, showing a radiant woman and a young boy sitting under a tree in the sunshine. The boy's face was lit up, vibrant brown against the blue sky, giving the smile that everyone said was just like his father's. No one said that anymore. The screen was browning, faded in spots where the weather had defied warrantees and guarantees and made itself known. Freeman rubbed it with his sleeve, but it wouldn't come off, hidden safely beneath the impenetrable glass.

He fumbled with the pen light, turning it off, and then looked at the woman again, hands clasped together, trying to put words to the thoughts that had been running through his mind all day. Instead, he closed his eyes, spoke a quiet prayer, hoping they were happy in heaven, getting by fine without him, not seeing what he'd become with them. When he opened his eyes, the screen had dimmed. He touched the woman's lips lightly, and she came back to full brightness.

"Asha," he said, then cleared his throat. He fixed his tie, his jacket, as if waiting for an interview, as if there was someone to impress here. She'd have hated that. She hated his artifice, loved it when he was just the way he started out. He took another breath, letting his shoulder slump a bit, and tried again. "Asha," he said. "Sorry I'm late. It's… well, it's been a long day today. I… oh, wait. Here, I brought you something."

He carefully removed a small bouquet of flowers from his jacket, placed them on the grave, leaning up against the tombstone. He couldn't see colour in the darkness, but he hoped they stood up well to the others he'd planted, years before. He stood back, nodded to himself, content. Somewhat content, at least.

"They're dried out," he said. "Sat in the car too long." He nodded to the air. "I guess you knew that. I like to think you still know these things. I know I shouldn't… they said I shouldn't, that I need to give up on things like that. Let go, or whatever. But you know me. I'm not the kind to give up. Not about you, anyway. Not anymore."

He stared at the ground, the long shadows from the screen stretching along his legs, and listening to the traffic in the distance, the quiet hum of the city.

"I guess you're mad," he said finally. "If you can see any of this, I guess you're mad as hell. I went and let my duties come before my family again. Same old, same old. I'll never learn, will I? I can hear you saying it."

He rubbed his forehead, pushing back a breakdown long overdue.

"I'd give anything to hear you say it," he said. "God, I'd give anything to hear you say anything again. I want to let go, I do, but I just… I have these dreams sometimes where you're here, and we're together, and it's like none of it… and it's like I can fix it, if I just keep from waking up. But what always gets me is that I can't hear your voice in my dreams. I can't hear you speak, and that's how I know it's not real. And I can't stand it, so I wake up. And I…"

He saw the screen had dimmed again, and he reached forward, touched it again. This time, the photo changed. The two of them at home, lying on the couch in their old house, laughing together, not knowing how many days they had left to laugh. He sighed, covered his eyes with his hand.

"I'm not learning," he said. "I'm not learning to adjust. I'm just… I'm treading water here, Asha. I don't know what I'm doing without you. I wish you'd give me a hint, because sometimes I just don't know if I'm doing it right at all."

He knelt down in the flowers, brushed some dirt away from the engraving on the front. Asha and Nicolas Freeman, died May 19, 2034. His finger paused at the base of the nine. Nicolas was five years old. Five. Every time he saw it, it hurt him like it had just happened. He spoke softly, whispering to them in the darkness as the screen shimmered above him.

"There was this guy today. Great guy. Dedicated. The kind of man I'd have killed to have on my team, back in the day. Works hard and has no complaints. And he's been working towards his dreams for so long. Longer than me, anyway. Longer than most. And today, his last day, after all this time… it all got taken away. He's got to come back again. He's got to put in on the line another day, and I can't… I don't know. I don't know what I think."

He got to his feet, clasped his hands, and closed his eyes.

"I've been asking myself: if I had it to do over again… if I could have said no that last time, said I was done, that I'd done my bit… would I do it any different? Even if I knew what was coming, would I treat it different? And I don't know. I can't imagine doing it different. And I feel like that makes me a monster."

He shook his head, took a step back, let the screen turn right off.

"I don't know," he said. "I want to take care of my family. Not my real family. Too late for that. I failed once, but I can do better this time. I feel like… like I *need* to do better. I know it won't make up for what happened to you. And I know I can't be forgiven, but… I just wish there was something I could do for this guy. Save him that last trip. Because that last trip can be where it all falls down. And when it falls down, there's nothing left to come home to."

His phone rang. He exhaled, looked into the darkness, trying to see the grave somehow, but had no sense of space. He stepped back, wiping his eyes with the back of his hand, walked back down the row, taking the phone from his pocket and putting it to his ear, trying not to let his voice crack.

"Hello?" he said.

"Rook?" came a voice. Old and French.

"Lucet," he said, emotion dissolving and hardness returning. "You heard?"

"I did," said Lucet. "What went wrong?"

"Tundra went wrong. Where did you find her?"

"She came recommended. Independent confirmations."

"She seemed new to it. Complete disaster. If I'd had any sense, I'd have put her on point guard and let Elvis do the codes."

"You had no way of knowing."

"Yeah," he said, leaving the gate and waving a thanks to the groundskeeper, who made his way over to close it up. Freeman got into the truck, closed the door, and left the lights off. The groundskeeper watched from a distance, then shook his head and went back to his station. Cars roared past on the highway, noise in the background like a calming ocean for him. The sound of home.

"What about Gossamer?" he asked. "Any word yet?"

"I do not know. I have stayed at arm's length. If there were something to it, I am sure I would have heard."

"This is going to get messy," said Freeman.

"It already is messy," said Lucet, voice noticeably tired, frustrated. "It got messy the second he stole that plane. I do not know if anyone can protect him after that."

"Never mind him, I'm worried about *you*."

"You leave me to me," said the Frenchman. "I can take care of myself."

"Of course," said Freeman. "What's this I hear about Sri Lankan handlers for Indian drop zones? That's a change, isn't it?"

"The Indian handlers were arrested yesterday. Someone on the inside, working with police. We are investigating, but it will take time to find out where the leak came from. We need to move carefully on this. Our best team is on it, but it will take time to know for sure."

"I'm just wondering how this is going to change the game plan, now that we're into typhoon season. There aren't many good drop zones outside the Indian Ocean, so..."

The line went to static for a moment, and Freeman lost the start of the answer. When it came back, Lucet was in mid-sentence...

"... ask about Tundra. I have heard from Kaso that she is in trouble, and is requesting assistance. I wanted your opinion, if it is safe to intervene."

"Safe?" asked Freeman. "Or smart?"

"Same thing, I think."

Freeman sighed, checked the rear view mirror, cricked his neck. Whatever he'd said in the cemetery, it was over now. This was business, and business had no room for empathy, sympathy or remorse. He saw himself in the mirror, the coldness in his eyes, and it didn't bother him one bit.

"If she's really a vet, she shouldn't be that bad," he said. "And if she's new, she's not Tundra. Either way, we can't take the risk. Leave her."

Fast Lives

The lightbulb in the shed kept swinging long after it turned on, throwing moving shadows around the room, to the point that Kani started to feel sick again. She had no idea where they were anymore, but it was cold and damp and somehow stuffy at the same time, blood caked on the edges of the farm tools hanging on the walls. The nausea had been getting worse and worse since she got into Fantoni's truck, but now, with the pungent smells and the damn light moving so fast, moving so much, so fast… she was about to vomit.

Her arms were bound behind her back, fastened so tight it felt like she'd have to strip off her skin to get free. She was strapped to a rusted metal chair that squeaked every time she shifted her weight, and every time it squeaked, Erlenmeyer glared at her, warning her to stay put. The floor around her was plain dirt, uncluttered and clean. Ready to swallow evidence whole.

Fantoni sat on the work bench at the far end of the room, gun in his lap, and picked at his teeth with a toothpick. He'd been doing it for a few minutes already, and it was making Kani frantic. He seemed to enjoy it, the panic in her eyes.

"Listen," she said, glancing between Fantoni and Erlenmeyer, unsure who she was really pleading with. "Listen, I'll do anything you want. I can do anything you want, just please—"

She'd never been punched before. She'd been slapped, and for whatever reason, she thought it would be something like that: a sharp bite to the skin, shock and fear flooding from the cheek on out. But it was nothing like that. Her teeth shifted, her bones cried out, her eyes immediately watered, and she felt a deep, penetrating panic like she'd never experienced before. Her jaw screamed at her, and she desperately wanted to feel for blood, find out what kind of damage had been done. Her hands tugged at their bonds without asking, and she gasped for breath, trying not to cry.

"You know what they told me, back when I got the ship?" Fantoni said, tossing the toothpick away. "They told me this: do not hire young girls for these jobs. They said young girls will come, they will work for whatever you want, and you will look into their sad little eyes and feel pity, and you will say yes. But do not say yes. Because little girls will ruin you."

She looked at him through her tears, swallowed the vomit that was bubbling up inside. She refused to let him see her break.

"They never said why," he continued. "Me, I thought it was because they were weak, or slow, or just not so good at flying. But that is not it, because I've seen good pilots and bad, and the girls, they are good. Almost every one. Best of the best, and they never think they're as good as they are. Were you good up there, girlie?"

She glowered at him. "I'd never flown before."

"Oh, we are way past excuses now," he laughed, rubbing his eyebrow with his thumbnail. "The damage is done. The kind of mess you made, I don't even know how to clean up. You've put me in a very hard spot, girlie. Very hard. And I do not like being here."

He pulled a chair across the floor and set it down across from her, sat himself on it, and turned the gun over in his hand, like he was appreciating the texture and the build, instead of callously calculating how to terrify her. Even in the moving shadows, Kani could see dark circles under his eyes, a pale cast to his skin. He was under pressure. Terrible pressure. But he was taking the time to pass some of it on.

"After Stacey disappeared on me, I did some checking," he said, not looking her in the eye, still examining the gun. "It seems you girls go flying a lot. More than I thought, anyway. And the interesting statistic I found is this: half of you end up going to the cops."

This time, their eyes met. She couldn't see it, but she knew his finger was on the trigger.

"I didn't—"

"Half of you go to the cops," he said quietly. "And the other half die trying."

"I won't tell anyone what I did," she pleaded. "I just want this to be over."

"Oh, it's over," he laughed. "Maybe for me. Definitely for you."

He checked the gun one last time, then with an air of unhappy concession, put the muzzle against her forehead. She gasped, closed her eyes, and the tears came flooding out. She didn't want to give in, but it was too much. Too much.

"Please!" she cried. "Please, I will do anything you want! Please don't kill me! Please! You don't need to do this!"

He took the gun away, and though her eyes were closed, she could smell the garlic on his breath as he leaned close. "I don't *need* to," he said. "It's all about *want*."

She opened her eyes finally, looked at him with as much sincerity as she could push through her terror, and said: "I can make it worth your while," she said. "Whatever you want. I screwed up, but I can fix it for you. I'll make it work. Please."

"Your heart's not in it," he said. "I can find another girl who won't insult me to my face."

"Please don't!" Kani sobbed, hysterical. "Please… I can fix this…"

His finger moved to the trigger, and just as it touched, his phone rang. He watched her, listened to her sobbing, and then the phone rang again. He put a hand in his pocket, pulled out the handset, and checked the number. No recognition on his face, but no confusion, either. He put a finger to his lips to tell her to quiet down, and then pushed a button on the phone, and put it to his ear.

"What?" he said.

"Hello is this the mob?" said Kaso through the speakerphone, making Fantoni wince at the volume blasting into his ear. He tried pushing buttons, but the speakerphone seemed locked in place. He dropped the phone to his side, gun still trained on Kani's forehead.

"Who is this?" he snapped.

"This is Kaso. Who is this?"

Fantoni seemed genuinely put off the insolence of this fool on the phone. He stood a bit taller, grunted as he spoke. "It's Augusto Fantoni. How did you get this number?"

"Listen, Fat Tony," said Kaso, completely ignoring him. "That girl you've got there? She's one of ours. I think you know what that means."

"*Fantoni.* And it don't matter what that means. She owes me money, which means she belongs to me right now."

Kaso laughed. A little too long. "Oh poor, sad Fat Tony," he said. "I can't let you kill her. She has secrets. Important secrets. Secrets worth dying for."

"Secrets?" asked Fantoni, taking the gun away. Kani exhaled, still trembling. "What kind of secrets?" Kani wondered what kinds of secrets she had, too. Given Kaso's general personality, she assumed he was lying, and if so, there was only a limited amount of time before Fantoni figured that out, too. She had to find a way out, but Erlenmeyer was less interested in the phone conversation than he was in which direction she was looking.

"Don't be a putz," said Kaso. "I don't know *what secrets*. Obviously. Otherwise she wouldn't be important."

Fantoni turned away, a grin on his face. "So how much are those secrets worth to ya?" he said.

"Oh what, is this extortion now? Is that honestly all you've got? Killing and extortion?"

"That's what I do best," beamed Fantoni.

Kaso said nothing for a moment, and Kani was terrified he'd hung up by mistake again. "All right," he said. "I was told to let her die, but she's smokin' hot, so I'm going out on a limb here. How much does she owe you?"

"Twelve grand."

"Twelve thousand?" gasped Kaso. "Oh my small fry. Let's see. Okay. Carry the two, square root of four thousand and fifty-seven and if I can just round to the nearest…" Fantoni smiled at Erlenmeyer. His extortion schemes never paid off so easily. "Right," said Kaso. "If you don't let her go, I'm going to withdraw one hundred and twenty thousand dollars from your offshore bank account in the Seychelles."

Fantoni's smile disappeared. He checked with Erlenmeyer, ashen complexion losing even more colour. "How do you know about that?"

"How do I know about that? I know *everything*, Fat Tony. I'm like a fiery ball of perlite, I am. Wait, not perlite. That's potting soil. What was the word I was looking for…?"

Fantoni ran his hand through his hair, turning around in circles like a dog looking to sit. Erlenmeyer, too, was upset, and Kani knew it was now or never. To her right, just a metre away, was a hole half-dug under the edge of the shack; a trough animals must have dug to get in and out in the winter. It was just enough space for her to slip through if she tried. She checked her captors again, saw them muttering to each other, and knew she couldn't wait any longer.

She shifted her chair sideways, inching bit by bit. The thing creaked loudly at the first movement, but neither man seemed to notice, so she pushed harder, moved faster. Three squeaks later, the chair leg caught on a rock, and

Kani fell hard onto her side, smacking her punched cheek against the dirt and yelping involuntarily.

Now, both men noticed her. Erlenmeyer walked over, grabbed her by the shoulders and lifted her upright again, giving her a warning look as he left. Fantoni rolled his eyes, hand cupped over the phone, and said: "Vertigo, girlie. Shoulda taken those pills after all."

Stacey's phone began to ring in Kani's pocket, and she flinched at the sound. Erlenmeyer reached over, fished around in both her pockets until he found it, then showed the display to Fantoni. A shake of the head, and the phone was tossed on the ground at her feet.

"I don't have all day here, guys," said Kaso from Fantoni's phone.

"We're thinking," spat Fantoni.

"Yeah, I can hear the gears turning."

Kani saw the phone on the ground, the thing she needed to connect with Kaso, to escape this place, to get her life back. Without that, she was doomed. She reached her foot out, trying to slide it closer, so she could keep it safe. Her toe nudged it, then turned it to the right, and then—

A gunshot hit the ground next to her foot, shocking the breath out of her.

"Hey!" shouted Kaso. "What was that? Did you just kill her?"

"No," said Fantoni. "But the next one, that *will* kill her, capice? No more games from you. You do what I say here. I want—" He paused as his phone chimed, frowned at it. He tapped its screen three times, and then his face dropped. He looked to Erlenmeyer.

"What is it?" Erlenmeyer asked.

"It is... a confirmation of a twenty-thousand dollar withdrawal from my offshore account."

"My bad," said Kaso. "I've got a jumpy trigger finger, and the gun shot just... you know, let's let bygones be bygones and—"

"Give it back!" shouted Fantoni.

"Give me the girl!" Kaso shouted back, equally deranged. "Or you know what? I'll do it again, only I'll add a zero or two!"

Fantoni looked to Kani, then to Erlenmeyer. He nodded bitterly, turned away, and hissed into the phone: "She's free. Now give me the money back."

"When I know she's safe. Not a second sooner. And if I hear one more gunshot, I'm emptying the whole thing."

Erlenmeyer tugged her arms free and pushed her off the chair. She snatched the phone off the ground, made sure she still had her own, and carefully slid out the door, watching Fantoni's face turn red.

They were at the edge of a forest, not too far from the highway, but far enough that no one would have heard the gunshot. She climbed over the fence that laced around the trees and ducked into the darkness, using the light from her phone's display to guide her. It was a little warmer outside than it had been in that shack, but the air was still biting at her skin, giving her a shiver she couldn't shake. She nearly tripped over a fallen tree, stumbling into a pile of leaves and wondering if she should just stay there.

Stacey's phone rang. She took a deep breath, and answered.

"Hello Tundra baby. Did you miss me?"

"Jesus, you scared me."

"I was hoping for praise, actually. Let's try this again. Hello Tundra baby. Did you miss me?"

"Gee, Kaso, that was great," she said dryly. "You're more useful than I thought."

Kaso said nothing for a moment. When he came back, he was morose. "That was kinda fake."

"I'm not in the mood for acting," she said.

"No, not you. Well, yes, you too, but I forgive you. Amen. No, I mean the email. I spoofed the email he got, about the withdrawal. I actually have no idea if they have an account in the Seychelles at all. Wait. Scratch that. I have no idea if the Seychelles are even a part of the world. Totally made it up as I went along."

"Oh," she said.

"It's called social hacking."

"You should stop talking now."

"Ruining the mystique?"

"Yeah."

"Gotcha."

She kept walking through the forest, checking behind herself at every little noise, but feeling relieved for the first time in hours. Any other day of her life, walking in a thick, dark forest at night would have scared too much to move. But tonight, the solitude felt wonderful. She stopped and leaned against a tree, smiling at the freedom she felt.

"Kaso," she said. "You're actually pretty—"

"Um, not to interrupt," he said, "but you'll want to move a bit faster. I mean, it won't take them long to figure out the email was fake, and then they're going to be mad. *Madder*. And they have guns, and all I've got is a phone and a fantastic sense of humour. So, er... maybe running is a better idea. And, y'know, maybe soon, too. Soon is good."

Last Friend

The red-shirt kept the knife out, circling Yuri, ready to strike. He was bruised and battered, but his ego was ready to go again. Yuri shook his head slowly, turned away, resting his arms on the bar, leaving his back fully exposed. Like a fool. Or a martyr. He took his beer, chugged it, pushed the glass to the side. He saw himself in the mirror, thought he looked more tired than before, if that was possible.

"Do what you like," he said. "I do not care anymore."

The red-shirt, unfazed by the words and apparently fully prepared to stab an unarmed man in the back, took a confident step forward, holding the knife low, ready to attack.

He stopped suddenly, frowning at the sight of the bartender with a cricket bat held loosely in his hands. It was one young-and-able man against two old-timers, and this newest one looked about as strong as a chewed-up pencil. The red-shirt smirked.

"You want to play, old man?" he asked.

"Who're you calling old?" said the bartender, bat trembling like it was caught in its own personal earthquake. "I've still got punch left in me."

The red-shirt walked closer, face full of cocky fearlessness. The old man backed up a step, tensing, bat still shaking like mad. The punk waved the knife around to make his presence known, laughing. "Let's do it."

The knife flew across the room so fast he didn't feel it leave his hand. By the time the pain registered up his arm, the bat had swung back around, and sent five of his teeth flying, too. He landed on the floor behind Yuri, blood

pouring from his mouth, and tried to get his bearings. He grabbed hold of the
back of Yuri's stool, pulled himself up, and worked to have his eyes look in the
same direction, until the bartender came back into focus. He held the bat
loose in his hands, trembling slightly, but his face was devoid of emotion.

"Get out," he said. "Before I get mad."

The red-shirt choked on some blood, then pointed a warning finger at
Yuri, like an unspoken threat, and backed out of the place, falling into the
street and running away. His Paris vacation had cost him a little more than
he'd bargained for, but the dental bill was going to be horrendous.

The bartender waited until the door closed and the street was clear, then
poured Yuri another drink. "You all right?" he asked. Yuri shrugged, put his
head down on his arms on the bar. Neither man said a word for some time,
until the bartender tapped his shoulder, nudged the beer closer. "Don't waste
it, Yuri. It's on the house."

Yuri looked up, took the beer and began drinking. "Thank you, Bernard,"
he said.

"Two things I can do for free," said the old man. "Free beer, and free
beatings. Can't say which one I like more."

"I am in your debt," Yuri said, raising the glass.

"Don't be," said Bernard. "You've got enough to worry about. I can see it."

"Is not easy," nodded Yuri. "Is not simple."

"So what is it? What's wrong? You've been coming here a long time, but
I've never seen you this bad. Is it Anya? How's she doing?"

"Worse," said Yuri, and left it at that.

"Damn bureaucrats," cursed Bernard. It was a common refrain in France
these days, but he felt it more than others. His pacemaker was failing, and
though he refused to admit it to anyone that asked, the wait list to fix it was
years long. Years too long. His bitterness wasn't for himself, so much as it was
for the state of the world. He poured himself a drink, too. "Still no word on
the health care? Nothing they can do?"

"No word," Yuri said. "It is not so surprising. I cannot take personally. Is like
this everywhere now. If you want to survive, you must make your own way."

"Tell me about it," said Bernard, wiping down the countertops. "Economy's
in the pits. Worse than the pits. The pits were the last recession. This is just…
I don't even know what to call it anymore. You know how I know? Weekly
profits. Haven't *had* any for months."

"I will pay for beer—"

"No," he said. "No, it's not you, Yuri. It's nothing to do with you. It's just… the world, you know? There's no bottom to it. Don't know what else to do. My daughter moved into the projects, the ones they built in the old shipyards. What was it, three years ago? The *revival*? And they're being torn down. Three years on. Owned by Kenyans now. *Kenyans*, Yuri. How did we get here?"

Yuri said nothing, just sipped his beer.

"I'll tell you what," Bernard continued. "We used to take care of our own here. The ones that made something of France. Now the only ones left are the bums, the hooligans, and the ones too poor to run. No offence."

"None taken," said Yuri.

"Have you seen the cars on the streets now? None built domestically. Every last one of them an import. I saw one yesterday, and it had exhaust. Black smoke. Haven't seen that in… god knows how long. Imports, all of them, because there's nothing left of us anymore. It's sickening. Sickening."

Yuri downed the rest of his drink. "Is the same in Russia," he said. "And they had no investment in tourism. Nothing to lose, but somehow they lost everything."

"Screw them," Bernard said. "They voted the wrong way. They deserve what they got."

Yuri nodded, said nothing.

"How's work?" Bernard said, sensing the shift in mood. "You're busy?"

Yuri stared into his empty glass. "It has been better," he said. "And worse."

Bernard swapped in another pint, sat down with his own. "There's no work anywhere. Be glad you have something. Most of my regulars don't come anymore, since they lost their jobs. King/Western folded with the Abu Dhabi spaceport. Took the soul out of France."

"The soul left before that," Yuri said. "The UN made sure of that."

"What do you think of this new Secretary-General?" asked Bernard. "She seems to know what she's doing."

"Oda? Maybe. I will believe when I see it. I do not know anyone can survive that place."

"Amen," said Bernard, holding up his glass.

They sat in silence for a moment, Yuri playing with his beer, turning it in circles, biding his time. When he spoke, he didn't look up. "Bernard," he said, "I need loan. For Anya."

"Oh, Yuri. Please don't do that."

"I'm sorry. If I had another choice, you know I would—"

"Yuri, I don't have anything to loan. The fools I kicked out tonight will probably be the end of me. The only consolation I have is that I went out on principle, you know?"

Yuri nodded, but his face was white. He pushed the glass forward, looking away. "Another, please?"

Bernard smiled, filled it up.

"Why not," he said. "My retirement party."

Yuri closed his eyes.

"Why don't you ask Pellier for a loan?" Bernard said. "He's keeping half the city afloat these days. What's one more? He might even have a soft spot for a sick little girl if you tell it right."

Yuri shook his head. "I already owe Pellier money. Too much to go back for more. And I do not think he has soft spot in him. He seems cold straight through."

Bernard nodded, sipped his own beer.

"You must know someone else, Yuri. Think hard. You don't have friends *anywhere*?"

Interrupted

FIVE YEARS EARLIER

The rain started the second he left the station, and by the time he was three blocks away, Yuri's jacket was soaked through. He put his briefcase over his head for shelter and started running, feet disappearing into massive puddles as the storm drains backed up, flooding Paris for the third time that season. A shopkeeper at the side of the street, putting the finishing touches on his new walls after the last major disaster, threw his brushes to the ground and wept openly as sewage flowed out of his back room. Little things, all unpleasant, but for Yuri, it was just a rainstorm.

He paused at the warm glow of a café sign at the side of the road, up a few steps and beckoning to him. A place called Duschennes, swirly letters glowing with faint faux-neon, a shade of pinkish red that felt lovely somehow. Inviting, with their coffee. Pastries. Dryness.

The bell chimed softly as he entered, the heaters blasting him with a toasty breeze, followed by the smell of croissants and danishes, and it devoured the last bits of doubt in his mind. He took the first seat by the door, hung his coat over the back of his chair, and stared out the window at the soggy mess outside. The table, made up like a little mosaic of shining gems, wobbled at the slightest touch, but when it moved, it reflected the lights above in such a beautiful way, he found himself lost in it for a minute.

He absentmindedly pulled his phone from his pocket, wiped the water off and turned it back on. It took a minute, but still registered a signal through the rain, and he dialled quickly, putting it to his ear while he tried to roll up his sleeves, so the chill he felt would be minimized.

"Hello, Sabina?" he said. "You are not out yet? Is raining. No, *really* raining. Find cover for stroller when you come. Is worse than looks. I am at Duschennes, café near station. Yes. I will see you soon."

He hung up, wiping the phone on the dry part of his shirt, and left it on the table, where it almost disappeared into the mosaic itself. He loosened his tie, undid his top button, and scratched his neck, trying to catch the water and sweat as it made its way through his beard. The waitress appeared next to him, paper notepad ready, black-painted fingernails scratching the edge of the pen.

"Just coffee for now. Thank you," he said, checking out the window.

"Right away," she said, and the voice made him turn around. The hair was brown, the lip was healed, but it was unmistakable. Rache.

"Thank you," he said again, looking straight at her, and she nodded to him, went back to the counter without saying another word. She looked so different now, out of her torn-up clothes, wrapped in a crisp white shirt, apron wrapped around her slim waist, grey skirt and feminine shoes. She was like any other pretty girl in town, which seemed strange to him, and he laughed that it would be. She'd forgotten him, forgotten that night entirely, and the life that went with it. She was just another waitress in just another café in Paris, working her way up, or out. He was happy for her. Happy she didn't remember him at all, too. He went back to looking out the window, putting her out of his mind.

On the screen in the corner, the news began playing. Kana Choi began the hourly refresh like clockwork, her French impeccable, but thankfully not too fast for Yuri to follow. He watched the streets clear of the remaining brave souls, even as the rain tapered off, listening to the sounds of the state of the world, nearly missing the first story to daydreams.

"... promised increased support to the space enforcement fund," said the broadcast, and Yuri looked around. "President Campbell also backtracked on her commitment to supplying a new squadron of King/Western ships to the SEF after criticism American-based companies were not given adequate time to prepare bids for the contract."

A coffee slid onto the table, and Yuri looked around. Rache was standing there, looking out the window, like she was tired of her job already. A button hanging off her chest read "I love smiling", but there was no sign of it on her face. She sighed, hands on her hips.

"Anything else?" she asked, tugging at the vibrant yellow apron.

"No," he said. "Thank you."

She left, hips swaying with mock dramatics as she slid into the back room. He watched the door close, then sniffled, went back to the news.

"Chromoco profits topped analyst expectations of $2.21 a share, sending the stock soaring in after-hours trading in New York. Estimates of breaking the six-hundred barrier seemed more and more likely after a preliminary report from the European Space Agency suggested there may be more palladium in the asteroid belt than previously thought. Chromoco CEO Armin Harte welcomed the news, telling investors it marked a new high point in the quest to build a brighter future—"

Yuri laughed at the words, sipped his coffee. The slogan worked on so many people, giving them hope for tomorrow, even as things tumbled downhill. He couldn't stand the wording himself. In Russian, it was even more blunt, translating more into "*we* will make *you* a better future than you can do yourselves." To him, it was just a gimmick, one he saw far too often. A joke more than a promise.

Just as he set his coffee down, Rache sat in the seat opposite, apron off.

"Something funny about Chromoco profits?" she asked.

He let go of the cup, smiled. "I thought you were working."

"I'm on a break."

"Come to antagonize customer on break?"

"Only if I can, old man," she said with a smile. "What's so funny about Chromoco?"

He laughed again, shook his head. "Come, let me buy you coffee. You looked tired."

She didn't switch her gaze, bearing down on him, the fire in her eyes like she'd had back in the detention centre. Her shirt looked less like a uniform, and more like a disguise; one she was itching to strip off and reveal the black-and-red t-shirt below, ready for war. His heart ached, thinking he'd been deceived, and just as he was about to excuse himself, she smiled a radiant, comforting smile, and it was like a whole new person sitting across from him.

"I'm joking," she said. "Don't be so serious. You look like you're about to have a heart attack."

"I could be, talking with you."

She laughed, leaned back in her chair. "How's life?" she said. "I heard something about a stroller."

"Life is good," he nodded. "Baby born last month. Girl named Anya. You see her when she arrive. Beautiful thing."

"And work? You never told me what you do."

"Work is good," he said. "Long hours, but still good. And you? You seem happy here."

"It's a job," she shrugged.

"Any job is good," he said. "Trust me on this. I am glad you are doing better. You seem so angry last time we meet. Also, less red in hair is good."

She smiled at him. "I'd keep the red, but they won't let me," she said. "I think it fits the decor, but what do I know. It's about the smiles here, and I really do love smiling."

She gave as wooden a smile as she could. He laughed, nodded. "I can see."

She crossed her legs, started tapping on the table with her black fingernails, wire bracelets making counter-point noises for every movement. He couldn't wait to see Sabina, to show her Rache, the change brought about in such a short time. Sabina never believed people could change, that the world could change… but here it was. The proof. There was hope yet for humanity.

Rache nodded, traced around the mosaic with her finger. "But yeah. I *am* doing better. Sleeping better, too. I can't tell you how long it had been since I'd really slept."

"Do you have family here?" he asked, and she flinched, looked away. "Sorry," he said quickly. "Too many questions. I am nosy sometimes."

"No," she said. "It's fine. My family's all back in Sillery. I moved here a few years ago for school."

"Where is Sillery?"

"Québec. Canada."

"Oh," he said. "Long way."

"In so many ways," she smiled. "I'm actually back in school now. Working my way through again."

"Studying what, if I may ask?"

"Political science," she said, and he laughed loudly.

"Is good. I am sorry, is good. The world needs more passion in politics, yes? Is good."

She got up and left, ducking into the back room again, and he sipped his coffee, smiling to himself. Maybe he'd offended her, but there was something too funny about this young woman, so proper and *average*, hiding a secret anarchist agenda beneath her yellow apron. Sneaking into the UN unnoticed. Maybe ten, twenty years from now, but no one being the wiser.

She came back a moment later with a piece of tiramisu and two forks.

"Celebration," she said. "To your baby, and my passion."

He laughed, picked up a fork. "May they both do well in life," he said.

They ate in silence, watching the dwindling rain outside. Yuri glanced at her from time to time. It was like time had washed away all the anger she'd had on her, and what he saw now was a beautiful young woman, ready for life. She caught him staring, raised an eyebrow.

"What's up, old man?" she asked.

"Nothing," he said, reaching for money and putting it out on the table. "Is good to see you."

She pushed the coins toward him. "It's on the house," she said.

He pushed it back. "Then is tip. You deserve, for turning life around so well. Is not easy, doing that. I know. But you are doing wonderful job." She started to protest, but he put his hand over hers, pressing it onto the coins. "Is investment in future for me, yes?" he said. "Maybe some day you use this investment, you fix problems in world. Things you were so angry about."

Her expression changed, and she made a fist under his hand.

"*Were*?" she said. "You think I stopped? You think I *could* stop? Don't you watch the news?"

"Oh no," he sighed. "Is bear trap, I can feel it."

"Things aren't getting *better* out there, they're getting worse. I'm doing what I have to do, but there's no time to do this slowly."

"Fast never solve problem," he said.

"No?" she snapped. "We'll see."

"We'll see how? You do school faster?"

"I have other ways," she said. "I know someone…" She leaned in closer, voice low. He did too, but stiffly. "I know someone with access to a space fighter." Yuri sat back quickly. She continued in a not-so-quiet whisper, eyes narrow. "I can still go the legitimate route," she said. "But I can make a difference in a cockpit. I can be a pirate. One of the 'dustrunners' everyone talks about."

"Not in good way," he breathed. "Not in way you want."

"I'll take my chances," she said.

"You are fool," he said, grabbing his money back. "You are fool! You have so many chances, and you do this? Fool!"

He left her there, alone at the table with half-finished coffee. She didn't say a word back.

Villains and Lies

The room was stuffy from the second Freeman got in, thick air smelling like sweat and anxiety and a dozen different spices from every corner of the world. The seats all creaked, and they creaked often as the participants in the circle shifted uncomfortably, trying to find the best way to look at ease. No one wore their rank, but you could tell the officers by the slump in their shoulders. The defeat in their eyes.

They hadn't used the church hall that long — maybe five months at most — but it had been obvious from the start that it had been a bad decision. It was hard to make confessions this raw in the presence of the Almighty. Harder, still, in the porous antechamber of a run-down building in the poor part of town. The walls were cheap plaster, painted over enough times to seem thick, the wooden beams nicked and scratched from all the years of abuse, of other visitors letting their own demons out. They took down the flag that usually hung in the back of the room, put it respectfully outside the door. It would have been too much to have it there, too. They already had enough to deal with.

Jack was talking about Afghanistan again. He was a broad fellow, sandy hair sprinkled with grey, lines around his eyes from squinting into the desert or mountains, trying to see his fate through the glare of the sun. Civilian clothes sat on him funny, like no matter how hard he tried, he couldn't fit in anymore. He had a belly now, the beginnings of a second chin, but his arms were tough and lean, and there was no doubt he could break any man he chose. He just chose not to.

He was talking about how the things he saw in his last tour had made him relapse. Car bomb, shredding a woman and her baby to bits. A man shot in the gut, no medics in sight, bleeding to death, begging to be saved in a language Jack barely understood. He understood it now, after years of studying, but he couldn't remember those words anymore. And that was what did it. The agony of not remembering one tiny thing pushed him that inch too far, and he did it. One drink. Just one drink, but it broke four years of trying. He was ashamed, kept staring at the floor. Everyone gave him support, sympathy, regret.

"We've got the tallest hill to climb, sir," said one woman.

"And longest way to fall," agreed another.

It went like this around the circle. Military precision and rules, but without the burden of rank. Everyone called everyone "sir", even if they knew better. Not every time, but once, at least, to show you remembered. To go without it was insulting, like they'd not only lost their lives, but their dignity as well. Everyone deserved respect, most of all these people, fighting this war. When it was Freeman's turn, he thanked the man before him, cleared his throat, and spoke in a tiny fraction of his voice.

"I'm Marshall," he said. "Six hundred and thirteen days."

Everyone nodded appreciatively. He went back to silence.

"How was your week, sir?" asked Jack, knowing full well how it was. Jack had been there longer than Freeman, had been there last year on this day, when the weight of the anniversary was just too much to bear, and he'd fallen to pieces in the group. Better here than at home, or a bar, they'd said, and he'd believed them. But he didn't want to do it again. It was catharsis for the others, but hell for him. He wanted none of it.

"My week was hard," he said.

"How's the job? Getting better?"

"It's fine," Freeman said, staring at the floor. The others shifted uncomfortably. You didn't push those that wanted to stay quiet, and you didn't go places they didn't offer themselves. "Today was fine."

"Are you all right, sir?" Jack asked, and he was sincere and kind, but it was still too much.

"I'll survive it," Freeman said. "I'm here, aren't I?"

They all nodded at that, happy to be done with the conversation. Freeman let out a tense breath, looked to his left, at the new member: a fresh-faced boy — a private at best — with a north-east accent. His eyes were a piercing blue, jaw and brow the hallmarks of an Irish lineage, and when he sat, he sat without the rigid structure of the others. He was too young for that. It was like he'd been transplanted out of a Boston nightclub directly, but was playing the part of an alcoholic until he knew what was what.

"Your turn, sir," Freeman said, and went back to looking at the floor, letting the noise wash over him.

"Hi," said the kid. "I'm Neil. About... twenty-one days, I think."

There was a murmuring of approval. The first month was the hardest. And then the second. And then the third.

"What made you stop drinking?" asked Jack, always helpful, always gentle. Neil seemed unprepared for the question, started picking at his fingernails, frowning, trying to put words to his thoughts.

"I guess... I guess it was seeing the way it affected my family," he said.

"Have you told them you're sorry for what you've done?" asked Jack softly. Forgiveness was a big part of the recovery process. For those with someone left to ask.

"No," said Neil.

Freeman looked up at him, eyes narrow. "You ought to try, sir," he said, voice even and neutral. Give the kid a chance. He'd forgotten the basic rules, but he'd get them eventually.

"I don't know if I can. It's too soon."

Freeman straightened his back. "How did it affect your family, sir?" he asked. Another hint. The rest of the group watched Freeman, not Neil, waiting to see the reaction. It must have caught their attention, too, but they were going to let him deal with it. No one relished confrontation like him.

"They stopped talking to me," said Neil. "Kept their distance when I was around."

Freeman nodded, leaned back in his chair. It creaked loudly.

"Where were you stationed, sir?" he asked.

"Marshall..." warned Jack, but was ignored. You didn't go places they didn't want to go. Not to help, and certainly not to hunt.

"Fort Bragg," said Neil. "For a few months, anyway. Never got deployed before I moved here."

Freeman smiled. "Fort Bragg is a great place. Do you know Gary Weiss? 33rd Airborne?"

Neil looked away, into the air, squinted to pull a memory into focus. No one said a word. One woman shook her head slightly, knowing what was coming. Finally, Neil answered: "Yeah," he said. "Gary. Great guy. Don't know him well, but I've heard stories, right?"

Freeman nodded again, said nothing more.

"Frankly," said Neil, "I'm mostly worried about how my drinking will affect my chances of getting a job in the SEF. I've had my name in for months, but no word yet. I know they do blood tests, but man, they can't disqualify you for a little alcohol in the system, right?"

"How would you feel if they did, sir?" asked Jack.

"Wronged," said Neil. "That's my calling, you know? What I'm headed for. I wanna beat those dustrunner scum in the face."

"Amen," said Karen, and then added a hasty, "Sir," after a glare from Freeman.

"Not that it'll be hard," said Neil. "They're all halfwit scumbags anyway. Don't know how to fly a jet without assistance, can't get real jobs..."

The others were joining in now, throwing barbs into the ring, letting their frustrations flow at an absent enemy. None of them would have gone up there. None of them were young enough or dumb enough to try. The SEF was a show force of military has-beens, the ones who screwed up so bad they were literally sent off-planet as penance. That, or dishonourable discharge. Nothing to aspire to. But still, to the people in this room, the enemy was the enemy, and they deserved what they got, even if it was just words.

"That Gossamer joker's going to blow the whole thing wide open," said Neil. "Wide open."

"I hope so, sir," said Jack. "God, I hope so."

"I heard there's chatter they've got a big bust planned," said Neil. "It's downside, not in the SEF, but I'll be damned if I don't want to be there when they snag the bastards."

"Yes sir!" agreed Karen.

"Ain't that right, Marshall?" asked Neil, voice sharp.

Freeman looked at him, and the conversation stopped.

"Yes. Sir," he said.

"They're sitting ducks," said Neil, directly to Marshall. "And they don't know it. Even the ones that do, don't."

There was something in the turn of his head, the half-smile on his face, the way his eyes were locked, that seemed threatening. The punk kid with no respect, coming here to threaten him? Here? Now? No, that was not going to happen. Freeman looked at his hands, checked his watch, and sighed. He'd had enough, and it was time to go.

"They're all goners," said Neil, and Freeman leapt at him. He caught the punk in the face with a powerful blow, sending him flailing onto the floor, and tossed his chair across the room. The rest of the circle jumped off their seats, backing away, as Freeman continued beating the newbie.

"Marshall!" yelled Jack from a safe distance. "Marshall, stop it!"

"You don't know Gary Weiss!" yelled Freeman. "Gary died six years ago! Who the hell are you?" Neil put his arms up to protect himself, but it made no difference. Freeman felt strong arms lock around his shoulders, and he was pulled off, held back, heart racing and teeth clenched tight. "He's not one of us!" he screamed, trying to get free. "He's not one of us!"

Jack checked on Neil, looked up at Freeman angrily.

"No, Marshall, *you're* not one of us."

"But he—"

"You know the rules. No violence in the group. No exceptions. It's just not allowed."

Freeman stopped fighting, caught his breath, and was let go. He slumped forward, like falling out of a dream, and started towards the door.

"I'm… I'm sorry, sir," said Neil through a bloodied face.

Freeman glowered at him, pushed outside without a word. In the parking lot, he leaned against his truck, resting his head against the glass and sighing a rattled sigh. Anyone nearby enough to see him had also heard what he'd just done, and they were keeping to themselves. He felt their eyes on him. All their eyes. Especially the ones hunting for him. He took his phone from his jacket, dialled blind and put it to his ear.

"Elvis," he said. "I made a mistake. Horrible mistake." There was a pause. "You there?" Freeman asked.

"I'm here. What happened?"

"I just beat the bejeesus out of a kid, and I don't even know if I was right."

"You're having a bad day."

"That's no excuse. I don't know what I was thinking."

"Listen, Rook," Elvis said, "everyone's on edge these days. I'd be more worried if you were holding it all together."

Freeman got into the truck, closed the door. "I don't want to stand out," he said, putting the keys in the ignition. "I try so hard to stay under the radar, and do something like that."

"Don't worry about it," said Elvis. "Seriously. Let it go. Nobody stands out with all this stuff going on. Us or them."

Freeman nodded, checked back towards the church doors. Nobody was leaving. The meeting was going strong. He was outside in the cold, alone.

"Have you heard anything about Gossamer?" Freeman asked. "They were talking about him flipping. Rumours."

"I don't know about that. I know he's scheduled to testify. He got sick, and they've moved him. I know there's talk of someone trying to assassinate him before he gets to the stand, but beyond that… it's all speculation these days. Everything's speculation."

"Yeah," nodded Freeman. "We're on our way out, aren't we?"

"How so? Over Gossamer? He's a lackey, Rook. He knows so little, it's a wonder he ever got in a plane to start. Don't worry about it."

"It's not that. It's… things are picking up speed. We're surrounded by all these rotten apples, and we don't know which are which. Lucet seems more in the dark than some idiot kid in a meeting."

"There's chatter, but Lucet knows what to ignore."

"Maybe he *did*, but does he still? Maybe he's missing something important."

Elvis paused, exhaled, and Freeman rested his head on the steering wheel. The wind whistled through the window.

"If they're right, there's something coming," Elvis said finally. "I guess there's no harm in being cautious. Caution keeps you alive. But don't let it eat you, Rook. You'll never survive if you let it eat you."

"I know," Freeman said, turning on the truck.

"So what are you going to do now? Go apologize?"

Freeman laughed, put it into reverse and pulled into the street.

"Only one thing *to* do. Find myself a drink."

Imperative

Kani squeezed herself behind a dumpster in the alley next to a Chinese restaurant, curling into a ball and trying not to make a sound. She'd been running for over an hour, jumping at every crack and rustle of the forest, then every car or voice that called out any louder than a whisper. She'd ended up in the trashy part of north Toronto, only a few blocks from the CRA office she'd worked at last summer, but an entire world away from the streets she remembered. The place was run-down by day, but utterly terrifying by night. When she couldn't take it anymore, she hid herself in the darkest, dingiest place she could find. Someplace no rational person would go.

She sat there in a puddle of something sticky, listening to the sounds of the night around her. Chattering in Chinese; a woman laughing, talking a loud kind of sultry in words Kani couldn't make out; two men arguing, another man moaning; the songs of a drunk swaying his way down the boulevard. The place smelled terrible, like pineapples and wine, trash and something rotting, but for whatever reason, it smelled better than the forest.

She took the phone out of her pocket again, turned it over and slid her finger along the side. It came to life, and she covered it up with her hands, trying to keep the light from seeping out. The battery had plenty of life left, but the signal was weak behind the dumpster. She inched further back until she could see the night sky beyond the balconies above. The signal improved marginally.

She skimmed through the memory banks again, pausing at number twenty-seven, then hit "dial." It rang four times, followed by a click, but no voice.

"Kaso?" she asked.

"Please hold," he said, and started singing a tune to himself. "Hello, Kaso Industries, Kaso speaking. How many I help you?"

"What am I going to do..." she said, her voice cracking. The long day was getting to her. Her hands were constantly trembling. She rested her head against the dumpster, ignoring the dripping that started beating down on her scalp. Kaso said nothing for a minute, then cleared his throat.

"You're going to put on a happy face," he said. "It's never as bad as it seems!"

"It isn't?"

"Well, in your case it is, but I'm working on *optimism* here, okay? Play along."

She shook her head. "Why are you helping me?" she asked. "They said to let me die, right? Why are you helping me?"

Kaso sighed. "You're cute, and I need a girlfriend. No, just kidding. You're way too young for me. Well, maybe. When's your birthday? Don't answer that."

She laughed, rubbed tears from her eyes. "You're an idiot," she said.

"On the surface, yes," he said. "But underneath, I'm all man. Man and cheese puffs. Hmm. Too much information, I guess."

"Slightly."

"Right. Well, to answer your question seriously: I helped you because I have this feeling you're not as bad as they think you are. It's hard these days, all the rotten apples in the tree, and you never know who you can trust. But I like you, Tundra. I trust you. And if someone I like and trust is in trouble, I'll do just about anything to help them."

"Thanks," she sniffled.

"Except leave my room. I have my limits." She laughed again, pushed back the tears. His voice got bouncier, even more playful. "I made you laugh! We're meant to be together. How bout you drop this piracy thing and come live with me? I have a narrow mattress, but we can overcome any obstacle if we try."

"No thanks," she smiled.

"You're missing oooout..."

"I doubt it," she said.

"Why? What have you heard? If it's that Debbie chick, she's totally lying. I mean for one, she said she was under thirty. And two, three nipples? No sir. Not my thing. I mean, you'd have trouble performing too if—"

"Too much information," she said, trying not to laugh.

"Oh, so you haven't seen the photos, then."

"Back to me, Kaso. Please."

"Wow. Prima donna, aren't we? *Look at me, I'm being hunted by the mob! Ooo! Aren't I special?* So. Um. Yeah, okay, where was I?"

"Three nipples."

"Not funny. C'mon. Work with me here. Oh right. You. How could I forget? You're going to need some cash, so if you can give me your bank ID, I'll see what I can route to the nearest outlet. Get you some liquid assets, if you know what I mean."

"My bank ID?"

"The one we transfer to. I've got a big list here of everyone in your team, and when you finish a job — not to rub it in, right? — I move the cash from the *here* to the *there* so everyone's happy. Thing is, I don't know which number goes with which person, so… I kinda need to know your number. Just this once. I won't write it down or anything. You can trust me."

"I trust you," she said, searching her memory for anything that might pass as a bank ID. She just had no idea how many digits she was looking for, which made it impossible to even start to guess. If she got it wrong, he'd know in an instant, and he'd also know she wasn't really Tundra. "I just… I don't know any…"

"You don't *know?*" he gasped, horror hanging over every word. "Okay, well maybe just the first few digits. That oughta help lots. Just the first three. You gotta remember that much, right?"

"I think I may have stored it on my phone," she said, and started checking, but he yelped so loudly she listened to him instead.

"Not on your phone. Please say you didn't put it on your phone. Holy security risk."

"Oh. Right," she laughed, nervously. "I don't know what I was thinking."

Kaso sighed. She heard a pen clicking in the background, and a few heavy thumps on a table. "All right," he said. "We'll just see if we can take a look. How much money do you have in there?"

"I don't know," she muttered.

"Ballpark. Anything."

"I really don't know. The mob… I think they took it all out, so I probably don't have any—"

"Let me worry about that. You sure you don't have the number? Anywhere? You wrote it down, stuck it in your underwear? Here, use the phone's camera and I'll take a look."

"In your dreams," she said.

"You can see my dreams? Oh, this is awkward. I should explain about the suspenders…"

"You know what?" she said, going out on a bit of a limb, "I think I know where the number is. I wrote it on a scrap of paper, and I hid it. In my room. At home. So, you know, I guess that's not going to—"

"Excellent!" he said. "Let's go get it."

"Police, remember?"

"Right. Contiguous thoughts are not my forte."

The door to the Chinese restaurant opened and two men walked out, talking rapidly, urgently, and coming to a stop a short distance from where Kani was hiding. She saw the closer man, stocky and covered with grease, taking his cap off and running a rough hand through his hair. He seemed angry, kept yelling sharp words at the other man, stomping his foot for effect. She pushed the phone to her chest to keep it quiet, lowered her head slowly, and watched them.

The other man started rambling on, a few English words falling out that she caught: "Johnny", "bitches", "cops." The last word made her sink a bit lower, and the stocky man seemed to shrink, too, fists tightening at his sides. Finally, he snapped, waved an impatient hand back towards the kitchen, and stomped his feet for each of the words he said. The other man said something under his breath and the door slammed shut.

The stocky man leaned against the wall, looking up into the sky like Kani had earlier, and pulled a cigarette out of his pocket. He lit it, took a long drag, and blew the smoke into the air, watching it dissolve into the stars. The smell made her gag — the only smokes you could buy were smuggled in from the States through the First Nations reserves, and they didn't always come out the same as they went in. But somehow, it was a better deal than the trash she was living in.

The man shook his head, closing his eyes and speaking something to the sky that, to Kani, sounded like the kind of thing she wanted to say. *Please save me from this mess I've got myself into.* He opened his eyes, turned towards the dumpster, and unzipped his fly to relieve himself directly on her. She covered her eyes and hoped for the best, but then the door opened again, and the other man called out in sharp tones. The stocky man zipped back up, stomping his foot again, and waved the other man away. He took another drag on the cigarette, and tossed it into the darkness behind the dumpster. It landed on Kani's lap, but she couldn't do a thing about it.

Finally, the door closed again, and she snatched the thing off, tossing it into a puddle, where it fizzled and died. She put the phone back to her ear, trembling.

"That was a whole lot of rubbing sounds," Kaso said. "Was that phone sex? 'Cause I was totally unprepared."

"I have to get out here," she said. "I really need to get out of here."

"Gotcha," he said, back to seriousness. "We can skip money for now. You've got the encoder chip, right?"

"The which?"

"The encoder chip. The thing that… we gave you when you… did you hit your head or something?"

"No, I'm sorry, I didn't know what you meant," she said, wincing, hoping she was better at lying than she felt. "I left that at my house too. Sorry."

Kaso sighed. "Well, nothing left to do but go get it."

This woke Kani right up. "Go… to my house?"

"The chip is important, Tundra. You know that. If it got into the wrong hands, there'd be deaths and suicides and various forms of artichokes falling from the sky. Madness and stuff."

"Right," she said, and got to her feet. "I've got to get it back."

"Don't worry," Kaso said cheerfully, "the cops probably left hours ago."

The police cars were still there. Worse yet, there were more of them than before, parked in the driveway and down the street, officers milling about, on phones and taking photos. Kani had to cut through her neighbours' backyards, keeping out of sight, to get a good view of her home.

The front curtains were open, the lights all on, and she could see the command centre set up in her living room. Her father was sitting on the couch, head in his hands as detectives stood around him, asking questions, passing around the photos from the mantle. When he looked up, his face was more tired than it had ever been, mouth turned down into a fearful shape, hands pushed together, pressed against his lips, trying to hold in anguish in. She felt awful for him. Truly awful.

Her grandfather was in the back of the room, sitting on his usual chair, staring down at a teddy bear he'd given her when she was a baby. He was wearing his best suit, and she noticed her father was, too. *The memorial.* Her grandfather's face was a mix of concern and deep resentment. If they'd missed today of all days, he was going to be furious. She'd better come home in a coffin, or not at all. He wouldn't accept anything less.

She put the phone back to her ear, lowered herself back behind the bushes in her neighbour's front yard.

"There are a lot of police," she said.

"But you're there? Right now, you're there?"

"Yeah," she said. "Across the street."

"Okay. One second, just going to *holy crap* are your relatives cops? That's one, two, three, you know what? Screw this, head downtown and start knocking over liquor stores, because the police are obviously occupied."

"You're not helping."

"I'm helping in my own special way."

"Try a different way."

"Fine," he said, curt. "Something different. Something *boring*, obviously, but different. Let's see. Hold on. Here we go. It's comin'… it's comin'… Oooh, that's a good one."

"What are you—"

"Don't fret, I'll make a distraction."

"Kaso, wait—"

But he was gone.

Inside the house, the detectives were going over the day for the hundredth time, trying to figure out if Kani had made any hint about where she'd really been going, what she was up to. The school had no idea where she was, Stacey's mother hadn't seen either of them in days, and the cameras at the train station lost the trail so early in the day, it was like she'd just disappeared off the face of the Earth. Did she have a boyfriend? Yes, but he hadn't seen her, either. What about other friends? No one had heard from her all day. And on and on, with no resolution.

No sign of her at hospitals, no arrests anywhere in the Greater Toronto Area. Nothing useful. Nothing to go on. Kani's father lost more and more hope, the longer it went on. Girls her age ran away all the time, but she wasn't unhappy. There were no signs. And if she hadn't run away…

"We're going to find her," said the detective, sitting down next to him, offering him a coffee. "We're going to find her, and it's going to be okay."

He took the drink, stared into it, trying to think of what to say. "I can't... I can't thank you enough. For all this. I know it's more than you'd do, but—"

"Your father-in-law's a good man," said the detective. "Your family's been through enough. Anything we can do to help you out, just ask."

"Thank you," her father said, nodding. "Thank you so much."

The phone rang, and the entire room froze. The detective picked up the handset, nodded to his tech, and handed it over to Kani's father. He lifted it to his ear with shaking hands, pushed the button, and spoke with a tiny shadow of his usual voice. "Hello?" he said.

"Hello," said the words, distorted and serious. "We have your daughter."

The phone hit the ground and the detectives in the room scrambled to listen in on the line. Two computers started tracing the call, and the detective put his hand on Kani's father's shoulder, squeezing gently, trying to give him the strength to get through what was coming. He picked the phone back up, put it to his ear, and listened. There was crackling, like static, and the soft breathing of a person waiting to be spoken to.

"Y-y-you have Kani?" he asked.

"Yes," said the voice. "She is safe. For now."

"What do you want?" he asked, watching the police motion to keep talking as they continued to trace the call. He nodded to them, swallowed. "Is she safe? I want to talk to her."

"She's busy right now."

"Busy where?" he asked, voice cracking. "Why did you take her?"

"You've heard of Russian brides?"

Her father's mouth dropped open, mind racing. Had they kidnapped her, sold her into slavery? Where? Why would they do that? His poor little girl... what had they done to her? He took a breath, answered slowly: "Y-y-yes?"

"It's like that, but kind of in reverse."

Half the detectives in the room frowned at this.

"You're sending her to Russia?" her father asked, uncertain how to respond.

"Well. No. Bulgaria. Close enough, right? Not a nice place. All the women left when they realized what a crap part of the world it is. Seriously. Look it up. But anyway, the men are lonely there."

Kani's father stood up, looked out the window, tears in his eyes. The police worked furiously in the background, their traces never resolving to the same place twice. The kidnappers were playing with him, and he couldn't stand it. He wanted his daughter back, and the anger came boiling over, and he shouted into the phone: "How much do you want? Just tell me what you want!"

"We don't want money," said the kidnapper.

Her father's fury evaporated instantly. He sat back down, looked at the detectives. They shrugged. "You don't want... money?"

"No," the voice said. "We want to know the square root of twenty-five."

The detectives were stumped in so many ways.

"Um. Is it five?"

"Hold on. Carry the two and... Yes, yes it is five. All right. You pass. I'll tell you where she is."

The detectives were shaking their heads, but looked so uncertain, Kani's father couldn't stop himself.

"Where is she? Where's my Kani?"

The police cars kicked into reverse and tore down the street away from the house, sirens blaring. Inside, half the police had packed up their gear, and the other half were racing through screens of data on their laptops, trying to sort out the unsortable. The noise of so many sirens was so loud, Kani almost didn't hear the phone.

"Kaso?" she asked. "What did you do?"

"I sent them on a very long trip."

"For what?"

"You. You're kidnapped, you know. Now get your kidnapped ass into that house and find the bank ID and the encoder chip!"

She shoved the phone into her pocket and dashed across the street, ducking into the neighbour's yard and back to the fence that ran between their two properties. She reached over the gate and pulled the latch, letting herself through and closing it gently. These people heard everything, and she wasn't going to get caught by them now, not after everything she'd been through.

The crabapple tree that dropped rotten fruit into her kiddie pool as a child was not as easy to climb as she thought it would be, but she managed to pull herself up enough to get a foot on the top of her fence, and then drop herself over into her own backyard, keeping low and out of sight. She slid her key into the lock and turned it as slowly as she could manage, so it only made the slightest click. She opened the door, crept inside, and closed it behind her.

The laundry room was right off the kitchen, and from the half-closed doorway, she could see a broad police officer making himself coffee at the kitchen sink. He poured some cream into his cup, then opened the drawers, looking for a spoon. There weren't any. Not clean ones, anyway. He gave up, swished it around with his pinkie, and headed back to the living room.

Kani left the laundry room, inching towards the stairs, pausing only briefly to see her father looking at the photos of her from when she was a kid, playing with her mother, happy and innocent and nothing like what she felt like now.

"Don't worry, sir," said the detective at his side. "We'll get her."

Kani inched up the stairs to the second floor, wondering if Kaso was tracking her movements, waiting to see if she'd done what she said she was going to do. She had no idea what she'd do when she got to her room, though… she had no encoder chip, no way to fake one, and if she failed that test, how would she stop him from turning her in to the police? Something like that was trivial for him.

By the time she got into her room, she was on the verge of a full-blown panic. She left the lights off, the door ajar, and stared at her bed. She so desperately wanted to sleep. Instead, she took the phone from her pocket, and continued the game.

"Are you there?" Kaso asked. "Can you see it?"

"Yeah," she said, looking around the room, standing in front of her shelves, trying to look like she was doing something other than faking. "It's here. Underneath my DVD player."

"Wait, your what?"

"DVD player."

"Oh, optical media. I get it. Nostalgia. Quaint. Now hurry!"

She looked at a photo on her shelf, the one of her and Stacey and Simon at the Ex last summer. Back when the biggest worry was what your boyfriend thought about your choice of clothes. She touched Stacey's face with her fingertip, hoping she was still alive, and then went back for the door. She stopped short, listening carefully to the sound of footsteps coming up the stairs. Panicked, she turned off the phone, slid it back in her pocket, and quickly dove into the closet, closing the door.

A shaft of light broke the darkness as the hallway light turned on, and her father came in, head low, looking around much the same as she just had. He sat on the edge of her bed and started to cry, quiet and personal, running his hand along her mattress.

"My baby," he said to himself. "What am I going to do?"

Kani desperately wanted to open the closet, to tell him she was fine, that she'd be fine… She wanted to hug him and just let all the tension and agony of the day disappear, to let him finally have some peace, and maybe they could figure out her problems together. She wanted to stop running, stop depending on a lunatic voice on the phone, and go back to her old life.

But she knew it was impossible.

She clenched her fist, closed her eyes and waited for it to end. Willed him to go. Please, just go. Instead, he picked the phone off her dresser, turned it on, and started dialling.

"Come on," he said quietly. "Please pick up. Please be okay…"

Kani sniffled quietly, watching him suffer.

And then the phone in her pocket rang.

"Crap," she mouthed.

Nowhere to Run

Kani's father leapt off the bed and backed into the door so hard it closed. He fumbled for the light switch, turning it on and squinting at the brightness, looking around the room as Kani turned off her ringer, cursing silently to herself.

"Who's there?" he called. "Who is it?"

She wrapped her fingers around the closet door, and after a brief pause to hold on to her composure, slid it open. She wanted to look apologetic, but the second she saw his face, she started fighting back genuine tears. He dropped to his knees at the sight of her, gaping. His expression was a mix of joy and horror and confusion.

"Kani..." he gasped.

She took a steeling breath and held Stacey's phone tight. Faced with this, with this moment to escape, she knew it would be too easy to give up, take the easy way out. But the easy way would end badly. She knew it.

"Sorry," she said, not looking him in the eye. "I'm sorry."

She ran past him, opening the door and bouncing off the far wall as she raced to the stairs. He tried to grab her, but she pulled free, falling partway to the ground floor and then back through the kitchen, out the rear door and into the yard. Shouting erupted from inside the house, panicked, urgent, desperate shouting, and when she pushed through her gate into the front yard, the shouts took a different tone: orders. The police were coming.

Her father's truck was in the driveway, free of obstructions, flanked on either side by police cruisers, but beckoning her as a means of escape. She ducked low and ran as fast as she could, pressing her finger against the passenger-side lock and crawling into the leather seat. Police were shouting louder now, trying to figure out where she'd gone. They were racing down the neighbour's lawns, flashlights out, calling her name. She pulled at the car door to close it, but it bounced off her foot, and she stifled a cry. One of the officers nearby turned in her direction, pointing the flashlight into the truck, and then settling on the open door.

"I've got her!" he called, and started running.

Kani sat in the driver's seat, pushed her finger on the ignition, and knocked the gear into reverse. She prayed there'd be nobody behind her, and then put her foot hard on the gas, powering out of the driveway, electric engine tearing up the air with a furious charge. The right door swung open as she moved, and as she arced around onto the street, it caught on one of the cruisers, ripping itself off before she had a chance to react.

"Crap," she muttered to herself, "dad's gonna have a fit."

Police were running at her, hands on their guns, but not sure how to react. They were calling for her to stop, to stay still, but she switched gears again, put her foot straight to the floor, and the truck tore down the road, fishtailing as the tires tried to get purchase.

The phone rang once, and she slammed it in the dashboard cradle.

"You and me have different ideas of 'subtle,'" Kaso said.

"Shut up," she said. "Tell me what to do."

"Did you get the encoder chip?"

Kani bit her lip, checked the mirrors. Red and blue lights were chasing her. She pushed the gas down harder, though it made no difference. The engine was working overtime, after a life of sub-60 travel.

"I got it," she lied. "I got the chip, but it got smashed when I fell out a window."

"How smashed?" he asked, cautious.

"Totally."

"Hmm," he said.

She took a quick right turn onto the highway, swerving into traffic so fast she nearly flipped the whole car. She'd never driven so fast, never had the sensation that tiny movements could make the difference between living and death. She reached over her shoulder, grabbed at the seat belt, and clicked it into place. She had a feeling it wouldn't help her, but she felt naked without it. Her heart was beating so fast she was having trouble hearing anything else.

"What do I do?" she shouted. "I need a plan! Think!"

"Whistlepig!" Kaso shouted back.

"*What?*"

"Stop yelling at me! I'm working!" he snapped. "Okay. Get off the highway. It's too easy to trap you there."

She swerved around a pair of slow-moving cars and then shot through an opening, down the next exit. It warned her to slow to 30 km/h, but that was far too much of a drop for her to handle at this point: she eased off the gas just enough to make the turn in one piece, then pushed back down when she saw the police were following close behind. In the second she'd taken her eyes off the road, her truck had strayed from her lane, and she had to turn back, clipping a parked car and bouncing back into incoming traffic. Cars honked their horns, spun to get out of the way, and all she could do was work her way back to something resembling safety.

"Where am I going?" she yelled.

"South, I think. Just keep going."

"There's a red light ahead…"

"Just keep going!"

She tore through the intersection and the lights changed behind her. Traffic on either side started moving in, barely missing the police in pursuit. One of the cruisers crashed, trying to avoid a collision. The other four made it through unscathed.

"Damn. Network lag," swore Kaso. "You've gotta put some space between you. Step on it."

"This *is* stepping!"

"What kind of crappy car are you driving?" Kaso snapped.

"Shut up, you hermit!"

Kaso laughed hysterically. "That's the spirit! Woo!"

She raced through another intersection, dodging turning cars by a fraction of a second, and this time, the lights changed fast enough that the police were blocked by crossing traffic, easing out in front of them. They blared their horns, worked their way through, but it put at least a few more seconds between them and Kani.

"Okay, I've got your plan here," said Kaso. "Ready? It's going to be hard."

"Just tell me!"

"All right… here we go… take the next left—"

Kani turned the corner so fast she nearly smashed into a lamp post. She switched gears, tires skidding on the wet pavement, and raced off again.

"Another left!" shouted Kaso, and she barely made the turn in time.

"Give me a warning next time!" she yelled.

"Sorry! It's another left, then right, and then keep going straight until you see the ostrich farm on your... hold on, this is the wrong map."

"Dammit!" she shouted, slamming her hand on the dashboard. She spun the wheel back towards the highway, pushing hard on the brake. The truck nearly toppled, rocking into position in the middle of the road, facing the highway. She pushed her foot down again, one last time, straight past the police cruisers who had just turned to pursue her. They scrambled to follow, making sloppy movements that bought her even more time.

She passed under a rail overpass, saw the train above her, heading south, outside lights flashing on as they approached the station up ahead. She turned right again, bounding over a curb, onto the street running parallel to the tracks.

"Where're you going?" Kaso asked. "This looks like a dead end to me."

"Shut up and watch," she said, switching gears and keeping her foot to the floor. She would only beat the train to the station by seconds, but it would be plenty. She careened into the parking lot, skidding to a halt just short of the entrance, and kicked open her door. The seatbelt pulled her back in, and she struggled with it, punching madly until it let her go. She snatched the phone off the cradle, fell out onto the sidewalk, and then ran for the stairs. The few people on the steps moved out of the way as she ran past, jumping over the broken stalls and down the long hallway.

The police arrived, coming to quick stops all around the truck, jumping out with guns drawn, covering it from every angle. They ran through the station, yelling at everyone they passed to get down, get on the ground, but they knew where she was going. They got to the platform just as the doors were starting to close, and barely made it inside.

"Split up," the senior officer yelled to the others, and they took off through the mostly-empty cars, roughly turning around any women to check their faces. They finally arrived at the last car, and at the very back they saw a figure hunched over in a seat, head out of sight, hiding.

Hiding badly.

Grabbing at Life

Yuri fell out the door and into the cold night air, grabbing hold of a fence to get his balance back. He stunk of beer and wine and whatever else the bar had left in stock, and he knew it. He wasn't just drunk, he was *gloriously* drunk, and he didn't care who knew it. He waved to Bernard, a big, dramatic wave that nearly threw him over, and inhaled deeply.

"Thank you," he said, switching between Russian and French mid-word. "Thank you. You are good friend."

"Sorry I couldn't be more help, Yuri," said Bernard from the door. "Let me know how things turn out."

"I will," Yuri promised, then saluted, and started on his way home. One foot after another, down cobbled steps, past the chains that kept him in bounds, and into the empty streets where dreams came to die. Paris at night was still beautiful, bright lights in every tree, even if some were faded, dying. There was no one out to see it but him, but he relished every moment. It was one of the great marvels of the world, and he lived here every day. Well, most every day.

He'd been gone for the start of the Memorial — starting in September, marking the hundredth anniversary of the invasion of Poland and running for another six years after that — but it was hard to imagine the city could pull itself out of its stupor in time to remember the German occupation. Events planned years ago were all half-realized, and when the leaders of the world made their way here next summer, everyone wondered what they'd see.

France under the Nazis had been a shambles, but a proud one. France under the depression had nothing to show at all.

Yuri stumbled down a ramp until he ended up at the Seine, followed it through town, swaying dangerously close to the edge. Then, stopping and turning around in a full circle, certain he had no idea where he was anymore, he fell to his knees.

"I'm okay," he said to himself. "Is good. I'm okay."

He threw up into the water, licked his lips and sat down. He spat the rest on the walkway, took off his tie and threw it into the Seine as well. The stars were out, and they were beautiful. Especially when he turned his head, and they kept moving without him. He smiled at the sky, wondering how soon he'd go back. He lay down, tried to pick out constellations as the stars swirled above him. He laughed at it, how familiar it was, seeing that sight. Not from his angle, normally, but still so comforting.

"You!" came a sharp call from his side, and a police officer marched forward, hand on his stun stick. "Did you just—"

Yuri vomited again, this time on the sidewalk by the officer's shoes. The man backed up in disgust, arms crossed, jaw clenching. "Move on, sir," he warned.

Yuri nodded, got to his feet, shifting involuntarily towards the water. He took a moment, breathed in some fresh air, and got lost in the act, closing his eyes and spreading his arms out wide like he was flying. The cop lost patience, gave him a push in the arm. "Move it," he said.

Yuri shoved back, and with his massive size, knocked the cop down into the vomit. He got up quickly, checking his uniform, his ears turning bright red.

"That's it," he snarled, throwing Yuri into a wall. "You should learn to do what you're told."

"I always do what I am told," Yuri slurred. "Is how I get into trouble."

"Your bad luck, then," said the cop, pushing the scanner against Yuri's finger. "Your luck's only getting worse."

"Worse is not possible," Yuri sighed. "I am like stupid dog getting kicked by owner. I go back for more every day. Even I do not understand myself. I must be broken somewhere, yes?" The cop waited for the scan results to come in, kept pressing Yuri against the wall with his arm. "My daughter is dying," Yuri continued. "She is in hospital now, dying, and I cannot help her. I try, but my luck, it does not work for me. She is dying and I have no way to help."

"Getting drunk is always a good start," snapped the cop.

"Healthcare will not cover her," Yuri sighed. "My wife and I are not French, so they would let my little girl die. Seems wrong, no? So wrong to me."

"How about you go back where you came from?" said the cop. "That would solve all your problems. All *my* problems, anyway. Maybe you're having trouble because you're in the wrong country."

"Maybe," Yuri sighed.

The cop eased up, looked back at his handheld. "You worked at King/Western?" he asked.

"Yes, sir. Ten years."

"What job? Management? All the management were foreigners. Not a Frenchman in sight. That was some take-over we funded."

Yuri shook his head, rested his forehead on the wall. "I was not management," he said. "Engineer. Always engineer. Back-thrust adjustment. Later, RCS shielding."

The cop let him go, stepped back. "No kidding. My brother worked on the assembly line. What models did you do?"

"Many pleasure craft like R-12 and RF-31. At what factory was your brother?"

"L'Amaury," said the cop. "Six years until they closed."

"I visited often. They made good ships there. Best in fleet, I say. What is brother doing now?"

The cop pocketed his handheld, stared at the river. "He killed himself two years ago. He was too much of a company man, in the end. Couldn't move on. Couldn't see past what they did to his work."

"Yes," nodded Yuri. "I know feeling."

"It's the national psyche," the cop said. "Living a dream. Same reason they keep maintaining the spaceport at de Gaulle. It's like my old man says, you know... the ban is absolute, but we just won't see it. We can't let go of what this all should be."

"Is hard to give up. France was leader. I came to be part of history."

"Different kind of history, now."

"Yes," Yuri nodded. "Different."

The cop clapped Yuri on the shoulder, smiled a weary smile. "You should join the force. We could use big guys like you. As long as you're not usually this drunk."

Yuri smiled, shook his head. "No, just bad day is all. I am much better normally."

"Think about it. And have a good night!"

Yuri waved to him. "Good night! And I am sorry about uniform!"

"Don't be! It'll get me off early tonight!" The cop laughed and ran up the steps to the street. Yuri watched him go, felt the pit of despair growing deeper inside him. That man's brother had worked on the ships used by the wealthiest aristocrats the world had to offer. The sleekest, most perfectly-engineered spacecraft the human race had ever designed. They were the things you would tell your grandchildren about, pointing to the sky and remembering the great things you did.

Now the aristocrats had fled France, the factories were gone, and the ships he'd made were stocked with ice cannons and voice changers, and flown by faceless pirates like Chenne. If the cop's brother could see what she did with his work, what she made it do... would that bring him peace, or make it worse? It was hard to decide. It was hard to decide for Yuri, too.

He walked back along the water's edge, watching the lights from the nearby buildings shimmer in the reflections there, and stopped to stare. His phone rang and he answered blindly.

"Hello?" he said.

"Redux. Elvis."

"Hello, Elvis. It is late where you are?"

"Not yet," Elvis said. "I wanted to call and tell you how sorry I am, Redux. It's got to be hard, losing that retirement at the last second. I'd cover it for you, but I'm still a few months away from paying off my own fighter."

"Is okay. Is not your problem. Thank you for thinking."

He looked up at the actual buildings causing reflections in the water, felt let down by their worn exteriors. They were so much more romantic when he didn't see them directly. He wanted to hang up the phone and mourn them, but Elvis kept talking.

"Listen, I just found out about another mission in a few hours. It's not on any of the networks because of the typhoon in the drop zone, but I was thinking... this might be something that could help you."

"You are going too?" Yuri asked, stumbling a bit on the edge of the sidewalk.

"No, I'm busy all day. I just didn't want it to go to waste. It seems right up your alley."

"Thank you. I will think on it. It may be bad time for me too," he said, and his face lost its happy glow. "I will think."

Elvis cleared his throat, and his voice quieted. "You've heard about the rotten apple problem, right?" he said. "There's a lot of speculation right now about who it could be."

"Is not me," Yuri laughed.

"Yeah, nobody'd think that. You've been at this longer than anyone. We were thinking of someone else."

"Tundra is fool, but not mole. If they want to spy on us, they send better pilot. She sticking out like sore... sore..."

"Thumb."

"Yes. Thumb. She is new apple, not rotten."

"Troubling either way."

"Yes," Yuri nodded.

"What about Chenne? Nobody knows anything about her, and she *is* a good pilot. Do you have anything on her, one way or another?"

"She is good at job," Yuri said, thinking. "I do not know. She could be. But if so, she is working very slow. She has been with team for two years. What is she waiting for?"

"That's what worries me. All right, Redux. Thanks. I'll—"

"I am having problem," Yuri said, stopping. He stared at the pavement, held his breath. "I need to switch team, if I can. Do you know who can arrange?"

"Whoa," said Elvis, "are you sure about that?"

"I cannot trust Rook. He brought Tundra in. She has... damaged my life now, Elvis. Damaged badly. I cannot face her again, but I cannot face Rook either. He is meant to protect us from these things, and he... if I go back there, I cannot face him again."

Elvis said nothing for a moment.

"I understand," he offered, finally. "I'll see what I can do."

"Thank you," Yuri said, and started walking again. His foot slipped on the edge of the curb, and he dropped the phone onto the ground. He scrambled to pick it up, but it was off when he found it. He cursed, turned it back on, and kept walking. It rang almost immediately.

"Elvis?" he said, but heard crying on the other end.

"Yuri," sobbed Sabina. "Come quickly. Please, come quickly."

In a Bad Place

The door chimed loudly as Freeman entered, nodding to the clerk behind the counter, but keeping his face away from the security cameras up above. The clerk, an older man with a bowling shirt and high-top sneakers, tipped his cap and nodded back.

"Good evenin'," he said.

Freeman forced a smile, went straight into the aisles without a word. He made his way to the middle of the store, surrounded by hundreds and hundreds of bottles of every type and brand of liquor, and knew at a glance he'd tried them all at least once before. When he passed them on the street, or in the supermarket, they called out to him, begging for attention, for one more go… but now that he was here, ready to act on his impulses, they sat silently, waiting, hoping today would be *their* day.

He picked up a bottle of scotch, turning it over as calmly as he could manage, pretending to check the price, but mostly having a battle with himself, with his conscience. He knew this place: the top of the slope, straight on down into self-destruction. It was a steep drop, too. He thought of Asha, of what she'd say, but knew it didn't matter. She'd never seen him like that before. She'd never had to see him fall apart like that.

He looked at himself in the windows facing the street, glass reflecting the aisles like a mirror. What he saw was a tall, proud black man, a military man, someone unbowed by the certainty of death and the collapse of everything he knew. He saw someone able to put the bottle down, double-up his efforts and push past adversity like he'd done a thousand times before.

What he saw was a lie, and he new it. He was just *that* good at hiding the truth, even from himself. He picked up a different brand of scotch instead. One that wouldn't make him remember this moment again. And when he looked back to the glass, he saw himself breaking.

At the same time, he noticed a man, mid-twenties with unkempt black hair, baggy jacket hanging loose over his wiry frame, eating a Pocky and staring back at him through the reflection. The man bit down on the stick, swivelled his head ever so slightly, but kept his eyes locked. Freeman picked up another bottle of scotch, nodding to himself that it would be enough, and made his way to the counter.

Halfway there, he slowed at the sight of a second man entering from the street, hands in the pockets of a big, bulky Raiders jacket, bobbing his head to music, though there was none, and he had no earbuds in. The man glared at him sideways, but kept up his pace, and Freeman did his best not to notice. He went straight for the counter, put his bottles up for the clerk, and a took a handful of mini-mixers from a display nearby.

"Major?" came a voice from behind, and Freeman whirled around, ready to strike. It was a young man in military clothes, dog tag at his neck, arms held behind his back like he was saluting a commanding officer, which in a way, he was. His red hair was cut so short it almost looked blond, which was a flash of a memory all its own, but it was the smile on his face that triggered Freeman's memory. The kid always smiled like he'd just won the lottery.

"Lieutenant Armstrong," Freeman said, saluting. "How've you been?"

Armstrong saluted back, shrugged. "Same old, sir. How've *you* been? The guys all miss you. Haven't seen you in ages."

"I've been around," Freeman said, holding the scotch behind himself. "Are you back now? Back for good?"

"No sir. Short breather, sir. We ship out next week. Militia's been using the proceeds from piracy to buy new guns, so there's a never-ending supply of bad guys to kill. You know how it is. What they say on TV is half as bad as it is."

Freeman nodded, felt a jolt of anxiety and checked over his shoulder, trying to get a sense of what was going on. The two other men were on opposite sides of the store, reading bottles without using their eyes. Looking busy.

"Wish you were still with us, sir," said Armstrong.

Freeman laughed. "I doubt anyone else feels that way," he said.

"No, sir, that's just not the case. The guys have no hard feelings. None at all, sir. We all wish things had gone differently. More than anything. Hell, if it had been any of us, getting that news, we'd have been on the first plane back. You can count on it."

"It wasn't an easy decision to make," Freeman said quietly.

"It was an easy one to accept, sir. You've got my word on that. AWOL isn't always AWOL."

Freeman shrugged, smiled weakly.

"Let me get your drinks for you, sir," said Armstrong, reaching for the bottles, "It's the least I can do. Saying thanks for all the times you saved my ass."

Freeman pulled the scotch away, shaking his head, trying not to let the cracks show. The hardest part of drinking was imagining someone you knew would see, judge you. He couldn't let this happen.

"No, Lieutenant," he said. "I can't let you do that. I've got expensive tastes."

"It's okay, sir. I'm not a lieutenant anymore. Got promoted to captain last year. Now come on, I want to do something with my captain's pay, and something tells me this is gonna be as good as it gets for a while."

"Captain," he said, voice thick with disbelief.

"Yes, sir. Feels strange, don't it?"

"Feels right to me, Captain. It just won't to you, not for a while yet. And by then, you'll be Major Armstrong, bustin' heads in places we've never heard of."

"Yes sir," smiled Armstrong, and knocked on the counter twice, getting the attention of the clerk. "This man's a hero," he said proudly. "And I'm buyin' him some scotch."

The clerk looked between the two. "Good for you," he said.

Freeman let a smile creep onto his face, turning back to the rest of the store just in time to see the two men at the back burst forward, guns out, shoving their hands along the lines of bottles, glass shattering everywhere.

"Down on the ground!" they yelled. "Get down now!"

Freeman turned back to the clerk, but was lost in the chaos of the moment. The first man grabbed Armstrong by the jacket and tossed him onto the floor, stepping on his neck and aiming a gun at his head. Armstrong made no move to fight, knowing perfectly well that he was outgunned and outflanked, and anything he tried would end in bloodshed extending far beyond just him.

"No heroics, army-boy!" snapped the gunman, then looked at the clerk and bellowed: "Empty the register now!"

Freeman sighed, and the other gunman put him clear in his sights. "On the ground!" he shouted. "Get on the goddamn ground!"

"What do you want?" Freeman asked, not moving.

"Cash! Now get down! Now shut up before I—"

The scotch bottle exploded across the robber's head, spraying glass, blood and booze everywhere before he fell over in a heap. The second thug started to turn, but Freeman hit his wrist so hard the gun dropped, sliding across the floor and under a display case. The two of them faced each other, the world stopping around them: one frantic and cornered, the other eerily calm.

The robber reached into his jeans and began pulling out a second weapon, but it caught on his belt, and before he could get it loose, Freeman's boot caught him in the throat. He felt a crack, a stunning pain, and he landed on his back, gagging, grasping at his neck.

Freeman turned to Armstrong, helped him up, and patted his shoulder. "Nice talking with you, Captain. Tell the men I'm counting on them."

"Yes, sir," nodded Armstrong, dazed but understanding exactly what had happened. Not everyone got outflanked in impossible situations.

Freeman started towards the door, but the clerk called out: "Wait! The police will be here and…"

"I've got to run," Freeman said. "Places to be. That all right with you?"

The clerk nodded, smiled nervously, still shaking from the ordeal. "Please, take a case of beer. It's free. As thanks."

Freeman grabbed a six pack from the display at the front. The cheapest stuff in the store. He held it up, smiled. "Thanks."

He ran back to his car as the sirens closed in from all sides.

Something Small

The hospital was a monolith. From blocks away, it was visible, towering over the other native buildings like a massive sheet of glass and metal, like an alien spacecraft that had landed in the middle of Paris. At night, every floor was lit up, bright lights beaming out into the streets below, refusing to be constrained by things like nature or the position of the sun and moon. The old Seizu sign had been switched off years before, but it stayed up there at the top of the building, backlit and ominous, like a curse that would never fade.

Inside, it was like being transported from France to a metropolitan hospital in Tokyo: sharp lines, sterile, white walls made of metal and glass that seemed impervious to dust and grime, even while the rest of the city decayed. Every sign was trilingual: Japanese, French and English, and some of the computers still had kanji-enabled keyboards. As if anyone knew how to use them anymore.

Seizu had built the place for its employees — the world leaders in cockpit design at the time — because the French healthcare system was deemed too backward, too reactionary, too lazy. A year after it opened, the Seizu hospital was ordered by the government to take in anyone needing help, to spread their legendary care more freely. Still, backed by shareholders terrified of losing their shirts, the directors ran the place like a Japanese hospital, turning away those unlikely to heal to keep their ratings up and their reputation intact. That lasted another year, before the directors were deported and the hospital nationalized.

In the elevators, it was hard to miss the fact there was no fourth floor. Four is the number of death in Japan; especially taboo in a place meant to heal. After the takeover, even when run by the best the French system had to offer, the place fell from grace. To the last Seizu employees stranded in town after their plant shut down, it became known as "the hospital with fifteen fourth floors." It was a place for the impossibly-ill, staffed by doctors at the end of their careers, or those who thought technical marvels could somehow overcome any adversity, even if they weren't used quite right.

Yuri's family lived on the twelfth floor these last few years, and he knew it so well it made him sick. He ran down the hallway to room C-27, hand resting on a glowing white wall as he caught his breath. The door slid open — another odd culturalism of the Japanese era — and a doctor came out of the room, chart in hand. Yuri swallowed hard, tried not to panic.

"Doctor Olivette," he said. "Is she…"

"She's resting," said Olivette slowly, making sure to speak as clearly as possible. He seemed unable to believe Yuri would ever be fluent in French. "She is very ill. She cannot be stressed under any circumstances."

"No," Yuri agreed.

"Your wife was upset earlier. You cannot bring that into the room. Anya can't take it. You understand me?"

"Yes. Yes, I understand."

Olivette checked his notepad, scrolling through pages. He frowned. "I don't see any record of financing yet. Are you making arrangements tonight?"

"No. I have none. None yet." The doctor nodded, looked away. "Is there…" Yuri said, and Olivette turned back. "Is there some way you can do operation, and we pay later?"

The expression said it all, but Olivette still took the time to speak kindly, calmly. "I'm afraid not," he said. "There is a policy against it. Too many patients in your circumstances skip out on the bill when it comes due, and the hospital cannot afford any more losses, especially for expensive gene therapy."

Yuri stood there, nodding blankly, not surprised by the answer, but silently wishing there could be something more. Some sliver of hope. Olivette slipped the pen into his pocket and made his way down the hall, leaving Yuri in the pale light of the far wall, waiting to regain his composure.

Anya was not asleep. She was tucked into her bed, tubes running everywhere, blue knitted blanket askew from when the nurses had been in to run her nightly check-up. Her hair, so faint it was almost white, peeked out from the scarf tied over her head. Her smile widened the second he walked in the room, and she put out her hands to him, as if she could hug him. As if she could move.

"Papa, you came!" she said. Her voice was weak, scratchy, but full of life somehow. More so in French, a language he'd never master the way she had. "Did you have a good trip?"

"Yes, my darling," he said, sitting on the stool next to her, sticking with the Russian he hoped she'd remember when she was older. When she was older. "How are you feeling?"

"The doctors are nice to me," she said. "One of them brought me crayons."

"Oh? What did you draw?"

"You and mama in the park."

He smiled. "And where were you?" he asked.

"In bed, of course!" She reached for the papers on her bedside table, but her arms were too weighed down with wires to make it. Yuri reached over, grabbed the bundle, and sorted through them one by one. The drawings were crude and halting, but they were hers, and he loved them.

"This is me?" he asked, pointing to a drawing of a man with a beard, bent over so he took up half the page.

"You duck when you come in the room," Anya said, smiling. "It's funny."

"It's not ducking, darling," he said. "It's me bowing to you, when I come near." She giggled, and her heart monitor beeped slightly. He watched it, touched her hand, stroked gently.

"You are doing fine," he said. "You are doing so well. I am so proud of you. When I was your age, I thought taking cough syrup was worst thing in the world. But you... you sit here without complaint. You are magnificent."

She darted a look left and right, leaned forward. "I have a complaint, papa."

"It's okay, darling. You can tell me."

"The morning nurse smells like onions," she giggled.

"Some people do, darling," he laughed. "Some people smell terrible."

She took his hand and squeezed a finger. "You look sad, papa," she said. "Me?"

"Why are you sad? Is it me?"

Yuri looked down at her hand, squeezed it gently. "It's not you, darling. It could never be you."

"I can cheer you up," she said, and her heart rate picked up. "I have a story. I had an adventure."

He smiled, met her eyes again. "Ah, well! When did you have this adventure?"

"Last week," she whispered. "It's a secret."

"I will never tell."

Her gapped smile grew bigger. She tried to sit up, but couldn't make it. The scarf around her head came off, revealing the last wisps of her beautiful blond hair. He caught his breath, looking at it.

"I made a new friend," she said. "His name is Pierre. He lives at the hospital."

Yuri stiffened, kept his smile intact. "Where does he live here?" he asked.

"Under the bed. Don't look! He's sleeping!" Yuri hesitated. "He is a wombat," she continued. "They are very sleepy animals. They sleep all the time. But Pierre had trouble sleeping. He was scared, I think. And I told him not to worry, and I helped him count sheep until he fell asleep."

"You are a kind, kind girl."

"It was no trouble," she grinned. "I was tired too."

He kissed her small hand. She pulled it away, tickled by his beard.

"When you get better, darling, where would you like to go? I will bring you on vacation. Anywhere you like. Anything you like. What do you like?"

She thought, biting her lower lip and staring into the sky as if the answer were written on the ceiling. Then she smiled broadly, looked back to him.

"Ash Wednesday," she said.

"Ash Wednesday," he repeated, uncertain.

"Last year for Ash Wednesday, you took mama to Church and it made her so happy. When I get better, I want to go there too. It sounds wonderful."

"Yes, darling. Then that is where we'll go. I promise."

He kissed her forehead, trying not to cry, to make her worry, but it was so much, seeing her like this. He squeezed his eyes shut, prayed for a miracle, some miracle that would get him the money to save her. Anything. He'd do anything.

The heart monitor started whining, and he pulled back from her in time to see her eyes roll back in her head. He let her go, stepped away, hands trembling as doctors raced in, pushing him aside, ordering him out. Get out now! He stumbled back, eyes never leaving his daughter's poor little face, and almost fell into the hallway, tears streaming down his cheeks.

"Yuri," said Sabina, in the hall, half-empty coffee in her hand. "What happened? What did you do?"

"Nothing, I just..."

"Jesus, Yuri, they warned us to keep her calm. You have to be careful. You have to be think about someone other than *yourself!*" He nodded, sat on a chair by the door, expressionless, listening carefully. "Did you find money yet?" Sabina snapped. "Or did you just drink whatever we had left? That's an excellent plan, Yuri. Maybe beer will cure Anya."

"I have options," he said quietly.

"Options? What options? I need to hear *real* options, Yuri. Not dreams, not promises. I need *answers.*"

The heart monitor was silent in the room, and he held his breath, waiting for word.

"What answers, Yuri? Tell me."

He looked at the floor, avoiding her. "I will look to join police force," he said. "They want people like me. Get medical coverage for Anya."

Sabina threw her coffee against the wall, paced away, holding her head. "That's no answer, Yuri. It'll take months for you to get hired, to get coverage. *If* they cover you. Anya needs help *now*. Not tomorrow, not next year… *now.*"

He nodded, breathing ragged, and stood up. He couldn't look her in the eye, even if she had wanted it. He wanted to apologize, but words were meaningless anymore. Most actions were, too. He reached out to her, hoping he could show her how awful he felt, but she slapped his hand away.

"Don't," she snapped. "Just don't."

The door slid open and Olivette stuck his head out. "I need you two to stay quiet," he said. "She's fine, but your voices are frightening her. Please. Quiet down."

Yuri nodded, took his phone in his hand.

"Do not worry," he said. "I will leave. You may have peace."

He left them there, dragging his problems with him like a noose.

Killing Fate

The train rocked through a turn, but the police didn't lose their footing, keeping their guns aimed at the figure in the back. The senior officer moved forward carefully until he was almost within reach, then let loose with the loudest voice he had.

"You!" he shouted. "Show me your hands! Now!"

The figure jerked to attention, didn't turn, just waited.

"I want to see your hands!" yelled the officer. "Nice and slow!"

The figure barely moved, hands raising up into the air at a glacial pace, and then turned around to face them.

"Do you have any tea?" asked the man with the missing teeth.

"Dammit!" spat the officer, losing his balance as the train rocketed down the tracks towards Guelph.

Kani was winded, still buzzing from the adrenaline of the chase, but fading fast. She leapt down the stairs, ducking behind one of the vending machines and pulling the phone out of her pocket. She held down the power button until the thing shut off completely, and she put it away. She didn't want to be tracked anymore, by anyone. She ran back down the hallway and out into the open, moving fast and letting herself into a yellow cab that was waiting by the doors. The driver peered over his shoulder, squinting at her. Teenagers were notoriously bad fares, and she smelled like trash, so she was half-expecting to be kicked to the curb at any time. He looked at her, up and down, and then tapped the fare sheet on the bulletproof glass with his knuckle.

"Pre-pay the first twenty," he said. "Pre-pay, or get out."

Below the fare sheet was a thumbprint scanner, poking out of the glass partition. She hesitated, not wanting to create a trail the cops could use to follow her movements, but she had no cash, and no way of getting away without this ride. She winced, put her thumb down, and waited for it to process her account. If the police had locked it down, she'd know right away.

The driver watched her watching the display, snorted loudly. He could smell trouble.

The light flashed green. The payment cleared. She let out her held breath, trying not to look too obvious about it. The cabbie smiled at her; a thin, plastic smile. "Welcome aboard," he said. "Where to?"

Kani looked up at the horizon, weighed her options. She was so tired, she just needed a place to rest, to disappear for a while until her head stopped spinning. Exhaustion weighed on her more than anything. Around here, in the outer cities, there was no place to hide. Everyone watched everything. She'd never stand a chance.

She looked the cabbie straight in the eye. "Toronto. Downtown. Eaton Centre."

"That's a long way, miss."

"I'm good for it. Just drive."

The driver sighed, put the car into gear and drove off, turning towards the highway, pausing to let another fleet of police cars into the station. They screeched to a halt and more officers flowed up into the station. The cabbie watched it all from his mirrors.

"Wonder what's goin' on?" he said, almost like an accusation.

"Some idiot's lying on the tracks," she lied. "Won't get off."

The cabbie laughed, shook his head. "Damn fools," he said, as if that covered it.

Kani watched the highway ahead, saw flashing lights and slowing traffic. The signs above the road said, "Expect delays", but she knew hers would be more than most. She tapped the window lightly, motioned to the right.

"I need time to think," she said. "Take the side roads."

The cabbie turned again, scowling at her. "Listen, kid," he said. "I'm fine doin' whatever you want. But side roads're expensive. Real expensive. Pre-pay another eighty, and I'll consider it."

She put her thumb on the pad without hesitation, and the cabbie glanced over his shoulder, and sighed. "Your funeral," he said.

They turned off at the next exit, still a few kilometres from the roadblock ahead, and looped around some slower streets until they came to rougher, old municipal road that ran parallel to the highway, a wide grassy ditch separating them from the faster-moving traffic. Lampposts lit the street every half block, illuminating trees, the narrow gravel shoulder, and the occasional mailbox at the end of a long, rural driveway. It reminded her of the forest near the shack, and it gave her a shiver she couldn't get past.

She lowered herself in her seat, leaning her head against the door, and took Stacey's phone out of her pocket again. She wiped the dirt off the edge, staring at it like it held the answers.

The cab stopped suddenly, and she almost flew out of her seat. The cabbie turned around, nostrils flaring, and pounded on the glass partition.

"What's that s'posed to mean?" he demanded. She leaned forward, read the display on the scanner, and saw "Credit exceeded. Payment declined."

"I…" she said, but her door opened before she could think of a good explanation.

"Out!" the cabbie snapped. "Before I call the cops."

Kani let herself out onto the dark highway, reaching to close the door, but it closed on its own, and the cab tore off into the distance, moving so fast its tail lights were gone in less than a minute. She turned around, standing in the blackness in the middle of nowhere, and suddenly felt so much colder than before. She was invisible to the world — even to herself — and it didn't feel good. She started walking back the way she'd come, feet kicking the gravel, trying to think of a way out.

If she turned herself in, she'd be arrested for sure. Maybe she could cut a deal. The world was going mad over Gossamer's trial, and from what she could tell, he was refusing to cooperate. If she told them what she knew, maybe it would be enough to buy immunity? Forgiveness? She didn't need to be a hero, she just needed to get her life back.

But then Stacey would go to prison. Or if not, she'd certainly never talk to Kani again. That is, Kani realized, if Stacey were still alive. Once Fantoni realized the email from Kaso was fake, would he have kept Stacey around, or killed her horribly, out of revenge? The thought made Kani panic, and the panic gave way to a pulsing agony in her head. She pushed her palms against her temples, closed her eyes tight as a wave of swirling pain washed over her. When she opened her eyes again, the world was spinning. Vertigo, and worse than ever. She fought to keep her balance, to avoid falling into the black hole of the world around her.

Bright lights caught her attention, jarring after so much rural darkness, and she moved faster to see tall lamps beaming hot white light into a football field. Out on the blue-green grass were the familiar colours of the Trudeau High squad, wrapping up after a home game. It felt so good to see them, the pain in her head disappeared for a second. She was at the back entrance to her school, way out near the student parking lot she hadn't used since she broke up with Simon.

If the game was still on, the school would be open. If the school was open, she might be able to hide there overnight, like her teammates did the night before an early practice. All she needed was a little time to sleep, so she'd be more alert. She could shower, maybe clean her clothes a little... she could get her bearings. It wasn't a long-term plan, but it was better than anything she'd had so far. She headed for the lights, aiming to slip past the bleachers without being noticed.

"Hey, Kani!" called a girl from her calculus class. "Great game, eh?"

She smiled, nodding as best she could, but her smile disappeared when she saw the massive crowd ahead of her. The game was over. There was nowhere for her to hide from the glares and stares of her schoolmates, whispering too loudly about how she looked and how bad she smelled. They jostled her back and forth until she couldn't tell which way was forward anymore, and the world started spinning like it had in the fighter — gravity was an illusion, everything she knew as true was wrong — and she felt viciously ill again.

She put out a hand to brace herself, but was knocked from the side and stumbled, arms flailing, into one of the football players, his shoulder pads cracking at her head. He pushed her back without looking, and she hit the grass, gripping it tight in her hands, trying to stop the world from shifting beneath her.

"Help..." she whispered, but no one could hear her. She put a foot down ahead of her, braced both hands on her knee, and pushed herself up, swaying in the suffocating crowd. She could see the school between the heads all around her, and she knew it was going to be a very, very long walk.

A squeal and a laugh cut through the haze, and two girls rushed past behind, knocking her forward, between two jocks and straight into a peppy blonde in a cheerleading uniform. The blonde spun around, face twisted in righteous indignation, put her hands on her hips and looked Kani up and down.

"What the *hell* do you think you're doing?" she snapped.

Kani pulled herself back up to full height, tried to hold back vomit. "I..." she said, and then doubled over. The adrenaline was long gone now, and all she had left was stress and confusion. The blonde cleared her throat loudly, stomped her foot on the ground, trying to make a scene.

"You smell disgusting," she said. "Ever heard of bathing?"

"Sorry," Kani gasped, trying to move forward. "I just need to—"

"Kani?" came a voice from the side, and she wheeled around to see Simon pushing through the crowd, face awash in concern. She felt like she could collapse into his arms and somehow the agony would disappear. But before he could reach her, the blonde hopped between them, wrapping herself around him and giving him a long, long kiss that said she was staking her territory.

The rest of Simon's crew filtered into view, standing around her like she was a caged animal at the zoo. She recognized most of them, particularly Oak, mouth the size of his foot after years of practice. Simon himself had grown since she'd seen him last. His sideburns had come in more, hair cut a bit shorter, too, and he seemed to fit his shirt more ably than before. Or maybe it was just the way the girl was wrapped around him. She couldn't tell. Didn't want to tell.

"Kani," he said, breaking free of the blonde, "what's... are you okay?"

"All good," she wheezed. "Just gotta get to the school."

"You don't look like you'll make it," he said, stepping forward and leaving his girlfriend behind. "Maybe I should—"

"Simon!" whined the blonde. "We're on a *date!*" She scowled at Kani. They were so different, the two of them, it was hard to imagine he found them both attractive. Kani was plain and tough, straightforward and maybe even a little sly; her darker skin had turned heads when she and Simon had first started dating, but only because her grandfather was so infamously insular. This girl, though, she was like an American prom queen: blonde, perky, able to get her way through well-practised moves and poses meant to break down any man's resistance. But still, he was ignoring her and grabbing Kani's shoulder, keeping her up.

"Let me help you," he said.

"I'm fine," she said. "Stay with your girlfriend." She knocked his hand off her shoulder and tried to keep walking, but her first step missed its mark, and she started to fall. As she dropped, the world blacked out on her, sucking her into delirium. She felt herself turning her head, swaying side to side and she tried to hold on to her goals. She was going to get to the school. She was going to the school. She was going to wake up, and then she would—

Her eyes rolled forward and she was in Simon's car, strapped into the passenger seat as he raced down the side road so fast the streetlights barely registered as more than a strobe in her peripheral vision. He looked over at her, eyes in a panic, and betrayed a smile when he saw she was awake.

"Hold on," he said. "I'm getting you to the hospital."

Hospital! The thought of it was too terrifying to manage for Kani. As soon as he told them who she was, the police would show up, and then the game would be over for sure. She couldn't go to the hospital. She reached out and grabbed the steering wheel, yanking it sideways, and the car lurched towards the trees.

"Kani!" Simon yelled, and hit the brakes, spinning the car around in a wide arc, crashing its tail into a set of bushes just short of a telephone pole. Kani was flung into the car door, smacking her head on the window. Simon grabbed her face and turned her towards him, staring at her furiously. "Kani, what the hell is going on? You almost killed us!"

"I'm sorry about your girlfriend."

"My *girlfriend*? After *that*? You owe me an explanation, and fast. Your face looks bruised. Are you okay? Did someone hurt you?"

She turned away, ran her hand through her hair to cover her cheek, though it didn't reach. "It's…" she began, then trailed off. She couldn't find the words. Her head was swimming, and nothing was coming to her mouth the way it should have.

"Kani, stop screwing around. What's wrong? I can't help you if you keep secrets from me."

She stared at her hands, trying to put her thoughts in order. She needed to hide from the police and the mob and everyone else in the world, but there was no way she was getting into the school now. Too many people had seen her, had seen what had happened. That plan was gone. She'd run out of options, so she looked at Simon, tears in her eyes, and did what she did worst with him: she told him the truth.

"I need a place to say," she said. "I don't know where to go. I just need a place to stay."

"Why?"

"I don't want to—"

"Dammit, Kani! This is exactly the same as when you dumped me! No communication! Happy one day, split the next."

This pushed a button she didn't realize she had. The haziness melted away, and she felt energetic again, ready for whatever the world decided to throw at her next. Her shoulders squared and eyes narrowed, and when she spoke, she felt the venom on her tongue. "You landed on your feet all right," she snapped. "Must be hard, having a girlfriend like that."

"Trudy's nice," he said, half-heartedly.

"Yeah, *real* nice," Kani laughed.

"She's had a tough time," Simon argued. "She's not normally that angry."

"Boo hoo, boob jobs make me cry," Kani said, feeling a bit better every time she picked on the blonde. And a little bit worse, too. "She's as shallow as they come. I can see why you like her."

He leaned back, his expression changing, too. The kindness was gone, replaced with the cocky veneer he'd adopted since their break-up. "Oh, that's rich!" he laughed. "Coming from you? That's just too funny."

"I don't treat people like they're meat!" she yelled. "Ooh, look at me, I'm all blond and bouncy and—"

"So what? You're *jealous*? You don't get to be jealous, Kani! *You* broke up with *me*! If I offended you that much, why do you care?"

She rolled her eyes, looked back out the window. "You didn't offend me," she grumbled.

"So what? Why did you break up with me? And don't give me that crap about growing apart. You know it's not true."

"You wouldn't understand," she muttered. "It's complicated. You're probably not used to complex thoughts anymore."

"Try me."

She banged her head against the glass, closed her eyes.

"My grandfather found out about us," she said.

"I thought he already knew we were—"

"I lied," she said. "You know him. He's conservative. He didn't even like me going to normal school. If he found out his only granddaughter was fooling around with—"

He touched her hand and she looked up at him. His face was kind again. The one that came to her when she was in trouble, despite all their history. "Since when have you ever cared about stuff like that?" he asked.

"I don't," she said. "Or at least I try not to. I just get it from all sides, and I don't know… sometimes it's just easier to go along with it, you know?"

He rolled his eyes. "I don't buy it. You don't believe that."

She shrugged, wiped a tear from her eye.

"I guess I had to learn why I believed it," she said. "See it for myself."

"And now?" he asked softly.

"My grandfather's a loon," she said, and smiled. "But I guess I already screwed up." He touched her cheek, was about to speak, but she had to stay on track. Her head was pounding, and she didn't know how much longer she could stay awake before the day caught up with her. "Simon," she said. "I need a place to stay."

She took his hand in hers, holding it tight, silently pleading that he wouldn't question why, but knowing that he would. "I wish I didn't have to ask, but it's important, Simon. Please. Please help me."

He nodded. "I can have my mom make up the guest room, but—"

"No. No, I can't let my dad find out."

He moved closer, brushed the hair from the side of her face, met her eyes. "You could sneak in the back," he whispered. "Hide out in my room."

She held her breath. "Are you sure? You can't tell anyone. No one, no matter what happens."

He nodded, didn't speak. She flashed a smile, leaned closer. "You know," he said, "it's a good thing you dumped me for a dumb reason." She looked at him, waiting. "Because it means there's still hope for us."

She smiled, and closed her eyes, leaned closer still.

"God, Kani," he said suddenly, pulling back. "What's wrong?"

She felt a trickle on her upper lip, touched it with a shaking hand, and came back with dark blood.

Not the Same

Five times he'd passed it, and five times he lost his nerve. The café's sign had lost some of its lustre, the inside looked more worn, less fresh and cheery, but it wasn't that that kept Yuri out. It was what he was going to say to her. On the sixth time around the block, he paused across the street, gathered his courage, and took a chance.

The bell over the door rang, he was hit by the same blast of warm air, but no one welcomed him, said hello. He passed by the rickety tables, standing by the edge of the kitchen, waiting for someone to stop by. The only other customer, a man with a weed of a moustache, read his book in silence, sipping at his cappuccino at every page turn. Finally, a waitress came through the door, saw Yuri, and turned with a smile.

"Hello, can I help you with something?" she asked.

"Yes," he said, standing on the precipice of a bold commitment. "Is… is Rache working today?"

The waitress' smile faded fast, and she shrugged, grabbed an American-style coffee pot off the counter, throwing a towel over her shoulder. "Rache quit months ago," she said. "She got into a fight with the manager and left. I don't think she even picked up her last paycheque. Dumbest kid I've ever seen, that one."

"Oh," said Yuri blankly. "Thank you."

The waitress was already gone, so he shoved his hands back in his pockets and pushed into the autumn air once more. He stood at the street corner, looking across the river at the people busying to get to work or home or wherever else was left, and felt like a part of his life had finished, finally. Every time the leaves changed, he thought of Rache, and wondered how she was doing. Now all he'd remember was that she was there, briefly, lost her temper and moved on. It made him laugh, such a fitting epitaph to their relationship.

A hand touched his arm, and he turned to see another waitress, faded apron squeezed far too tight around her waist, looking at him. "You were asking about Rache?" she asked in a quiet voice.

"Yes. But is okay. She is gone, I hear."

"Yeah," nodded the girl. "But if you want to find her, I think I saw her once, just a few weeks ago, down by the club called Spangles." He stared at her, then laughed. "Does that help at all?" she asked.

"Yes," he said, nodding. "Yes, is great help. Thank you."

He set off down the street, grinning broadly. It seemed he had written off their relationship far too soon.

Spangles was in a part of town packed with dance clubs, bars and gambling parlours, but it was not operating at the same level of respectability as its brethren. From the outside, it was clear they provided exotic dancing, a place to unwind without fear of being watched... but something in the way the building sat on the street said it was housing something... more. A pair of own-on-their-luck men sat at the curb, wearing lean, grey business suits, ripped at the sleeves and doused with dirt. One was playing a guitar, the other was singing a song; neither was paying any attention to the other, and it showed. People threw insults at them rather than coins, but they seemed too stoned to notice.

Yuri checked out the club on his first pass by, then decided the main entrance was too obvious. Sabina was not the jealous type, but this was no ordinary club. He had to be discrete, and for a moment, he wondered what he was doing, even considering going into a place like that. For a reason like he had, too. It seemed like madness.

And yet...

He walked down the sidewalk, ducking around the corner to the side-entrance he'd seen another man use a minute before. The alley was pitch black, only a faint red glow from a coloured ring around the doorknob lighting the way, but when he got closer, he paused at the sight of two heavy-set men, arms crossed, grinning at him.

"Sneaking in?" asked the bald one, wearing a name tag that read "Jean-Louis-Michel." He seemed made of pure muscle, wearing a skin-tight t-shirt even in the biting cold, and not even caring. He looked Yuri up and down, taking stock, probably making a list of ways to make him break.

"Main entrance is too bright," Yuri said, trying to sound like he fit in. "I prefer quiet, you know?"

"We need to see some identification," said the other. Roger, by the name tag. His appearance and accent said Indian, or Pakistani, but the look in his eye said he was best left alone. "ID card, driver's license, fingerprint."

Yuri held out his hand and let them scan him. He smiled at Jean-Louis-Michel. "It is early in day to be so busy, yes?"

"It's always busy," he sighed. "Always. What're you here for, friend?"

Yuri looked between them. "Do I need to give reason?"

"If we ask, yeah."

"Is personal."

"They're *all* personal," Roger said. "We've heard them all, too. We just like to be sure."

Yuri took a step back, crossed his arms. "I am curious. What would I do? What is wrong?"

"Well," said Roger, "if you were a cop, for instance, we'd have to ask you to leave."

"I am not cop," said Yuri with a smile.

"Some guys want to come in here to beat up the girls," said Jean-Louis-Michel, watching his reaction carefully. "Get confused about where the lines are drawn. And you're a pretty big guy, so…"

"I do not hurt fly. Very peaceful. I promise."

They looked to each other, grinned in perfect unison. "Then what d'you have to hide?" Jean-Louis-Michel asked. "Sounds like there's nothing to it."

"I like privacy," Yuri said.

They laughed, shook their heads and stepped aside, letting the red-handled door swing open. "Privacy," snickered Jean-Louis-Michel. "Love it. Good luck, friend. *Behave.*"

"Always," said Yuri, and went inside.

The music, barely audible from outside, was throbbing and enveloping in the club. A heavy, pulsing beat so loud he could tell he'd hear it in his dreams for weeks; like Russian techno, but more manic, raw, almost organic. He felt it on his skin, it carried so much power. The room was huge, much bigger than

it looked from the street. It had been made to mimic the popular Pleasure
Palace motif — like an industrial warehouse gone chic, then dilapidated —
but without the brightness that played so well on camera. The only real
lighting in the place shone on certain high-value areas like the pole dancers
and the cages suspended over dinner tables.

A trio of businessmen sat at one table, eating sushi with their hands as a
nearly-naked woman dressed as a panther prowled in a spherical cage above
them. Only the woman in the party paid any attention. Shock, maybe.
Curiosity, too.

Yuri ignored all the sights, making his way to the bar, and resting his
hands on the cool marble surface. "Do you have beer?" he shouted over the
noise, and the bartender nodded, poured him a pint. Yuri fished a large
banknote out of his pocket and passed it across, waving away the change.
There was no way he was going to pay by thumbprint here, and no way he was
going to take any money home. Clubs were notorious for bugging their
change, carving out the insides so they could see where their customers lived.
Or that was the rumour. The other half of the story is that the rumour was
started by the clubs themselves, so nobody would want to keep their change.
Yuri couldn't decide which sounded more likely.

When he turned back to the room, a blonde woman in a revealing blouse
was at his side, twirling her long curled locks between her fingers, tongue
playing with her upper lip in something resembling seduction. "Hello," she
said in a too-deep voice, like she was trying to sound older than she was. "I
am Helga."

He laughed, sipped his beer. "Hello, Helga. Is what accent you are using?"

"Svedish," she said, tripping over the "v."

"Is very good," Yuri said. "You are from France, yes?"

She shook her head, rubbed up against him.

"No," she said. "I am Sv-v-vedish."

He looked down at her, cocked an eyebrow. He spoke as quietly as one
could in a place this loud. "You are paid by customer, or hour?"

"Now ve are talking!" she swooned, grabbing at his belt. He put his hand
over her face and pushed her back. She stumbled into a stool, confused and
upset.

"You want to find someone else, Helga. Customer or hour, I am not good
fit for you."

She hissed at him, turned and walked into the darkness, swinging her hips far too much, trying to be sultry. Yuri leaned back towards the bartender.

"She is funny girl," he said. "Not my type."

"What is your type?" asked the bartender, scanning the available hostesses around the room. This was the key part of his job, selling the merchandise. His voice took on a salesman's tone. "We've got all kinds. Just tell me what you dream about, and it can be yours."

"Brunette," Yuri said, "Short hair."

"That, I can—"

"Her name is Rache."

The bartender paused, and Yuri nodded. He supposed that "by name" arrangements were made ahead of time, set up as something special for an extra cost, but he wasn't coming back here again. He put on a pleasant smile and waited. The bartender checked his computer, shrugged, and looked back up.

"It's not really a good time for her," he said. "I can find you someone that looks almost exactly—"

"Will not take long," Yuri said. "I promise."

The bartender, winced, then sighed and pointed to the back of the club, back where there was no lighting at all. "Red room," he said. "Wait for her on the bench. She'll be out any minute now."

"Thank you," Yuri said, handing over another banknote.

As he crossed the club, the occasional flash illuminated where he was going. There was an arch over the doorway, tall and menacing, like a twisted rendition of an Egyptian sculpture, doused in black. Etched on it were figures in all kinds of poses, none of them for the faint of heart. As he got closer, he could see dim lighting inside, bodies in motion, satin and sequins and gold.

The right side of the corridor was made up of ornate stalls, big enough for two or three beds, doors held on by silver hinges shaped like women's hands. Those that were closed had a red sash overtop; those that weren't had girls inviting him in. All kinds of sounds echoed from the place. Most happy, some not. All pleased.

A few stalls in, he smelled burnt rubber, scented oil and cinnamon. A man nearby was crying "it hurts! Oh, it hurts!" … but he was not complaining. A girl by an open door sat, knees up to cover her naked body, with a wide grin across her face. Every time the man yelped, she jutted her tongue out a bit. Yuri kept walking.

He finally found the stall with the red door, and paused there, looking for the bench. There was a wooden plank along the wall behind him, but it was strewn with other hostesses, writhing around with wires fastened on their temples, breasts and hands, lost in another world. He was about to make room for himself when the red door opened, and a man with a heavy stick — a table leg — shoved a woman out onto the floor. The man stomped forward, held the stick high, and beat her back again and again. Yuri moved to stop him, but it took on a new urgency when he saw the woman was Rache, her back purple with wretched bruises.

Yuri caught the stick before it hit her again. "You will stop that," he said to the man, not even half the Russian's size.

"She stole my money!" the man spat. "Ask her!"

"I didn't!" Rache cried. "I didn't, I swear I didn't!"

"Lying bitch!" yelled the man, and tried to swing again. He yanked back on the stick, but felt it twist suddenly, his arm locking in a painful position.

Yuri leaned down into the man's face, spoke quietly. "You will *stop* that."

The man let go of the stick and punched Yuri in the stomach with all the energy he had in him. It had no effect. In return, he got a face full of wood.

"Rache!" came a man's voice, German and hysterical, from the back rooms. "What the hell is going on?"

She got up off the ground, pulling the straps to her bra over her shoulders, and pointed between Yuri and the bleeding customer, mouth moving, but no words coming out. The German, her boss, glared at Yuri furiously.

Yuri shrugged.

"Is baseball fantasy," he offered.

Rache hit the sidewalk and collapsed, but Yuri kept his balance despite the shoving. The front doors closed behind them, and locked, too, putting off a pair of customers who had been hoping for some lunchtime fun.

Yuri put a hand on Rache's shoulder, holding her hand as she got off the ground, shivering in the cold. Her back looked worse in the light, bleeding and ruined by the sharp edges of the table leg. Whatever guilt Yuri had felt about that customer's face, it was gone. He took off his jacket and wrapped it around her shoulders, squeezing her arms to help her warm up.

She slapped his hands away, rearing on him with tears in her eyes. "What the hell was that?" she snapped. "I'm fired, you idiot! Fired!"

"Is not good job for you," he said.

"No? What's a better job? Tell me that! What's better?"

"Anything better. Place where they do not beat you is better."

"Well *obviously!*" she yelled. "But it paid the rent, you know! Are you going to do that, old man? Are you?"

He sighed, shook his head. He could do a lot of things to help her, but that was not one of them. That wasn't what he wanted for her. He paused, wondered for a moment what it *was* that he wanted for her. What was he here for? Why couldn't he let her go?

"So what?" she snapped. "What did you want to do today? Ruin my life? Is that it? Just ruin it, and go home to your wonderful wife and kid? Because congratulations, you did a great job!"

"Is not what I wanted," he said, finding the easiest reason and clinging to it. "I came to say sorry. For last time, at café. I left in hurry, should not have been so…"

She sat on the sidewalk, started crying into the sleeve of his jacket. Her eye shadow was leaving streaks everywhere, turning her face into a blur of black, blue and purple. He sat down beside her, put his arm over her shoulder, and pulled her close. Protecting, he told himself. Keeping her safe.

"Is not all bad," he said. "Will be okay. You will be okay."

She looked up at him, face so close her nose brushed his cheek, and held her breath. "Do you want me?" she whispered. There was hope in her eyes. Not love or lust or need, but *hope*. He let her go, but she stayed there, breathing on his neck, moving in gentle motions.

"I… I do not…" he stammered.

"Is that what this is?" she asked. "If you want me, you can have me. This is what it's been the whole time. That first night in the cells, then the café, and now this? You want me, and you don't know how to say it. I should have known, but I… I just didn't… I didn't see it."

He stood up quickly, backing away. She reached for him, caught his hand.

"It doesn't need to cost much," she said. "I just need rent."

"Is not right," he said, not even sure himself. "Is not why I am here. I wanted to be sure you were… safe."

"I'd be safer with you," she said, and tried pulling him down. He didn't budge. She kissed his fingers, keeping her eyes locked on him.

"Is not what I am here for, Rache," he said. "Will not help anyone."

She got to her knees, running her hands up his chest, clawing at his back and trying to pull him down. "It'll help me," she whispered. "Help me, Yuri. Help me please…"

He pulled away, and she stumbled, landing a hand on the pavement, and looked up longingly. He took another step back, suddenly aware of the people around them, the audience of drunks and beggars all waiting to see how this drama would play out. Yuri straightened, shook his head.

"I can find place for you to live," he said. "Safe place until you find your own way, yes? Rent is no problem. This, I can do. We can fix."

"Whatever," she said, getting to her feet, kicking off her heels and walking away. The coldness was back with a vengeance.

"Rache!" he called to her, desperate for her to stay, but not sure why anymore. "You can fix this! You can live important life!" She wheeled on him, gave him the finger, and kept walking. "Do not lose purpose!" he yelled. "Is not too late!"

She stopped, hands making fists, and seemed to be debating with herself. Her head lowered, then she turned suddenly, and stormed back.

"Not too late?" she yelled. "It's been too late *forever*! You think anyone can undo the… the *shit* we're in? You, me, the whole damn *country*? You think that's fixable? You're out of your mind, old man. This is all there is! Just be thankful you have a place to stay, food to eat! Half the world is *starving*, and you think there's *anything* about it that can be fixed? Out of your mind! So what? What? You give me a place to say, but what's that going to do? Drop in the bucket! Nothing's getting done like that!"

"We start small and then—"

"Too small!" she screamed. "I've got problems, alright? I have problems that don't go away with a warm bed at night. Not by a long shot." Her eyes were red, purple streaking down her face, and she pulled his jacket tight around her shoulders.

"Tell me other problems. Maybe I can fix—"

"Dammit, you can't *fix* everything, you know!"

Yuri stepped closer, lowering his voice, trying to close down the scene that was being watched by so many. "Is problem to do with money?" he asked.

"Money's just the start of it," she said, sniffling.

"Maybe I can—"

"It's heroin, okay? Heroin." Her voice dropped, quiet, urgent. "I don't need you to care. I don't need your sympathy, or your fixing. Just forget about that.

We'll forget all this. All this stuff today. Never happened." She stepped closer again, eyes half-closed, breathing into him. "You want me. You can have me. Any time. Any time. I just need some cash—" he stepped away, and she got more frantic. "Please! Please, you've got to give me some cash!"

He shook his head slowly, his hand over his mouth, stunned at what he'd been a part of. "You were so good," he said, voice hollow. "You were going to be so good. I do not know what went wrong."

She slapped him, spat in his face.

"Get over yourself," she snapped. "You're not a saint, and you're *not* God."

She took his jacket and left him alone in the cold.

On Your Knees

The house was far down the street, down where the streetlights were broken and the city knew not to care. It was older than the rest, built up over the last century until it was like a rolling anachronism, no two parts exactly misaligned, but somehow the whole feeling off-kilter. It was large, to be sure. The size of three other homes, a long stone wall around it, grown over with moss and vines. It was a palatial home, cloaked in the darkness of a Paris night, and it scared Yuri more than anything he'd seen.

He came at it as calmly as he could, arms out at his sides, palms facing forward, trying to show how non-threatening he was. The look on his face did that for him. His heart was pounding so hard it was like another set of steps pacing him, walking just a bit faster than he was.

He opened the gate and looked down the walkway, at the two figures silhouetted by the single light over the door. They adjusted their stances, and he put out his hands, showed he was unarmed, and shuffled carefully towards them. Two steps away, the backlighting eased, and he could see their faces. He smiled, despite himself.

"I must see Mr Pellier, please," he said to the bald man, nodding in turn to his Pakistani partner. "Is urgent."

Roger laughed, crossed his arms over his formidable chest. "Do you have an appointment, friend?"

"No," said Yuri, almost pleading. "Is urgent."

"So you said," grunted Jean-Louis-Michel. "What do you want to see him about?"

Yuri lowered his gaze, shifted uncomfortably. "Is private," he said.

"I thought you looked familiar," said Roger. "You're even dressed the same."

"Same haircut, too," said Jean-Louis-Michel.

Yuri glanced at the man's bald head, said nothing.

"You here to cause trouble?" asked Roger, looking Yuri up and down. If it came to it, he knew neither one of them could take him alone, but together, he didn't stand a chance. He slumped his shoulders as much as he could, tried to look pitiable.

"No," he said. "I only need to speak for minute."

Jean-Louis-Michel spoke into his sleeve, listened at the earpiece that hung loose down his neck, and then nodded. He motioned to a camera above the door, a tiny thing you wouldn't see unless you were looking for it. Yuri stared up at it, tried to look composed. He felt a moment of panic, not knowing what they might do next. He wasn't sure if they'd be running his face through a program, or passing it by some kind of security protocol, or maybe even—

The door buzzed, and Roger reached a hand out, took the handle, and with a warning look to Yuri, opened it.

"Don't beat anyone up this time," Jean-Louis-Michel cracked.

The foyer was immense, a magnificent chandelier hanging down from the storey above, the last of its crystal shards hanging at Yuri's eye level, casting glimmers around the room like he was underwater, and it was the sunlight flooding through. The walls were covered with artwork spanning the ages, paintings from private collectors who hadn't been able to pay their debts, or those who fled the city with only what they could carry. There was a Picasso by the drawing room, in a frame so gaudy, it would have made the artist turn in his grave. The whole place reeked of uninformed decadence.

Yuri was guided to the wide spiral staircase, around to the back, and down into the basement where all the walls were the original stonework, but painted over in gold to make it seem richer than it was. The floor in the basement was lined with thick velvet carpeting, so padded Yuri found it hard to keep his balance the first few steps. He waited outside a pair of grand double doors, standing in a pool of darkness while his guide knocked three times on the wall to his right.

"Come!" bellowed a Frenchman, and the doors opened to reveal Pellier at his desk, bathed in warm light, face twisted in furious concentration. He was older than Yuri, but by how much, it was hard to tell. His hair was mostly gone, the skin on his face re-formed many years ago in a race against time, and his body fit enough to forty, but wizened enough to be seventy. His wide-collared shirt was undone midway down his chest, black jacket hanging on his shoulders loosely. He'd lost weight, and hadn't bothered to change his wardrobe. The hallmark of a man who thought it would come back.

There were two more guards flanking the inside of the door, another four off to the sides near the desk. Yuri stood in the middle of all this, watching Pellier fidget at his desk, whittling a piece of wood into something resembling a horse without legs. The knife might have been an antique, but he used it roughly, jabbing and scraping, not once moving with the grace his craft required.

Pellier looked up after a few seconds, seemed annoyed he had a visitor, and motioned to the chair with the knife. "I hear congratulations are in order," he said, trying to smile through his concentration. "Your last mission today, wasn't it? It's been a long time, Yuri. A long time. Marcel, get him a drink. What are you taking, Yuri?"

"Nothing, thank you," he said to Marcel.

"Nonsense, Yuri. Vodka for my Russian friend. Something with vodka." Pellier leaned forward, held up the wood, the shavings on the desk, squinted at it. He blew on it, but there was nothing to come off. He snorted, turned it around. "Do you know anything about whittling?"

"No sir," said Yuri, watching the guards around him. Their gazes stayed locked near the top of the room, hands crossed neatly.

"My doctor has me doing this to relax," Pellier said. "Whittling and a vegetarian diet. Sickening stuff. I can't stand it. God gave me these —" he tapped his canine teeth with the tip of the knife, "— for a reason. For *tearing*. Brussels sprouts and beans. Nonsense!" He thumped his fist on the desk, then blew the shavings towards Yuri, setting the carving down. "What does this look like to you? Hmm?"

Yuri looked at the wood, then back to Pellier. His face stayed blank. "A stallion, sir," he said.

"Excellent," said Pellier. "I'm improving. My wife said it was a penguin earlier. Dumb cunt. A penguin. Marcel! Drinks!"

Marcel handed Yuri a drink, set a small paper napkin on his wrist. The glass was thin crystal, gold-rimmed, with two perfect ice cubes inside. Yuri took a sip, tasted peach and vodka, badly-mixed. He cupped the glass in both hands, playing the part of house guest.

"I admit it, Yuri, I'm going to miss having you around," said Pellier, picking the penguin back up and continuing to shave it to oblivion. "It's been quite the adventure. More than I'd have thought." Yuri said nothing. "Buying you that ship wasn't the best investment I've ever made, but it's been the most interesting. I can't tell you how much fun it is to tell people at parties that I'm a dustrunner sponsor. The madness, I tell you! They all want to know what it's like. I should bring you along some time."

"Yes sir," Yuri said, wondering if the man was stupid, or just too powerful to care. He prayed it would never come to refusing that request.

"How is Sabina?" said Pellier, smiling to himself at remembering Yuri's wife's name. "And little Anya? Is she well?"

"Sir," Yuri said suddenly. "I must tell you something."

"Anything Yuri! Anything!"

Yuri drank half the glass, held it in tightening hands. It give him no courage, no focus either. All it did was make his fears of what was coming seem more terrifying. "The mission today," he said carefully. "Was failure."

Pellier's knife slipped and cut his thumb.

"Repeat that," he said.

"Mission failed. Was not my fault, but—"

Pellier slammed the knife deep into the desk, kicking his chair back as he stood up, face turning red. He picked his drink off its coaster and threw it against the wall, glass flying everywhere.

"What do you mean *it failed?*" he roared. "How does it fail? You've been doing this long enough to get it done, haven't you? What in the *hell* happened?"

"Was new—"

"No!" shouted Pellier. "I don't want to hear it! You idiot, get out of my sight! Now! Get out! Don't come back until you've paid it all back. All of it! There's interest on this payment, you know! Interest!"

Yuri got up to go, head hung low, but he paused. Paused at the thought of Anya, of the doctor's warnings, of Sabina's face if he told her he had nothing to give. He looked over his shoulder at the knife in the desk, at the guards in the room, thought about his chances in any scenario he might imagine. He watched Pellier as he stormed around the room, kicking at walls, spittle flying from his mouth.

"Sir," Yuri said. "I must ask… for loan."

Pellier turned on him, nostrils flaring. "You must be joking."

"Anya is sick in hospital and I—"

Pellier snapped his fingers and one of the guards stepped towards Yuri. He thought he was about to be carted away, but instead, the guard punched him hard across the face. He stumbled, catching himself on his chair, and took a moment to recover. Then he stood again, bowing his head low, and continued...

"My daughter Anya is sick and needs operation today if she—"

He was punched again. This time, he hit the floor, knocking the chair over as he went. He sucked blood back into his mouth and swallowed, blinking to keep the world from spinning any more. He pulled his arms under him, pushed his palms into the carpet, and got up, slowly, regaining at least some of his composure.

"I will pay back," he said. "You have my word."

"I don't care," Pellier said. "You broke your word to me, I don't care for your word anymore."

"But my daughter!" Yuri said, and got on his knees, pleading, begging. "Please save her! Please!"

Pellier rolled his eyes, picked up the knife again and started whittling at a furious pace. He left bloody smears on the wood. "Yuri, I've seen more people die than you can possibly imagine. The one thing I know — and you'll do well to learn — is that you get over it. Even your children. You get over it."

"Please," Yuri cried. "I do not want to get over. I do not want to." He stood up, held out his hands, tears in his eyes.

"Boss," said the guard with the quick fists. "Maybe it's a good investment. Pay a bit now, save the girl, right? Get paid back, *plus,* when she's old enough, you can pimp her out and earn even—"

The guard's nose cracked so fast he didn't know what hit him. Yuri turned savagely to the sight of six guns aimed at his chest. His breath rumbled with anger.

"Yuri, Yuri, Yuri," said Pellier. "This is no way to get what you want."

Yuri slowed his breathing, opened his fists and let the anger dissipate. The guard stumbled out of the room, spilling blood everywhere. The other guards stifled their laughter at the fool. He deserved it.

"I will tell you what," said Pellier. "I never make two loans to the same man. But I will offer you a fair trade instead. You'll still owe me for the fighter, but you'll get the cash you need to save your daughter."

Yuri checked the guns. All still aimed. "What do I do?" he asked.

Pellier reached into his desk drawer and pulled out a folder. He tossed it across to Yuri. Inside were photos of a middle-aged man getting out of a government car. Taken from afar. Yuri looked to Pellier.

"Duplessis," said Pellier. "Transport minister. He's corrupt, of course, but not in the right way. Selling France to the foreigners. He needs to be taken care of."

Yuri said nothing. He nodded.

Pellier took a cloth out of the drawer, unwrapped it, and shoved the pistol over to Yuri. The guards kept their aim at him.

"It's very simple, Yuri," said Pellier. "Kill him, and save Anya."

Wild Disintegration

Kani wiped the blood from her nose, spread it on her shirt without thinking. Her head was spinning, vision filled with spots, and the blood was flowing faster. She felt like she was trapped in the fighter again, floating free and unable to tell which way was up. She fumbled at the car door, panicking and pounding at it, finally falling out into the gravel, crawling for safety she couldn't see.

"Kani!" Simon shouted, running after her. "What's going on?"

"D-d-don't know," she said, trying to stand, but the world shifted and she fell back. Simon caught her, brushed the hair from her face, tired to clean the blood away from her nose. Her eyes were rolling back in her head, snapping into focus, then drifting apart. He dragged her to the car, throwing open the door and carefully lowering her into the back seat. He crawled in on top of her, put his hand to her forehead. She stared up at him, half-smiling.

"What are you doing?" she asked.

"I don't know," he said. "I don't know at all. You don't have a fever. I don't know what's wrong. We need to get you to a hospital."

She grabbed his arm urgently, tried to sit up, but couldn't manage it. "No!" she gasped. "No, I can't!"

"Kani, you're white as a sheet. I don't want you dying in my car. We have to get you professional help."

"I'll be fine," she said. "Please, just give me a minute..."

She put her sleeve to her nose, pushed hard and felt the warmth of her blood seeping into the fabric, up her arm. She inhaled deeply, exhaled, and repeated that five times until the stars stopped moving in her vision, and she felt something close to normal.

"There," she said, and tried to sit up. The world blacked out on her, leaving her weightless again, and she fell back into the seat with a thud.

When she opened her eyes next, they were racing down the road. She put her hand on the back of Simon's seat and tried to move, to lift herself up, but she couldn't make it. He must have strapped her down — or she was too weak — but she couldn't make it, couldn't make her body obey even simple commands.

"Simon..." she called. "Simon, please..."

Things blurred again, and the next thing she knew, she was being carried out of the car, her arm over Simon's shoulder. She couldn't see where they were or what was happening, but she heard voices, urgent voices, and some she knew. Or one. The words were hard to hold on to, but she heard Simon arguing with someone, handing her over, she thought... and then she was sitting in a waiting room, struggling to keep her head up.

"Are you hurt?" asked voice from beside her. She turned her head and saw a small boy with a nail stuck through his hand. It was wrapped in gauze, and he held it out in front of him like it was odd, but not worrying. He stared up at her with wide eyes, oblivious to his own ordeal.

"I'm good," she said, clearing her throat. "How are you?"

"I fell in the garden."

"Looks painful," she said. "Does it hurt?"

"No," he shrugged. "It's not as bad as it looks. How about you?"

"It's a girl thing," she said, and tried to smile. He did not look amused.

"You've got blood on your shirt," he said. "And your face. What's wrong with you?"

"Nothing," she said, and looked around. Things weren't so swirly anymore, and she could see across the room. Simon was at the nurses' station, making broad motions in her direction, but she still couldn't quite make out what he was saying. Her vision shifted, and she saw something else: behind Simon, a security guard strode into the room, talking on his radio. He was sweeping his gaze across the patients, watching carefully, eyes narrow and ruthlessly precise. Kani turned around, trying to keep her balance, and talked to the boy some more.

"Are you scared?" she asked him.

He seemed caught off guard by this. "What? No."

"I'd be scared. How are they going to get that nail out of your hand?"

"I… I don't know…"

"If you hear them talking about a saw," she said. "Run."

The boy's carefully-crafted bravery shattered in an instant, and he started bawling loudly. Kani got to her feet and rushed to the door, hand at the side of her face in case the security guard saw her moving. The boy was hysterical, his parents rushing back to calm him, and just as she cleared the sliding doors, they started screaming at him to leave the nail where it was, leave it alone!

Kani thought she was free and clear, but then she heard Simon shout: "Wait! No!" and she took off running. She only made it a few steps before her vision got spotty again, and she had to fight to keep herself upright. It was a battle she lost quickly, toppling over, landing on her shoulder, and blacking out.

She woke up in a gurney, wheeling backwards, Simon at her side. He squeezed her hand, and she squeezed back.

"… only family," said a nurse, and Kani nearly cried at the thought of being alone. She tightened her grip on his hand.

"She's my sister," Simon explained. The nurse looked at Kani's dark hand interlocked with Simon's white one, and raised an eyebrow. "Half-sister, obviously," he said, and the nurse rolled her eyes.

Kani was set up in a curtained partition, IV in her arm, heart monitor chirping away. She had a clear view of the central area where the nurses worked, doctors milling about as they hopped from patient to patient. As her vision came back, she saw a young man covered in hives, fighting against restraints like he was going mad. It made her anxious, seeing the restraints. She could be a prisoner here just as easily as anywhere else.

The doctor came by, checking her chart and watching the machines. He seemed tired, kept rubbing his right eye with the heel of his hand.

"I'm Doctor Stanwick. You're miss… Davenport, is it?"

"Yes," Simon blurted, and the doctor looked between the two of them with a flash of a question that quickly disappeared.

"Do you know what might have caused this?" Stanwick asked. "Anything at all. Help us focus our testing."

Kani looked at her feet, squinted. She had no idea what to say. The truth and anything like it would have the police on her in a heartbeat. She tried to think of any medical condition that caused nosebleeds, but her mind just wasn't working that well yet. She remembered the last time she had a nosebleed at all was swimming lessons in fifth grade, when a classmate had kicked her in the face by mistake. It was all she could think to say.

"I was diving earlier," she lied. "Came up too fast."

"Diving?"

She had to think of a place they could never verify, never confirm one way or another. Someplace big and unguarded and— "Lake Ontario," she said. "Looking for sunken treasure."

Stanwick stared at her for a moment, tapped some buttons on the chart, and took out his pen light. "Bends have very specific symptoms," he said. "They're similar to other conditions, but there are some important differences."

"Like what?" Kani asked.

"Bleeding isn't very common from the bends. Not to this extent, anyway."

"I went really deep."

"You'd have to go to the bottom of the ocean floor."

She let him check her pupils, momentarily returning to that state where she couldn't see through the spots and stars. Simon gripped her hand, and she squeezed back, trying to forget the panic that was growing in her mind. She felt a tightness in her arm, her left arm, and her lungs felt smaller somehow, tighter, harder to use.

"I… I don't feel so good," she said, trying to sit up, and failing.

A searing jolt shot through her chest, and she twisted back, feeling incredible pain but unable to make a noise to show it. Simon looked to the doctor in a panic, and in an instant, Stanwick dropped the bed back and hit the panic button.

"Cardiac arrest!" he shouted. "I need some help over here!"

Indecent

Yuri sat down to a Tandoori chicken, only to realize he'd forgotten utensils. He made a quick dash into the kitchen, pulling open the drawer and fishing out the right combination: two forks, two knives, and a little spoon for Anya. He hopped back around the counter, put the silverware on the table like a waiter in a fancy restaurant, and then sat himself back down as if nothing had happened. Anya took the spoon in her little hand, burbling happily in her high chair, smacking her plastic bowl like a drum.

"I hope this worked," Sabina said with a nervous smile, serving the food. Yuri took his plate, turned it twice until it seemed positioned right, and then scooped a forkful.

"Is excellent," he said, then sneezed at the spices.

Sabina put down the serving spoon. "Don't be like that," she said.

"Like what? I like chicken."

She scowled at him, picked up her fork. "You lie badly."

"Is no lie! I love your cooking, Sabina. Truly."

He put the fork to his mouth, and the doorbell rang. He smiled, knowing it looked like a last-minute reprieve, trying to avoid Sabina's wrathful glare. He put his fork down carefully, kissed his wife on the cheek, and walked down the hall, ready to thank whoever had decided to call at dinnertime. The bell rang again, and he unlocked the deadbolt, opened the door.

It was Rache. The makeup around her eyes was dark, but her eyes were clearly sunken, drug-addled. She had on a black tank top, perfect for the summer heat, but she was shivering like it was the dead of winter, hands frantically rubbing at her arms to keep herself warm. She kept her elbows bent, hiding any traces of track marks. When she saw him, a smile crept across her face, and she stepped forward.

"Yuri!" she said. "It *is* you!"

He stepped outside the apartment urgently, closing the door behind him. She didn't back up to give him room, stayed close, touching his arm lightly with her fidgeting fingers.

"What do you want, Rache?" he said, voice low, rumbling. "How did you find me?"

"The bouncers at the club," she said, biting her lower lip. "They scanned your fingerprint when you came in. I... *persuaded* them to share it." She had a playful smile on her face, like none of what she said meant anything more than a game. Like nothing had happened at all. He turned his head away, but she stroked his neck, resting her head on his chest. He pulled back, bumping into the door.

"What do you want?" he asked, his voice hollow. "Just tell me. What?"

"I need some money," she said, wincing like it was hard to say, but it was clearly not. "Just a little money. I'm not offering anything. It's not like last time. I learned my lesson. I just need some cash, Yuri. Please."

He shook his head, trying to put words to the anger he was feeling. She rested a hand on his shoulder, pinned him to the door, pushing herself against him. Not to have him, not in a sexual way... like she was curling up to sleep. She tilted her head up, spoke softly into his neck, a breathy, quiet voice.

"Please, Yuri," she said. "I'm getting clean. I swear."

"You do not look clean," he said, taking her by the shoulders and holding her back. "You look worse. How is heroin treating you?"

She didn't react, just smiled. Smiled and ran a finger down his chest, dropping off at his belt. The door behind him opened and Sabina came to an abrupt halt at the sight of her husband holding a strange girl by the arms.

"What..." he began, then started over. "What's going on here, Yuri? The food is..." She looked Rache up and down, and then at Yuri. He held his head away from Rache, obviously uncomfortable. "Who is this?" Sabina asked.

"Is no one," Yuri said stiffly.

"Then get rid of her," Sabina said, simmering. "We're having dinner." She went back to her food, closing the door carefully. A peaceful kind of motion that betrayed a firestorm inside.

Yuri looked across at Rache, and she smiled hopefully, reached towards him. He squeezed her shoulders and she moaned like she liked it, like she thought he'd like her to… but then he pushed her away, and she stumbled into the far wall. She stood there in silence for a moment, shocked, hurt, angry, and a dozen other emotions he couldn't begin to put words to. Then she started to cry, sniffled suddenly, stood straighter, and set her jaw. Her eyes narrowed. Ready for battle. A range of emotions playing so quickly, it was like there was no "real" for her anymore. She was as changeable as the drugs wanted her to be.

"Rache," Yuri said carefully, "you are not my problem. I cannot fix life for you. You have parents. Call them. They can help you."

She laughed, shook her head, rubbed her forearm across her eyes and cried for an instant before catching herself. "My parents died a few months ago," she said.

"I am sorry," Yuri said, stiff and formal, giving no ground.

"It was a car accident," she said, fishing for sympathy. Empathy. Anything. "They were decapitated. I saw the morgue photos. It was horrible."

Yuri said nothing. He couldn't decide if she was telling the truth, but what made it worse was that he realized he couldn't trust her even that far. He had no doubt she'd use the deaths of her parents as currency get what she needed… what she wanted… and he wouldn't be a part of it. Not anymore.

"I am sorry," he said. "But is still not my problem."

"They left me with so much debt, Yuri," she said, stepping closer, but he held out a warning hand, and she paused. "They had so much debt. I need help, Yuri. I can get back on my feet, I just need some help."

"No," he said. "Is too late for that."

She took his hand in hers, placed it on her chest, above her heart. He tried to pull back, but she was strong, kept it steady, staring into his eyes.

"Do you feel that?" she asked quietly. He wouldn't answer. "My heartbeat. That's the sound of me. That's the sound of my honesty. I'm being honest with you, Yuri. I am."

"You do not know honesty," he sighed.

She kept her eyes on him, started sliding his hand lower, but he pulled back suddenly, slamming his fist into the door frame and cursing as the wood cut his knuckles. He sucked on them, tasting blood, feeling shame for having been so stupid as to care for her at all. When he looked past his injury, she was at his side, digging through his pockets, throwing receipts and tissues on the ground in manic fury. He grabbed her wrist, pulled her out, and threw her on the floor. She looked up, panting, desperate.

"I need it," she pleaded.

"Somewhere else," he whispered, keeping his voice as low as he could. "Please, go somewhere else."

She picked herself up off the ground, straightening her tank top and trying to hold on to some dignity for a moment. She stepped forward, looked him in the eye, and slapped him hard across the cheek.

He didn't react. She reached back to do it again, and he caught her arm.

"You had chance to fix life, Rache, and you did nothing with chance you had. I try to help you so many times, and so many times you ruin for yourself. I cannot do anymore. You choose life, and this is life you get. If you do not like, you have no one to blame but yourself."

He let her go, checked his knuckles again, and turned to go back inside, back to his family and their dinner. He put his hand on the doorknob, and Rache grabbed the back of his shirt, pulled so hard the top button popped off.

"Who are you to tell me this?" she snapped. "What have you done with your life that makes you do high and mighty? You have money? Money means nothing! Money is a symptom of corruption, and you're just on your way to hell, Yuri! To *hell!*" He paused at the door. Her grip tightened. "Chromoco is killing children, the UN stands by and watches, and all the while you just sit here, eating your dinner and loving life, and you let—"

"Rache," he said, turning around. "None is about you. Chromoco is not you. The UN is not you. Learn to see small picture first." He opened the door and pulled free.

Rache screamed suddenly.

"Stop it! Give me my money! I need it! You *owe* me! You owe me for what I've done for you! Dammit, Yuri, you owe me!" She started pounding on the wall next to his door, eyes streaming with tears, and he stepped away, stunned at the transformation. He had no idea what she'd become, but it scared him.

Rache stopped the second the crying started. Anya was upset, and the cries penetrated the door like a knife. Rache backed away from it like it hurt, hand over her mouth. She looked to Yuri, back to the door, then ran to the stairs, and away.

No Life to Live

At three in the morning, the city was finally falling asleep, or nearly so. A light rain was falling, coating the street and anyone about. A cold drizzle that cut through clothing like it wasn't there, setting a chill to the bone. Yuri hovered at the edge of the building across from Duplessis', tucked in a shadow, hands deep in his pockets. A car hummed down the street, headlights catching him briefly, but he didn't move. His eyes were locked on the house across the way.

It was a converted shop, redone to look like a metropolitan townhouse: a broad set of stairs led up to a large-paned door, not two feet from a giant bay window that was lit up with a fierce orange glow, a bright square amid the darkness. A man stood there, cigarette in his hand, smart vest undone but not removed; he was watching the rain the way Yuri was watching him. He was a fit forty-year-old, well coiffed and alert, white shirt and slacks kept in perfect condition after what must have been a painfully-long day. He looked exactly like his photo, which did nothing to calm Yuri's nerves. Duplessis put the cigarette to his lips, paused, and then exhaled smoke into the window.

A woman — his wife, probably — came from the back of the room with coffee, and he took it gladly, saying something quiet and inconsequential with a smile. She plucked the cigarette out of his mouth, and he gave her a kiss on the cheek, after which she kept the smoke and disappeared into the back once more. He sipped his coffee, seemed lost in thought again, watching the rain, but not really seeing it.

Yuri gripped the gun in his pocket, the cold metal feeling icier than it ought to, finger dancing off the trigger, afraid of what it might do. He checked Duplessis once more, then took a step into the street.

A young girl ran up to the man in the window, wrapped her arms around his legs and nearly spilled his drink. She was five at most, brown hair in curls, pink nightgown drifting as she moved. Duplessis laughed, knelt down next to her, placing his coffee on the floor, and put her on his knee. She showed him a paper, indecipherable from across the street, but it made him smile so much it hurt Yuri to watch. Things he had to trade to get the same.

He stepped back into the shadows, hand leaving the gun for his phone, and dialled with shaking fingers, putting it to his ear and waiting while it rang, rang, rang... He cleared his throat, wiping the rainwater from his hair as the voicemail message played. When it beeped, it took him a moment to put his words together.

"Hello Sabina," he said, under his breath, fighting to stay composed. "Is Yuri. I hope all is good there. I am calling to say... to say I will have money soon. Anya will have money soon. Please do not worry." He lowered the phone, looked at the display, at the red button that ended the call, and stopped. He put it back to his ear, spoke louder this time. "I love you," he said, and hung up.

This time, he just walked. One foot in a puddle, but his stride never faltered; down onto the street, up the sidewalk, past the gate and up to the stairs. He stood beside the door, hand in his pocket, gripping the gun so tight it might have split in two. Rain funnelled off the roof in a sharp line onto the top of his head, but he had to stay there, stay ready, in the darkness. He reached a trembling hand over, caught the edge of the doorbell, and pushed it before he lost his nerve. The doorknob didn't turn, but he watched it, needing it to turn, needing it to be over.

Finally, the lock jerked out of place, the doorknob began to wiggle, and he stepped into the welcome mat, hand wrapped round the gun in his pocket, aimed dead-centre into the house. The door opened slowly, and his finger nudged the trigger, and he—

He let go quickly. The girl stood there, frowning at him, blue eyes boring into his soul in a way that was too much like Anya to bear. He nearly fell off the steps, he was so stunned by her.

"Are you the taxi driver?" she asked without judgement.

He couldn't find the words.

She held up a doll to him — plastic and beautiful, like the one he'd bought last Christmas and lost on the train — hair cut at different lengths, frayed in every direction, wearing a sparkling blue ball gown. He knelt down instinctively, staring at the doll like it was some holy relic, something didn't want to do, but couldn't stop himself.

"This is Elizabeth," said the girl. "She's English." Yuri watched the girl speak, saw the interest, the passion in the simple things, the way the doll moved its legs. He fought back a smile. He couldn't smile. Not here.

"Jacques cut her hair last week, and he lost his allowance for a month," she declared. "Mama said he got off easy." Yuri stood up, took a step back, not knowing what he'd do. How he'd follow through. How he could *not*. "We're going to Fiji tonight," said the girl, brushing Elizabeth's hair with her fingers. "I get to stay up past my bedtime. Do you know where Fiji is?"

"Hello?" said Duplessis, coming down the stairs, pulling his jacket on, checking his watch, trying to figure out if he was late or the driver was early. When he saw Yuri, he rushed forward, took the girl by the shoulder and moved her inside, out of the way. Yuri looked at them both, wondered what this girl would think of him, once he killed her papa. Would it haunt her forever? Would he be a demon to her like he was to Rache? He nearly fell down the stairs, feeling faint, pale.

"Is he sick, papa?" the girl asked.

"No, darling," said Duplessis. "He's not sick."

The way the man was looking at him helped Yuri get his nerve back. He stood straight and tried to control his fate again. "I must speak outside," he said, his voice hoarse.

Duplessis looked down at his daughter, Elizabeth in hand, and then back to Yuri. If he knew what was coming, he was exceedingly brave. It would have been a surprise, except Yuri knew the sentiment. He would protect his daughter at all costs, even when he faced death. He nodded to his assassin, knelt down and patted the girl on the head, gave her a kiss on the cheek. She wrapped her little arms around his neck, and he whispered in her ear, sending her rushing up the stairs and out of sight. He got to his feet, straightened out his jacket, and let himself into the night, closing the door behind him.

Yuri aimed the gun at Duplessis' gut, fingers fumbling into place, trying to keep steady long enough to do the job. The politician watched the pocket shift, and looked up with understanding. "What is this about?" he asked.

Yuri flipped off the safety. "You should know," he said, and took another step back so he might save himself the blood spatter.

Duplessis puffed his chest, shook his head in disbelief. He was a proud man, and would not go easily. Not with actions, but with words. "You think this will stop us?" he snapped. "You're naïve. There are more in my party ready to stand up to corruption. You can't stop it like this!"

Ah, the last roar of a lion. Hunting without mercy, now caught in a trap of his own making. Yuri's guilt melted away by the second, replaced by a searing anger made real by all the hurt he felt in his adopted city. The policeman's brother called for vengeance, and he was there to deliver it.

"Corruption?" Yuri growled. "Who are you to say this? You sold countrymen to dogs for your place in power. You and your party deserve to burn. You are hypocrite."

Duplessis stepped toward him cheeks rumbling with fury. "How *dare* you!" he snapped. "I've dedicated my *life* to overturning those damn piracy laws! Don't you *dare* lecture me about hypocrisy, you cowardly swine!"

Yuri's hand let go of the gun involuntarily, and he stumbled back. Piracy laws. The knife in the back of the French space tourism boom. With them in place, there was no way forward, no way to recover. "You… overturn laws…"

"Kill me, fine, but do not fool yourself: we *will* bring France back to life! It's beyond me, beyond my life. Do what you like. People will find out. People will care!"

Yuri let go of the gun, shaking badly. He pushed Duplessis against the door and ran, ran down the walkway, through the gate, and into the street, falling into a puddle and scrambling on, trying to see through the strengthening rain. He didn't know what he was doing anymore, but he knew he couldn't kill this man. If there was a soul left in him at the end of the day, after all he'd done, it wouldn't survive that murder. He wept for Anya, wept for the promises he couldn't keep, but he couldn't pull the trigger. Not tonight, not like this.

Duplessis' voice rang out over the sound of traffic, calling for help, crackling like thunder. Yuri kept on running, panicked as a chorus of angry shouts joined in, and he heard splashing behind him, flashlights marking his way as he raced ahead. Their feet pounded after him faster than he could bear, and then they tackled him, slamming him into the ground, pushing his head into the grit as his arms fell loose at his sides, and they dragged him away.

Goodbyes

First came the sounds. Distant, echoing, and missing the bass that made them seem real, but she could hear the slow, steady beep of the heart monitor, filling the void. That was the first thing she heard, and it took her forever to know what it meant. She was swimming without moving, laid back in a sea of black and purple and swaths of blue that moved her this way and that, so she never felt steady, but never felt so calm.

The second thing she heard was Simon, anxious and close, calling her name in the soft voice he'd had when she'd fallen asleep on his chest in the field behind his house. The memory was sharp but indistinct. She remembered the shirt he wore, blue checked and dirty, the brush of his fingertips on her bare arm. She reached out to feel it again, and he caught her hand, squeezing it tight in his, and she knew that was a different self altogether.

She felt the weight of the blanket on her chest, the mask on her face, and her eyelids fought to open, to stay open against the bright lights above her. She turned her head, halting and slow, and as the spotlight faded, the world came rushing back. Simon held her hand tighter, smiled like he'd never been happy before, and lowered his head to the bed.

"Kani," he breathed. "Thank god."

She looked around, her strength and anxiety coming back in a rush. They'd moved her to a private room, windowless and dark beyond her bed. The door to the hall was open, dimly-lit but still coursing with doctors and nurses. She was deep inside the hospital. Trapped.

"How do you feel?" Simon asked gently, and she looked back, confused. "You had a heart attack," he said, voice weak, like he didn't believe the words himself. "They say you'll be fine. They said not to worry. They're just being careful."

She reached up, took the mask off her face, trying to keep her hand from shaking. She was wearing a hospital gown, and she couldn't see her clothes anywhere. She smelled blood everywhere: in her nose, her throat, all around. It made her nauseous again.

"How long have I been here?" she asked, nearly coughing. It hurt to breathe. "What time is it?"

"A little past one in the morning," he said. "Not that long. Listen, Kani—"

"Excuse us for a minute, young man," said a doctor from the door. He was older than the one from before, seemed less concerned with bedside manner at all. His white hair was close-cropped, thin eyes looking out over glasses shaped like blades. He held a clipboard under his arm like a soldier, regarded them like a king. Kani squeezed Simon's hand tighter. The doctor saw it, and seemed unimpressed. "I need to talk to the patient alone."

Simon shook his head, held his ground. "I'm going to stay," he said. "She needs me here."

"And I need you out," said the doctor, pointing to the door. He had a phone on his belt, uncovered while he held out his arm, and they both knew he could have security on-site without a second thought. Simon looked to Kani, and she nodded, giving him permission. She'd beaten enough odds today. A doctor wouldn't best her now. Simon slipped past the doctor, out into the hall, and the door closed behind him.

"Hello, Alanna," said the stranger, pulling up a stool and sitting next to her. He smelled like blood, too, but he was spotless, clean. "I'm Dr McGruther. You're feeling better, I see. You gave us quite a scare for a minute there. Do you know what happened?"

Kani shrugged, looked away. "Nose bleed and heart attack," she said.

"Yes," he said, speaking softly. "Do you know how it started?"

Kani cleared her throat, remembering her earlier lie. "I was diving and—"

"Young lady, please save us some time and tell me the truth. I know that's not your brother outside, and I know you weren't diving. This is not the bends. I don't care if you want your boyfriend here to comfort you, and I won't call your parents unless you ask me to. My concern is what's going on with you. I need you to be honest with me."

Kani didn't say anything.

Dr McGruther rolled closer, lowered his voice: "Your blood work indicates you've been exposed to constant low levels of radiation for several hours. I don't know if it's what caused your bleeding and the heart attack, but I've got a pretty good idea they're related somehow. And if it keeps up, I'm sure you're aware the damage could be much worse than what you've experienced so far."

Kani bit her lip, looked at him in flickering glances. "I don't know what it could be," she lied.

"I don't believe you," he said. She shrugged, looked down at her hands, picked at her nails. He put his hand over hers, but she refused to make eye contact. "I have a daughter about your age," he said. "She's in that rebellious stage. The one I'm sure you don't think you're in. I understand rebellion, wanting to be your own person. I do. I've been there myself. But there's a difference between being your own person, and putting yourself in *danger* for the wrong reasons."

Kani looked him in the eye. She was shaking.

"I don't care what you've done," McGruther continued. "I don't care where you've been, or why you did it. I can't talk about it even if I knew, because you're my patient, and I need you to trust me. All I care about — all I want from you now — is that you tell me the things I need to know to treat you properly."

Kani was crying, trying to wring her hands, but he wouldn't let go. She saw Stacey at the side of the river, her hand broken open, the blood on the ground, the pitiable look of fear and pleading on her face, and she couldn't help but wish it had been her there instead. She felt sick with herself.

"You're young," he said. "You've got so much life left to live. Don't waste it like this. Let me help you. Please."

She nodded, caught her breath, and looked up again. She opened her mouth to speak, but remembered Stacey again, Stacey in the black truck, being stolen away.

"I…" she said.

"Yes…" he nodded.

She blinked, and Stacey was gone. "I'd like to see Simon for a bit, please."

He held her hand, squinting at the decision she'd made, as if he could see through it to the truth. She didn't care about looking innocent anymore. She just wanted him to accept that she wasn't ever going to tell him what he wanted to hear, and to leave her alone. He seemed to sense it, because he patted her hand, stood up, slipping the clipboard back under his arm, and walked to the door.

"I'll be outside," he said. "Please, Alanna. Please trust me enough to let me save you."

He left, and she fell back into her pillow, squeezing her eyes shut, wondering if she'd done the right thing or just doomed herself, and if maybe those two concepts were one and the same. Simon back came in, rushing to her side and taking her hand again. He knelt down beside her, speaking softly.

"Are you okay?" he asked. Did they tell you anything? You're going to get better, right?"

"I think so," she said. "I think so."

"Oh thank god," he said, smiling a hopeful smile she felt guilty for causing. She was drowning in lies today. That thought caught on a memory, and she sat up, whispering: "You told them I was Alanna?"

"They knew her name from the health records. It was the easiest way to play it. I thought someone would realize we look nothing like brother and sister, but no one said a word."

"I think they know," she said, glancing at the door. "But I'll play along, just in case." She sat up, wincing at the ache in her chest. "What floor are we on? Do you think we can get out of here without anyone seeing?"

"It's not safe, Kani. You're—"

"I'll be fine," she said. "Don't worry about me."

"It's not that," he said, pushing her back into bed. "I saw the news while I was waiting. It's... it's Stacey, Kani... they think she was kidnapped. It's everywhere. Her parents are freaking out. And I... I don't mean this the wrong way... but I think you know something about it, don't you?"

She said nothing, offered nothing.

"That's why you're hiding. You're afraid."

"It's not that, Simon."

"Why are you lying to me?" he asked. "Why won't you tell me the truth?"

"It's not that simple," she said. "I can't get you involved. I can't. I'm sorry, but it's just not possible."

"Kani..." he said, and kissed her. It caught her by surprise, but she didn't resist. Their hands locked together, and her dug her fingers into him, trying to hold on to the safety, the moment. She felt dizzy again, but didn't mind at all. He kissed her mouth, her cheek, kept his mouth so close to her ear she could hear him catch his breath. "Kani," he said softly. "Tell me the truth."

She couldn't say no, couldn't avoid the question. Without his eyes on her, judging her, weighing decisions she'd made without time or preparation... it was somehow easier. She wrapped her arm around him, held him there, kissed his ear and whispered: "Stacey was kidnapped. I was there." He tensed, but she wouldn't let him go. "It's the mob. She got caught up in some dangerous... in some stupid things. They're going to kill her, Simon. They're going to kill her, and there's no one that can help her but me."

"You can't blame yourself for—"

"I'm not blaming myself. But I *will* if anything happens to her. I can't let that happen."

Simon pulled back, smiled softly. "So what's our plan?" he asked.

"No," she whispered. "I can't do that to you. I don't want to be part of this, but I *really* don't want you getting hurt."

"You're going to have to try extra hard to stop me, Kani. You should know that by now."

"Simon, I'm not—" she began, and looked quickly to the door as McGruther peeked his head in, glasses off and expression dire. "I'm fine," Kani said to him. "Really. Fine. You don't need to—"

"It's not that," said the Doctor said. "It's not that at all. Alanna, there's someone here to see you. From the government." She started to sit up, pulling back in bed. "I don't know how they found out," McGruther said, "but they think you know something about a kidnapping."

Kani and Simon exchanged glances. McGruther cleared his throat: "They want to see her alone, young man. You can talk to your sister later."

Simon looked for guidance, and once again, Kani nodded to him. What choice did she have? If he stayed, she'd be dooming him. This was the only way to play the hand she'd been dealt, no matter how much it scared her. Simon leaned in and kissed her cheek, awkward and hesitant, and then let the doctor lead him out into the hall.

Kani was left alone in the room with no place left to run. Were there no windows in here for that reason, or was it just luck of the draw? She couldn't find her clothes, couldn't see a way out, but a sudden burst of adrenaline shot through her, and she felt *desperate* to escape. She pushed at the railing at the side of her bed, trying to get it down, when suddenly the door creaked open, and she froze mid-motion.

Into the room walked a man in a black suit, stocky with ghostly white skin and a head of fiery hair. He closed the door behind him with the utmost care, meandering to the foot of her bed, playing with the pages of a Bible left on a table there. He seemed lost in his own world, and for a moment, she thought he might not have anything to do with her at all.

But then he looked up, and saw straight through her, she could tell.

"Hello, Kani," he said. "You and I need to talk."

How It Works

"How do you feel?" asked the suit, pausing on a page in the Bible and smiling at it. "I hear you've had quite the day."

Kani didn't speak.

He smiled, nodded, kept flipping pages. "Radiation can be very painful the first go around," he said. "The body adjusts over time, but that first dose is the one you remember. Rips your guts out, makes you wish you hadn't been born." He laughed to himself, turned and started checking around the room, staring at random objects that weren't even hers. "Hadn't been born," he said. "Tired expression, I'm sorry. Did you take the pills like they told you to?" He checked over his shoulder. "You didn't, did you?" She clenched a fist.

"They wouldn't help you anyway. Not on such short notice. Don't believe them if they say otherwise. It's a popular lie. It takes weeks to build enough to do you any good. And you haven't had weeks, have you, Kani?"

He turned, leaned against the cupboard across from her, scratched his chin. His nails were sharp, dry-looking, and they grated on his nearly-invisible stubble in a sound that was awful from across the room.

"I'm Mr Andrews, by the way. I'm on your side. Not in the generic sense, either. *Your* side. I hope you understand the distinction."

"What do you want?" she asked.

"Ah, a voice! Well done. Let's keep this progress going." He stopped at the foot of her bed, played with the Bible again. "I want you to have children, Kani. That's not a come-on. No, I want you to get past this predicament, and have kids running around you some day. And you still can, but you need to stick to the regimen they'll prescribe today. Stick to it to the second, because you've still got a chance. Your uterus still has a fighting chance. Ignore it, and… well, it won't be the only organ that will look like a cancerous raisin, will it?"

She clenched her teeth, and he cocked his head.

"Didn't they explain the risks to you? They didn't clarify things? Oh dear. Oh dear." He closed the Bible. "Here's what I think happened to you today, Kani, and you can tell me how close I am." He clasped his hands, stared up, as if reciting a speech he only half-remembered. "Stacey is your schoolmate. Your friend, maybe. Probably. And Stacey got mixed up in some bad things, with some bad people, and she's in trouble. Present tense. She's in *serious* trouble."

Kani shuddered.

"You want to help," Mr Andrews continued. "You're a good friend. You've done more than any friend would: you've gone on a mission to help her. You've strapped yourself in and done what no one would ever expect of you. You've seen Earth from a distance. Maybe it was beautiful. But it was the biggest mistake of your life."

Kani looked away, and he wheeled the stool next to her, perched at the edge like a gargoyle.

"I see a lot of people going up there, Kani, for so many reasons. So many reasons, and most of them seem noble. Oh, you know… poverty, fighting injustice, starving children. For every out-of-cash pirate, there are ten more out there that think they're saving the world when they put on that helmet. They're saving the *world*. And maybe they are. It's not my job to decide."

He wheeled across the room suddenly, and she turned to watch him go. He seemed to enjoy the ride. "Your teammate, Spastik," he said. "He nearly killed a hundred thousand people when he lost control of a freighter over Victoria. Showed no remorse. Did he seem troubled to you?" She thought back to Spastik's games, his trivia, the way nothing seemed to faze him at all. He didn't seem troubled. Not one bit.

"Or Chenne!" he said. "She's disabled a ship in such a dangerous place, the pilot nearly ran out of oxygen before they could get him back home. Think of that. Think of being in that cockpit, knowing you're going to die. Think of what that's like."

Kani could. She really could.

"Rook has fired on unarmed cargo ships from law-abiding companies. There are politics to it, as I'm sure you've learned. For all the passion, no one wants a death in space. It brings the conflict to a whole new level. Something no one can control."

He stood up, walked back, and started flipping through the Bible again. He said nothing for a moment, pausing at a page and reading a passage, and it was as if Kani had disappeared from his life entirely. Then he tapped a finger down, smiled, and continued talking. "These things I'm telling you, these aren't the statistics you hear in the news, Kani. These aren't dressed up to bother the public. Inflated, sensationalized. These are *real*. This is the life you're on the brink of."

He stared directly at her, and she couldn't tear her eyes away. He was looming over her from across the room somehow. "Honestly, Kani, the companies aren't perfect. And it's not a *just* world, either. I've seen enough things to make me doubt humanity. But when you put your faith in the kinds of people that dustrunning attracts, you're putting your faith in the basest of human nature."

He turned his head suddenly, squinted into the heart monitor. "Do you know where the word 'dustrunner' comes from? Most don't. I know 'pirate' is more *en vogue* these days, but if you'll forgive my diversion for a minute?" He waited for her to give him permission, but she was having none of it. He nodded to her as if she had, and continued: "The 'runner', as you know, refers to bringing contraband across enemy lines. Blockade runners were famous in the American Civil war. Gun runners, what have you. The 'dust' refers to the loose particles outside the freighter when they reach cruising speed. Floats around the ships like a cloud. Dust. It's poetic, don't you think? Dust?"

Kani looked away, but he didn't seem to notice.

"You're trying to save Stacey," he said. "You're not one of them. You're trying to do what's right, and it's killing you. And I know... I know why you're not answering. You don't know who you can trust. They've got you scared of everything. It's part of the game. Paranoia. More dustrunners commit suicide than are caught, did you know? Terrible statistic. Entirely avoidable."

He threw the Bible onto the bed, startling her. "I don't know any passages that cover this," he said. "God has never been my strong suit. I represent something more basic. Something man-made, and powerful. And I want to help you, Kani."

There was something in his eyes that made her panic. She'd seen killers today, seen the look of insanity, of callous cruelty, but this was nothing like that. This was the look of someone who could kill her without noticing, shoot her through the heart in the same way he ran off statistics and philosophies. It would almost be better to be arrested than have to see what lay at the end of his talk, because she felt certain she wouldn't survive it. She reached for the emergency call button, hand trembling, eyes not straying from his. He saw her do it, yet he didn't move a muscle.

"You can protect Stacey," he said. "The police will find her, and if you tell them what they need to know, they might find her faster. That's within your power. That's something you can do.

"I know it's hard to trust, but if you don't do this, you'll be an accomplice, and the longer it goes on, the less sympathy anyone in law enforcement will have for what you've gone through today. Everything you've done so far, we can call it fear, or shock, or just plain old desperation. But everything from this moment on? That's you. It's all on you."

Their eyes met, and his smile disappeared. "If you co-operate, none of this will be on your record in the morning. We'll make up any story you like, and everyone *will* believe it. That I can guarantee."

She inhaled, said nothing.

"Or," he said, smile coming back. "If you prefer, I am prepared to offer you assistance. Assistance in the form of advice and material support — one hundred and fifty-thousand to start — if you will consider working for me instead."

She looked into the face of the devil, and his smile didn't falter.

"Who are you?" she asked.

"I am one of the good guys, Kani."

Owing Things

Yuri's elbow hit the glass, and it tipped over onto the table, spilling water everywhere. He dropped the remnants of his meal back down on the placemat and tried to use his napkin to soak up the mess, but the water was getting the better of him. He dashed back into the kitchen, grabbing a roll of paper towels, and laid them out all along the table and the floor, sloshing them around until the damage was contained. He scooped up the soggy towels, put them on his plate, and was halfway to the kitchen when the doorbell rang.

He opened the door with slippery hands, and froze in shock. It was Rache, but not like before... not like ever before. Her hair was neat — still short, but more contained now — and she wore tidy glasses, a businesslike sweater and skirt, and held a briefcase between her hands. Her eyes looked healthy. *She* looked healthy, and Yuri almost gasped at the sight of her. It was like she was an entirely different person than the one he knew.

Still, he couldn't fight instinct, so he slammed the door in her face and stepped away, like she might break the thing down.

"Please, Yuri," she said from outside, her voice never above an urgent whisper. "Let me explain."

He rested his head against the door. He remembered her screaming at him, tearing a hole in his marriage that hadn't yet healed. He shook his head, closed his eyes. "I cannot do any more, Rache," he said. "Please go."

"Give me five minutes," she said. "I can explain. Please."

"Is not enough," he said, laying a hand on the doorknob. Tentative. "You do too much damage."

She said nothing for a moment — a long moment, and one that begged him to take a chance and open up and see if she'd left him, if he'd dealt the final blow and that was it. He let go the doorknob, stepped back, ready to move on. But then she spoke.

"I'm back in school," she said, voice clear in the hall, but not angry this time. "I've given up my old habits. I'm better now. I haven't used heroin in months. I just wanted you to know. That I'm doing something about it now. I'm fixing it." He didn't move. He didn't know what to do. "I wanted to thank you," she said. "So. Good-bye, Yuri. Thank you."

His fists tightened as her footsteps clicked down the hall, and he ran through all the reasons to just let her go, to let it go… but those reasons weighed nothing against the irrational need to see things done, so he opened the door, leaned out, and she paused, half-turned in the hallway, a look of surprise and tentative happiness on her face. She didn't speak, and neither did he, not really knowing what to say.

He motioned for her to come, come closer, and she nodded slightly, came back to him, standing a safe distance away in the hall, both hands still gripping the handle to her briefcase like it would keep her together. Yuri looked her up and down, then shrugged, motioned inside. "Is wrong place to talk," he said, and let her in.

He brought her a cup of tea as she settled at the table, upright and aloof, like she expected Sabina to jump out at any second. He sat across from her, heavy arms on the place mat, fidgeting with his ring. Rache smiled at the cornucopia in the centre of the table, turned it slightly, investigating. It was a polite moment of silence, but it had to end.

"Thank you," she said. "Thank you for understanding. I know it can't be easy, after last time. I wouldn't be so forgiving."

"I am not sure I am either," he said, leaning back and crossing his arms. She didn't react to the words, just sipped her tea quietly. Her arms were covered by her clothes, and it sparked suspicion he couldn't keep down. "No heroin?" he said, more harshly than he'd expected.

"None," she said. "I got out of the rehab clinic three months ago, and I honestly haven't even thought about it since then. I've been too busy."

"What clinic?" he asked, shocked by his tone. She smiled uneasily, nodded, turned her tea on the saucer.

"St Lucienne," she said. "Outside the old city. I can bring you if you like. There's this odd fellow there... a writer who thinks he's Billy the Kid. He writes the most fantastic prose. Sometimes in French, sometimes in English, but he's mastered them both. He's just lonely, so I go back as often as I can." She smiled, but he didn't. She sipped her tea again, watching him carefully.

"You are dressed well," he said. "What do you do now? Is not café, yes?"

"No, I'm back in school again. On my way to a degree in international relations. I'll get there this time. I know what I'm after. It's a lot of small motions, but they'll get me there someday." He nodded, sipped his tea. "I just needed to tell you how sorry I am for how I behaved last time. You didn't deserve it. I know that. I know it, and I'm sorry for dragging you through it with me. It was wrong. I'm sorry."

She started to stand, taking her bag off the ground, but he reached a hand over, not touching her, but pausing.

"How can I trust?" he asked. "I do not know how I can trust anymore."

"You can't," she shrugged. "And it's my fault. I accept that. But hopefully you'll be the last one to have that experience. I honestly hope so." She walked around the table, right past him, but before she could leave, he caught her hand, and she turned, looked at him, though he was staring into his tea. He took a moment, thinking things over, then spoke.

"Students do not need such fancy clothes."

She nodded. "I've got a part-time job working for the United Nations. As a translator." He looked at her and she smiled. "It's not where I'm going," she said. "It's a step on the way."

"At UN," he said.

"There are better ways to make a difference than I was willing to admit," she said. "You taught me that. I just didn't see it until recently."

He tugged on her hand, and she sat again, right next to him. So close. He passed her tea over, and she sipped it slowly, eyes locked on his. She left lipstick on the edge. It wasn't black or purple, which seemed odd to him.

"You are done with Chromoco?" he asked. "When I say word, you do not feel burn inside? Do not want to scream?"

She smiled. "Oh, I still hate them, Yuri. I can't lie about that. I'll see them destroyed one day, but it won't be with a protest sign or a Molotov cocktail. It'll be at the end of a vote in an international committee. It'll be *just*."

He let his breath go, tried to hide a smile, but it was impossible. "You have grown up, Rache," he said.

She flashed a smile at him, and it was brilliant. "Not as much as you, old man." She stood up, took her case and pushed in her chair. "Thank you for the tea, Yuri. And thank you for letting me explain. I'm sorry for disturbing you, and please tell your wife I'm sorry. I wish I could have done it in person."

"Sabina is away with Anya, visiting grandparents," he said. "But I will pass on message. I do not know if Sabina will be happy, but I am."

He opened the door for her, and she turned to him like she was about to kiss him good-bye... but instead she smiled with confidence, and looked up until their eyes met, and she knew he was listening to every word she said. "Good-bye, Yuri," she whispered. "And good luck to you."

He couldn't close the door.

Where You Go to Die

The light in the basement was pleasant and soft, but nothing else was. Yuri was hit again, face spiking with pain as a tooth broke loose, splattering blood on the plastic sheet that covered the floor. He coughed, tried to recover his composure, but another blow knocked him back again. The cuffs shook, cutting into his wrists as he jerked back in his seat.

The guard, a slim man with a fierce brow and tattooed arms, massaged his bloodied knuckles, his face devoid of emotion. His right ear was crumpled, a deep scar along the side of his head. He almost purred as he breathed. He could kill Yuri like this. It was just a matter of permission.

Duplessis sat at the desk across from them, sorting through papers, wrapped in coloured folders and elastic bands, seemingly unaware of the violence going on around him. He took a pen from the desk, marked a few spots in the middle of a document, then looked up, frowning.

"I appreciate your loyalty to your employer, but I'm sure you know we can do this all night. I'll ask you again: who sent you? The party hardliners? Was that it?"

Yuri let the blood fall out of his mouth, barely able to keep his eyes in focus anymore. He didn't nod, didn't shake his head, just sat there, drifting. Duplessis snapped his fingers, brought his attention back.

"Valneuve and the rest are in Chromoco's pocket, you know. They're just the buffer to keep the mothership safe. I don't care what they promised you, just tell me who they are."

Yuri dribbled blood onto the plastic, turned his swollen face up again. "I am…" he wheezed. "I am not on that side. On *your* side."

Duplessis laughed, went back to his reading. "I find that hard to believe," he said.

"They lie to me," Yuri said. "I do not fight against France. I do not fight you. You are ally."

"You must take me for a fool," Duplessis said. "My *ally?* You tried to kill me in front of my children."

"I did not know that you…" Yuri said, trying to form the sentences, but the language was fleeting, a theory in the back of his mind. "They lie to me. They said you were corrupt, taking money to sell out—"

"Yes, yes," Duplessis said. "We've been over this already."

Yuri shook from another blow to the stomach. He fought back the urge to vomit. "I am with you," he gurgled. "I am on your side. Piracy… not bad. Should not be illegal."

Duplessis looked across at him, eyes narrow. "What did you say?"

"Piracy steals from poor, not from rich," Yuri said, the words coming back in a flood. "Is all game to protect big players. Laws much change, protect the poor. I know. I know it all. No one says, but I have seen. Chromoco stealing freighters from un… unaffiliated miners and use for profit."

Duplessis stood up, moved across the room and stood before Yuri, arms crossed. When he spoke, his voice was low, rumbling. "How do you know that?"

"Check radiation levels," Yuri wheezed. "You will see."

Duplessis laughed. "I don't have that kind of equipment in my *house*. Who does? Now tell me how you know."

Yuri looked up, shuddered. "I hear on grapevine." Duplessis shook his head. He snatched Yuri's wallet off the table, flipped out his ID card and passed it to one of his guards.

"Send someone to his house, find out everything they can."

"No!" Yuri cried. "Leave my family alone!"

"You don't give me much choice, do you?" Duplessis said. "You know quite a lot about things you shouldn't, and I don't know *anything* about you."

He nodded to his guard, and two of them left, checking their weapons as they walked. Yuri yelled furiously, shaking the cuffs behind him, unable to get free. "I am dustrunner!" he shouted. "I am on your side. I am not assassin."

Duplessis bent down, shook his head. "Recent experience suggests otherwise," he said.

"I owe money to Pellier," he said. "Pellier told me to kill you, that he would save my daughter. I do not kill. Am not assassin. But my daughter will die, and he will pay for operation. You must believe!"

Duplessis stood straight, adjusted his jacket, and nodded to Yuri, clapped him on the shoulder. "Excellent," he said. "That's all we needed. It changes a lot. I thank you for helping me understand things. You're a brave man." Yuri looked up at him, his left eye swollen shut. "Sadly," Duplessis said, "Pellier has forced my hand. We can't keep you around. If word got out that I had dealings with an actual pirate, my career would be over. It's one thing to say you're a victim in a global conspiracy, but quite another to have you over for tea. And I can't risk that. I'm sure you understand. This is bigger than either of us."

Yuri trembled as the guards came to take him off the chair. "Please..." he gasped. "Please, no."

"Pellier isn't a fool," Duplessis said. "When he learns you didn't do your job, he'll shine a light on our meeting. The only hope we have is if you disappear." He looked to the guard at Yuri's right. "Throw him in the river," he said. "Make it look like the mafia. I want nothing more to do with this."

He left the room as Yuri screamed. The guards pulled a sack over his head, tied it tight around his neck until he could barely breathe. They knocked him to his back, pulled the chair out from under him, and kicked him in the stomach to keep him down. The air around him thickened, and he heard a zipper close, pulling his limbs in tighter, locking him down. He began to thrash around, trying to break free, but he was wrapped in a bag, tight and restrictive, with no hope of escape. They lifted him up, carried him upstairs and into the rain. With a jolt, he landed in the trunk of a car, hitting so hard he saw stars.

He reached for his phone, maybe still in his pocket, but his arms were too bound to make it. He couldn't have heard it even if he'd found it. He started to scream, hoping that someone — anyone — would hear him and come to help. All he heard was the sound of the tires in the rain, the soft bump as they turned a corner, and the frantic terror of his own breath.

He slid back as the car turned down a hill, bouncing more on the cobblestones as they made the final descent to the river. There was no time left. He knew he had no time. He started kicking out again, trying to break loose, but then the car stopped and the trunk opened, and rain tumbled down and hit the bag on his back, then his face, and he roared furiously as they lifted him out, holding him between them, swinging him side to side until he felt weightless.

"Please god, spare Anya," he whispered to himself, and they threw him in the river. He repeated his prayer ten times before he blacked out from the cold and lack of air.

Ideas and Actions

The water was freezing when she reached her hand in, but after a minute, the shower's temperature shifted to something like warmth, prickling Kani's skin and sending a wave of comfort up her arm. She checked over her shoulder at the closed door to the other room, and shivered. The light shone under the door in a solid beam, except for two breaks where Mr Andrews' feet were. Waiting.

She undid the bow at the back of her hospital gown and slipped into the shower as fast and silently as she could. She meant to keep watching the door, but the water on her face and body tore her out of the moment and put her in a place where the stress of the day was a fading memory. The filth and stench and blood washed off her, and she stood there, stream pounding into her face, letting everything disappear in the sound of the water pouring down the drain. It was like the world didn't exist anymore, and somehow, she was fine with that.

She poured shampoo into her shaking hand, so much it spilled out onto her feet, and washed her hair furiously, scrubbing out whatever memories she could reach. When she rinsed, she felt lighter, less burdened, more like herself again.

The door opened and she nearly screamed. She turned into the corner, out of the water, feeling so exposed she wanted to cry. But then a nurse leaned in, eyes averted and smiling, sensing the distress in the air.

"I brought you some clothes," she said, laying a set of hospital scrubs down on the counter. "They'll be more comfortable for your trip." Kani said nothing, stayed huddled in the corner, shivering. She wanted to thank the nurse, but the words wouldn't come. "Take your time," the nurse said, opening the door again. "There's no rush. He's gone for some food, so just take your time, dear."

The door closed, and Kani's eyes shot to the clothes. She jumped out of the shower, leaving the water on full blast, and dried herself furiously with every towel she could find. She was still dirty, but cleaning could wait. She threw the towels into the tub and grabbed the scrubs, shaking them open and pulling them over her shivering body. They were loose and starchy, but so much better than the blood-stained clothes she'd worn half the day.

She turned the doorknob carefully, peeking out into the main room. The hall outside was still dim with sporadic movement, but there was no one between her and freedom. She dashed to the bed, slipping her feet into her sneakers and carefully opening the plastic bag that held her belongings. She gripped her wallet in her teeth, and tried to push her phone into her pocket. But there was no pocket, and the phone slipped out of her hand and onto the floor with a loud bang.

She didn't move, listening for noises in the hall. Recognition. Concern. But all she heard were the quiet moans of a patient in another room, and the hum of the air conditioning switching on. She picked the phone off the ground, bundled both handsets in her fist, and ran for the door.

She came around the corner so fast she nearly fell into Simon, laying across a pair of waiting chairs, sleeping as peacefully as he could on seats made of metal and sharp plastic. She shook him until he opened his eyes, then put a hand over his mouth to keep him quiet.

"Don't talk," she whispered. "We have to go."

He nodded and she pulled him to his feet, grabbing hold of his arm and yanking him down the hall. She had no idea where they were, and all the signs pointed every direction but where they were headed. All Kani knew for sure was that she didn't want to be caught... the rest were peripheral details. She saw a sign pointing to stairwell A, and ran that way, shoes squeaking loudly every time she turned a corner. Finally, up ahead, she saw the stairs, and was about to push herself faster when an orderly wheeling a trolley pulled out in front of them, and she ducked into a side room, down and out of sight. Simon pushed against her shoulder, panting from the sudden exercise, and rubbing the sleep from his eyes.

"Are you sure it's safe to leave?" he whispered urgently.

"Yeah," she said. "It's recommended."

The orderly wheeled into view and stopped right in front of them, frowning deeply. He looked strong enough to disable either of them, but what scared Kani more than anything was the phone hanging off his belt. If Mr Andrews had any idea she'd run, that would be the quickest way to find her. She tried to push herself right into the wall, wishing she could disappear entirely.

The orderly walked towards them, hands on his hips, frown deepening with every step. He paused, so close Kani could smell the antibacterial cleanser on him, and she closed her eyes, waiting to be caught.

"What the hell," he said, and she nearly stood up and surrendered. But then she heard the soft sound of a fingernail on glass, and when she looked up, he was tapping a dead lightbulb embedded in the ceiling. It flickered every time he touched it, which seemed to make him more agitated. He unscrewed it carefully, took it down, and shook it by his ear. "Still good," he said, and blew on the end twice, then screwed it back in. Four twists in, it lit up brightly, shining down and highlighting Kani and Simon hiding just across the threshold.

The orderly squinted at the light, smiling, and went back to his trolley. Kani leaned into the hall, waiting until he was a few doors away, and then she and Simon ran for the stairs, heading down.

Simon jumped down a flight and took the lead, holding a hand back to Kani as if he were protecting her, keeping her safe. She almost laughed at it, seeing him acting so noble. They were in way over *both* of their heads, but the sentiment was nice. But then she collided with his hand, stumbling back, and gasping for breath. He put a finger to his lips and motioned over his shoulder. "Security one floor down," he whispered. "Not what we're looking for, right?"

She shook her head, and he nodded. They backed up slowly, pushing open the door to the second floor ducking into a ward with pastel-painted walls and clouds on the ceilings. The lighting here was brighter than upstairs, but softer, more comforting. Kani glanced at the signs on the walls, at the large lettering above the directions to radiology, imaging, palliative care, psychology and surgery: the oncology ward. She almost stepped back into the stairwell.

"Come on," Simon said, pointing down the hall. "There's another exit that way." He pulled her through, walking past darkened rooms, patients moaning in their sleep, the sounds of machines measuring life, doling out extensions in drops of medicine, oxygen and electric pulses. Without the visitors, the place felt like a wasteland of despair. No husbands comforting, no daughters wishing their mothers well. Hope sucked right out of the air, and it was suffocating.

One room's lights were on while the woman inside thrashed around in her bed, sleepy nurses trying to calm her down. "It's not supposed to be this way!" she screamed. "No! Stop it! Please!" Kani slowed to see, unable to take her eyes off the commotion. The woman had blood all down the front of her gown, down the front of her face. She kicked her dinner tray, and a bowl skidded across the floor, off-colour jello sliding to Kani's feet. She stared down, shaking. Simon took her by the shoulders, kept her walking.

"Come on," he said. "Let's go."

He pulled her through a set of doors, down some stairs that seemed slippery and uneven, and then out into the cold night air. She took a deep breath, letting the chill wake her up, and she looked back to Simon, took his hands in hers.

"Sorry," she said. "I just—"

The door swung open and a security guard pointed a flashlight at them, square jaw cricking as he reached for his radio. That was it. They were caught. There was no way they'd get away now. Kani's legs felt weak, and she reached to Simon for support, but his hands had let go, making tight fists.

He spun around, catching the guard in the neck so hard he slammed into the door frame, gasping desperately, his radio flying across the floor and shattering. Simon grabbed the open door and shoved it into the guard. Once, twice, and the third time, the man slumped to the ground, eyes rolled back in his head, breathing raspy and pained.

Simon looked back to Kani, eyes wide open, and hiccuped.

"Wow," he said.

"Yeah, wow," she agreed. They pulled the guard outside, closed the door behind him and handcuffed him to the railing by the stairs leading to the parking lot below.

By the time they got in Simon's old T-bird, he was practically electric with energy, switching gears like they needed to know who was boss, and ploughing straight through the parking gate, splintered wood flying everywhere.

He raced down the road, kicking leaves into a whirlwind in his wake, and when he crossed 140 he howled into the sky. Kani laughed, put a hand on the back of his neck, and almost instantly, he geared down and turned onto a darkened side road, jerking to a stop in a small clearing with no one around.

The car switched off as powerfully as it had turned on, and he sat there in silence, hands still on the wheel.

"Simon, I—"

He turned suddenly and kissed her, pulling her close, needing her close. Her hand touched his chest, and she felt his heart racing, the energy in his movements. The urgency. He felt as alive as she had earlier, back in the fighter. It was an amazing sensation, and infectious too. She let him lift her onto his lap, mouths desperate for each other, hands moving to drink each other in, as much and as fast as possible. She laced her fingers into his and squeezed, and he yelped, bit his lip and kept kissing her, trying to pretend it hadn't hurt. The hand he'd used to hit the guard. It felt bruised, swollen.

She saw Stacey in a flash, lying at the side of the river, hand mangled and bleeding, and the moment was over, the rush was gone, and she pulled down her shirt, resting her arms on his shoulders, and kissed his face softly.

"I'm sorry," she said. "I'm sorry."

"What?" he asked, still manic, hands feeling caressing, up and down. "What's wrong? Are you okay?"

"It's Stacey," she said, and his hands stopped. He looked at her, eyes clear for the first time since they'd left, and nodded.

"We're going to get her back," he said. "From the mob."

"Yeah," said Kani. "She's in a lot of trouble. She owes them money, and they're going to kill her if I don't pay it off."

"How much are we talking about here?" he asked. "Maybe I can—"

"Twelve thousand," she said, and he gasped. "I know. I know, it's a lot. But it is what it is, and if I can't pay it, I need to think of some other way to get her away from them. Something to get her to safety."

Simon brushed hair from her face, kissed her gently.

"You know what?" he asked. "You're too good."

"How so?"

"You're trying to find a way to save your friend — and I mean this in as nice a way as possible, Kani — but you're saving her from her own stupid mistakes."

"I know it's stupid, but she—"

"There's a point after which this stops being noble, and it starts being insane, Kani. I think you know that."

She looked into his eyes, saw the concern, the fear. She kissed him again. "Would you do it for me? Would you save me from the mob?" she asked.

"Of course," he said. "You know that. I'd do anything for you. But unless you're saying Stacey is your secret girlfriend, I don't think we're talking about the same thing."

"She's been my best friend forever," Kani said. "I can't lose her, Simon. Not when there's a chance I can get her back."

He watched her, then sighed, shook his head. "Fine," he said. "So what are we doing to do? Run a bake sale to earn the twelve grand? Or do you have something else in mind?"

Kani took out Stacey's phone and turned it on. "We're going to set a trap," she said, and then redialled the only number she knew wasn't Kaso. The other end rang twice, and then a sleepy Erlenmeyer answered, yawning midway through his greeting.

"What?" he grunted. "I'm sleeping."

"Tell Fantoni I've got his money," Kani said confidently. "Tell him to meet me at the Trudeau High football field in one hour. Bring Stacey. I'll bring the cash. Don't be late."

"Wait, what time is it?" grunted Erlenmeyer. "Oh my god, you want us to go *where*?"

"Trudeau High. Football field by the bleachers. One hour."

She hung up. Simon's eyes were wide open in shock.

"You're pretty badass when you want to be," he said. "I haven't seen that side of you since—"

"Don't say it."

"— since the day you broke up with me. Vicious. I like it! So what's the plan? It's a sting? We're going to call the police and get them arrested? Is that it?"

"No," she said, shaking her head. "I meant it when I said we can't involve the police. The kind of trouble Stacey's in, that'll only make things worse. We need to solve this ourselves. Somehow."

Simon's confidence faltered. "So... wait. You don't have a plan?"

"Nothing really defined yet, no."

"Then what—" Stacey's phone rang, and a quick glance told Kani it was Kaso. She powered it off, squeezed it between her palms, and winced. "Who was that?" Simon asked.

"Long story," she said. "I think we need to go now."

"Go?" Simon breathed, running his hand under her shirt, up her back, pushing her towards him again. "But we've got a whole hour to spare." He kissed her, and for a moment she thought about giving in. But she knew Kaso would be worried about her, and would be tracking her phone, and if he got really spooked, he might arrange for someone to find them. And she couldn't take that risk. Part one of the strategy was getting Stacey away from Fantoni. Part two was getting herself away from dustrunning.

"We've got to get ready," she said, turning her face away from Simon, but he kissed her neck instead. "We need to get ready, because this meeting... *oh...* this meeting is going to take a lot of work to pull off."

"Speaking of pulling off..." Simon purred, lifting her shirt. She pushed it back down, clasped his hand between hers, and spoke very clearly to him.

"We need to get ready," she said. "As great as they are, your fists aren't going to solve this problem. This is the mob. They have guns. We need to have a real plan, or we're going to get killed."

His hands let go over her, and he nodded seriously.

"All right," he said. "What do we do?"

"I don't know," said Kani, dropping into the passenger seat again. "But I'll think of something."

Terminus

Freeman sat on the hood of his truck watching the city lights shine brighter than stars in the sky ever could. They were just a line to him from this distance, a sprinkling in the dark, but they were beautiful, captivating. Planes drifted into the mix, losing their identity as they drew closer, the distant humming the only sound he heard at all. The world was a giant sinkhole, a sensory null, except for that line of stars on the horizon, set perfectly between two halves of utter black.

He finished another beer, threw the can into the pile at his feet.

A car came down the gravel road, winding around rocks and across a little bridge that hadn't seen water in decades. The engine made a heavy purring noise, a little louder than average, but so much quieter than the trucks of Freeman's youth. He used to stand on the bridge over the interstate by his house, picking out the cars by the grit in their engines, the torque he could hear, that he wanted to hear when he was old enough to drive one himself. He was old enough now, but the sounds were all tamed.

The car stopped but left its lights on, beams cutting through the swirling dust kicked up by their arrival. A moment later, the driver's side door opened and a pair of work boots scuffed out. Freeman didn't turn to look, just pulled the last beer from his pack and cracked it open.

"I thought you didn't drink," said Elvis, stretching like he'd just woken up from a long sleep. He passed around the front of his car, stood in the headlights, completely ignoring the city. "You don't drink, do you."

"Two years," said Freeman, shaking his head. "That's a damn long time to go without a beer."

"You sure you want to be doing this, then?"

Freeman shrugged, drank some more. The magic of it was long gone; the actions were all automatic now. He didn't care for the taste, and the stuff was warm, sickening to swallow. But he knew every gulp brought the day a little further out of his mind. He'd keep drinking until even that thought was gone, too. He swayed in the breeze, kept up only by sheer will and a lack of movement.

"I'll survive," he slurred. "I'll just start counting again tomorrow. It's all part of the plan."

"Oh, so you have a plan?"

"Yeah. First part is: did you bring more beer?"

Elvis smiled. "Another eighteen. In the car. You really need it?"

"I will in a second. Get one for you, too."

Elvis leaned in the back of his car and came out with two cans. He tossed one to Freeman, who fumbled the catch, and the thing exploded on the rocks, spraying his truck with beer. "Dammit," he cursed, checking over the edge and almost falling off.

Elvis watched him for a second, finger on the tab of his beer, trying to decide what to do, as Freeman slipped and scurried back into position, lolling his head back and staring into the sky. There were a dozen empty cans on the ground, some crumpled, but all empty, and the place smelled strongly of booze. Too strongly.

"Listen," Elvis said. "Maybe we should—"

"Pass me another," said Freeman. "Just one. Please."

Elvis shook his head, but ducked into his car again, pulling out another can, and walking over to the truck. He handed the drink over, then climbed up next to Freeman, looking out at the city.

"You're not doing well," he said, after a time.

"No I'm not," Freeman agreed. "Today's been a bitch of a day. Special anniversary."

Elvis said nothing.

"Back in the service," Freeman said, leaning back on the windshield, "how did you do it? How did you deal with letting your men die? You knew something was a trap, but you sent them in anyway. How did you deal?"

"In the service?" Elvis asked, opening his beer. "Never did deal. Still don't."

"I never had problems, staring down death," Freeman sighed. "Death is easy. But asking someone else to do it… that's hard."

"Soldiers know that's in the cards," said Elvis, sipping lightly. "They know it could happen. They can cope. You don't need to worry for them, 'cause it's part of the job."

"Dustrunners don't know it's in the cards," Freeman said. "They can't cope."

"No, they can't," Elvis nodded.

They sat in silence for a while longer, watched another two planes come by, the lights in the distance shifting on and off. Rook observed his friend, the changes since they'd last met. Elvis was a military man, a Marine, spine still straight like a rod and hair cut close, however many years after he'd hung up the uniform. He was thinner now, still muscular, but like his training had come at the expense of food. Freeman had seen men like that in Mexico. The ones stationed in the desert, trying to ration food because they had no faith in the supply lines. Men like that lost their nerve fast. He'd never let himself be that kind of soldier.

On his third round, Elvis laughed suddenly, threw the rest into the bushes, letting the beer seep into the soil. "It's too bad about Redux," he said. "I tried to find money to cover him, but I'm so far from being clear. I almost got my loan called tonight, just for asking. But damn, I wish I could help him. He's a good guy."

Freeman lay there, can on his chest, listening to the crickets. "I don't think he'd take the money anyway," he said. "That's a lot to ask of a man of his stature. A lot to ask."

"Might be a good idea to find out," Elvis said.

"Yeah," agreed Freeman.

"You want me to see if I can work a deal with Lucet? Figure things out?"

"He won't get involved."

"I can still ask."

"He won't take your call," sighed Freeman. "And I can't do it for you. Things are shaky enough as it is. I just can't."

Silence returned. An awkward silence, made worse by the unspoken words between them: *you don't have the standing and I do.* A difference of rank in a game that had no rank. Freeman had no doubt Elvis had been at this as long as he had, but for whatever reason, he hadn't been chosen to move into the inner circle, to hear the things the burdened leaders got to hear. He had his finger on the pulse of more rumours and truths than anyone in the game, but for whatever reason, he never got to make truths of his own. Freeman wanted to help him… he'd almost done it so many times, but that was the quickest way to end up on the outside of everything. At that level, people were chosen, not recommended.

"You ever think about signing up to go out there?" asked Elvis, staring at the sky. "I mean, *way* out there? To the belt? Ceres?"

"No," said Freeman. "You?"

"Sometimes. Sometimes I think it's simpler that way. You do your work, you send it back, and whatever happens, happens. Fruits of your labour, one way or another. None of the politics, the hiding, the… the paranoia. I don't even know what kind of tools they use out there. Jackhammers or something. Something meaty. Something where you come back to the base feeling like you did something. Something real."

"It wouldn't bother you, knowing someone had hijacked your shipment at the end?" Freeman asked.

"I don't know," Elvis said, squinting at the moon. "I don't know what really bothers me in this. They call us pirates, but all we're doing is protecting an honest day's work. They call themselves good, but they're raiding someone else's pantry."

"That's poetic."

"I don't know," he sighed. "I just feel like I'm making tiny dents in a very big tank. I've done that before. It's not a fun feeling."

"No it's not," said Freeman. "No it's not."

"Still," smiled Elvis, "Our ships are better. And that's saying something. I spent half of August pipe-cleaning out the damn ice channels on my bird, and she still jams half the time."

"It's the glue," said Freeman. "You must be using too much glue."

"Could be. Could be."

Freeman drank more of his beer, closed his eyes and nearly fell asleep as the world swayed gently around him. This is what he missed: sitting around with friends, talking shop and little bits of nonsense after a hard day's work. Conversation was easy enough to buy, but understanding… that was a valuable commodity.

"You heard anything new about Gossamer?" asked Elvis, breaking the spell. "The trial should be underway by now. In the morning, maybe. He was sick, but I didn't hear if that's over, or if he's testifying, or what."

"Haven't heard," said Freeman. "Information's tight, I guess."

"I'm hearing chatter about it. People are worried that if he talks, it'll run down the chain. If they snag Lucet, it takes us all down. That's the big flaw in the system. Nobody knows what Gossamer knows. They're all scared shitless."

"Lucet isn't worried."

"He wouldn't tell you if he was, Rook. That's his job. He needs to instil calm and confidence in his agents."

Freeman laughed. "That's a tall order."

Elvis closed his eyes and leaned back onto the truck, head knocking the windshield, hair bristling as he rolled it from side to side. It was getting colder. September was a bitter month round here. Stifling heat or too damn cold. Freeman could see his breath.

"Well," sighed Elvis. "Even if they get all of us, at least Kaso would be safe."

"Yeah."

"We'll have someone to call from prison."

"Hell no," said Freeman, and they both laughed.

A minute passed with no noise at all.

"How about the rotten apple," Elvis said. "Any thoughts on that? I know every team thinks they've got one, but something smells wrong, doesn't it?"

"It's Tundra," Freeman said, like it was the end of the topic.

"I don't know," said Elvis. "Redux had a point. He said if they wanted to plant a mole, they'd pick someone who knew what they were doing. Sabotaging us so obviously… it just makes no sense. Not in the long run, anyway."

Freeman grunted. "I don't understand how she got on our team in the first place. Lucet said she came recommended."

"That's a loose term, though," said Elvis. "Recommended isn't some standardized metric you can count on. I mean, you've only worked with the best, so maybe you don't know. Get on a team with someone like Captain Poultry, and let me tell you: Tundra's like an idiot savant next to him."

Freeman laughed again, but not happily. "Don't depress me any more. I might throw up."

"No, I don't think it's her," said Elvis. "But then who? Spastik? Not a chance. Chenne? Maybe. She's a great pilot, but… well, it's never easy to tell. I'd say it was you, but you're way too paranoid to be working for the cops."

Freeman sat up, threw the rest of his beer away and rubbed his face to wake himself up. "Redux needed one more mission," he said. "And now he's still on the hook. One more mission. One more. And I can't get out of my head the thought that that 'one more' is going to hurt him like it hurt me."

"Rook, Asha's accident is not your fault. That's something that happened independent of whatever choice you made..."

Freeman turned away, slid off the truck, catching his balance with a firm hand on the mirror. He was burdened, but not by the anniversary or the drink or the day that was over. He was terrified of the day that was coming. Maybe not for him, but for people he cared about. It was making him sick.

"Are you going on the mission this morning?" Elvis asked. "I'm still trying to find someone willing. Favour for a friend."

"No," Freeman sighed. "The typhoon makes it too dangerous, and without the Indian agents on the ground, I don't really know if it's worth trying."

"Yeah," said Elvis. "I figured as much."

"I keep waiting for the other shoe to drop," Freeman said, swaying in the darkness. "I know it's coming, and the tension is killing me."

"Well," said Elvis distantly, "if it's going to drop, it'll have to drop soon."

Asymmetrical Force

Without the flood lights, the football field was pitch black, an imprecise space you could get lost in easily. They parked in the bushes out by the road, out of view of anyone coming in, and walked across the field, duffel bag in hand. When they got to the hill at the far end, Simon stopped, looked down at the scenario they were creating, and slumped his shoulders.

"You can't see a thing down there," he said. "And the school's lights are going to make it easy to spot *you*."

"That's the idea," Kani said, setting down the bag and leading him back to the school, outside lights shining onto the surrounding area, as if anyone believed teachers or security would be hanging out so late on a Friday night.

The place was built like a fortress, four storeys and made of imposing concrete and reflective glass. The principal's office was at the top of a tower at the south end of the building, looking out over the entire area like the eye of god. Ten years ago, the administration had wanted to build a fence around the lot — ostensibly to protect students from predators or drug dealers or themselves — but it had been voted down because the plans looked too much like a medieval castle, and the principal a deranged king.

The main gym doors were locked tight, but a side entrance, used to cut in and out of the change rooms during practice, that was kept open by a small wedge of wood set in the door. To the casual observer, there was no way in, but to Kani, with a tiny tug, the door swung open.

"Excellent," smiled Simon. "You sure nobody's around?"

"It's the weekend," she said. "If anyone's here, they deserve what they get."

They crept inside, looking around at the empty gym, the lights all off, but the orange beams from outside shining through the windows, giving just enough illumination to navigate by. Kani pointed down to the far end of the space, where a pair of double doors led to the main part of the building.

"They chase me in here, and I'll run up to the third floor and then right back down to the front hall. The science rooms up there make clicking noises all the time, so they'll probably get distracted for a while, and by the time they know what's happened, I'll be outside at the front entrance, waiting for you."

"Right," Simon nodded. "And I'm getting Stacey from *their* car, putting her in *my* car, and meeting you there in... what, like five minutes?"

"As fast as you can," she said. "If I'm not there, wait for me. I won't be long."

"What if they catch you?" he asked, touching her arm. She stared at him, shrugged and smiled.

"They won't," she said. "I know this place inside out. Even if the plan doesn't go exactly the way I want, I can improvise better than they can."

"Right," nodded Simon, and she brought him back outside. A crisp wind blew past, and she shivered, rubbing her bare arms, wishing she had something more than just hospital scrubs to wear in this weather. Simon noticed her, took off his school jacket and draped his over her shoulders. She gave him a kiss on the cheek, and they walked back to the field, watching the street for movement.

"Good luck," he said, stepping down the hill towards the parking lot.

"You too," she nodded, and buried her hands in the jacket pockets, leaving the phones there, and zipping it up. Simon disappeared into the darkness, and soon she was totally alone, backlit by the school lights, a solitary figure standing against what would soon be impossible odds. She stomped her feet to stay warm, repeating to herself the only thing she truly cared about anymore: *get Stacey away from the mob, get myself away from Tundra*. She said it almost a hundred times before lights appeared in the distance, and a black car pulled into the parking lot, leaving its headlights shining straight at her.

She saw two figures get out. One was Erlenmeyer, his massive frame recognizable even from so far away. The other was shorter, wispier, but she couldn't be sure it was Fantoni until he stopped midway down the field, hands in his pockets, and called out to her.

"You better not be lyin' to me, girlie," he said. "It's too early in th'morning to be dealing with liars."

"I've got your money," she said, holding up the duffel bag. "Now tell me where Stacey is."

Erlenmeyer pulled a gun from his jacket, aiming it at the ground, but making it very clear he could point it anywhere he chose. Kani's heart starting beating furiously, but she stood her ground. This was part of the plan. She knew this would happen. This was part of the plan.

"How about you give me my money, and then we can discuss this like reasonable people?" snarled Fantoni. "And I'll give you to the count of five."

Kani didn't wait for him to start counting. She wound back with the bag, and after a quick spin, threw it at them. It landed at Erlenmeyer's feet with a solid thump, and the two mobsters chuckled to themselves.

"Nice throw," Fantoni said, motioning for Erlenmeyer to check it out. The larger man tugged the zipper open, reached inside, and pulled out a pile of crumpled-up laundry, damp and stinky. He threw it on the grass, tried again, and only found more of the same. He turned the whole bag upside down and shook it, but only thing in there besides dirty uniforms were soccer cleats and a mouth guard.

"What the hell is this?" Fantoni barked, but when he looked up, Kani was already running fast. "Dammit! Get her!"

Kani glanced over her shoulder and grinned when she saw both men were chasing her. With the head start she had and the speed she could move, her biggest problem would be getting so far ahead of them they wouldn't know where to look. She guessed they wouldn't start shooting at her as long as they thought they could get something out of her, and that theory made her brazen, confident, and just a little too sure of herself. When she got to the school, she turned back and laughed at them as obviously as she could. She was just a teenager, but she'd outsmarted the mob.

She grabbed the side door and pulled. And it didn't move. She yanked again, but still, it was locked. "What the hell…" she gasped, and looked down to see the thin piece of wood had fallen out of the door after she and Simon had left earlier. The school was locked. She was locked out. And Fantoni and Erlenmeyer were catching up.

She dashed around the side of the gym, sprinting past the windows, heart pounding in her ears, the world feeling mercifully sharp and clear after so much trauma. She skidded into the front walkway, saw the school sign down by the road, down where Simon would come and get her in four minutes or less. She didn't have four minutes, though. She had to find another way to keep the mobsters busy.

She ran down the front of the school until she came to the junior wing, where a staircase ran along the outside of the building, zigzagging up until it reached the classes on the top floor. It was the emergency exit in case of a fire, but to Kani, this emergency was far more critical. She jumped up the steps four at a time, hearing Fantoni yelling after her from the ground. When she finally reached the top level, she realized she had nowhere else to go.

Erlenmeyer was running up after her, heavy breaths getting closer and closer. Kani looked around frantically, trying to think of where to hide. She could break in a window, but she had no idea how she could do that with her bare hands. It was too far to jump down, and Fantoni was waiting for her if she did. She looked to the side and saw the roof only a metre away. Just close enough to reach! She climbed up on the thin metal railing that kept her safe, fighting to balance in the strengthening breeze, and she leapt.

Her fingers caught the edge of the roof, legs smacking into the wall with enough force to wind her. She cried out, redoubled her grip, and pulled... pulled so hard she saw spots in her vision, and for a terrible moment she thought she might black out again. But with another agonizing effort, she lifted herself up and out of the way as Erlenmeyer snatched for her, missing her ankle by centimetres.

Kani didn't wait around to gloat. She ran along the roof, staying low to keep Fantoni in the dark about her whereabouts, then jumped down a slope until she landed in the third-floor greenhouse, a kind of courtyard in the centre of the building connected to the science labs all around. She pulled on the closest door, and it opened, letting her in to the school at last!

The classrooms were dark, but there were dim emergency lights that kept the place illuminated enough to move. She stayed low between the desks, stopping to listen every few steps, in case she was really being followed. She got to the door and paused one last time, but there were no sounds other than her own ragged breathing. She opened the door and crept into the hall.

The far staircase would bring her down to the ground floor, but there was still the issue of how to get Fantoni and Erlenmeyer to stay at the back, near the field, while she was escaping out the front. She'd have to improvise a distraction somehow. She started looking around the halls, hoping to see something that might do the trick, something loud or bright or...

"Magnesium!" she said, remembering her ninth-grade science class, where the teacher had burnt magnesium, stunning everyone with the power of chemistry. The magnesium would be in the main lab, around the corner and—

"Hello girlie," snarled Erlenmeyer, stepping out of a shadow.

Kani screamed, turned and ran as fast as she could move. She heard his heavy footsteps behind her, pumping furiously as she sprinted down the hall towards the stairs. He was a big man and very fit, and she could even smell him coming up behind, so fast it felt like a losing battle from the second she started. But she pushed herself harder than she'd ever done before, flying down the first flight of stairs and colliding with the wall, stumbling back and leaping down again, not even knowing which way was up anymore. Erlenmeyer jumped too, but he hit the wall harder, took longer to recover. By the time she got to the ground floor, he was still on the second, roaring furiously at losing his prey.

Instead of running out the front doors which were right in front of her, she turned the corner and raced back toward the gym, exploding through the double doors, shoes squeaking like mad as she cleared the basketball court in record time. She fell out into the back field again, gasping for breath, but not giving up. If she kept up this pace, she could put just enough distance between her an Erlenmeyer that when she got to the front, she'd have enough time to get into the car and escape. All she needed to do was move this fast for a minute longer... just a minute longer...

Just as she was about to round the corner at the far end of the school, she heard Fantoni call to her, and it scared her so much she almost fell into the dirt. She grabbed the edge of the building and swung herself around, but something she heard cut through her panic...

"*Kani!*" she heard Simon call. "Kani, wait!"

She stopped, stumbling to a halt, muscles on fire and heart beating so fast she almost fainted from the simple act of not moving. She struggled to catch her breath, turned, and peered around the corner again, down into the field.

Fantoni had a gun to Simon's head.

"No!" she yelled stepping out into the open, and was suddenly ploughed right over by Erlenmeyer, shoulder cracking painfully as she hit the ground. He pushed down on her face, grabbing her arm and yanking her up, making her cry out as he shoved her down the hill, into the field where Fantoni and Simon were waiting, the third mobster standing a little ways in the back, arms crossed, a self-satisfied grin on his face. She'd forgotten there were three of them. Simon must have walked right into a trap of his own.

"This is what passes for strategy?" Fantoni sighed, cocking the gun. "Send your boy toy to save your friend, and what? You think we would let you go if you pulled it off? You must be stupid."

"Where's Stacey?" Kani spat, seeing their car in the distance, all the doors open, but no one inside.

"First rule of negotiation," grinned Fantoni. "Lie."

"Is she still alive?" Kani asked. "You said she was still alive!"

"She is," he shrugged. "For now, at least. But something tells me there *is* no money, is there? You don't have it, and you can't get it, neither. So you make me wonder why I should keep you alive at all. You and your pretty boy here, who can't even pull off a simple kidnapping without getting caught. You're idiots, both of you."

"So why don't you hire us? We'd fit right in."

Fantoni laughed a big, booming laugh. "You're got a tongue, girlie. A good tongue. But you're right. Why don't I hire you?" Kani's stomach twisted at the words, the greedy look in his eyes. "You mentioned it before, but it seems the only way you're going to pay off what you owe. Get you into a better outfit, and I bet you'll make back that twelve grand in four, five years tops."

She drew in a deep breath, staring him down. It was a terrible situation, but she'd run away before, and she could do it again. She'd done some terrible things in the last twenty-four hours, and she could do worse if she had to. Erlenmeyer twisted her arm tighter, but she didn't give them the satisfaction of showing pain.

"If I do," she said, "you promise—"

"Kani, no!" Simon pleaded.

"—you promise to let Stacey go?"

Fantoni shrugged. "You buy her debt, I have no problems with her anymore. But it's twenty grand now, girlie. Interest is steep."

She held herself together, ignoring the pain and the swimming feeling in her head, and the thoughts of what would come in the hours, days and months ahead. She pushed all that aside, set her jaw tight, and nodded.

"Fine," she said. "Just let him go."

"*Kani!*"

"What, him?" Fantoni laughed, switching the safety off the gun. "No, for twenty grand, you can't buy him too. He kicked me in the shin earlier. He's gonna die."

He put his finger on the trigger, and Kani screamed, tried to get free. "Wait!" she yelled. "Wait, I can fix this! I can get you whatever you want!"

Fantoni rolled his eyes at her, but took his finger off the trigger. "Anything I want?" he laughed. "So if I say… thirty grand? That's okay with you? You'd pay that to have your boy toy see another day?"

Kani was crying, even though her body refused to sob. She sniffled, looked at Simon, his face twisted in agony and despair, and she nodded again. "I can do it," she said. "I just… I just need to make a call."

Fantoni lowered the gun, squinting at her. He seemed amused. Intrigued. He snapped his fingers and Erlenmeyer let her arm go. She stretched it out, letting the blood run back to her hand.

"You're gonna try to go back," Fantoni said, stepping towards her. "You really think they'd take you back?"

"I know they will," Kani said, locking eyes with him and refusing to betray her looming sense of doubt. She unzipped the pocket, reached a trembling hand inside and pulled out Stacey's phone. A quick slide of the finger turned it on, and she stared at the display as it booted. She scrolled through the memory banks until she reached number twenty-seven. If this went well, Simon and Stacey would survive. If it didn't, her two best friends would be dead by morning.

Either way, she was doomed.

"It's-a me, Kaso!" said Kaso in the worst Italian accent of all time. "I thought you'd gone AWOL. Or MIA. Or SPCA. Something. Good to have you back. What can I do you for, babe? And why are you in a football field? Oh no, you're not doing *sports*, are you?"

"I… I need another mission," she said so Fantoni could hear it. "Something good, and something fast."

"You've got twelve hours," said Fantoni. "Three tomorrow. If I don't have the money by then, I kill them both. You understand me?"

"You heard that?" Kani asked.

"His accent's worse than mine."

"*Kaso*. Focus."

"Sorry. Mission. Right. And soon, too. This isn't going to be easy. They send those freighters off every few weeks, not days."

"Please, Kaso. Please."

"That's it!" Fantoni yelled, pointing the gun at Simon's head. "You're just stalling. We're killing the boy, and you can do lap dances in my private club."

"Did he just say lap dan—"

"*Kaso!*"

She heard furious typing in the background, and Kaso's voice went from bouncy to scolded. "Fine," he said. "Give me a minute."

She covered the phone, nodded to Fantoni. "He said give him a minute. Please. Just another minute. That's all I need."

Fantoni turned the gun to the side, checked his aim at Simon's head.

"A minute's all you've got," he said.

Life and Death

Elvis' car turned from a speck of light in the distance to nothing at all, and Freeman blinked a few times to make sure he was seeing it right. He snatched up the beer cans from the base of his car, one by one, dropping them into the empty box in the trunk, trying to impose some order on the night's ordeal. He was reaching for the fifth can when his phone rang, and he slid it open so smoothly, it was like he wasn't drunk at all.

"Yeah," he said.

"Rook," said Lucet. "We have a problem."

Freeman let go a rattled breath, nodded. "All right," he said.

"Tundra is in trouble."

Freeman sat forward, cocked his head. "Wait, again?"

"My bad," said Kaso, cutting in. "I misheard you earlier. I thought you said 'save her at all costs,' when you really said 'let her die.' Funny how those two thing sound so al—"

"Same answer," said Freeman. "Let her die."

"There is more this time," said Lucet. "She is requesting another mission. I trust you have heard about the shipment Elvis has been trying to sell? Due in a few hours? I do not have independent confirmation, but if you—"

"There's a typhoon in the drop zone," said Freeman. "It's a no-go."

"You could change the corridor ahead of splashdown."

"Look, even if I could, with only two fighters, the SEF would be all over us, and we'd have no way to stop them."

"The SEF will not be looking for you, given the typhoon," said Lucet. "You would have an open field in which to work. If you move fast enough, they may not even reach you before you are done."

Freeman sighed, threw the sixth can into the box angrily, order be damned. The world was swaying slowly, and he still felt ill. It would take a lot of coffee to sober up in time for a morning run.

"If Tundra's the rotten apple—" he growled.

"She's not," said Kaso. "Uh. Sir."

"If she is not," said Lucet, "you have a two-way split of the proceeds. Which is agreeable to her."

"Then let her go up on her own," snapped Freeman.

"You know I cannot do that. It would ruin my credibility, as well as yours. We are professionals, Rook. Whatever else we do, we are professionals. Tundra needs you there for support. If she is good enough, you get paid. And if she is bad—"

"I ditch her in the atmosphere and we call it an accident."

There was a moment of silence. Even Kaso stayed quiet.

"Agreed," said Lucet. "If she betrays us, kill her."

Last Chance

When she hung up the phone, Kani's hands were shaking.

They shook as she told Fantoni the news, saw the smirk on his face as his gamble paid off. Another mission like this would cover off Stacey's debt, and add much more than he'd expected. He wished her luck and gave her a rough kiss on the forehead, like everything was forgiven and she was one of the family. She wanted to stab him in the neck when he touched her, but she knew she'd never survive it.

Her hands shook as she hugged Simon good-bye, telling him to be safe, to keep Stacey safe and not worry. He had no idea what she was going to do, but the look on his face said he expected the worst. She wanted to tell him, help ease his worries, but she knew there was no way the truth would do that. She kissed him lightly, held his hands and whispered: "It's okay. I know what I'm doing."

He kissed her back, pulling her tight, and she wrapped her arms around him, overcome by the moment. When she let go, she held on to that kiss. She held on to it as she left Simon in the park, as Erlenmeyer drove her to the station in the dead of night. She wouldn't let go of the kiss. That was what kept the shaking at bay. It fought against reality, the terror of what came next.

There was no moon to navigate by, no lights in the field at all, but still she trudged onward, pushing through the same corn, stumbling over the same rocks, coming out to the same clearing where her life had started to go all wrong. She slipped in the side door, opened the cockpit, pulled out the flight suit and zipped it overtop the hospital scrubs. She was still shivering, but at least she knew it wasn't the cold anymore.

She sat on the bundled tarp in the corner of the shack, back against the creaking walls, listening to the sounds of night. The crickets were all gone this late in the year, but the hinge on the door made a kind of chirping noise, soft and regular, so much so she felt like she might fall asleep. She closed her eyes and saw the woman from the hospital, face covered with blood, pleading with the nurses. With fate. It's not supposed to be this way.

Stacey's phone rang, jarring her out of her daze. She pulled it from the flight suit pocket and put it to her ear, but couldn't bring herself to say hello.

"Hey kid," said Kaso. "How you holding up?"

She swallowed, smiled into the darkness. "I'm good," she lied.

"You sound it. You know if you stay in one place for as long as you have, you're gonna get blood clots and die, right? Happened to a friend. Gamer. Lotsa gold, not too many brains. Don't do it. Get up and walk."

"I'm okay," she said. "Stop spying on me."

"Me? Spying? Never!" He coughed awkwardly, and she laughed.

"You're a good guy, Kaso," she said.

"I know. Thanks for confirming it, though."

She said nothing for a few moments, watching the wheels of the Incessna in the glow of the phone's screen.

"You know what I just realized?" Kaso said, breaking the silence. "You and me, we both have four letters in our first names, and they both start with the letter 'K.'"

"Yeah," she said. "You're really quick, aren't you?"

"That's nothing!" he said. "Try this on for size: Kilt. Kebab. Kerfluffle. Kin. Um... kiss..."

"Stop hitting on me," she said, and sat up a bit straighter, stretching her back. He started to whistle innocently, and she smiled, despite her best efforts not to.

"Say Tundra," he said. "You can tell me things, you know. I'm not like a lawyer or anything, but you know I have your back, right?"

"I know," she muttered.

"So if there's something you need to talk about, I'm ready to—"

"There's nothing," she said. "I'm fine, Kaso. Really."

"Okay," he said. He started whistling again — a tune with no melody that he seemed to enjoy — then stopped abruptly. "You know what's funny?" he asked.

"I have a feeling I'm about to find out."

"When you were having that trouble with Fat Tony, I was searching through your transcripts, trying to see which members of your old teams you might've got along with. See if I could hit 'em up for money on your behalf."

"That's really not—"

"Turns out you weren't very popular. Can't see why not. Well, except for losing freighters. That's definitely full-on suckage." She lay down, covering her head with her arm, like maybe she could fall asleep and he'd lose his train of thought. "Anyway, one thing I wanted to ask you. And I dunno how to say this, but… back on your first mission, Ricochet asked you what your name was, and you said what sounded a lot like 'stay.'"

Kani froze, held her breath.

"And I guess I'm just wondering," he said, "if that makes any sense to you. Because it's confusing the hell outta me."

She didn't move, didn't breathe, didn't know what to say. Stacey had said her name. The only thing keeping them from knowing she was the wrong Tundra was the code of secrecy they all lived by. You never give your name, one way or another. And now there was evidence — solid, real evidence! — that she wasn't who she said she was. Never mind Fantoni, if Rook found out about this, she would die alone in space. She opened her mouth to reply, but he beat her to it.

"You were trying to double-cover," he said. "It's pretty common with newbies. They use some other name instead of their own, thinking that'll throw the SEF off. Make 'em go looking for the wrong person. Like I'd say Darien is my name, because Darien is the hot chick who delivers my mail, and if anyone goes looking for her, they'd find out pretty quick that she's really not me. I mean *wow* is she not me. If I had an ass like that, I'd—"

"Kaso?"

"Right, sorry," he said. "I get distracted sometimes. But really, Tundra, you shouldn't use your best friend's name out there. You could get her in trouble."

"Oh. I… thanks for the tip."

"I live to serve," he said. "Any time. My door's always open. Really. Stop by. I'm lonely."

She laughed, sniffled, sat herself back up. "How do you do this?" she asked. "Doesn't it just drain you? The fear? The paranoia?"

"Me? I'm safe where I am. Guess it doesn't hit me as much. I can appreciate why it sucks for you guys, but to me, it's like a game. Find the spy, catch the mole, that kinda thing. It's just a game."

"Yeah," she said, but knew it was anything but.

"*Speaking of which*," he said. "One game I love to play to catch moles is this thing called the 'encoder chip game.' It's great fun. Really easy to play, too, if you're interested. All you do is make the mole go running around looking for something that doesn't exist. Call it the encoder chip for best results. Then you just sit there and laugh about how dumb they look, pretending to have something you made up on the spot."

"Oh," she said.

"Great for laughs. Well, on my end. When I tell the higher-ups, they're never laughing."

"I—"

"So yeah, *Tundra*. If you ever get told to look for an encoder chip, make sure you laugh it off, or people'll get the wrong idea, right?"

"Right," she said. "Thanks."

"Especially Rook. You know what I'm saying? He's already jumpy. You've got to be extra careful around him."

"I got it," she said. "And I noticed."

"Okay, then. You should get some sleep. Big day today. Stop bugging me, all right? Calling me at all times of the night, wanting to chat about your girl problems. Sheesh. I've got things to do, lady. Things!"

She laughed, probably more than she would have on any other day. "Thank you, Kaso," she said. "You're a good friend."

"Oh go on."

"I'll talk to you soon."

"You'd better, or I'm gonna come over there and kick your ass."

"Good luck leaving your room," she said, and turned the phone off right before he started howling.

She let the phone light the ship for a few more seconds, studying the shape, the smooth lines punctuated with sharp corners and cracking paint. The phone shut off and she was in the dark again, staring into the night.

She put her head down on the tarp, closed her eyes, and let the stress of the last twenty-four hours carry her off to sleep.

It was a short sleep.

Escape

Yuri couldn't close the door, kept his hand tight around the doorknob. He watched Rache walk down the hall alone, heels clicking on the wood floor, and he leaned against the door frame, wincing at the thoughts racing through his mind. She started down the stairs, and he pushed his forehead into the wall, squeezing his eyes shut so he wouldn't see her leave. When he opened them again, she was gone.

He stepped back inside and started to close the door, but stopped halfway. The words were crawling out of his mouth, filling his brain so fast he knew he'd never think another thought until he acted. Until he did what needed to be done. He ran down the hall, grabbing hold of the railing and sucking in enough breath to boom her name across the city. But when he looked down, she was standing on the first landing, staring back at him.

He cleared his throat, motioned back to his apartment.

"Another minute," he said. "Please."

She didn't say a word, just came back up to meet him at his floor, and he showed her through to his apartment, closing the door behind him.

"Please, sit," he said, and she set herself on the chair closest to the window, so the light from the late afternoon sun lit her up from behind, giving her hair a tinge of the red he hadn't seen in years. Her fingers danced over the cornucopia, eyes anywhere but on him. He sat next to her, hands folded, and thought of what he wanted to say first.

"Is all right?" he asked finally. "Are you happy?"

She laughed a bit, shrugged. "Not yet," she said. "I guess not yet. But I'll get there." He took her hand in his, but she pulled back, smiled awkwardly at him. "What's wrong, Yuri?" she asked.

"What about passion? What will happen to passion if you go to UN?"

Her smile got an edge, like she was about to cry. She laughed, cut it off, looked away. "What are you talking about?" she said. "This is what you were asking for. This is what you wanted…"

"But is what *you* want, Rache? Will it… kill you?"

"I'll be fine—"

"No, I mean… will it kill who you *are*?"

She pushed her chair back, stood up, blinking back tears. This was the Rache from outside his apartment, the one hurt and confused. Using drugs as a crutch to hold up her delicate existence. He'd just replaced the drugs with his dreams for her. He was no better than the dealers and pimps that had abused her before. He was shaping her into something he wanted, using all the same tricks, just different rewards.

She touched his shoulder gently as she passed on the way to the door, hand over her mouth to stop herself from crying. Just as her fingers slipped off, he caught her arm, held her there. She didn't say a thing, and neither did he, until he knew exactly what he wanted to say.

"I worry I have doomed you," he said. "Doomed the world. Not helped. Ruined hope."

"You make no sense," she said, wiping her eyes.

"I had passion once," he said. "I did good work. Work I believed in. Work that made difference. I followed dream and every day it hurt, but I kept living for dream anyway. Was nothing I would not do. But in time, hurt got bigger, and dream got… got harder… and soon I do not know how to go on. And when day came, I traded this dream… I traded for work that pays bills. Was not right. Was not good. Was compromise to keep lights on. And I stopped being right. Every day since, I… I do not know if I am living *my* life anymore, or life of someone else."

"I don't know what you want from me," she said.

"Live right life," he said. "Save the world."

She looked at him, smiled. "Sometimes saving yourself is all you can do," she said. "I didn't understand it before, but I do now. Nobody can change the world. They can just change enough parts of it, that it looks different at the end. Thank you for teaching me that. Even if it hurt both of us."

She leaned forward and kissed him, softly at first, but then a second time, holding her lips against his, and he let go of her arm, put his hand on the table for support. They stood there, frozen in time, his heart paused mid-beat, waiting for instruction. Her mouth moved away, nose brushing his, the weight of her body just beyond him, but crushing him all the same. He couldn't look at her.

Her hand touched the back of his neck, up into his hair, and then her arm wrapped around, and she pulled herself close, sliding up him until they were wrapped tight, and he breathed her in, looked at her face, dark eyes searching his, mouth so near. He kissed her again, putting a strong hand down her back and pushing her into him, feeling her wrap around him, hands tracing to his chest, grabbing his collar and ripping his shirt open.

He spun her around, sitting her on the edge of the table, and she kept him close with legs wrapped around his waist while she kissed his chest. His hands ran down her, pulling her sweater over her head, pressing his mouth to her neck, and she moaned. His fingers danced on her skin, across her body, down her waist to where she was unzipping her skirt, and he grabbed her and held her and tasted the sweat on her chest, her lipstick, her...

He stood back, hands shaking.

"What is it?" she asked, fingers falling short of his belt. He couldn't look at her anymore. Her skin, her face, her eyes... He couldn't look at her anymore. It was too much. "Yuri?"

He ran to the bedroom, closed the door, and sat against it, holding his head in his hands, waiting for her to hate him enough to leave for good.

Not the Same

Yuri gasped for breath, fighting for life as the water drained away. He felt heavy, sluggish and exhausted, but the first thing he thought was so clear: he was still alive! He tried to get free, but his arms were still stuck at his sides, the body bag even tighter now that it was wet. He choked, rolled to his side, coughing out water and vomit that stayed on his face, made him ill.

A man cried out in pain, and there was a heavy splash close by. He jerked around, as if he could see where it had come from, but then a strong arm wrapped around his neck, pulling him to his feet. He was pressed back against someone who was shaking uncontrollably. He heard the sound of a gun clicking itself into readiness, and a gentle tap on the side of his head. He stayed very, very still.

"Another step and he dies," said a voice at his ear. One of the guards. Trembling. "One step, and I swear—"

The guard jerked suddenly, and Yuri was free, stumbling forward and crashing to the ground. The bag was suffocating, holding him in so perfectly he couldn't stand it. He was blind and powerless and the world was going mad around him, and all he could do was sit and listen and wait for death to catch him too? He roared, pulled as hard as he could, and the zipper gave way, tearing open. He ripped the bag off himself, stumbling forward, and then saw the figure before him… and he dropped to his knees.

"Well," said Rache. "I was afraid it was you."

He stumbled back, back onto the guard behind him. A knife was embedded in his forehead, his eyes rolled up like he was trying to see where it had gone. Yuri looked between the guard and Rache, unable to connect the two concepts at all.

"We have to move," Rache said. "Can you walk?"

He nodded, but didn't move. His body was frozen, wrapped up in something like fear, but it felt like betrayal. Like a nightmare that was playing on the last thoughts in his head before he died. He didn't know what to do.

She held a hand out to him, winked. "Get up," she said. "Come on. I'm not supposed to be out here."

He took her hand and she pulled him up, giving him a quick, distant hug before slapping his cheek lightly. "You look good," she said, and ran up the steps to the street, not stopping to see if he followed. But follow he did, out onto the main drag, around the side streets and across the bridge to the other side of town.

All the way, he watched in silence, amazed at what he saw. It was the same Rache as ever, but she was confident, composed, precise in her movements. It was like all the pieces of her from the years had come together to form this perfect creature of beauty and strength, not afraid of the world and what it could bring, but ready to show it that *she* was the one to fear. She wore a black biker jacket, slim-fitting cargo pants and boots that clicked when she walked. On her belt were six thin knives and a pistol holstered up in her mid-back, the tip of the grip peeking out beneath her jacket as she moved.

She stopped at the corner of Mazarine and Guénégaud, looking down the narrow streets spread around her, and seemed to be listening to the wind. No one was around but the two of them, but watching her, it was like they had an audience no one but she could see or hear. After a long minute of silence, she smiled to him, opened the door to an all-night café, and led him in.

Food service in Paris had gone one of two ways in the last decade: those that were desperate started serving alcohol in the hopes of holding on to customers running away from despair through a tall glass of beer. Those that were smart realized booze is too expensive for the unemployed, so they stripped away all pretence and served half-baked coffee every hour they had left before bankruptcy. *Le Balto* had been a sports bar once — and a good one at that — but their walls of screens had been replaced with walls of offers of packaged food they didn't serve anymore. The place wasn't even called *Le Balto* anymore, but that's what the locals knew it as, so that's what it remained.

At five in the morning at the end of September, it was all but empty. Rache moved straight to the back, sweeping the other tables for a stray glance or movement that looked out of place. She settled on a booth in the corner with a good view of the door, set herself up and placed a menu at the edge of the table like a screen, and leaned forward.

"We have to be careful," she said. "No names. You understand, Redux?" He blinked, stunned, said nothing. "We've been wiretapping Duplessis' house for a few months," she said. "We suspected he was using his contacts to run a moonshine operation. Moonshine doesn't mean what you think it does. Ask me later."

He nodded.

"We heard you talking to him, and my bosses thought you were ratting on us, going to turn us in. They wanted me to make sure you didn't get out of the river, Redux. You have to know what kind of trouble you're in over that."

"Yes," he said, scolded.

"When I saw the size of the bag, I knew it had to be you. You're pretty distinctive. How've you been?"

"I… I am confused, I think."

She smiled, accepted a coffee from a waitress Yuri hadn't seen coming. She smiled innocently, like they were just two friends out for an early-morning chat, like nothing was wrong. The waitress didn't seem to see Yuri's battered face or the fact that he was soaking wet. She'd probably seen it all. Rache shook two packets of sugar and emptied them into her cup, waiting for the waitress to leave. "I understand your confusion. I'll cover everything eventually, but right now I want to talk about *you*. Your daughter. She's in bad shape?"

"Yes… she… last mission, it failed, and is bad for her."

"I understand," she said. "I'd help you with that, but I don't have the resources right now. I give all my money to sustain our operations here."

"Operations…?"

"Doing good," she smiled. "Saving the world."

"I do not understand… what are you?"

"I'm on your side," she said. "I'm part of the team that makes sure everyone else plays nice."

He squinted at her, leaned close. "Since… since when?"

"Two years ago? Maybe less. I didn't have the job when we last saw each other, if that's what you're asking. It came after. I bummed around a while and I met the right people and I moved up. Fast. Because I knew what I wanted, I guess."

"Wait… you were… were *out there*…"

"Absolutely," she said, smiling. "I've been out there and down here, setting things right. And I'm sorry I didn't say hello before now, but you have to understand, Redux, secrecy is how we survive. I would have told you all this sooner, but I had no idea who *you* were."

"Who are you? I still do not—"

"Chenne," she said, and all he could do was nod. "I found my purpose after all, I guess."

"You are very good," he said.

"I try," she smiled. "But now listen. I know you need some money, and I think I've picked up a solution on the wire. There's a shipment coming through in about four hours, and so far nobody seems to want it."

"There is typhoon, yes? Elvis told me."

"If we do it together, I think we can make it work," she said. "Three freighters, the two of us. And as a thanks for kicking my ass three years ago, I'll give you the whole take."

He gasped, shook his head. "No," he said. "No, I cannot do that. Is not right."

"Redux, listen. If you hadn't treated me the way you did, I never would have gotten my ship, I never would have done what I've been able to do, and I can promise you, the world would be a worse-off place as a result. You're taking the money. There's no debating it."

He smiled, trying to remain calm. "We must go then, yes? Time is short."

"Yeah, we should head out," she said. "I'll have the co-ordinates sent to your phone—"

"My phone is dead," he said. "In water."

She nodded, reached into a pocket and pulled out a tiny black one. She passed it across. "That'll do for now. You should be good with that."

They stood, and while she walked to the door, he didn't move, eyes searching left and right, like he was trying to piece together a puzzle.

"I must make little stop," he said. "One stop first."

Damned

Sabina had stopped crying hours ago, the flood drying out to a trickle, then an agonizing stillness that made her face ache for want of tears. Something to show she was still alive inside, when she felt nothing like it. The doctors stayed away, not wanting to give hope when there was none. Every move they made was like a death sentence, cut into pieces and scattered through the night; it was nothing they'd done, it was what they weren't going to do that hurt.

She was stuck in the seat by Anya's door, hands clasped so tight they were white and red from squeezing, stumbling through prayers long forgotten, listening for the sound of her poor daughter sleeping, breathing, something... Several times she thought she heard the sound of a whine, that final callous tone that said she'd lost the battle, that her prayers meant nothing after all. Sometimes it was a dream that she woke up from with a jolt, so thankful she had a few minutes more. Sometimes it felt like her mind was preparing her for the inevitable. She hated that idea.

Light pierced through the windows, casting long shadows in the orange hue around her, signalling another day she'd get to spend with her daughter, however brief. The shadows crept along the floor as time slipped past, and she measured it in movements that were so slow, no one else would know to look.

She glanced up at the sound of footsteps, down the hall, rushing towards her. She got to her feet, hands clasping her bag, face swelling with emotion that had no tears left to show, terrified at what she'd see. Maybe the whine was silent.

Maybe the doctors already knew what she didn't hear. Maybe the end had come while she'd been watching shadows, and she hadn't even thought to notice.

She gasped when she saw them: Yuri, face a battered mess, drenched like he'd been swimming, eyes red with fear. And that girl from the hall, Rache, the one who'd sent their marriage on the downward trajectory she knew it would never pull out from. She felt ill, seeing them together, no matter the reason, standing there so close to her dying daughter.

"Is Anya awake?" Yuri asked, voice low, tired.

"No," said Sabina. "We're not allowed in. *None* of us." She glared at Rache, wanting to scream, but knowing she had to keep Anya calm. Rache looked away, held her arms behind her back, like she was here as an observer and nothing more. Sabina felt bile in her mouth, fury at the sight of her husband's mistress: young, sharp and clever, dressed to draw men in no matter the consequences. But there *were* consequences.

Yuri stepped softly to the door, leaning against the wood and resting a hand on in it, eyes closed as he spoke, like he was seeing inside, pushing past the barriers the world had made for him. Sabina wanted to stop him, but he seemed so sincere... so honest, she couldn't help but watch.

"Anya, darling," he said in French, voice cracking. "Is papa. I know you are sleeping, but I need to say good-bye again. I hope you have beautiful dreams, my angel. Beautiful dreams. Take care of mama for me. I love you, Anya. Sleep well."

Sabina nearly broke, put her hands to her face to try to keep herself from falling apart. Yuri put a firm hand on her shoulder, squeezed gently, and leaned his head near hers. Then he kissed the side of her head, then her hand, and moved away.

"You will have money today," he said quietly. "One way or another, you will have money. Take good care of her."

She moved to speak, turning with questions and theories and recriminations to shout, but when she spun she saw Rache staring straight at her — straight into her — and her mouth stayed shut.

Yuri lumbered into the orange sun, and left her there, alone.

Synchronicity

The sun left a bright white streak across the ocean, like a line along the Earth, pointing to the mass of white cloud inching into darkness. The sight was beautiful and terrifying, but Rook wasted no time with sightseeing.

He switched his view on and off, toggling the sensors, listening through the static of the debris to pick up a sign of something that wasn't coming. Tundra had lied about the mission, putting him at enormous risk for no reason. He had ideas of how to punish her for it, but his head was so leaden from all the drinking that he knew he had to leave the answers for later. He switched his grid again, still saw no sign of her, and fought the urge to punch a wall.

He looked into the darkness around him, trying to figure a way to make things happen. Working alone, could he bring in three freighters at all? There were no spotters and defence, the roles he usually played, but the most critical role was entering the code and guiding the freighters into the right spot. If he were left completely alone, he might be able to play all the parts himself. But if the SEF caught wind, he could have freighters flying lop-sided through the atmosphere, dumping ore and metal all over the world. Populated areas. It had never happened before, and he wasn't about to go down as the one that made the fears a reality. Let the SEF have these ones. He'd find another way to help Redux.

He punched codes into his console to initiate the re-entry sequence when he caught sight of a green triangle on his grid. He tapped it, zoomed, and saw the call sign. Before he could speak, his radio crackled to life.

"Sorry I'm late," said Tundra. "Traffic."

"I swear to god," he fumed, "if you don't take this seriously, you will never fly again."

"Sorry," she said meekly.

"Follow orders and keep your mouth shut."

"Yes sir," she said, dropping all attitude and behaving like a proper soldier. It was comforting to hear, but something about it made him anxious. Dustrunners never did what you expected, what you needed. Something about this felt *wrong*.

He sent her the co-ordinates he'd been fed by the mission database, an obscure, distributed network of trusted sources spiking innocuous traffic with strings of numbers that acted as three-dimensional maps. The position over the globe at a certain time on a certain day, looking out at an angle that the freighters would travel on. Sometimes the numbers were off, but not often. There were smart people behind them; people who knew a fraction of a degree could cost billions when the day was done. This time, a corridor appeared before him, tracing a gentle arc around the planet, into the darkness. Right past the typhoon.

He pushed his throttle, bringing himself in line with the corridor, and drifting gently from side to side as the RCS jets worked to keep him stable. Flying in space was a complex operation, and sometimes, when the job was done and the enemy gone, he would turn off all the assistance and let himself feel the unencumbered chaos of it all. You could move in any direction forever if you tried, could move at impossible angles like there were no physics and sense to the world. It was all physics, of course, and he knew it… but it felt like magic, drifting without purpose or intelligent oversight. The dream of space tourism, alive and well in the new owners of their spacecraft. Maybe as a side show, but alive all the same.

He punched numbers into his console, singling on Tundra's private channel, and waited for her to authorize him. He cleared his throat. "Kaso tells me you can't go home after this."

There was a pause, like she was trying to decide how to react. Of course Kaso told him everything. Was she surprised at her position in the pecking order? Did she really think she had anything resembling privacy, doing what they did? Or was she just upset about her life being ruined, about losing her home? Maybe it was the hangover. Maybe he was being irrational. He kept himself in check, waiting for her to answer.

"I… I guess not," she said. Humility. Good.

"We have a protocol for dealing with this," he said. "But you're going to have to trust me. Can you do that?"

"Yes sir," she said immediately. Smartly. The continuing change in attitude was enough to make him suspicious on its own, but he kept it stowed, focused on what had to happen next.

"All right," he said. "When we're done here, I'll send you landing co-ordinates where I can find you, and I will help you get set up in a different life."

A longer pause this time. "Okay," she said.

"You hesitated."

"No sir, it's just… leaving my—"

An alarm sounded and he looked up to see two ships closing in on the horizon. The trick of their mission database was that most people saw the same numbers at the same time, and there were limited means to avoid duplicating efforts. It rarely happened, but there were incidents where two teams had had to haggle over capture rights. By and large, priority went to the first on the scene. He needed to make that clear, because the more fingers in the pie, the less money there'd be to take home. He needed this to count. He switched on his ice cannons, dimmed his cockpit and kept his finger on the navigation sphere.

"Behind me," he said sharply. "And don't shoot me in the back."

The sun caught the wing of one of the ships, washing out his vision and tinting his visor so fast it was like he was going blind out of nowhere. The sensation was jarring, but at least he knew who he was dealing with.

"Chenne?" he asked. "What are…"

"Hello, Rook," said Redux. "You are here for shipment too?"

He held his breath, tried to think of how to express what he was trying to do, what this mission was really about. Telling the truth would be too awkward: Redux would accept no charity. Not from him, anyway. But he felt like he had to explain, to let him know they were all on the same side. They'd always been on the same side.

"I'm letting Tundra make up for her mistake," he said, wincing as the words left his mouth.

"She is here?" Redux asked, his voice dull. Rook understood it perfectly well, the sentiment. She botched the last mission — *his* last mission — and now she was back for more. But more than anything, he knew the accusation was aimed at him. *Why did you bring her here?*

"Do you have a plan?" Rook asked. "Or is four a crowd today?"

"Sir—" protested Tundra.

"I said no speaking!" he snapped, and no one said anything for a moment. He calmed himself, then continued: "We'll go back home if you'd prefer a two-way split. *We* owe you that much."

"No," said Redux. "Four is good. Thank you for offer. You are true gentleman."

Rook laughed, wished it were true. "I'm just fixing things that need fixing," he said, and sent the corridor information to all three ships. "Here's the game plan. Chenne and I will run interference on whatever fighters the SEF send our way. Intelligence and common sense suggest it won't be much. Redux, you're the spotter. The freighters are programmed to come down in the middle of the typhoon zone, so we need to act fast when we see them. Tundra will change the splashdown co-ordinates and enter the landing—"

"Excuse me," said Redux. "I do not want Tundra near codes this time."

Rook nodded, wincing to himself. "Sorry, I should have—"

"I'll… be the… uh… spotter," Tundra said, quiet and careful, like she knew how precarious her place was. "I can make sure they re-enter properly."

"Good," said Redux. "I do not want to hear your voice again."

He flew out, straight past them all, to the bright blue line that showed the Ten Minute Mark — the point at which the freighters would turn and decelerate enough to enter the atmosphere roughly ten minutes later. No one moved to follow. Rook hesitated, hand on the throttle, and considered calling it off, leaving Chenne and Redux alone, and leaving Tundra to her own problems.

"You and me, Rook?" asked Chenne, catching him by surprise. She rarely spoke, and almost never so casually. She took off to the rendezvous. Rook pushed his own throttle, racing to catch up before the freighters made their appearance. The mission stopped being about charity or obligations or anything like that. It was a mission, and there were ways missions had to proceed. He spun around, getting into position at the blue line, watching Tundra follow silently behind, playing the shunned outsider perfectly.

"Just to be clear, we're aiming for an alternate drop zone because of the typhoon," Rook said. "You need to make sure you enter the data before they reach the five minute mark, or they won't have time to adjust their burn, and we'll have to scuttle the operation."

"I am good," Redux said.

"If anything goes wrong, you ask for help. We're a team here. No proud heroics, all right?"

Everyone voiced agreement except Tundra. It was better that way.

The clock on his console was counting down the seconds until the freighters would hit the mark. Usually, the last thirty or so seconds would be bursting with trajectory warnings, SEF alerts and a barrage of debris noise as the computer tried to keep the ship safe and stable in the madness of space. This time, though, it was silent. No enemies trying to engage, no debris big enough to worry about, and most worrying, no freighters. Not on target, and not even on the horizon. Rook switched his grid on and off, hoping it might reset something, give him the information he needed.

"They're overdue," he said.

"They have no guide," said Redux, referring to his usual job of escorting the freighters from further out than anyone bothered flying anymore. A lost art, and maybe an essential one after all. "Is easy to lose. May be off-course."

"Stay ready," Rook said.

He searched the grid again and again, switching the sensitivity of his sensors until the entire screen lit up with inconsequential debris, and then dialling it back so all he saw was blackness. Even if the freighters were off-course, they shouldn't have been completely missing like this. The only possibility was they were coming in so shallow, they were on the other side of the planet. And if that were the case, they'd be extremely hard to wrangle.

"Hey," said Tundra, piercing the silence. "Are those—"

"What did we tell you?" Rook snapped.

"I'm just saying—"

"Redux, I'm sorry," he said. "I don't know why she has to much trouble listening to—"

"Freighters at six o'clock!" Tundra shouted.

Rook looked over his shoulder, trying to see behind, but there was nothing there. But then he realized what she meant: six o'clock... *down*. He spun himself downward, and his screen lit up with red, alarms blaring. Three freighters, racing in on a collision course!

"Move!" he shouted, and hit his thrusters hard. His ship slipped and fishtailed as it raced to escape, but he saw the freighters were moving too fast to avoid. He'd never clear them in time. His ship screamed at him, flooding with more red than he could process, and he slammed it into a spin, hitting a sideways drift that put him straight in line with an empty gap between the second and third freighter. They shot past, long antenna barely missing his wings, showering him with so much dust he couldn't see anything but tiny particles reflecting sunlight, sticking to his canopy like a film. His ears were full of collision pings, as the computer reported every single fleck of dust that shot by.

He activated his window jets, and compressed air blew the junk off his viewport. What replaced it was far more dangerous: twelve SEF ships, ice cannons firing straight at him.

No Chance

Kani must have done something wrong when the freighters passed, because her ship went into a spin that she couldn't break out of. The blue of the planet rushed around her so fast she felt ill, but no matter how much she worked the controls, she couldn't get it to stop. She closed her eyes and the sickness eased: there was no momentum to her predicament, it was like she was just sitting still. She twisted the controls left and right, feeling the change in pressure, and when she opened her eyes again, things felt much more controlled. She couldn't help but smile.

A barrage of ice pelted her, and she let out a yelp, catching heavy fire on the underside of her ship that made her spin out of control towards Earth's shadow.

"It's a trap!" shouted Rook beyond the noise of impacts. "Everyone move! Regroup in the—"

Kani lost the rest of the sentence as she was hit by another round. She switched her grid on and off, trying to see where the SEF ships were coming from, but the picture distorted, being replaced with a warning: "40% sensor coverage. Cannot generate map."

"Mute off," she said, and the computer welcomed her back. She looked out the top of the ship for the sun — her one hope at getting back in the game — and saw a swirling beat of light through the ice. It was dizzying, moving so fast, but she knew what she had to do. She pulled her helmet off and set it in her lap, closed her eyes and felt the quick flash of heat every time she spun round. The computer blared at her to put her helmet back on, that this was dangerous, oxygen and radiation and everything else… but she kept feeling the pace of the spin, *feeling* it… until she was ready.

She pushed her throttle and the ship lurched forward, pressing her back into her seat. The sun swept around in front of her, burning off the ice and making her face sear with pain so fast she let go of the controls and dove back into her helmet. When she looked back up, the ice was gone, white distortion replaced with a shocking, loud red triangle and a freighter dead ahead.

"Warning!" said the console. "Impact danger!"

"Got it," she said, and spun the controls confidently. But the ship didn't react the way she expected: it turned her sideways, her right wing closing in on the side of the freighter. If she lost that wing, she might not die out here, but she'd never be able to get back home. She pushed down on the throttle, but all it accomplished was to move her closer to the freighter, not away. No matter how much she worked, she couldn't get out of the way.

"Dammit!" she shouted. "Move!"

She pushed the sphere downwards and the ship rocked, flipped around so she couldn't see the freighter at all anymore.

"Warning!" said the console. "Impact—"

"Zip it!" she snapped, and turned some more. She yelled a furious battle cry and spun the sphere as hard as she could, and the ship rolled in space, missing the freighter by centimetres. She gasped for air as the console stopped warning of danger.

"Decell in five!" yelled Rook from the chaos. "Everyone clear!"

Kani looked out her window and saw the freighters all rotate around 180 degrees, massive thrusters pointing straight at her. "Oh damn," she said.

She pushed down on the accelerator, trying to escape, but her steering was still off, and all she did was veer closer to the first freighter's engines, where the first signs of ignition were already apparent. Little bits of rock and dust were flaring up, bursting away like they were embers in a fire. Off to her side, an SEF ship was firing at her, his ice pellets disintegrating in the thruster heat, but it didn't stop him trying.

"Come on you stupid piece of sh—"

The freighter's thrusters ignited suddenly, white-hot ripples shooting out, and in an instant, the ice on the side of Kani's ship melted away. Her eyes shot open, and she turned hard right, punching it as fast as it would go. The computer screamed at the danger, but she arced away, blindly racing out of the blast zone, trailing ice and dust behind her.

The SEF fighter wasn't so lucky. It shot into the area too close, catching the flame directly at its side. The ship burst apart, throwing briefly-molten fragments all around. Kani's ears screamed with warnings as the console tracked every bit of the SEF wreckage, tumbling past her as she swung back around behind the freighters. This was what everyone was scared of, what everyone worked so hard to avoid. Inside that ship, there had been a man or a woman trying their best to survive, and now they were... they weren't anything. Only the metal seemed to exist anymore, lumpy bits of melted *junk*. The rest of it was just gone. Kani felt violently ill.

"Everyone report!" yelled Rook. "Chenne!"

"Here. Safe. I have you covered."

"Redux!"

"Working on co-ordinates now," he said.

"Tundra!"

"What do I do?" she gasped, ducking out of the way as another SEF ship shot past her. "They're everywhere!"

"You're on the front lines," Rook ordered. "Keep them off Redux."

"Yes sir!" she said, and turned her ship around. She felt like she should mourn the lost pilot, but his comrades weren't even taking the time for that. She had work to do, the largest part being the hardest: stay alive. She swished her controls left and right to get her bearings. It was an odd feeling, drifting backwards so fast. In regular planes, it would have been impossible, a sign of distress. But out here, it was one of the tricks of the trade. Now that she had the hang of it, it seemed to her it was almost like ice skating. A dangerous thrill.

The grid was a mess of yellow squares, shifting corridors and rapid green triangles. There were more obstacles than she could possibly get a handle on. She tried to pick out which one was Redux, but it was too hard to see.

"Redux!" she said. "Say something."

"Not now!" he snapped, and his green marker lit up.

"Thanks!" she said, and raced towards him. An SEF ship took a pass at her, but the ice only hit the tip of her wing. She ignored the challenge, kept charging forward.

"Rook," said Redux, panic in his voice. "Co-ordinates are not accepting. Freighter codes not accepting. Something is wrong!"

Kani opened fire with her cannons, shooting straight over Redux, pounding an SEF ship that was coming around to attack. Collision pings whined from behind, and she spun herself around and fired again, catching the side of another as he swept past.

"This is insane," she said to herself. "There are too many of them!"

"There's something wrong with the freighters," said Rook, his voice cracking. "They're not ours."

"They must be," said Chenne. "Where else did they—"

Kani looked around at the swarming SEF ships, and her mouth fell open. They weren't moving the way they had last time: they were ganging up, three for each dustrunner, boxing them in. It wasn't interference at all. It was corralling. "They're trying to catch us," she gasped.

"Chenne!" yelled Rook. "You and I are cover. Redux and Tundra, head for home. Abort the mission."

"But—" said Redux.

"There's nothing to do! Move!"

Kani turned her ship towards Earth, looking through the mass of ships coming at her from every side. They'd chase her every step of the way, and they'd stop her from getting the money she needed to keep Stacey and Simon alive. There was no way around that. If she left now, her friends were dead. She looked over at Redux's ship, saw he hadn't moved either, and ground her teeth.

"Redux, can you crack it if I give you some time?" she asked him.

Three SEF ships raced towards them, ice firing wildly.

"I can try," he said, no emotion in his voice.

"Then let's do it," she said, and spun herself around, blasting off into the fray. She rotated around the first volley of ice and fired her own shots at the cockpits of two of the ships, knocking them off-course and away from Redux. She doubled back to pursue the third, weaving where it weaved, slicing through space as it looped around towards the dark side of the planet, its engines the only light in the sky. The pilot was trying to trap her, trying to pin her down in the shadow of the planet, where the ice wouldn't melt. It was a showdown with only one chance at success, one ship coming out the victor. She kept after him, holding her fire, but letting him know he was cornered.

"How's it going, Redux?" she called.

"Maybe progress," he said.

"You two should be going home!" Rook yelled. "Leave the freighters!"

Kani was jolted by the sound of ice hitting the rear of her ship, and she looked up to see a second and third SEF ship tear past. She broke off pursuit and went after the new target, locking on her weapons and opening fire.

The ship dodged ably, shifting impossibly smoothly to avoid every blast that came at it. Kani tried rushing faster, but a warning from behind made her duck, and the two other SEF ships shot over her, their ice missing her, but pounding into their friend, layering up so much ice that his smooth motions turned into a deadly spin. The two SEF ships took off, leaving their comrade tumbling towards the planet, no way to recover, but moving so fast he was headed for disaster.

"Mayday!" shouted the pilot, and she recognized it from the first time up. It was Ares, the SEF commander. They were abandoning their own commander! "Mayday! I need help here!"

Kani looked back, but none of the other ships were coming to his aid. They were actually leaving him to die. She looked back, and her console warned he was about to hit the upper atmosphere of the planet. Something about the colour of the wording and the panic in his voice told her hitting the upper atmosphere would be bad news.

"Redux!" she called. "Any luck?"

"I think maybe," he said.

"Keep working. I'll be right back."

She shot towards Ares, trying to think of a way to pull him out of his descent when she had nothing but more ice to use. Then it came to her.

"Drop landing gear," she said.

"Command not found."

"Lower landing gear."

"Command not found."

"Put down the wheels!" she shouted, and she heard a ker-chunk as the landing gear moved out. "Thank you," she said, moving forward until she was pacing him exactly. She turned the sphere, twisting it until her ship's movements were in sync with his, moving belly-to-belly. She gently pushed her ship in towards his, like a mirror image converging with its parent, until they were almost connecting.

"Warning: dangerous re-entry angle," blared her console.

"I know," she said. "Stop bugging me."

With one last move of the sphere, she felt a shudder as her wheels connected with Ares' ship.

"Get out of here!" he barked.

"That's the plan!" Kani yelled back, and throttled up.

The two of them pushed up and out of the atmosphere, the rattling easing to nothing, and the console calming itself as the danger passed. She pushed him until he was in the sunlight again, and the ice melted off his ship and she could read the "FC-01" on his wing. Then, without warning, he broke off her, drifting for a moment before racing back to the battle.

"You're welcome," she muttered.

She was about to follow him when she saw a twinkle on the horizon. The space station again. Closer than ever, too. She could see the solar arrays, the expanded living quarters, the...

"Computer, magnify that area."

"Command not found."

"Help."

"Help menu. Please choose option."

"Magnify."

"Command not found."

"Dammit, how do I zoom?"

A yellow grid appeared over her viewport. She reached out and touched the square where the space station was floating, and it enlarged immediately.

Floating next to the solar arrays were three motionless freighters.

Escape

Redux finally pulled away from the freighters, watching as they moved into slow Earth orbit, gracefully avoiding re-entry and sliding around the planet like tiny moons. Rook pounded his leg with his fist, barely able to control himself.

"They were decoys," he fumed. "Dammit. It was a set-up."

SEF ships buzzed past him, and he turned to return fire.

"How did they get information into network?" asked Redux, arcing back towards Rook and Chenne. "This is serious issue, yes?"

"Yes," said Chenne, her voice darker than usual.

"Where's Tundra?" asked Rook, checking the grid, trying to get a handle on the noise he was seeing. "Wasn't she guarding you?"

"She was here second ago," he said. "Maybe she is captured?"

"Or maybe she got out of the mess while she could," said Rook. "Went back to her people."

"Wait, are you saying... she is rotten apple?"

Rook looked through the racing SEF ships, didn't see a third green triangle. "I think she is," he said. "I think she's the traitor."

Maryann Lewis was in the crew quarters of the old section of Alpha One, fighting with a socket that hadn't been upgraded with the rest of the space station fifteen years earlier. The newer parts of the station had integrated heating systems that worked flawlessly, but in certain areas, it could get damn near freezing without a little help. She'd requisitioned a space heater for the crew area months ago, and now that it had finally arrived, she was eager to try it out.

The only problem was this: the space heater had four prongs, and the socket had three, and try as she did, she couldn't find a way to make them connect. Maybe it was the lack of gravity. Maybe she was just having a bad day.

She set the heater back on the counter and pulled the cord over to a newer socket at the other side of the cabin, but the cord was too short, and the heater drifted off the counter and knocked her in the head.

She grumbled, put it back in its place, lifted her feet so she was free-floating in the centre of the room, and gently reached across with the plug, watching the slack on the cord to make sure everything would stay in place.

She was only a tiny distance away from the socket when the room suddenly shifted around her, and she completed her motion by jamming the plug into a window.

She looked up, uncertain.

And then the alarms started.

Kani had her landing gear hooked over the nose of the frontmost freighter, thrusters on full, ignoring the console warnings as she pushed the row of them away from the space station. She had no idea if her landing gear could withstand that kind of pressure, but she had a feeling the computer would tell her if she were about to ruin the ship. Hopefully. The freighters, as big as they were, weren't moving at the moment, making them remarkably easy to steal. She just had to keep at it, and she'd be able to bring them back to Rook and the others.

The more the freighters moved, the more the tether cord attaching them to the space station pulled tight, and she suddenly realized the whole place was starting to pivot. The solar arrays caught the sunlight, blinding her with a brilliant reflection.

"Come on…" she muttered, watching the freighters almost slip away from the SEF's control. "Just a little further…"

Then something caught her eye. A glow off the back freighter. It wasn't sunlight… it was something else.

"Oh no," she sighed.

Maryann was racing through commands at her computer, watching out the window as the three freighters lurched away from her. She finished the order and hit "send", then scrambled to the window, holding on with anxious fingers as the rear-most freighter's engines powered up. She grinned confidently.

"Take *that*," she said.

Kani's console warned her she was moving backwards, despite all her throttle pushing her forward. She looked out to the left and saw the space station coming back into view, the tether cord slackening. She pushed the throttle harder, but it made no difference.

"Warning," said the console. "Damage to landing gear detected."

"Dammit!" she cursed, hearing the creaking beneath her. "Move!"

Maryann laughed as the tiny F-422 slid backwards under the mighty boost of the freighter's engines. She tapped a button on the keyboard and watched the flame intensify, watched the dustrunner slip even further back. It was almost cruel, playing this game with such a tiny vessel. But she was in a bad mood, and she didn't care about cruelty.

"That'll teach you," she said, collecting her space heater and taking a closer look at the plug.

Outside, the F-422 made a quick manoeuvre, lifting itself off the top of the freighters. Suddenly free, the three of them shot off at full speed, out and away from Alpha One. The tether cable tightened quickly, and before Maryann could react, the room spun around her, and she found her face colliding with the floating base heater.

Kani retracted her landing gear and raced after the freighters. They were moving fast, and even at full speed, she was having trouble catching up. She saw the console calculating corridors for them, flashing options until it settled on a solid green path. A moment later, a warning came on-screen.

"Warning: Fatal re-entry angle. Catastrophic outcome predicted."

"Great," she sighed, and charged forward.

Stranglehold

The first freighter hit the atmosphere at an angle, and the friction made it pivot just enough that the other two broke free. The middle one deflected away from the planet, and the last one kept firing its thrusters straight towards the blue ocean below. No matter which way she looked, the outcome seemed bad, and Kani was at a loss at how to proceed. Losing the freighters in the first place was a big mistake, but if one or more of them crashed into the planet… that would be horrific. She had no idea what to do.

Without warning, Chenne shot through the mess, looping back and charging into the fray, following the first one like a silver arrow in the sky. "I have this one," she said.

"Good," said Rook. "Redux, catch the outbound one. Tundra and I will take care of the other re-entry."

"Understood," said Redux, and turning back into the void.

"What do I do?" Kani asked, hands shaking like mad.

"Get out your Bible and pray," Rook said.

The freighter Chenne was chasing had turned upside-down, dropping so fast its antenna array had dissolved from the heat. The huge tiles along its nose were aimed out towards space, doing it no good against the incredible heat it was absorbing. Normally, they caught the brunt of the re-entry friction, using their carefully-designed surfaces to deflect the heat away. Instead, the weaker parts of the structure were being exposed to temperatures they were never meant to handle, turning bright orange, yellow and white.

"Calculate corridor," Chenne said, holding her ship steady in the wake of the freighter's fire trail. The corridor began changing beneath her as the computer worked out how to move things from disaster to recovery, analyzing wind currents and friction depth and a dozen other fragments of information that determined how to make things fall from the sky safely. The computer finally settled on a spot a few hundred metres to her left.

Her ship rocked as the freighter lurched suddenly, its top side gleaming and white, quickly dimming to orange. It was getting spun by the atmosphere. There wasn't much time left to act.

"Map," she said, and the planet beneath her lit up with a grid of latitude and longitude, continent and countries outlined to help read the massiveness of the objects below. She cursed under her breath: the corridor was wrong. It ended up in south eastern Australia.

"Merde," she spat, and reached a hand out against the gravity to pull the corridor point back towards the Indian Ocean. It clicked into place, and the console re-calculated the corridor. It was to her right. Several kilometres to her right.

She pulled up her keyboard typing furiously to get the landing codes in place, took control of the freighter's engines. She activated the RCS jets closest to her, then looked over to watch. To her horror, she saw the cone-shaped jets were melting, white hot and bubbling.

"Not good," she said, and then they exploded out, spraying liquid metal towards her. She swept sideways and back, massive tremors shaking her ship as the atmosphere demanded she stop. Her console tracked the trajectory of the molten metal, whining urgently as little flecks barely missed her nose.

The freighter was rumbling towards the corridor, rotating gradually as the atmosphere thickened. A moment later, it completed its turn, and as the heat shield took the brunt of the friction, the whole freighter rocked smoothly into place. The difference was amazing to behold: once a gigantic box of fire and wreckage and death in the sky, when it was on-course, the thing just slid downward like an ice cube melting on gentle slope.

Chenne pulled her ship back, slowly shifting into a space-bound arc, watching the freighter make its descent below her.

"One freighter in," she called into the comm. "How are the rest?"

Kani's harness held her in, but her body felt like it was going to fly straight out of her ship. She'd never been under so much pressure before, it was like all the blood in her body was pooling in her head, making it hard to focus. Her ears felt like they were going to explode.

"What do we do?" she shouted over the roar of re-entry. "I can't see anything!"

Thin smoke shot out from the freighter's tail as it spun towards the planet, the smoke thickening every second it dropped deeper into the atmosphere. She and Rook were a short distance behind, catching the wake and trying not to get hit.

"Enter the code!" Rook yelled. "We need to get it stabilized!"

Kani pulled up the keyboard and hit the code, but the console flashed red. She tried again, but no luck. "It's not working!" she yelled.

The freighter hit a patch of friction and changed dynamics, tumbling headlong into the ocean, dropping bits of rock behind it that tore past them and burned up fast like giant sparks.

"The long-range communications melted," Rook yelled, and Kani saw all the antenna mounts on the freighter were burnt out of existence. She was sending codes to a ship that couldn't listen. "We need to get closer."

"*We?*" Kani squeaked. "You want me to—"

"Hurry!" Rook shouted, swinging in behind the freighter.

Kani rocketed forward, pounding "enter" on the console every few seconds, waiting for the light to turn green. Every time she let go of the controls, her ship started to buckle, but until the code stuck, she couldn't give up. One, two, three more times she did it, but still nothing! "It's not working!" she yelled.

The freighter hit another pocket, and the freighter pitched sideways.

"Tundra! Move!"

She banked right, spinning out of the way as the freighter swung towards her. The fire from the engines passed close to her, throwing warning upon warning across her screen. Every time she moved, she felt the pressure on her body change, and she realized she couldn't just shift anymore: the atmosphere and gravity were making her ship move like an airplane. She started to panic, terrified at the idea of having to fly for real, without any of the allowances made in space.

On its second rotation, Kani saw the tip of the freighter's heat shield glowing bright yellow. It cast streaks of white down the edge of the ship, down to the massive hinges, which were losing their definition.

"Oh no," said Rook. "Get out! Get out now!"

The freighter finished another spin and seemed to stick in place, suddenly motionless after all that tumbling. A huge rumble filled the air around them, rattling Kani's lungs with terror and awe, drowning out even her frantic heartbeat. The freighter stayed still for a second more, and then with a massive sucking noise, the heat shield caved into the body of the ship.

Kani pulled back, tried to pull up, but she was too thick in the atmosphere to stop herself. Little fragments of rock shot out from the sides of the freighter, screaming past her like stars falling upwards. She dodged them, pushing away as hard as she could, until they stopped, leaving the air rife with smoke trails, but otherwise calm.

But then the freighter imploded on itself, and her console lit up with a debris field the size of a football stadium.

Tragedy

"Flip and full blast!" Rook screamed, and Kani spun the sphere as hard as she could. The ship barely made the motion, lurching against the atmosphere, and the console immediately warned of structural damage to the rear engines.

She pushed down on the throttle and was pinned flat against her seat. She felt faint, her hands went numb, and for a second she thought the black sky grew bigger. The roar of the engines was deafening, bleeding through every cell in her body and making her cry out in pain. She screamed at the top of her lungs, a pained, terrified scream that trailed off as she cleared the atmosphere and the pressure all vanished. She was spinning through space, the debris from the freighter splaying out beneath her like a massive fireworks display in slow motion.

Rook shot past her, regained his orientation, and passed back around. "Dammit," he said. "Damn it all."

"I'm sorry," she gasped, fighting for breath. "I didn't—"

"Save it," he said. "There's one more, and I don't have the patience right now." He took off around the Earth.

Redux had the freighter on a corridor back to the planet, clear into the Indian Ocean, but the SEF were swarming him like flies, pelting him with ice from all sides. He returned fire sporadically, but his ship was too big and cumbersome to truly fight back, and even worse, every time he looked away, the landing codes were overridden. He had to watch them above all else. Without this shipment, he'd never be able to cover his debts.

"SEF!" called Ares over the comm. "We have an explosion in the atmosphere. I need eyes on the scene now. Go!"

Most of the ships took off immediately, leaving him in peace for a change. A few stragglers were moving slowly, not wanting to give up the fight, but he refused to engage them. He had bigger things to worry about. He pulled up the map and adjusted the splashdown zone again, tweaking the exact landing spot. There were certain areas of the Indian Ocean the trawlers could access easily, and the sooner they got to the freighter, the sooner he'd get paid. The freighter shifted into its new trajectory; a slow, gentle motion that would take a whole other orbit of the planet to complete, but would very safely make the trip down.

"Freighter is under control," he said into the comm. "How are others?"

Chenne was five minutes out by the time the two SEF ships tailing her were forced to retreat, cursing all the way that they'd *had* her, that they could have caught her. She spun herself around and powered up her guns, ready to show them how wrong they were, but something else caught her eye.

The decoy freighters were still orbiting, gently swinging along the equator, around the far side of the planet. Ahead of them, just at the edge of the disc, she saw the third of Tundra's freighters... the one Redux was shepherding. They were moving towards each other so slowly it was hard to tell, but something about it struck her as wrong.

"Show me corridors," she said, and the console threw up a set of green toughs that made an "X" over South America. A green pulse traced the projected movement of the two sets of ships, connecting directly at the centre. They were going to collide!

"Redux!" she shouted. "Watch your angle!"

There was no response, not even static. She powered her engines and shot forward, repeating her warning over and over, her voice getting hoarse from yelling. Redux never replied, never gave any indication he even knew what was going on.

"Rook!" she called. "I can't reach Redux! He is in danger!"

"Where is he?" Rook asked. "I can't see him."

"With the freighter, near Antarctica."

"On our way!"

Rook raced around the planet, Tundra close behind, until his console drew the triangles for Redux and the freighter in the distance. Off to his left, he saw the decoys moving at a solid clip. He drew the corridors onscreen and saw the meeting-point coming up fast.

"Redux!" he yelled. "You have to change the corridor!" There was no answer. "Dammit, he's in the shadow of the freighter. His antenna might be frozen. Tundra, see if you can—"

A sudden barrage of ice clipped his side, and two SEF ships shot past, turning in graceful arcs and coming back for another try. They were determined to capture a pirate, and even direct orders weren't going to keep them down.

"I've got them," Tundra said, turning.

"No!" Rook shouted. "Warn Redux. He needs to get out of there!"

"Yes sir," she said without hesitation, and shot into the distance. One of the SEF ships chased after her, while the other took a second pass at Rook, firing wildly. He rocked his ship sideways, catching his tail in the sunlight, trying to thaw himself out so he could fight back. The SEF ship hit him again, this time on the underside, and it knocked him into a spin. He fought to correct it, but it was no use. With every rotation, he lost a little more ice, but it wouldn't be fast enough.

He opened his thrusters to full blast and shot forward, straight into the atmosphere, jerking back as the friction hit his nose. His console whined, counted down the seconds until his heat shielding could buckle, but he kept charging forward, waiting until the last of the ice was gone. The SEF ship fired past his side, missing broadly, and he glared up at them, eyes narrow.

"You should learn when to quit," he said, and swung back into space, firing in a constant stream until his cannons ran dry and shut off to reload. The SEF ship was pelted with so much ice, its nose looked bulbous, and it drifted into the dark side of the planet, away into obscurity.

Rook turned himself around and took off after Tundra.

Kani heard the ice hitting her tail, but she didn't try to fight back. Her thruster was on so high, almost anything melted anyway. The distance to Redux was closing fast, but no matter how many times she called, he didn't respond.

The SEF pilot finally got his aim right, hit the back of her canopy with several successive bursts, and she checked over her shoulder to see the glass fully covered.

"Buzz off," she said into the comm.

"Suck my pipe," replied the SEF pilot in a weasely little voice.

"I'd have to be able to see it first," she snapped.

"Come 'ere and I'll show it to ya."

Her eyes narrowed. "I'll show you something," she said, and spun herself around. Her ice cannons blasted his nose, and he swerved down to escape, letting her coat the top of his ship as well. She gave him the finger as he ran for cover.

"Suck on that," she grinned, and turned back to the freighters, only to find she'd overshot her objective. The SEF ship she'd pummelled swung back down, ice cannons blasting at Redux as Kani struggled to slow herself enough to get back on target.

Chenne knew there was no hope. The freighters moved together in slow motion, their noses colliding, then buckling, and swinging inward like a massive book closing.

She pushed the throttle so hard it creaked, but then she saw it: the brief flash of an explosion, and a debris field drifting away from the scene.

"*Yuri!*"

Carefully Ruined

The debris scattered in a plume like a puff of smoke in space, catching the light as Chenne shot forward, gasping for air. The freighters swayed apart, dropping ore over the ocean, a flood of red warnings telling everyone to stay away, just stay back. Death ruled, here. There was glass in the debris, shining brighter than any metal would. A shattered cockpit. A dead pilot. No more second chances.

Tundra swung around, her engine flaring once or twice before she came to a stop, but she said nothing, did nothing. Like the others, she just stayed still, watching, mourning.

Chenne's eyes filled with tears that wouldn't fall, clouding her vision. She slid up her visor, wiped them away with rough, gloved hands, unable to catch her breath. The cockpit was so small. So small.

"Chenne," came a voice over the comm, slow and careful. "Is okay."

The freighters parted slowly, and then she could see him… Redux's ship drifting above the debris, red paint catching the sunlight. She froze in her seat, reached her hand to her lips, the life sucked out of her. Her hand was trembling, fingertips cold. He was alive, but he was… she had…

"Oh my god," she whispered. "Oh no…"

"Chenne!" shouted Rook. "What in the *hell* did you do?"

"I… I don't…"

"Is okay," said Redux, life gone from his voice. "Do not worry."

Chenne's hands floated above the controls. She couldn't touch them, couldn't move.

"What happened?" Tundra asked. "What's going on?"

"Not now," Rook snapped.

"Is old rule," said Redux serenely. "You don't speak names in ships, yes? SEF records all transmissions, compares for identification back home."

"But all they have is a first name. They can't—"

"It reduces error to small degree," he said. "You would be surprised how much they know by voice alone. First name, accent and voice? That is very small group of people in world. They will have me picked out like ripe apple by bed time."

Chenne lowered her head as far as she could, crying. "I'm so sorry, Redux," she said.

"Please," he said. "Is okay. Call me Yuri. Suits me better. Redux is silly name that came with ship. I sound like heart burn, yes?" She laughed a little, sniffled. "You got freighter in safely, yes? One out of three is not too bad. It should pay bills. Buy me new car for fast driving. Ha ha!"

"Redux," said Rook darkly. "I'll make sure your share gets—"

"No," said Chenne. "I will. I'll take care of it, Yuri."

"Thank you," he said. His ship powered up, turned gently, and moved towards the Earth. It paused for a moment, and they heard him sigh a long, deep sigh. "Is no one's fault," he said. "If I had seen my antenna frozen, I would have been fine. Is no one's fault. Is fate, yes? Do not blame anyone. Not even Tundra."

Chenne looked over at Tundra's ship, grit her teeth.

"Tundra is becoming good pilot now," Redux said. "I wish I could see how she changes world."

And with that, his engines flared brightly, and he took off into the atmosphere. They watched his re-entry fire burn brilliantly around him, and then he was gone, another pinpoint of light floating around the globe.

Rook and Tundra left next, slipping away without a word, leaving Chenne alone in the darkness. The puff of debris was bigger than the freighters now, and as it touched the edge of the planet, parts of it sparkled as they burned into nothing.

She watched until the last of it was gone.

Exception

THREE YEARS EARLIER

Rache picked her sweater off the table and pulled her bra back into place, watching the bedroom in silence. She walked over, hand touching the door lightly, and listened. She heard Yuri inside, his breathing raspy, distraught, and she closed her eyes. Her mouth opened to speak, but she couldn't decide what to say.

She stood back, hand clutching her clothes to her chest, and then sighed, pulled the sweater on, and let herself into the bathroom. The lights came on, flickering tiredly, and she leaned close to the mirror, fixing her hair, cleaning her smudged lipstick, the traces of his mouth on hers. She looked at herself, saw the hurt in her eyes, and tried to wipe it away. It was stubborn, though. More stubborn than her.

Out of the corner of her eye, she saw into the medicine cabinet, saw a row of bottles without labels. She opened the door carefully, took one of the bottles out, and unscrewed the lid. It was filled with an assortment of pills without brands; different shapes and sizes, textures, different purposes. She put the lid back on, replaced the bottle and closed the door back the way it had been, but stared at it a moment longer.

She picked up her bag from the floor by the table, looked back to the bedroom one last time. The closed door. The things she didn't say. A thought caught her, and she reached down, zipped her skirt the rest of the way up, and somehow felt more composed, like the hesitancy was gone.

On her way to the front, his phone lit up, chiming softly as a message came in. She looked at it, then reached down, flipping it open, and saw the note from his wife: "Anya is asking for you." This hurt, and she almost put it down, threw it down, but instead she deleted the message, and felt guilty the second it was gone.

What replaced it was a different note altogether: a short, cryptic scribble of letters and numbers, sent by a man named Pellier. None of it made any sense, except for two things that burned into her mind the second she saw them: the letters "DSR" — the insider term for dustrunners; and the last line, which read: "Good luck, Redux."

She jotted Pellier's address down in her own phone, a smile creeping across her face. "Redux," she said to herself. "Doesn't roll off the tongue like 'Yuri', does it?"

Passing Away

The hangar was bathed in orange light, long sheets of plastic draping down like cobwebs in an attic, casting half-shadows on the walls and floor. Rache ran her hand along the tarp, felt the roughened grit and the cold gloss of the machine beneath. It was the death mask of a hero, standing proud in its throne room, looming tall over all visitors. She knelt before it, for so many reasons.

She found the letter in a worn envelope by the front wheel, the small, precise letters of an engineer spelling "Chenne." She looked at it, running her fingers along the edge, the object she most wanted and most feared.

She opened it, unfolding the paper inside, and read in silence, tears held back to protect the words below.

Dear Chenne,

I will not see you again. I have turned myself in, and I hope you will understand why. They would find me someday, and I cannot live with that fear. It would not be a life.

You said you would take care of my money, and I hope you will still take that task. I would ask you to go to the hospital and make the payment yourself, so I can be sure it will be done. They will seize all I have, and I cannot lose my baby to such a reason.

Thank you for all you have done for me today. I will never forget it.

I asked you once if you were happy with your life. If you were happy giving up passion for safety. And in truth, I was looking for the answer myself. I think I have it now, and I regret it took such a day to become clear.

Get out of this game while you can. It will kill you. You will not change the world. The world will change everything you know as yourself, and you will not see it until you are two steps past the point of no return.

You can change things, Chenne. I need you to change things. But do not change yourself.

As always,

Yuri

She held the letter as she stood in the hospital, watching Anya wheeled to surgery, the bed making no noise as she floated down the hall like an angel.

She held the letter as she faced Sabina, lacking the words to tell her, only shaking her head and holding back her own tears out of respect. Playing the enemy. Making it easier.

"I'll make it better, Yuri," she said to no one at all, and she hoped he would know.

At Odds

America was noisy. Kani stood at the edge of the road, her back to a massive black truck, listening to the traffic roar down the highway. Rook watched her from safe distance, arms crossed, listening while looking like he wasn't. She wasn't sure how much he'd hear anyway, with the sound of the cars so near. Back home, electric engines were the norm. Here, she heard the sounds those tinny speakers were trying to emulate. It was deafening. She pushed the phone against her ear a little harder, cupped her hand over her mouth so she'd be heard.

"Thank you," she said. "Thank you for everything."

Kaso laughed. "You say that like I'm going somewhere," he said. "I was thinking we should move in together. Are you free Thursday?"

"No," she said. "I'm in hiding Thursday."

"All right, Friday. You're such a control freak."

She hid a laugh, ran her hand through her hair. "Have you heard anything about my friends?"

"I sent Fat Tony the cash myself," he said. "You guys didn't net the full amount, so I chipped in from my personal account."

She gasped. "Oh god, Kaso. Thank you so m—"

"Okay, I lied. It was some guy in Malaysia. But he won't notice, I think. I mean maybe he will. When they say, 'college fund', do they really mean it the same way we do? I can't tell. Let's move on, shall we?"

"Are you going to be okay? With the money, I mean?"

"I'm fine. And better yet, your friends are fine. Fat Tony even thanked them for being good hostages when he let them go."

"You're kidding."

"Okay, I'm kidding. I waited until they were out the door and called the cops on him. Apparently he collects very strange sub-genres of porn that are illegal where you live. Who knew gnomes and socks could do those things. It's sick, I tell you. Sick."

"You're insane."

"You're just noticing?"

"How can I ever repay you?" she asked, then frowned and added: "Don't answer that."

"I heard you did pretty good up there. Incident reports aren't out yet, but Rook said you were moving like a hummingbird, babe A hummingbird. Whatever that's supposed to mean. You should be proud! I think."

"I don't know how I did it," she smiled. "It just came to me. It just made sense."

"That's the Centrix system at work. Meant for gamers. Easier on the brain. Uh... which is not taking *anything* away from your skill. You are the master. Centrix? Feh. Centrix is like the... the diaper to your... your... help me out here."

"No thanks," she said, and glanced over her shoulder as Rook whistled for her. "I've gotta go."

"You're going to be okay?" he asked.

"I think so. Rook is taking me to a safe house somewhere."

"Remember what I said, okay? I looked up the old Tundra, and she sucked ass. You, I like. You should stick around."

"I think I don't have a choice," she said.

She got into the truck and strapped in as Rook pulled into traffic. They drove for ten minutes without a word, her stealing nervous peeks at his tense face, dark hands squeezing the steering wheel like it could feel pain. He was exactly the way she'd imagined him, but somehow more tired. He seemed like he'd been kicked in the gut too many times, and was trying to hold himself together.

They were riding down interstate 75, towards Dayton, the city far off in the distance, barely visible through the light sheen of rain in the air. When she'd left for the mission, it had been morning... but now it was already night. Another day completely lost, and yet somehow she felt years older. Every second she lived this life, this existence as Tundra, she found fewer things to scare her, and more things that terrified her to her core. Cars moved past them, engines cutting through the glass like it wasn't there, but even the shock of that was gone. She just stared at her hands, thinking.

"Can I ask a question?" she asked quietly.

"Speak up," he said. "Or don't talk at all."

"Can I ask a question?" she said again, louder.

"Go."

"What happened with those freighters? They were decoys?"

"I think so. They've never done that before, but it was always in the cards. We're going to have to work around it from now on. I just don't know *how* yet."

"But the information came from… inside…?"

"That's what worries me." He looked over at her, frowned. "You haven't had any pills since you landed, have you?"

"N-no," said Kani, remembering the hospital. "I didn't bring any with me."

"Glove compartment," he said. "And a bottle of water. Has some extra vitamins mixed it. Stops the vertigo, if you get that."

"Do I ever," she muttered.

She threw a handful of pills in her mouth and washed them down with water, choking at the end. Her throat was dry. She hadn't eaten for so long. She wasn't hungry yet, but she could feel the effects all the same. Something about fear sucked every other sensation out of you. She finished the water, closed it back up, held it between her knees.

"That was a stupid move with the freighters," he said. "You're lucky it worked."

"I couldn't just leave them there. The space station was totally unguarded."

Rook smiled, looked in the mirror for a moment. The heat was on, but she was still shivering, wearing only the hospital scrubs she'd kept under the flight suit. Rook turned the dial higher, adjusted the vents so she'd get more of the hot air the truck was blowing. It didn't seem to help.

"Who do you think the mole is?" he asked.

"There's a mole?" she asked. "I mean, we know it for sure?"

"We didn't end up in a trap by accident," Rook said. "Someone put us there."

"Well then I guess it's someone who wasn't there," she said. "Not Elvis, so maybe Spastik?"

"Spastik's crazy, but he's no mole. He's too reckless for that."

"So not Elvis?" she asked, and blinked away a spot in her vision.

"No, not Elvis," he said. "He thought Chenne was a good candidate, and after what happened tonight, I can almost see his point… but I don't think it's her. She cares about the team too much for that."

"So what," Kani asked. "Wait, are you saying it's me? I just got here!"

Her head flopped back, and she found it increasingly hard to focus on her surroundings. Rook took a hand off the wheel, felt the pulse on her neck, and pushed her head gently against the side of the car.

"You called it a space station," he said without judgement. "First thing you learn up there is the proper name. Alpha One. Anyone who says, 'space station' is going to get mocked to within an inch of their life. You never forget it. It's part of the culture. So there's no way you've been up there as long as you say you have, if you're making mistakes like that."

"Wait," she said. "I *am* Tundra… I…"

"Don't bother," he said. "I asked around. We know you're not Tundra, no matter what Kaso says. The question I have now is: who *are* you?"

"I told you—"

"You're going to want to think about your answer," he said. "Because in my position, I don't have many options to deal with moles."

She was looking out the window, but it was just a blur of light. Her hands moved slightly on her lap, but that was all she could manage. The water bottle fell from between her knees, landing on the floor, and she knew she'd been poisoned. She knew he'd tricked her, made her take pills she never should have swallowed, and now she was… now she… she took a deep breath.

"I'm not Tundra," she said. "Tundra is my friend. I had to take her place because she got hurt and—"

"You're going to have to do better than that," he said. "We don't just go recruiting anyone into this world. You had to have been vetted first."

"I swear, I'm not the mole. I only found out about this yesterday. I'm not who you think I am."

"Sure," he said. "Then you won't mind it if I…"

Rook's voice trailed off, then he grabbed her head and shoved it forward, into the dashboard. She started to cry out in pain, but glass shattered around her, and the car swerved to the left.

"Hold on!" he shouted. "This could get messy."

Sucker Punch

Freeman shot across the median and into oncoming traffic, but a pair of black sedans followed close behind, tires cutting through the rain like knives. He put his foot to the floor and swerved back to the other side, knocking a smaller car out of the way. A bullet caught his side mirror and shattered it completely.

"What's going on?" slurred Tundra from the seat beside him. "Where are we going?"

"We're being followed!" he shouted. "What did you do? Who did you tell?"

"I didn't tell anyone," she said, and another shot broke out the back window. He pulled aside a compact car, jerked the steering wheel left and smashed the tiny vehicle into the railing. The car spun out of control, bouncing straight into the path of one of the sedans, crumpling both cars in an explosion of glass and metal. The other sedan dodged the wreckage, revved loudly to keep up.

Freeman grabbed his phone from the dash and dialled, keeping an eye on the road behind him.

"Kaso!" he yelled. "I need help!"

"On it," Kaso said.

The second car raced ahead, pulling up beside him, jutting back and forth as other traffic got in the way. The rear window rolled down and a man in a dark suit aimed a gun towards the truck. Freeman double-checked his timing, and spun the wheel, smacking the car across two lanes, into the edge of a highway sign. The metal pole sliced straight through the centre of the sedan to the trunk, the two occupants mangled beyond recognition. Freeman raced forward without looking back.

"Dammit," said Kaso. "Dammit, there's a problem."

"What?" snapped Freeman. "What's wrong?"

But then he saw it. Up a head, across the highway, a roadblock. Five more sedans, agents on the ground. There was nowhere to go. He leaned Tundra back, made sure the seatbelt was tight, and floored it.

"Kaso," he yelled. "You have to warn them! The mole isn't Tundra. It *isn't* Tundra. It's—"

The front tires hit the roadblock, bursting on impact. The truck fishtailed and hit a concrete barrier, flipping into the air and landing on its roof. They skidded across the road in a sea of sparks and shattered glass, finally stopping under a massive blue highway sign. The world kept spinning as Freeman undid his seat belt, landing on his back, cutting himself with every movement. He pulled his gun from under the seat, crawled over to Tundra and checked for a pulse, then saw his phone in the glass, reached for it, trying to tell Kaso the name they needed to hear.

Footsteps came closer, guns clicking into place, and just as his fingers touched the edge of the phone, a hand grabbed him by the neck and dragged him out through the window. He tried to shoot, but a rifle butt hit his hand, then his head. He crumpled, eyes losing focus, waiting for the final blow. He coughed blood onto the ground.

Another set of footsteps moved towards him, and he looked up, lights blinding him, seeing just a shadow, a silhouette against the vibrant blue sign. The figure tilted his head to the side, then nodded.

"That's them," said Elvis. "Bring 'em in."

Author's Note

This book was written in three days.

You think I'm joking, don't you? But no, it's true: from October 6th to 8th, 2009, I sat down at my computer and wrote *Typhoon* with the help (and harassment) of a great many people on the internet. The project was called #3D1D (3 days, 1 draft) and it was my first foray into a process called livewriting.

To really understand *Typhoon*, you need to understand how it came about. I started with an outline and a general idea of who my characters were, aiming to write a new chapter every hour for three days straight (with a few sleep periods mixed in), and come out at exactly 51 chapters. Every hour, I would post a series of questions on Twitter, then randomly select answers to integrate into the story as I went. It wasn't complete unpredictability, but it was as close as I thought I could manage. It was a big gamble. If I failed, it would be well-known, and well-documented. I had no idea how it'd turn out.

Actually, it turned out pretty good. The experience was like nothing I'd ever done before. I liken it to a concert by a writer: the rush of performance, the instantaneous feedback from the audience, and the personal experience you share with those who were there with you. I made really great friends who have stuck with me past the end of this book, three of whom are mentioned at the start: Eli James, Jan Oda and A.M. (Anna) Harte. If you want to know why *Typhoon* worked, it's because of them.

There are things in this story that are entirely my creation, and things that are the result of odd answers to confusing questions. Why is Elvis called Elvis? Someone told me that was his name. Why Dayton, Ohio? Another user-submitted suggestion. Why, when things are getting really intense between Yuri and Rache, does he suddenly stop? I asked the question: "Stop or go?" with no context, and the chosen answer was "STOP!" I had a sex scene all planned out, but it never saw the light of day...

The first version of *Typhoon* was a slight touch-up on the original livewritten text, but this is a whole other beast. The original was 50,000 words, but this is more like 85,000. Most of the chapters have been at least partially rewritten, and some (like Kani and Simon trying to outsmart Fantoni at the school) are completely redone. There's more texture to everything, including a lot of subtle hints about things to come. I'm preparing to livewrite the second book in the series, *Polarity*, so those things are big in my mind right now. Suffice to say, if something in this version seemed left unfinished or half-defined, it's on purpose. And the answer is coming.

Writing a book like this is extremely hard work. I mean, writing it the first way was hard enough, but making it *perfect...* that takes a lot of brainpower. So I want to thank Jan again for taking the time to tell me where I was being stupid. She's a very supportive lady, but she's also ruthless, which is much appreciated!

Finally, I'd like to invite you to partake in *Polarity*. If you're reading this before the end of November, 2010, you can participate in the livewriting at http://1889.ca. If you're reading this any time after, keep an eye out for the ebook or print versions. I don't know exactly what the story will look like, but I've got a pretty good idea it's going to knock your socks off!

Thanks for being part of the problem!

— MCM
October, 2010

Appendix A: History of the Future

I generally don't believe in appendices for my stories. I have an intricate world built out in my head, and I prefer to give you glimpses into it through the actions of the characters, not some faux-encyclopedic analysis. That said, there's far more to the Dustrunners world than I can communicate in the course of my plotlines (without resorting to some crazy exposition)… so rather than tease you with it forever, I thought I would explain at least *some* of the things that make this world tick.

None of these things are spoilers. They're just background for those who are interested. It's also insanely dry. You've been warned.

SPACE TOURISM

Beginning with Virgin Galactic in the early part of the 2010s, space tourism looked to be a major part of the worldwide economic turnaround. What started as an expensive luxury for the super-elite came down in price so fast that by 2020, the idea of seeing the Earth from orbit was within the means of many upper-middle class families — if still only as a once-in-a-lifetime event.

Hoping to capitalize on this trend, the French government positioned itself to lead the way into the next generation of space exploitation. In 2018, new tax credits were implemented to lure aerospace companies into French cities. An immigration law passed in 2023 further incentivized firms to relocate, giving quick and immediate social benefits to employees certified as being essential to the space tourism industry. By 2026, over two-thirds of the world's aerospace companies were headquartered in France, creating better and more streamlined vessels than many had thought possible just ten years before.

In early 2025, French companies began creating a new class of spacecraft, forgoing the "carpooling" motif for high-fashion personalized ships. Using advancements in autopilot and heat shielding technology, the goal was to let the average person explore near Earth orbit on a recreational basis, with price tags starting at just under the cost of a small house. Analysts predicted massive market penetration within a decade, with the promise that, "every family will have a spaceship of their own" tantalizingly close.

In 2026, the world's second major commercial spaceport opened at de Gaulle airport, with satellite outposts planned for New York, Los Angeles, Tokyo and Buenos Aires. Many countries tried to stop or stall the expansion of space tourism, to little effect. Efforts loosen the French stranglehold on the industry were ultimately defeated when the World Trade Organization ruled a planned regional spacecraft re-regulation policy was overly cumbersome by design, with protectionist intent. The message to the world was clear: if you want to beat Paris to the stars, you need to invest in your own companies. Heavily.

By 2027, the French economy was booming as never before, even as the rest of the world stumbled under the weight of new emissions regulations, and the pre-emptive disintegration of the commercial airline industry (personalized spacecraft made round-the-world plane rides obsolete, analysts said). The world was on the verge of a major revolution in transportation. But it would be short-lived.

ENERGY CRISIS

Climate change had been on the world's radar for at least fifty years, but in 2020, after five consecutive years of damaging droughts, floods and storms — and the very real spectre of a fossil fuel shortage in the near future — a new environmental protection convention was signed with aggressive goals. As outlined in the Shanghai Accord, emissions standards in all countries would be increased to the point where new gasoline-powered vehicles would no longer be legal. Within five years, all new cars would be hydrogen or electric-based, with the remaining older-generation cars replaced or upgraded by 2035. Special exceptions were made for developing nations, but only until 2040, when the world would be officially "oil-free".

The Accord was ratified by most industrialized nations by the end of the year, though two holdouts prevented it from coming into full effect: China, a strong supporter of the text for years, insisted on American participation before committing. The United States, while supporting the Accord in principle, was wary of China's position as the leading exporter of the minerals used by most next-generation hybrid engines. Until China agreed to guarantee certain free trade provisions, the treaty was at a standstill.

Meanwhile, the rest of the world worked to implement the goals of Shanghai as quickly as possible, each country hoping to become the world leader in the emerging field of mainstream hydrogen power. "Trade or Upgrade" policies — adopted by many countries like the United Kingdom, Denmark, Spain, Germany and Canada — caused what economists called "hiccup recessions", where the sticker shock of being forced into environmental friendliness wiped out great amounts of wealth very suddenly, only to reverse itself when the auto industry reaped the rewards of the mandated upgrade regime. Overall, the world economy stalled heavily in 2023, the worst broad-based recession since 2009.

In mid-2023, the American government, led by an extremely popular Democratic president, rushed to appease the Chinese and ratify the Shanghai Accord before the upcoming elections, hoping to use it as a centrepiece in their list of legislative victories. After securing a twenty-five year agreement on exclusive (and attractive) export rates from Beijing, Congress agreed to the Accord and the Chinese followed suit, putting it into full force with only a year and a half to meet stringent standards. Unfortunately, the world recession caught up with politics in Washington, and the new Republican-controlled government quickly reversed the ratification, vowing to keep using gasoline and American-based fossil fuels, despite the howls of protest from the international community.

By 2036, the only countries in the world with laws permitting gas-powered engines were the United States, and the United Arab Emirates. Unfortunately, the new era of "clean" transportation was not as bright as it had once seemed.

ASTEROID MINING

In 2018, it was already clear the technological base for hybrid engines was too dependent on rare minerals found in only a small number of countries. While efforts continued to find alternative zero-emissions technologies, many nations began investing heavily in extra-terrestrial mining projects, hoping to harvest the necessary minerals from objects in the asteroid belt just beyond Mars. This process kicked into high gear once the Shanghai Accord became a reality, increasing the likelihood that the country that dominated space would dominate back home as well.

Piggybacking off the achievements in the French aerospace sector, the asteroid mining industry grew at a phenomenal rate, with competing nations (and their largely government-backed companies) constantly one-upping each other in a bid to reach the asteroid belt first. Though there were significant accidents between 2018 and 2027, the rate of progress incentivized most nations to allow a "wild west" mentality to permeate the industry, so long as the risks took place a safe distance from Earth. By 2026, the first shipments of asteroid ore were arriving at the International Space Station (revived and retrofitted to act as a gateway down to the planet), and the dreams gave way to cold practicality.

Companies around the globe bought out their government shareholders and began competing aggressively, resulting in cries of antitrust violations as the major players began to take shape. Just a decade into the Asteroid Age, the industry was valued at over $14 trillion, though very little revenue had been generated from the imported ore itself. Most of the successful attempts had been undertaken by smaller African-based companies, working without the cumbersome safety regulations imposed by the G12 nations.

In October 2027, a Kenyan-based freighter collided with a defunct communications satellite while trying to re-enter Earth's atmosphere. The wreckage burnt up harmlessly over the Pacific Ocean, but the accident provided easy ammunition to the "Big Five" mining companies in their quest to clamp down on their more nimble competitors. In April 2028, a solid majority of western powers signed two critical pieces of legislation: the Near Earth Safety Act, and the Bonn Convention.

REGULATIONS AND LAW ENFORCEMENT

The Near Earth Safety Act (NESA) dealt with the primary concerns of the Kenyan freighter accident, by creating strict safety guidelines and certifications for operating vehicles twelve kilometres above the Earth's surface. In particular, it required specially-trained United Nations overseers to be onboard to ensure the pilots (whose own certification process had become a complex endeavour) wouldn't pass through dangerous "junkyard" orbits. While ostensibly designed to ensure safety, NESA's true purpose was clear to even the most casual observer: it would make private spaceflight illegal. The French government protested the move strenuously, but in the end, too many bridges had been burned, and the act went into force. France briefly defied the ban, but crippling trade sanctions reversed that decision, and threw the French economy into one of the deepest depressions in world history.

The Bonn Convention was largely credited with making asteroid mining illegal, though in reality it only imposed many of the same strict regulations the "Big Five" struggled with before 2028. It specifically targeted the treatment of shipments coming from the asteroid belt, defining how fast they could travel and what their crew requirements were. However, due to the bureaucratic burden associated with meeting the Convention standards, many smaller companies were unable to become licensed, and either went out of business, or were absorbed by their larger competitors.

Seeing a potential windfall as the number of importing countries dwindled, the home nations of the Big Five imposed crippling export tariffs on unprocessed ore, guaranteeing manufacturing jobs in the hybrid engine sector. The automotive industry, seeing a windfall themselves, felt no reason to decrease the price of exports, because they had no effective competitors. Developing nations fought to overturn the Bonn Convention, or to reach a compromise to allow them to participate in the mining sector, but thanks to alternating vetoes by the United States and China — trying to capitalize on their existing domestic mineral agreement — the Bonn Convention seemed unstoppable.

Because actual asteroid mining was not covered under the convention, many poorer nations left teams in the asteroid belt and sent shipments back to Earth, hoping to negotiate transportation agreements with licensed operators when their freighters reached Earth orbit. However, once it became clear the fees would more than devour any profit they might have made, countries such as Kenya began designing new unmanned freighters intended to re-enter the atmosphere directly, and be recovered in special drop zones in and around the Indian Ocean. By 2032, the mining industry estimated illegal shipments made up over 80% of the asteroid ore consumed globally.

To combat the problem, the Big Five mining companies bankrolled a special United Nations-backed detachment of spaceships known as the Space Enforcement Fleet (SEF). The SEF's mandate was to seize illegal shipments and deliver them to the International Space Station (renamed Alpha One after protests by the last of the scientists evicted in favour of military personnel). In an attempt to appease (and prop up) France, the United Nations agreed to purchase its ships from the largely-defunct King/Western Aerospace assembly plants near Paris. The vessels were based on the old space tourism models, adding a hint of irony to a bad situation: one of the fleet's secondary missions was to monitor compliance with NESA. The SEF had many high-profile victories in the early 2030s, but by 2035, a new threat had emerged.

PIRACY

Having tasted the profits from unrestricted asteroid mining, the poorer nations of the world refused to back down to the SEF. Numerous international treaties made weaponizing space illegal, meaning the SEF was effectively toothless. In late 2033, a Somalian convoy was escorted back to Earth by a pair of mercenary ships — old French models bought on the black market — in direct defiance of the SEF. Within a year, the field was full of mercenaries trying to cash in on the craze. A repurposed ship might cost $5 million or more, but the rewards were exponentially better than any other line of work.

The Big Five, seeing public opinion favouring the mercenaries ("Robin Hood in space" read many newspapers) attempted to demonize their new enemy, branding them "pirates." As was pointed out in the media numerous times, the mercenaries were not actually pirates, because they never stole Big Five shipments, but rather escorted the unlicensed freighters through the SEF blockade. A new term emerged for them, drawing on the continued mystique of asteroid mining and a long history of naval defiance: dustrunners.

Appendix B: The Bonn Convention

CONVENTION FOR THE RIGHTS OF OWNERSHIP, SOVEREIGNTY, AND POLICING OF ASTEROIDS AND ASTEROID PRODUCT

Signed at Bonn, 25 April 2028

The undersigned plenipotentiaries of the Governments represented at the Diplomatic Conference held at Bonn from 5 February 2028 to 25 April 2028, have agreed as follows:

CHAPTER I
General Provisions

Article 1.1. All Contracting Parties undertake to respect and to ensure respect for the present Convention under all circumstances.

Art. 1.2. The Convention shall apply to any and all parties operating any activities, industrial, commercial, recreational or otherwise in outer space. Although a party performing such activities may not be a party to the present Convention, the Powers who are parties thereto shall remain bound by it in their mutual relations.

CHAPTER II
Outer Space

Art. 2.1. It is the responsibility of the owner of any satellite, ship, station, probe, or any other equipment purposefully placed into outer space by legal or illegal means to ensure that the said piece of equipment complies with all safety standards and does not interfere with the operation of any other piece of equipment owned and/or operated by a second party.

Should said equipment malfunction, work in a manner contrary to its design, or be it decided that said equipment is longer of use, the piece of equipment in question shall be disposed of by safe and proper means according to Article 6.1 of the Convention.

Art. 2.2. The United Nations Space Enforcement Fleet (UNSEF) will patrol and protect from offending parties all areas encompassed within an altitude of 2000 km from Earth. Conflicts and disputes within an altitude of 500,000 km are under the jurisdiction of the UNSEF, and any actions contrary to the Convention taken within this sphere of jurisdiction.

No ship or personed capsule of any kind may travel in the area of UNSEF jurisdiction without the express permission of the UNSEF by means of permit.

Art. 2.3. No natural satellite, including but not limited to asteroids, planetoids, comets, meteors, planets and moons may be controlled by any world power. Ownership in the form of corporate ownership may be exhibited within the terms of Article 3.1 of the Convention.

Areas of space relative to orbital positions of Earth may not be declared sovereign property, or property of any corporation or organization. The United Nations (UN) maintains control over outer space with specific control over certain relative areas, listed elsewhere.

Art. 2.4. All space vessels must bear the flag of their relative corporation, or government. Vessels must maintain radio channels open along UNSEF frequencies at all times and have installed a standard identification signal locator.

CHAPTER III
Interstellar Bodies

Art. 3.1. Any and all interstellar bodies of a size no greater than 1000 km in greatest diameter may be owned by private or public organizations for the purposes of mining operations, scientific endeavors, or government stations.

Any body laid claim to before the time of this Convention is henceforth deemed as owned by said claimant, unless a disagreement between parties exists. In case of disagreement, UN Tribunal will decide own ownership through due process.

Art. 3.2. Any party who does not hold ownership of a particular asteroid may not land any vehicle, personnel, probe or any other equipment on said asteroid. No equipment, interstellar body, or energy source may be directly or indirectly directed toward said asteroid without UN sanction.

If a state of emergency exists and emergency channels have been activated, or if a second party has reason to believe that lives are in danger on an asteroid surface, they have clearance to land sufficient help until emergency is declared over. After emergency has been declared over, the second party shall leave the asteroid surface along with any and all equipment at the discretion of the owner.

Art. 3.3. Ownership of an interstellar body carries with it the right to mine that body to exhaustion, providing that all necessary measures of safety are taken to ensure the safety of all personnel on, around and in the orbital path of the body. Mining refers to extraction of metals amd minerals for commercial or industrial use either on or near the base of operation, or for transport to Earth.

It is illegal to extract mass quantities of coinage material, including but not limited to gold and silver. This clause does not apply to the presence of coinage material in ppm quantities as impurities in legal shipments.

Any party who does not hold ownership of an asteroid may under no circumstances extract materials from said asteroid unless under direct contract from the owner. Any materials extracted in defiance of this Convention shall be turned over to the original owner at the expense of the offending party.

CHAPTER IV
Working Conditions

Art. 4.1. All personnel, government, corporate employees or otherwise must be provided with safe and reasonable conditions through launch, transport, living, and re-entry. Adequate protection from cold, heat, radiation and any physical dangers must be implemented before any person is subject to out of atmosphere conditions.

Art. 4.2. The UNSEF has the authority to stop any operations, commercial, industrial, government run or otherwise that put any person in danger of physical or psychological damage.

Art. 4.3. All ships, freighters, capsules or any method of transport must travel in a safe manner as per UNSEF regulations. No piece of equipment, piloted or otherwise, shall travel at speeds excess of 62,920 kph Earth relative.

Art. 4.4. UNSEF representatives must be present at all times on all flights sanctioned by the UN. The representatives must accompany the flights from origin to destination to ensure compliance of the Convention and to protect parties involved from any possible danger to the best of their ability.

CHAPTER V
Structures

Art. 5.1. The International Space Station (ISS) is directly under the jurisdiction of the UNSEF. No parties, commercial, government or otherwise may approach the ISS without the express permission of the UN. Permits may be obtained through the proper channels.

No ship, satellite, probe, or any other piece of equipment may pass within 10 km of the ISS on any orbital, transport or other path. Failure to comply will result in UNSEF intervention.

Any action of force against the ISS is considered an act of war against the UN and will be dealt with accordingly.

Art. 5.2. All structures used to house persons, equipment, asteroid material or otherwise must comply with UN safety standards for outer space structures. Airlocks and docking tubes must conform to UNSEF standards in all cases.

CHAPTER VI
Atmospheric Activities

Art. 6.1. All equipment, ships or otherwise set for re-entry into Earth's atmosphere must be controlled either by a land-based control centre or have persons piloting said equipment in situ.

Equipment being de-orbited must land in a designated splashdown point pre-determined in conjunction with the UN and NASA. Ships, freighters, satellites and otherwise that are equipped to land safely must do so at sanctioned airstrips in co-operation with the UN and NASA.

No cargo vessel may re-enter the atmosphere if it carries more than 5000 kg of material within. Material must be split between multiple cargo vessels to allow proper re-entry.

Art. 6.2. No party may deliberately send any piece of equipment, built or natural, into the atmosphere without the proper permit.

FINAL PROVISIONS

Art. F.1. The present Convention is established in English, Japanese and French. All texts are equally authentic.

Art. F.2. The present Convention, which bears the date of this day, is open to signature until 25 April 2029, in the name of the Powers represented at the Conference which opened at Bonn on 5 February 2028.

Art. F.3. The present Convention shall be ratified as soon as possible. A record shall be drawn up of the deposit of each instrument of ratification and certified copies of this record shall be transmitted by the United Nations to all the Powers in whose name the Convention has been signed, or whose accession has been notified.

Art. F.4. The present Convention has no relation to any previous Convention.

Art. F.5. The Convention parties shall register the present Convention with the Secretariat of the United Nations. The Convention shall also inform the Secretariat of the United Nations of all ratifications, accessions and denunciations received by it with respect to the present Conventions.

In witness whereof the undersigned, having deposited their respective full powers, have signed the present Convention.

Done at Bonn this twenty-fifth day of April 2028, in the English, French and Japanese languages. The original shall be deposited in the archives of the United Nations. The Convention shall transmit certified copies thereof to each of the Signatory and Acceding States.

(Here follow signatures)